Stars and Bones Book VI

Archmage in the Ruins

Beatrice B. Morgan

Authors 4 Authors Publishing
Marysville, WA, USA

Published by Authors 4 Authors Publishing
1214 6th St
Marysville, WA 98270
www.authors4authorspublishing.com

E-book ISBN: 978-1-64477-072-6
Paperback ISBN: 978-1-64477-096-2
Audiobook ISBN: 978-1-64477-191-4

Edited by Rebecca Mikkelson
Line edited by Renee Frey
Copyedited by Brandi Spencer

Cover design ©2024 Practically Perfect Covers. All rights reserved.
Interior design and map by Brandi Spencer.

Authors 4 Authors Publishing branding is set in Bavire. Book title is set in Allura and Bilbo Swash Caps. Series title and other headers are set in Cinzel. All other text is set in Garamond.

Archmage in the Ruins

BEATRICE B. MORGAN

Authors 4 Authors Content Rating

This title has been rated 17+, appropriate for older teens and adults, and contains:

- brief intense sex
- graphic violence
- moderate language

Please, keep the following in mind when using our rating system:

1. A content rating is not a measure of quality.

Great stories can be found for every audience. One book with many content warnings and another with none at all may be of equal depth and sophistication. Our ratings can work both ways: to avoid content or to find it.

2. Ratings are merely a tool.

For our young adult (YA) and children's titles, age ratings are generalized suggestions. For parents, our descriptive ratings can help you make informed decisions, but at the end of the day, only you know what kinds of content are appropriate for your individual child. This is why we provide details in addition to the general age rating.

For more information on our rating system, please, visit our Content Guide at: www.authors4authorspublishing.com/books/ratings

DEDICATION

To each and every one of you who saw this story through.

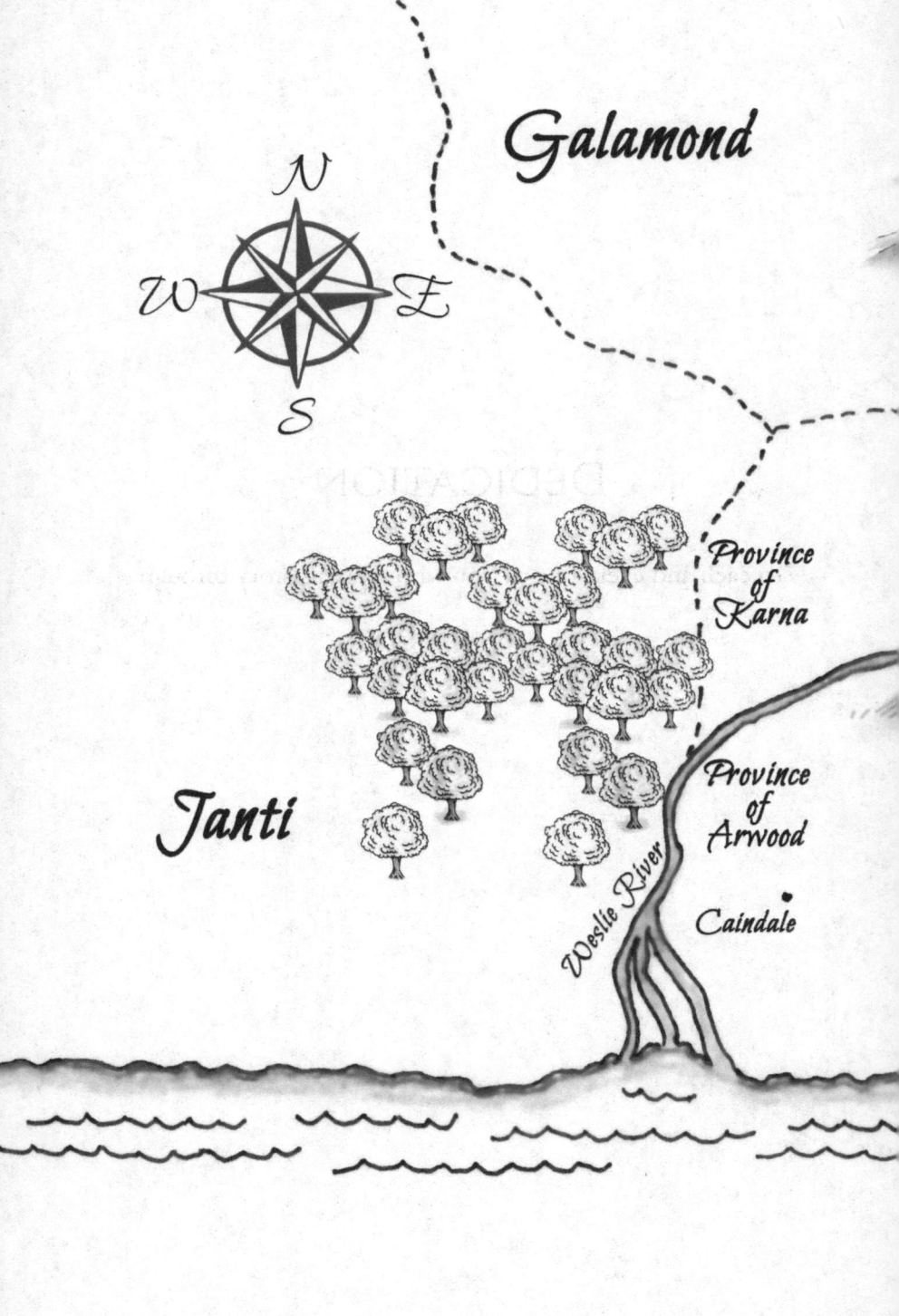

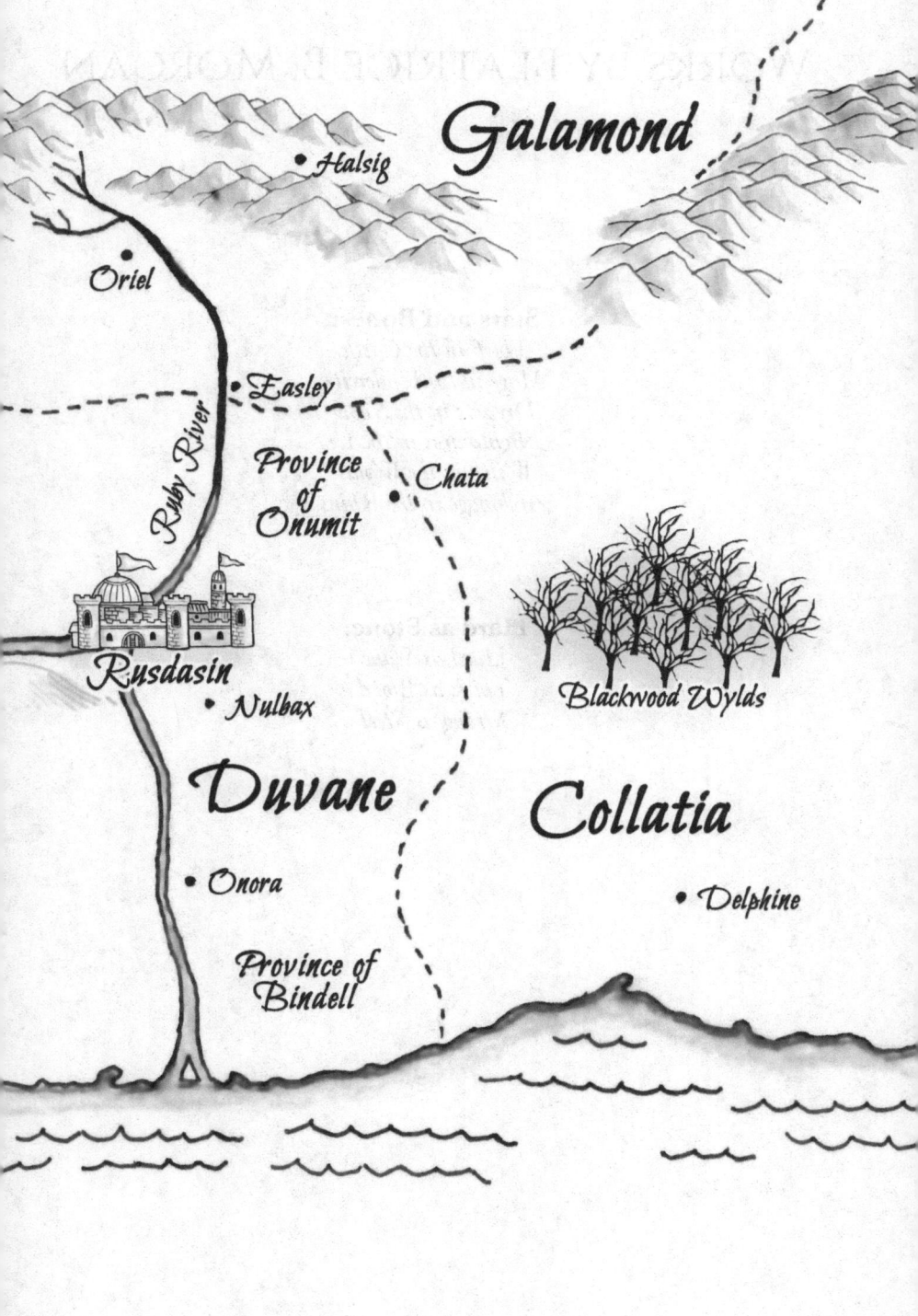

Galamond

Halsig

Oriel

Easley

Ruby River

Province of Onumit

Chata

Blackwood Wylds

Rusdasin

Nulbax

Duvane

Collatia

Onora

Delphine

Province of Bindell

WORKS BY BEATRICE B. MORGAN

TABLE OF CONTENTS

CHAPTER 1

Reid Sandpiper had endured pain and injury. He had devoted most of his twenty years to becoming a chivalrous and respected knight of the Order. He had believed in their ideals of truth and justice with his entire being. He had trained incessantly to withstand magic, to detect it, to combat it. He had endured injuries from battle, flesh torn by steel and iron and magic, burned and chaffed.

Yet he had never felt anything like what he felt now.

Darkness engulfed him. It pressed against his mind and clogged his lungs. He had fallen. He had struck something hard. More than bones had broken.

Shattered.

He had shattered. He couldn't move. The pain had been instantaneous but short lived. It had numbed into a blurry nothingness—the precursor of death.

Death. Reid felt it creeping closer with every shuddering, shallow breath. Hiada was pulling his soul onto the other side.

The glittering magic of the wellspring caressed him, as if trying to comfort him. It swirled in dark shades of marigold, sage, and charcoal. He had always imagined his death would come in battle, a grand battle that would stain the pages of history for centuries, not like this, in the bottom of a pit in the middle of the gods-forsaken Blackwood Wylds.

No one knew where he had gone. No one would know what had happened. That knowledge tugged at his silent heart. His uncle, his aunt—

The marigold magic gathered, and from within it, figures began to form. Those figures sharpened and became his uncle and aunt.

Reid tried to call out to them, but his broken body did not respond. He had to tell them what had happened!

The magic tilted. The figures shifted. The man looked like his uncle—he had the same chestnut hair, bronzed skin, broad shoulders, and green eyes—but his features were slightly different. He was taller, and his expression was not as stern. The woman beside him had pale gold skin, dark hair, and warm brown eyes that were bright and full of life.

His parents. He had nearly forgotten their faces. They had been ripped away from him so long ago, the memories had blurred, but these images were not memories. His still heart told him so. He knew then. He had died.

He tried to call out to them, but they did not respond. The magic shifted, and his parents became as he last remembered them: dead, glassy-eyed, and ashen, with terror and pain etched onto their expressions. The magic shifted again, and his parents were alive.

What sort of hell had Reid fallen into?

The marigold magic undulated, shimmered and rippled like water, and the image changed yet again. His parents stood closer, and their faces were smooth with youth. His father wore the black-and-gold doublet of the Royal Guard, and his mother wore a simple servant's dress. The marigold magic formed a ghostly corridor of stone around them. Torches burned in iron brackets, their flames lightless and frozen. Portraits formed along the walls, but the canvases within were blank.

"I haven't seen you before," said his father. His voice sounded as Reid remembered, strong and deep, somber and kind, yet boyish and unsure.

"This is my first day," said his mother, her voice sweet and joyful. "King Bradburn has graciously offered me work in his castle."

"My name is Corbin Sandpiper." He held out his hand. "Of the Royal guard."

"Marianne Hobbs." She took his hand. "It is a pleasure."

The magic shifted, and the image changed. Marianne stood before a hearth of frozen, lightless flames. She twirled a lock of hair around her finger. Reid recognized the room as the court magician's chambers in Bradburn Castle.

The court magician, Mason Hobbs, appeared. His white beard was several inches shorter, though he looked no younger. "I hear you've been getting along well with the older Sandpiper brother."

Marianne blushed. While staring absently into the fire, she said, "He's kind, he listens to me, and he looks dashing in the uniform."

Mason chuckled, though his eyes misted. "You sound like your grandmother. She played with her hair when she daydreamed."

Marianne's blush deepened. She pulled her hands from her hair and folded her fingers over her stomach.

"Don't misunderstand," Mason said, sitting in one of the cushy chairs before the hearth. "Corbin is a fine young man. As is his brother."

"Carter is stuffy and formal," Marianne whined. She meandered closer to the window, and closer to where Reid lingered. His mother gazed out of the window, fidgeting with the moonstone ring on her finger. Though the magic painted it in shades of gold, he would know it anywhere. She let out a dreamy sigh and added, "Corbin is... I don't know."

"More than you thought you wanted?" Mason asked, humming a note. "That is what I said about your grandmother. Gods, how long ago it seems."

The magic shifted again. Marianne raced into the court magician's study, wearing a plain nightdress and a cloak. Her feet were bare. A dark braid hung over her shoulder. Mason stood before the hearth, clutching a letter.

"What is it?" Marianne asked, breathless. "Has something happened?"

"My nephew has been killed." Mason threw the letter into the fire. The frozen flames did not lick at the edges like fire. The letter simply dissolved.

Marianne paled. She sank into one of the cushy chairs.

"It was Nexon. I am sure of it." Mason let out a grievous sigh. He looked decades older. "Our family has been systemically erased from this realm, save for myself and you. If we have played this correctly, Nexon doesn't know I have a granddaughter. It needs to stay that way. Marianne, I hate to ask this of you, but you need to leave Rusdasin. It isn't safe here. Take the ring, and vanish."

Marianne clutched her hand, hiding the moonstone ring from Reid's view. "What about you?"

"Don't worry about me," Mason said. "You are the remaining heir to the line, and you need to vanish before your existence is discovered. If Nexon hears even a rumor of your existence, he will not rest until you join the dead."

Marianne shook her head. Marigold tears lined her eyes. "No. I can't just leave you here. Where would I go?"

Mason frowned. His eyes reflected his own struggle. "I don't know. If you stay, you are a target. You have to survive. You need to leave as soon as possible, understand?"

"I understand," she whispered, though she looked terrified. She wiped a tear on her sleeve.

"Hide the ring somewhere no one will ever find it," Mason warned. "I recommend the bottom of the ocean. I should have thrown it to the depths when I had the chance."

The magic shifted again, rearranging the court magician's study into a dark chamber. A magelight glittered near the ceiling. Mason Hobbs had aged considerably. Chains of stone and steel held him against a spiked wall. His robes were torn and stained with blood. The old man clung to a shred of life. Runes marked his skin and the wall behind him—preventing his magic from healing, from saving him. Mason glanced up, and for a terrifying moment, his ancient gaze met Reid's. A strange expression came over Mason's bruised and bleeding face. The expression faded as footsteps approached.

A door opened, and a young man sauntered past Reid. He wore a fine suit and held himself like a king. Reid recognized him as Ron Hendle, the man whose body Nexon had taken for his own.

"Where is it?" Nexon demanded in a voice between Ron's and his own.

Mason didn't answer. The stone spikes grew longer, spearing his flesh. The old man groaned as fresh blood spilled, staining the wall, his robes, and floor. By the dark stains on the stones, his torture had been ongoing.

"Where did you hide it?" Nexon asked again, impatient and irritated.

"With any luck, it's resting at the deepest depths of the ocean," Mason managed to say, his voice raspy and cold.

Mason's eyes drifted to Reid once more. Nexon glanced toward him, but his eyes searched rather than saw. Nexon growled in frustration, and as he started to speak, the magic shifted. It did not form into a new chamber. It remained a thick marigold fog, undulating like light through water.

The wellspring, Reid remembered.

The cavern shuddered, but it felt far away, reminding Reid of the strange between-realm he stood in. As if summoned by his realization, the marigold magic thinned. His own body was sprawled on the ground, paled from blood loss, empty-eyed, and broken.

"You look so much like your father," came a voice.

A young woman stood on the other side of his body. She wasn't made of magic. She was tangible yet ghostly. Her dark hair was loosely braided, and she wore a pale blue dress and worn boots. She looked just like she had on the day she died.

"Mother," Reid said. Somehow, he felt no surprise.

Her honey-brown eyes softened. "I'm sorry for all the trouble. I couldn't let the ring fall into Nexon's hands. Reid, love, I don't have much time, and neither do you—your great-grandfather is dying."

"My great-grandfather," Reid repeated, realization sinking in. "Mason Hobbs."

"Yes. Nexon has kept him alive as long as he wants. Mason won't tell him where the ring is, and Nexon will kill him."

"Why?" Reid asked.

"Because he's a stubborn ass," his mother said, brows raised as if it were obvious. "Something you've inherited."

He frowned. "No, why the ring? What's so important about your ring that he would kill for it—"

And Reid understood why as soon as the question left his lips.

"It's a piece of him," his mother said. "Nexon needs it in order to become the monster he was a thousand years ago."

"Your ring…is a piece of Nexon?" Reid stumbled over the thought.

Guilt darkened her expression. "A piece of his power, yes. Moonstone is a clever material. It can contain magic without emitting it. The archmages used it to hold the pieces of Nexon's magic. But Nexon found out what they did and has spent the last few hundred years hunting them down. Each archmage took a piece and passed it down. My ring—your ring—is one of them."

She laced her fingers—she did not wear the ring.

"Luckily, you managed to find a safer place for it than I," she said, smiling. "I hear anyone who's tried to take the ring from Juniper has met an early end." His mother laughed, then added, "I like her."

Hearing those words from his mother melted tension he hadn't known he carried. His entire chest warmed and then immediately fell when he realized—his mother was dead, and so was he.

"Juniper," he whispered. He glanced around the magic-thick cavern, but he did not see her. He had a foggy memory of Juniper calling for him, screaming his name, crying, kneeling over him.

"Reid," his mother said, calling back his attention. She flickered, and her joyfulness diminished. "I'm running out of time. Reid, like it or not, you are the last direct descendant of the energy line. When your great-grandfather dies—"

She flickered again, as did the magic around them. She spoke again, but her words were muffled and distant. She flickered.

"Wait," Reid called. He reached out to his mother, but she faded into the magic. "Mother?"

An unseen force surged through the marigold magic. It rushed him from every direction and engulfed him within a fathomless abyss. Every thought shattered. The numbness vanished, and pain returned tenfold, needling his shattered bones, his broken lungs, his torn skin.

It consumed him.

CHAPTER 2

A chill seethed through Ison's fur-lined leathers. A layer of snow surrounded Baxion, and though the water mages kept the snow out of the city, and the fire mages kept the city from freezing, it was still blasted cold. He couldn't feel the tips of his fingers or his nose.

He stood in the dirt-floor arena where Nexon commanded his beasts to be trained—the beasts created from a black magic ritual that demanded the blood and souls of sacrifice. Ison had seen the ritual firsthand, when Nexon had possessed him and forced him to create the first beasts. That had been a year ago, in the bowels of Bradburn Castle. It seemed a lifetime ago. Ison had come to terms with what he had done, though guilt lingered like lead.

Ison had his redemption planned. He and his friends had infiltrated Nexon's stronghold of Baxion, and thanks to what Ison had come to think of as divine intervention, he had become the trainer for the beasts created in the dungeons below the city.

Ison had spent almost every waking moment in the arena working with the beasts. Whereas the beasts Ison had first encountered in Bradburn Castle were mindless and rabid, these beasts had a frightening intelligence. They knew what had happened to them, how Nexon's followers had kidnapped and killed them for his own beastly army.

No one else knew how smart they were, and Ison planned on keeping it that way as long as possible.

The sun had set, leaving the arena in hazy shadows. Magelights shone high on the stone walls, shading the center of the arena in snowy darkness. The fresh batch of beasts meandered about the floor, still getting used to their strange new bodies. Ison waited for them to understand and accept or suffer through madness. For each beast, for the souls locked within, it took time.

Ison had learned a lot in the past few weeks. When a new batch of beasts came to the surface for the first time, they needed time to realize and adjust to what had happened. In every batch, there were those unable to adjust. They were put down. That part never got easier to watch, though Ison had come to think of it as a release for the souls trapped within.

After the beasts adjusted, dominance was asserted. A leader came forward in each batch, and Ison then spoke to that leader.

The current alpha sat at Ison's side, watching the new beasts meander the arena, as they had with every new batch. The beasts stumbled around the arena's blood-stained dirt floor, getting used to their four legs and snouts, tails and claws, adjusting to the new weight and stance of their haunches, and to their new senses. They sniffed one another, snarled and barked and whined. Dominance was asserted, and eventually, a leader approached the alpha.

Ison stiffened. He hated this part too. The two beasts snarled at one another, and then after a moment, the newest leader lowered his head. The tension dissolved, and Ison released a breath of relief.

So far, no other beast had claimed dominance over the alpha at his side.

"All right," Ison announced to the arena. He lacked the volume to speak loudly, so the alpha let out a bark, gaining the attention of the others. "That's enough for today. Let's head back in."

The beasts followed the alpha, who walked beside Ison, back into the lift that carried them down into the dungeons, where they slept in cage-like cells. Ison made sure each had water and food and bedding, then headed back up to see to those things for himself. He tiptoed through the upper cells where the older beasts were asleep. Ison had stayed longer today than normal, and he suspected his housemates would be asleep too.

Ison didn't mind the lost sleep. All he was doing here would be worth it, he hoped.

He made his way to the stone stairwell and to the darkened upper floors. He started through the offices. With the other mages gone for the day, the entire arena was deathly quiet, so when he heard the whisper of urgent voices coming from the back office, the hairs on his neck stood straight, and gooseflesh crawled along his back.

"...are making remarkable progress," said a drawling and sharp female voice, one Ison had never heard before. "Nexon will be impressed."

"The boy's done far more than I thought possible," came Mercer's rough voice. Mercer headed the arena, and he didn't speak to the woman in the same harsh, commanding voice he spoke to Ison and other mages who worked in the arena. He spoke with respect.

That struck Ison as odd. Mercer didn't speak to anyone with respect, not even the superiors of Baxion.

Who was this woman?

"Nexon wants a scouting team to head south," said the woman.

"South? Into the Wylds?" Mercer barked a laugh. "There's nothing south of here but trees and cursed dirt."

"Don't ask questions," she snapped. "If Nexon wants to send a scouting team south, we will send a scouting team south. Understand?"

"Yes," Mercer said, the single word sharp. "May I ask why?"

"He thinks the girl is there, but he isn't sure."

"In the Wylds?"

"He didn't explain to me why he thinks that," the woman said, each word punctuated with annoyance. "There was…a disturbance. He felt it. I didn't. An archmage thing. Not for you to worry over or repeat like common gossip. Understand?"

"Yes, I understand," Mercer said without hesitation.

"Good. He wants a small scouting party, but he wants them to be ready for anything. A balanced team."

"All right, who do you want?"

"Mika."

Ison released a slow breath. He had feared his own name. Mika was another mage in the arena who had a talent for going undetected. He didn't talk about his past, but Ison suspected he had been an assassin or sellsword.

The woman started speaking again, but Ison didn't stay to listen. Ison tiptoed out of the offices and out of the arena. The chilly night air grazed his face, tousling his brown hair. It had grown out since he'd fled Bradburn Castle. Though his body craved a good wash and sleep, rather than head to the house, he went into the city.

This time of night, the magelights glowed in shades of soft blues and yellows, mimicking torchlight. The snowy sky looked ready to unleash a snowstorm enough to bury the city, but none fell. It if did, it never reached the ground. The air was dry. Cold, but not enough for someone to freeze to death. Just enough to remind everyone that winter had arrived. Ison stuffed his hands into his pockets and curled his fingers into fists.

Most residents were sleeping, as Ison should have been. He passed night workers and Baxion's green-robed version of the City Watch. No one stopped him or asked where he had been or where he was going or why he wasn't at home or in bed.

It had taken him a few weeks to get used to walking the streets. Baxion wasn't Rusdasin, and a mage could go anywhere and do anything.

Baxion was, to most mages, paradise.

And Ison had trekked across two kingdoms to bring it down. The more he had thought about it, he wanted a way to bring down Nexon and leave Baxion just the way it was.

But…could they do that? Ison made his way to the eastern square, where the taverns stayed open all night, to a quiet little place called Bee's. It had become a meeting place for his friends, and it specialized in delicious butter-toffee ale. He found Xavier lounging in a corner booth. Xavier had been assigned to the scouts patrolling around Baxion at all hours. He patrolled during the afternoons and evenings, and he would have recently returned to the city.

As Ison approached, Xavier glanced up from his tankard. His gray-blue eyes settled on Ison, and he witnessed the subtle shift from Xavier's casual coldness to something warmer. Xavier wore the dark leathers of the scouts and a fur cowl around his neck. His leather jacket hugged his lithe frame with buckles and dagger sheaths. The days in the sun had darkened his umber skin.

Ison sat on the leather-padded stone bench and slid closer to Xavier. He smelled like the forests outside the city, pine and snow and cold.

"How did you know I'd be here?" Xavier draped his arm behind Ison. He showed little affection, and Ison had come to appreciate the small acts.

"I didn't," Ison said.

The innkeeper waved, and Ison signaled for an ale. The barkeep set a full tankard on a stone platter and used earth magic to deliver it without leaving the bar. Ison accepted the drink; then the stone platter returned to the bar.

"I hoped you would." Ison whispered to Xavier what he had overheard in Mercer's office.

Xavier took in each word, his expression bored and observant. His gaze rarely lost that dangerous, vicious thrill. Ison didn't know if it had always been there, or if he had developed it in his years as an assassin.

"They're sending those scouts to find Jun. She's done something to draw Nexon's attention," Ison whispered. "We need to be ready for anything."

"Finally, *something's* happening," Xavier drawled. He sipped his ale. "I've been bored to death in his hellhole."

Ison tried to soak in Xavier's readiness. This is what they had come to Baxion for—to interrupt Nexon's plans and to destroy his followers from the inside. Ison's resolve hadn't altered and wouldn't, but it didn't make him any less nervous. He would do whatever he could to stop Nexon from hurting anything else, even if he had no idea how.

CHAPTER 3

Another tremor shook the wellspring. The knotted mass of agitated magic pulsed, and the sheer force knocked Juniper off her feet. Her back hit the uneven cavern floor and pushed the breath from her lungs. The pulse did not push Lilianna over. The druid girl held her ground.

Juniper staggered to her feet. Sweat sucked her clothes to her skin. Her arms and legs shook, and her lungs labored to draw in breath. It felt as if she had eaten something slimy and prickly, and it continued to stab her insides, steal her breath, and darken the edges of her vision. She felt like lying down and never getting back up.

Another tremor shook the cavern, knocking loose rocks from the walls and ceiling. Somewhere, rock slid again rock, pulling and pushing the earth above.

"If this keeps up, the village won't stand a chance," Lilianna gasped, her usual somber tone whittled by panic. Sweat glistened on her emerald skin.

Juniper didn't argue, though a part of her didn't care.

Maybe it would fall and crush them and end everything.

Juniper shoved away the darkness tearing at her heart. She had to help Lilianna. She was an archmage too.

Casting tendrils of her bright blue magic, Juniper felt along the tangled, knotted wellspring. The ancient magic was agitated, pulsing and trembling with festered rage and rotten betrayal. Juniper didn't know what she was feeling for, but Lilianna seemed to. Her spring green magic feathered over the knot with expert swiftness and slipped between the threads. It filled the cavern with a warm humid breeze that reminded Juniper of a summer storm.

Lilianna worked far faster. Juniper suspected it had everything to do with the nature of Lilianna's magical training. The previous archmage had been cultivating Lilianna's skill with the purpose of handling the cursed wellspring.

Juniper also suspected it had something to do with her own lack of enthusiasm. Right now, she didn't mind if the rocks crushed her into bits of bloodied bone and took the whole forest with her. If they did, she could see Reid again.

Her heart squeezed. Reid. He had fallen. His broken body stained the back of her eyelids.

You should have saved him.

A heavy tremor shook the cavern. Lose rocks and dirt and broken roots tumbled from the ceiling. Juniper pulled her magic back to give Lilianna more room to work. Clearly, the druid girl had a better mind for such things.

"There," Lilianna breathed. Her magic tugged on several threads at once, and the tension in the air loosened.

But not enough. Lilianna's sage magic encircled the wellspring and needled deeper, tugging and kneading the tangle. A few more tugs, and the tension lessened. The magic was still thick as fog and oppressive.

Juniper leaned forward, hands on her knees. Her head felt close to bursting.

"I can do it," Lilianna whispered. Hope threaded her words. Her golden eyes fixed on the knot, seeing things Juniper couldn't. "It will take time, but I can do it."

The cavern shifted. Rock ground against rock, thunderous and angry. Dirt and tree roots crashed down from above. Juniper summoned a shield of clear blue ice over herself and Lilianna. Debris rained against the ice and clattered on the stone floor. Lilianna gave no notice. She continued to test the tangle.

The oppressive magic slowly lessened. The wellspring continued to pulse, though the waves came less frequently and with less intensity. The tremors became fewer. The cavern still rumbled, though it felt less angry with every shattering heartbeat. All the while, Juniper's heartbeat thudded in her ears.

Lilianna stumbled back, sweaty and panting. Her magic vanished. "I—I can't do anymore. Not right now."

"It's all right," Juniper said. "You've made progress. We'll rest and come back."

Lilianna nodded. She looked close to passing out. Her green skin had paled, and sweat glistened along her brow and neck. She stumbled a step toward Juniper, and her golden eyes focused on something over Juniper's shoulder. Fear and dread and surprise wormed through her exhaustion.

Juniper braced herself. She readied her magic—she could fight off any cursed monster lurking in the depths of the earth, or worse. She curled icy tendrils around herself and whirled to attack.

Her heart stilled and then plummeted.

Reid stood in the mouth of the chamber.

Reid.

He stood hunched, a wild look in his molten brown eyes. Those eyes focused on her. His breaths came in raspy pants. He looked rabid, an animal acting on fear and defense, ready to tear her throat out. But, it was *Reid.*

Juniper stumbled over the debris strewn cavern floor and to him. She didn't know what to think. Reid was looking at her, yet she had felt the absence of his heartbeat. She had looked into his listless, dead eyes. Reid had been dead.

"Reid?" she asked, her breath shaky and uncertain.

His rabid eyes bore into hers. He didn't answer.

She looked him over. His chest rose and fell. He bore scrapes and bruises but otherwise looked unhurt. His shattered and broken bones had mended. Whatever force had mended his bones had also mended the worst dents in his silver armor. She dared a step closer and searched his face. Madness stared back at her, laced with fear and uncertainty. She reached for his scruffy jaw, lined with chestnut hair. Warmth radiated from his skin. Her fingertips grazed his pulse. It beat steadily, albeit rapidly.

"Reid?" she breathed. Seeing him lifted her heart, but it also terrified her. "You were dead."

"I was."

The sound that came out of her throat fell somewhere between a scream and a sob. She fell into him. She flattened her palms against his chest, over the scratched owl and chain insignia of the Order. Gathering herself, she looked into his face. His manic expression hadn't changed.

She whispered, "How?"

"That is…one thing we need to talk about." His voice came deep and husky and threaded with a darker emotion she couldn't identify.

"What else?"

"I…saw things." He shut his eyes, and his face contorted in anxiety. Fear flashed across his eyes. "My parents, my mother…she said…"

His madness crumbled into panic. She put her hand to his lips, ending the rambling. His panicked gaze flashed to hers.

"Reid," she begged. "It's all right. You don't have to explain it all right now."

"Mason Hobbs is dead," he said against her fingers, his breath hot. His voice cracked. "He's… He was my… Juniper, I'm an archmage."

Juniper blinked twice. Reid wore no humor. His wild gaze bore into her, fierce enough to make her bones tremble.

"I think you've inhaled too much of this cursed air," she said. She had too.

The ground trembled, and the entire cavern gave a dangerous growl. Reid wobbled and set a hand on her waist to steady himself.

"We need to leave," Lilianna said. She cast a shield of green over her head, but a rock punched right through it, narrowly missing her temple. Her magic flickered out.

"I've got the way out." Juniper gathered her magic and formed a staircase of blue ice. She angled the stairs to prevent anyone from slipping.

Lilianna went first, her limbs shaky and her steps uneven. Juniper glanced at Reid, who wore a faraway look.

"You first," Juniper said. "I'll close the ice behind us."

Reid's attention snapped to her. His gaze sharpened as if he feared she would attack. A jolt of predatory fear prickled along the back of her neck, and her magic stirred in instinctive defense.

The cavern shook, and a vicious creak of sliding stone sounded above them. Juniper pointed him to the staircase, and he stalked up. She followed a step behind him. She didn't want to be within a blade's range, not with Reid looking murderous and confused.

She glanced behind to the chamber where Reid had fallen, where he had died, and where he had reappeared. Something had happened in that chamber, and not knowing what made her stomach churn.

CHAPTER 4

Juniper's ice stairwell twisted and turned through the collapsing cavern. More than once, rocks smashed against the side, reverberating through the ice. Lilianna, despite her exhaustion and magical depletion, never slowed.

Reid remained silent and stoic. His footsteps thudded against her ice, and every third step wavered. She readied her magic to catch him should he fall, yet he trudged forward. She focused on her ice. Maybe he just needed time to gather his thoughts. Still, his words—*I'm an archmage*—resounded in her mind. What if it were true? How could it be true?

A large chunk of rock slammed into the ice above her head. She stumbled, her ice thinned, and she dropped onto the stairs. In reflex, she thickened her ice—the rock slid along her ice and fell to the cavern floor below, a thunderous crash.

"Juniper?" Lilianna called.

"I'm fine." Juniper stood on shaky legs.

Lilianna had paused, wide eyes pinned on Juniper. Reid paused and glanced behind him, but his face remained unchanged—unreadable and cold. Juniper ignored it and continued toward the stairwell.

She felt the sunlight on her ice before she saw it. It glittered through the clear blue ice like diamonds.

The stairwell ended somewhere near Blood Tree Pass. The gnarled black trees had lost most of their blood-red leaves. The tremors had destroyed much of the pass, leaving the narrow trail a mess of jutting stones, snapped trees, and straining and ripped roots. The earth creaked and groaned, unfinished with its destruction. The golden mist of the wellspring still floated upward through the cracks, filtering through the canopy and into the air.

Blugo, god of winter, had cast his chill over the forest. Juniper felt it down to her bones. Even for early winter, the Wylds were deathly quiet, save for the residual trembling. The cursed animals must have fled. Lingering golden mist hovered in the barren canopy, tucked in tangles of tree limbs. Not even a breeze blew. The sky above remained clouded in steely gray.

Juniper felt the difference immediately—the air no longer felt like a heavy blanket on her magic. The oppression of the Wylds was gone. She would be able to use her magic freely, without birthing more hideous, cursed creatures.

"Moss?" Lilianna called to the forest. The Shadow didn't appear. "Moss!"

"The tremors might have scared him," Juniper said.

Lilianna nodded, scanning the forest. "We should go to Enna first. On foot, I suppose."

"Lead the way," Juniper said.

Lilianna led the trek through the Blackwood Wylds. Juniper followed, and Reid walked behind her. She kept looking over her shoulder to make sure he followed—he did, looking forlorn and angry and confused. What had happened to him? He hadn't had a pulse. She had felt the absence of his heartbeat, and she had seen the emptiness of his eyes. His bones had been shattered and twisted, and yet he walked as if he hadn't fallen.

She kept waiting for him to collapse, for the gods to realize their mistake, for Hiada to steal him back.

The blood trees became fewer, and soon the towering cursed trees took their place. They grew thicker than houses and as tall as mountains, blackened and left barren by the curse. Their treacherous roots wove in and out of the hard ground, and it made the trek slow.

The timber wall of Sinjon came into view, or what was left of it. The village still smoked. The air reeked of ash and bitter magic. Lilianna led them to the nearest gate. With the holes in the wall, the gates mattered little, and they remained open. The sentries said nothing as Lilianna, Juniper, and Reid marched into the village.

Sinjon had not escaped the tremors. What hadn't been damaged by the Shadow attack had suffered in the earthquakes that followed. Houses had collapsed. Market stalls had burned. Many druids lingered in the streets, surveying the damage. Sobs echoed. As Lilianna, Juniper, and Reid passed, their hushed conversations paused. A few glared. They likely still blamed Juniper for everything.

It was their fault, Juniper thought bitterly. Though she knew it wasn't entirely their fault. The Wylds had turned against the druids centuries ago, and the curse had given them a sour taste for magic.

Lilianna led them to Enna's house on the outskirts of Sinjon. It had escaped the worst of the damage, though the sick rooms had been knocked in, the garden partially singed, and the vines climbing the chimney charred black. By the lack of bodies, Juniper assumed the sick had been moved before the collapse.

Enna stood in her shriveling herb garden, pruning what she could off a tree with blue leaves and deep orange bark. As they approached, Enna straightened and beheld them with a knowing cynicism. The deep wrinkles in her emerald skin stretched with her frown. Stray hairs had escaped her braid and hung around her face.

"Ah, good to see you're not dead," Enna said in her voice like a crow. She added the blue leaves to a basket resting on a knocked-over rain barrel. "And the forest seems to have lost a bit of its animosity. Might as well come inside before Jarek comes to demand an explanation."

They followed the old druid inside. The hearth room smelled strongly of cedar and lemongrass. Potted plants lined the windowsills and mantel, tins and jars of dried herbs lined the shelves two and three deep, and bundles of dried herbs hung from the ceilings to dry. Enna set a dented kettle over the hearth and gathered tea and herbs from her collection of cloudy, unlabeled jars. Lilianna collapsed before the fire. Juniper sat at the table, and Reid sat beside her.

"Well?" Enna set her hands on her hips. "Out with it."

Juniper and Lilianna took turns telling her what had happened since they had gone into the Wylds to stop the wellspring.

Reid remained deathly silent, enough so that Juniper glanced to make sure he still breathed. His chest rose and fell, he blinked, yet his predator's gaze bore into the hearth. His fists were clenched to white knuckles.

As Lilianna told her grandmother about Reid's fall and supposed death, Enna's eyes snapped to him and remained on him through the rest of the story. The old druid betrayed nothing as Juniper detailed how he had reappeared, but her words stumbled on the last thing he'd said—that he had become an archmage.

"Is that so?" Enna asked, her gaze still boring into Reid. "They say, in the moments before death, we are able to see both sides of the realm, this one and the beyond. Tell me, boy, what did you see? What stole your tongue?"

Reid remained silent and still as stone. Juniper feared that death had claimed him once again, but then he shifted his eyes from the flames to Enna. Juniper felt the air change. It thickened, intensified. It made her toes curl and the hair on the back of her neck stand on end. Lilianna's sudden inhale suggested she felt the same.

"My parents," he said, his voice rough. "I saw them meet. I saw my mother speaking to my...great-grandfather. I spoke to my mother's spirit."

A beat of silence.

Juniper's unease churned. Reid had spoken with his dead mother? Juniper had spoken with dead parents in Delphine, and the encounter had left her feeling off-put for days. However, she had never met her parents. Reid had witnessed the murder of his. She could only imagine how he felt, and she imagined a horrible dread.

"What did she tell you?" Enna asked. Her voice bore no sympathy nor compassion.

Reid's gaze moved to Juniper's hand, to the moonstone ring. In reflex, she curled her fist. She could imagine what his mother might say about her—thief, assassin, criminal, trash, scum. Nothing she hadn't heard countless times before.

"Mason Hobbs was her grandfather, my great-grandfather," Reid said, his words harsh and breathy. Like he struggled to draw breath. Like his lungs were slowly failing. "He told her to hide the ring because Nexon was looking for it. He hunted down Mason's family. She was the only one left."

"Why the ring?" Juniper asked.

Reid's expression hardened. His eyes remained on the stone. "It contains a piece of him."

The air fled Juniper's lungs. It felt as if something had taken hold of her insides and squeezed. She looked at her moonstone ring—her engagement ring. The smooth gem seemed to glow from within, as it always had. The aquamarines surrounding it glittered in the flickering fire light.

"Moonstone can…contain magic, she said." Reid's voice was flat and rough.

"The archmages hid the pieces of Nexon's power within moonstone," Juniper said in a single breath, the thoughts coming together with lightning speed, "which means we just happen to have the last two pieces he's been scouring the realm for. This ring and Angyla's brooch."

"Both passed down through an archmage line," Reid whispered.

The sheer coincidence pulled a ragged laugh out of Juniper's chest.

Footsteps thundered outside, and a heavy hand fell against the front door. Before Enna could stand or speak, Chief Jarek Hamish marched into the house from the garden. His broad frame f0illed the narrow doorway. The gloomy daylight filtered through the dusty air around him, and his furious gaze roamed over the three of them. His pale green skin had flushed with rage. A chunk was missing from his left ear.

"The sentries told me you'd returned," Jarek said.

"You missed the story," Enna said. The kettle began to hiss. "But you are just in time for tea. Sit."

CHAPTER 5

Juniper sipped her tea while Enna retold their tale to Jarek. No one else spoke. Lilianna sat before the fire, tea clutched in her hands. Reid stared into his untouched tea. A beat—he met her stare. His eyes were unreadable and distant. She held that gaze, willing it to change. It didn't.

Jarek listened without comment, though he looked ready to strangle the three of them. Enna left out Reid's strange death and return, and Juniper was grateful for it. The druids were incredibly ignorant and superstitious of magic. An angry mob had tried to kill Juniper after she had used her magic to save them. She didn't want to know what they would think if they knew Reid had returned from the dead.

She wasn't sure what she thought about it.

Though lessened, tremors continued. The jars of herbs and ointments rattled, as did the shutters and the floorboards. Even the flame flickered. Outside, stone creaked and timber collapsed.

"We'll be scrambling for beds tonight," Jarek said. His broad shoulders slumped. "More than half of the village has been destroyed, either by Shadow or the earth's trembling."

Juniper felt a pinch of guilt, and by the downcast look on Lilianna's face, she felt it too. Likely more so.

"Your friends from Delphine have camped by my house," Jarek said to Reid.

It took Juniper a moment to remember. A small group of Sentinels—anti-magic warriors—had arrived during the fight, turning the tide of battle.

"Lilianna," said Enna. "Your mother claims to have disowned you for running into the woods. I can't imagine what she'll think after this. You are welcome to stay here for as long as you like."

"Thank you," Lilianna said, though her words were weak.

"And you two best stay at my house," Jarek said to Juniper and Reid. By his tone, he'd rather them not. Juniper didn't mind. Her body ached and her mind spun. She needed rest, and a bed was a bed.

After tea, Juniper and Reid went to Jarek's house. Enna had sick and injured to tend to, and Lilianna silently retreated into the upstairs bedroom for much needed rest. Jarek's house sat on a grassy knoll slightly outside the village, perfect for a chief to overlook his charges, and perfect to see the vast destruction. So much had been lost in a single night, and more continued to crumble with each tremble of the earth. Many druids had resorted to pitching tents rather than begin repairs. With the continuous tremors, repairs would be futile.

A large tent had been erected beside Jarek's house. Typical camping equipment lay inside: cots, trunks, foldable wooden furniture, and a rug embroidered in gold with a rune of warmth. Two tapestries hung on the far wall: a crescent moon surrounded by a laurel wreath, the Collatian royal seal; and a stylized circle with half being the sun and half being the moon, the seal of the Sentinels. A laurel wreath surrounded the Sentinel seal, a nod to the crown they served. Juniper didn't see anyone inside. The Sentinels must have gone into the village to help.

Jarek let them into his house, then left to help with the villagers. Ingrid, Jarek's wife, was already in the village. The house was empty. Juniper didn't mind. Ingrid didn't like her, and the quiet gave Juniper a chance to think.

Juniper added a log to the low-burning hearth. Reid followed a step behind.

She knelt by the fire. "If only I could draw one of those runes for warmth," she mused. "I should have paid more attention in that class."

Reid didn't answer. She felt his presence behind her, stalking and lurking. If she didn't know better, she would feel threatened.

She held her hands out to the fire to melt the lingering chill in her skin. Her moonstone ring glinted in the flickering light.

"All this time," she said. "We had what he was looking for."

Reid stepped in her peripheral, quiet and stoic, looking around the house as if she hadn't spoken.

A memory floated to the front of her mind. "Reid, do you remember after you asked me to marry you, we met Ron in the corridor?"

He didn't answer. His gaze drifted to the fire as the log caught, brightening the flames and spitting a few embers into the air.

Her heart skipped. Had he even heard her? She twisted the ring around her finger. "He got a strange look on his face when he saw the ring," she continued. "And the enthralled knights kept trying to take it."

A long beat of silence followed. Juniper tore her eyes off Reid and looked instead at the moonstone. If it held a piece of Nexon's magic, had the ancient Balendin archmage carried it with him that day in the woods?

"I remember," Reid said, his voice low and breathy. He continued to stare into the fire, molten eyes full of churning thoughts she couldn't read.

A piece of the new log fell into the ashes, sending embers and a puff of smoke into the air.

If only she had known who and what Ron had been. She could have thrust an ice spike through his heart and been done with it.

Juniper stood. "I don't know about you, but I'm hungry."

She walked into the kitchen and fumbled her way through the hanging pots and pans. They were all slightly different, but essentially the same. Iron or earthenware. She chose a skillet at random and set it on the grate over the hearth. She magicked water from the pitcher—cleaned it of the sparse particles—and added it to the pan. She rifled through the jars of herbs and spices. The powdered bits all looked the same, and they all smelled like grass.

"Have you cooked before?" Reid asked.

The sound of his voice jarred her more than it should have. She turned. He was looking at her over the fire, his gaze sharp and unwelcoming. It gave her a feeling of having invaded or interrupted.

Never, not in all their times spent together, has Reid made her feel unwelcome. Juniper cleared her throat and pushed past the feeling.

"I've watched other people cook. It can't be that hard." She brought a few more jars of spices to her nose. She picked a few that looked familiar.

Reid appeared beside her. The suddenness of his approach made her tense. She had been so focused on the spices, she hadn't been paying attention to him. He examined her choice of spices, then put two of them back and carefully sorted through the cabinet until he found two others.

"These," he said.

"How can you tell which is which?" Juniper picked up the two new spices. They looked identical. "It all smells like weeds."

"It's subtle. The smells come out in the cooking."

Reid looked through the cooking supplies, added oil to the water, and chopped roots and onions. He added them to the water, then stirred in the spices. Juniper meandered to the opposite side of the hearth. Reid stood before the cooking pot, face empty of expression. He didn't even wear his stoic mask—his face showed nothing at all, and he reminded Juniper of a corpse set on display. The thought sent a shiver down her spine.

The silence between them stretched.

"How did you learn to cook?" Juniper asked. "Did they teach you that in squire school?"

Reid's blank expression shifted. "No. I learned from my aunt. She…" He paused, brow furrowed. He spoke slowly, as if he couldn't quite remember. "She taught me the basics. I spent a lot of time with her in the kitchen."

"You learned to cook between sword lessons with your uncle and history lessons with the castle scholars? Did you sleep?" Juniper wouldn't admit it, but she felt a pang of jealousy. She hadn't had someone to teach her how to cook, at least not lovingly so. She'd had Maddox Hawk, her guild master, who had taught her how to wield a blade and defend herself. She had learned survival on her own.

"My aunt always wanted a daughter." Reid absently stirred the sizzling roots around the skillet. "She often treated the servant girls as her own."

"She never had children," Juniper stated, though it came out as a question.

Reid shook his head. "She was with child once, but it made her sick. She lost the child, and she hadn't been able to carry one since."

Juniper's stomach knotted. "I'm sorry."

Reid's empty gaze remained on the skillet. He said nothing more.

The stew turned out to be delicious. Jarek and Ingrid remained in the village for the midday meal, and Reid and Juniper ate alone. They sat opposite each other at the wooden table.

"This isn't bad." Juniper pointed to her earthen bowl with her slightly bent fork.

"You thought it would be?"

"I was involved, so a little bit, yes." Juniper swallowed a spoonful and gave him a small smile. "Remind me to thank your aunt."

Reid did not mirror her smile. He didn't even look at her.

Juniper continued to eat in silence. Only after she set her empty bowl in the sink, she tested the waters again. "Do you want to talk about it?"

Silence. Then, Reid's calm footsteps approached the sink. He set his empty bowl with hers. She magicked hot water over the dishes and started to wash. This part, she knew. She had washed plenty of dishes in the Marca.

Reid remained beside her. He smelled of sweat, dank cavern air, and stale blood.

She set her clean bowl to dry.

"Which part?" he asked. Exasperation and dread wormed into those two words, and they settled like stones in her gut.

She started on his bowl. "Let's start with the archmage bit. Are you sure? I mean, if you weren't a mage to begin with, is it even possible to inherit archmage magic?"

"I don't know," he said. "So little is known about archmages. Until recently, I thought them a myth."

Juniper took her time washing. Reid stood close, and his voice trembled as if speaking took a great deal of concentration and effort. It broke her heart, but she feared she would shatter the moment if she moved.

"If what I saw is true, and Nexon has killed every other possible inheritor of the archmage magic, then I...I don't know." Reid released a quick, breathy sigh. "My mother said I was the only direct descendant left."

Juniper had washed the bowl three times to allow him time to speak. When Reid fell silent, she set the bowl beside the other. She turned to face him. His downcast eyes traveled from their faraway spot on the wall and to her. His expression had softened from predatory to wounded.

For a moment, they stared at one another.

"Can you…do magic?" she asked.

"I—I don't know," he whispered. His fear turned into something darker. His fingers curled into fists. "I can feel…something. Inside of me. It's moving, it's…alive."

He brought a hand to his chest and clutched at his shirt. It was the same place that Juniper imagined her magic to reside—that deeper-than-bone feeling.

Juniper magicked the water from her hands and flattened her hands on either side of his clenched fist. She didn't know what to look for, or how to, but she gently sank her magic into him. She expected him to be angry at the intrusion, to push her away, or swat her hands, but he did nothing. He stood stone still, watching her.

And she felt…*magic*.

She gasped—endless magic, warm and bright, rose up to greet her. That hadn't been there before. Her magic had felt Reid's being, and she would have felt *that*. His magic trembled at her touch and then engulfed her, stole her breath, and threw stars across her vision. She had never felt such magic before, like an entire ocean had crashed into her and pinned her at the bottom.

She tried to pull away, but Reid slapped his hands over hers. His wide eyes had gone wild, fearful and desperate.

"Do you feel it?" His whispered words shook.

"Gods," she gasped. "Yes."

The tide of magic receded, leaving her breathless.

His next breath shuddered. "What do I do?"

"Breathe," she said, to herself and to him.

Reid took a short breath, as did she. His eyes bore into hers.

"This magic is yours," she said, though her words trembled. "Take control of it. Don't let it bully you. You're Reid Sandpiper, knight prodigy. You fear no magic or mage."

Reid took in her words, but he didn't calm. He remained a wild-eyed predator, fearful and skittish. Juniper didn't know what else to tell him, how to calm him and his rampant magic. She was still having a hard time believing Reid was a mage, let alone an archmage.

He awaited her answer.

She didn't know if she liked his full attention better or worse than his indifference. Each put her on edge.

She swallowed. "It might take a few days."

That was the wrong answer. Reid blinked and looked away, expression unreadable.

"Anything else you'd like to talk about?" she asked.

"No." Reid dropped her hands and headed toward the stairs. "I need rest."

He retreated to the upstairs bedroom. Juniper stood by the sink, listening to his footsteps, the subtle squeak of the bed, the thunk of boots hitting the wooden floor. Something more than magic had happened to him in the cavern. She had the terrible feeling that there was nothing she could do and the worse feeling that it had been partially her fault.

CHAPTER 6

Juniper did not immediately join Reid. She instead sat by the hearth to think. Reid's indifference hurt, and his predatory stare worried her. The piece of Nexon on her finger worried her. The unknown fate of her friends a kingdom away bothered her.

She was still sitting by the hearth when Ingrid returned. A cold, ashy winter wind rushed in with her. Being a druid, Ingrid had emerald skin and dark brown hair. She hung her well-worn cloak by the door and did her best to avoid looking at Juniper. The firelight exaggerated the dark circles under her eyes and highlighted the soot on her dress and the rips at the hem.

"Is it as bad as it looks?" Juniper asked.

Ingrid sat at the table and dragged her fingers through her dirty hair. "The earth swallowed half of our crops, and the other half are burned. Most of our firewood was burned. We have enough food in our stores for a few weeks, and our song once again encourages the plants to grow. We won't go hungry. But we have lost other supplies, and we are scrambling to find places for everyone to sleep. So much of the village was destroyed, homes that have been standing for centuries, and it will take years to rebuild." Ingrid rubbed her eyes. Soot stained her hands, and dirt caked under her nails. "Your...friends from Delphine have been gracious enough to draw those...things. Those of our people sleeping in tents will not freeze to death tonight."

Juniper's guilt twisted. The druids had a way with vegetation. She had watched Enna coax lavender shoots and mint leaves back from frost by humming. It was old druid magic—their song could make anything grow, which is how they survived in the cursed Blackwood Wylds for a thousand years.

"Jarek told me what you did," Ingrid said nervously. "You and Lilianna. How you used magic to end the curse."

"Do you still hate me?" As the words left her lips, a tremor shook the earth. Dust from the rafters fell, the jars of herbs and spices rattled, and the flames of the hearth danced.

Wonderful timing, Juniper thought bitterly.

Ingrid waited for the shaking to end, then grimaced into the fire. "I don't know. Hate seems like a strong word. Distrust feels more appropriate."

Juniper was used to distrust. In her days as a thief, she hadn't been able to afford trust. The Undercity operated on distrust.

"Did you really do it?" Ingrid asked. "Did you really kill the witch?"

"She wasn't a witch." Juniper heaved an annoyed sigh, pushing down the urge to reprimand their backwater ideals. "She was an old, cranky mage, and she was the only thing keeping the curse in check. Without her, Sinjon would have fallen into the earth centuries ago."

She'd also been a bit mad, but Juniper kept that to herself.

"Jarek mentioned that Reid seemed distraught." Ingrid glanced toward the closed door at the top of the stairs. "Is he all right?"

Juniper held her tongue. She didn't know what Reid felt, other than confusion and dread, and she didn't know how to convey those to Ingrid. He had grown up hating mages for the murder of his family, and now he was a mage. She remembered the hate in his eyes when he had discovered her magic, and she couldn't imagine what he thought about himself.

Instead of lying, she simply smeared the truth. "We got separated in the caverns. The magic was thick as fog, and he saw things. He hasn't told me much."

Ingrid paled. Like most druids of Sinjon, she feared magic. They had grown up with the curse of the Wylds, and that was all they knew of magic. Ingrid and Jarek had lost their only son to it, and the recent events had only worsened their deep-seeded misunderstanding and hatred.

"Reid is a knight," Juniper assured Ingrid—and herself. "He is trained to handle magic. He just…needs time to sort out his thoughts."

"You look like you had a rough go of it too," Ingrid said. "Why don't you go on up and rest? You've been up all night and you look it. I'll make sure something is made for breakfast."

Juniper pulled herself up the stairs and into the smaller bedroom at the top of the stairs. The small woodstove burned low. Reid was lying on his side, facing the shuttered window. His silver armor hung on the lopsided stand, glinting in the dim orange light. The room smelled like woodsmoke and ash, but underneath it she caught the subtle floral scent. Most flowers had wilted with the curse or been trampled in the fight, and she hadn't been up there, which left only Reid. His magic, she realized.

She washed her hands and face in the small earthen basin, shed her dusty, torn, and musty dress and changed into a large tunic she found among the clothes in the wardrobe. Jarek must have procured it for Reid, for it hung to her thighs. She dug for a pair of socks, then tiptoed to the bed. Reid was sleeping, or at least his eyes were closed. She approached with caution, a thief sneaking up on a snoozing guard dog. She hadn't been nervous of approaching him in ages, not since those days in Bradburn Castle when he was the noble squire who hated magic and she was the thief and a reluctant mage.

Archmage in the Ruins

She sat on the bedside, jostling the old bed, but he didn't move. She tucked her toes under the quilt and crawled underneath. She set her head against the single pillow. The bed wasn't large enough to leave space between them, and her side pressed into his back. Warmth radiated from him. The warmth of a living body, with warm blood pumping through the veins.

She wanted to curl into his side—the heartbreak of his apparent death lingered, and she wanted the reminder that he lived, but she feared this feral version of him. She had read stories of people returning from the dead. They never returned as the same person. They either lacked vital parts of themselves or met terrible ends in which they poetically returned to the underworld. She wanted to believe the magic she'd stolen from the Spirit Gate in Delphine had done something to heal him, to pull him back before he crossed onto the other side. Enna had mentioned the in-between, and Juniper hoped Reid hadn't gone too far.

But if Hiada wanted Reid back in the underworld, he would have to fight Juniper first.

CHAPTER 7

Several tremors shook in the night. Juniper woke with each, hot and fluid panic pumping through her bones. Reid slept soundly, or at least he didn't move. Juniper slept in uneven, tumultuous bursts. What little sleep she found was riddled with nightmares—walking blood trees with glowing green eyes, crows with hinged jaws and razor-sharp teeth, and cracks in the earth that fell so far down that she would die before she hit the bottom.

Motion stirred her from the nightmares—Reid getting out of bed. Sunlight streamed through the closed shutters, illuminating the dust motes and stripping the far wall in pale gold. Juniper rubbed her sticky, groggy eyes.

Just dreams.

Reid went through the motions of washing his hands and face, dressing, attaching his Mage's Bane sword to his waist, and then headed downstairs without a word.

She sat up and hugged her knees to her chest. He hadn't even looked at her. She wanted to know what he was feeling, but she didn't know if she could handle it on top of her own stress. She sat there until Jarek's booming voice filtered upstairs. She washed, dressed, steeled herself, and opened the room just as the front door to the house closed.

"Jarek and Reid are off to help with repairs." Ingrid set a plate of toast and a jar of jam on the table. A pot of tea steamed. "I'm off too. You are free to stay here, unless you feel like helping. Right now, we could use all the hands we've got."

Ingrid pulled her cloak around her shoulders and left. Juniper nibbled on the toast. It wasn't that she didn't feel like helping the druids, she didn't feel like hard labor. She and Lilianna still had work to do with the wellspring. She forced down the toast and a cup of tea, then headed for the door. Outside, her breath puffed from her lips, and the cold penetrated straight to the bone.

The winter sun had finally broken through the steely sky. Thick gray clouds lingered, though they were thinning. Just as the curse thinned.

"Your Highness?" asked a husky female voice.

She bristled. From the tent beside Jarek's house, a familiar stranger exited. It was Rue Bellamy, a Sentinel. She was taller than Juniper and had deep golden skin and short caramel hair. She wore an infectious smile that warmed her entire face. Rue placed her hand over her heart and gave a quick bow.

"That's not necessary," Juniper said. "And I'd prefer if you didn't."

"My brother told me that you'd be stubborn," Rue said. Her brother was Captain Bellamy of the Collatian Royal Guard. "But you're still our princess."

Juniper sighed. "I'm not—"

"Oh, stop it," Rue snapped. She set her hand on her pommel. She held herself like Reid: proud, determined, and impassable. "You risked your neck for these people, despite how much they hated you, so stop saying you're not important. We didn't trek through these woods for nothing. We came looking for you. Now go do whatever it is you've been doing. We'll look after the village."

Juniper blinked at the Sentinel. No one in Delphine would have dared speak to her like that, and her fondness for Rue just doubled. Juniper half-laughed, jarring the recent injuries to her ribs and everywhere else, and then started toward Enna's to find Lilianna. The walk through the village let her see just how vast the devastation was, and how much the druids had lost. Holes had appeared in fields and paddocks, swallowing crops and livestock, while others had swallowed entire homes and parts of others. Druids, bundled in old wools and furs, salvaged what they could and swept debris into large piles. To Juniper's horror, they had started to build what looked like a massive pyre—person-shaped bundles had been laid out beside it, ready for their send off.

Juniper tore her eyes away. She didn't want to know how many. Too many.

Enna wasn't home, and Juniper found Lilianna behind the house. Moss basked in the sunlight, rolling in the grass. Like the Shadows that had plagued the Wylds for centuries, Moss was made of magic. His skin shimmered in shades of black and charcoal, undulating like contained smoke.

"There he is," Juniper said.

Moss let out a warble of welcoming, his pure white eyes wide. Where his body shimmered, his eyes remained steady.

"He was waiting outside this morning." Lilianna looked better, though exhaustion lingered under her eyes and in her movements. "Ready to go back to the wellspring?"

Moss rolled onto his feet and stretched his wings upward. No, but if her other option was helping with the repairs, she would go. "I doubt I'll be much help."

"I would rather you come with me," Lilianna said sheepishly. She looked at Moss, then the ground. "You know more about magic than I do."

"We're both archmages," Juniper said. "That technically makes us equals."

"You're more experienced." Lilianna's calm mask slipped, and uncertainty worried the edges. "I don't feel comfortable using my magic without…guidance. I suppose that's Angyla's doing. She taught me to be frugal with practicing, and I only ever practiced with her."

Juniper wanted to argue that she was a terrible teacher and had learned to use her magic as she went, but she held her tongue. She remembered being in Lilianna's position, a fledgling mage desperate to learn and not having many teachers to ask. Juniper had gotten lucky. Mason Hobbs had taught her the basics of control.

"Okay," Juniper said. "Let's get going."

Moss warbled and pranced through the grass. At Lilianna's command, he stilled and lowered his wings for them to climb onto his back. With a mighty flap of his leathery wings, they took off over the village. The destruction was even more apparent from above. Smoldering piles of ash and debris littered the outskirts, and the druids worked to pull apart the collapsed homes and structures. Her eyes caught on the pyre and the growing number of bodies to burn.

They flew over the timber wall and over the Wylds. Tremors continued, though with less intensity than the day before. Sunlight seeped through weak spots in the clouds, and in some places dappled the deadened forest below.

"It's strange to see the sun out here," Lilianna said. "Do you think that when we fix the wellspring, the forest will come back to life?"

"I hope so." Juniper had no idea. She wanted it to.

They flew over crags and fissures and fallen trees, fractured stone and ruptured earth, and finally came to the hole that led to the wellspring. The golden mist oozed upward, thinner than before. Moss landed on a mostly smooth piece of stone. He sniffed the misty air and snorted. He took a few steps back from the cavern.

"Stay here," Lilianna said kindly. She rubbed his snout. "We'll be back in a bit."

Moss warbled and wandered into the shade of the forest, and sat.

Juniper crafted a stairwell of blue ice that wound down through the uneven walls and to the bottom—the chamber of the wellspring. The tangled magic remained unchanged since the night before, though the air was not as stifling. Juniper didn't do much in regards to fixing the wellspring. She kept debris from hitting Lilianna as her sage magic tugged on the tangled threads, calming as she untangled.

Lilianna worked until she exhausted her magic, until sweat shimmered on her forehead and neck, until her knees trembled with the effort to stand, until her breathing turned labored. When she released her magic grip on the wellspring, she collapsed to the cavern floor, panting. She had unraveled the knotted magic considerably.

"I—I…I'm tired…" Lilianna said between gasps.

"You've depleted your magic," Juniper explained. "You can't do anything else right now. Come on, let's rest up and come back when you're full again."

They returned to the surface via Juniper's ice stairwell. The sun seemed brighter, although Juniper couldn't tell if it was because they had been underground or if the wellspring's curse had lessened that much more.

Moss was gone.

Juniper heaved a sigh. She would rather not walk all the way back to Sinjon. Lilianna, far more exhausted than Juniper, sat in the shade where Moss had been.

"Give me a minute," Lilianna said breathlessly.

"Don't pass out," Juniper warned. "I don't know if I could carry you to the village or not."

Lilianna didn't laugh.

Juniper meandered through the nearest trees, hoping Moss would pop out of the forest and save her feet from the walk. He didn't. Neither did anything else.

The Wylds were inexplicably silent.

"Lilianna," Juniper started. Her voice sounded far too loud in the quiet forest. "Where are all the Shadows?"

Lilianna glanced around the Wylds. "I…"

"You said Angyla controlled them. Can you do the same?"

Lilianna's brow furrowed, then she scanned the quiet forest. "Angyla said Shadows were made of magic," Lilianna said, almost to herself. "And if Shadows are made of magic and air…"

Lilianna stilled. Her gaze sharpened. She focused on something Juniper could not see.

The golden mist began to gravitate toward Lilianna, like blown smoke. The mist gathered at her feet, loosely at first, then pushed together into something solid. A shape took form. Lilianna's magic wove with the golden mist—four lean legs, a thick torso, a short snout, and a whip-like tail. The gold and sage swirled together into a deep shade of emerald, so dark it appeared black, shimmering and undulating like light through water.

The Shadow opened its pure white eyes and blinked at Lilianna. It stretched and flexed.

Lilianna released a sudden breath. Sweat beaded on her brow, despite how her breath clouded the air. Then she laughed.

Juniper couldn't believe it. Liliana had created a Shadow.

"What does that feel like?" Juniper asked.

"I don't know how to explain it," Lilianna said, her voice breathy but calm. "I can feel him, but not like a part of me. I mean, he is a part of me. It's my magic, but it is…part my magic and part the magic of the Wylds. I can sense his state. He's calm."

"He's connected to you just like the Shadows were connected to Angyla," Juniper said. When Angyla raged, the Shadows raged.

"It's incredible." Lilianna reached out her hand, and the Shadow nosed her palm. "And terrifying. I can't imagine having as many Shadows wandering through the Wylds as Angyla had. All at once. Do you think my magic will ever be that strong?"

"Of course it will," Juniper said.

Lilianna blinked at Juniper; the Shadow mimicked the gesture.

"You're the Archmage of Air," Juniper said firmly. "Your magic might not be as strong today, but give it some time. You'll grow into it. When I first decided I wanted to hone my magic, I could barely summon a handful of snowflakes."

"And now you're making entire stairwells of ice," Lilianna added.

Juniper nodded. "So, give it some time. You'll learn to control it."

As would Reid, she hoped.

CHAPTER 8

The next several days passed in a haze. Juniper helped Lilianna untangle the wellspring and coached her on the basics of magic. With every dawn, Lilianna could summon more Shadows. She tested her range by sending them into the forest as scouts. They brought her reports—though Juniper didn't understand *how* they reported—of fissures, collapsed caverns, and upturned trees.

Reid worked in the village with Jarek and the Sentinels. He spoke little to Juniper. She tried to hold a conversation with him at night, but he offered little in return. She kept telling herself that he had tired himself with all the repairs.

The druids remained leery of Juniper and Lilianna. Jarek assured his people that Juniper had saved them by defeating the witch, and that despite their prejudice, not all magic was bad. It seemed that Lilianna's being a mage had turned their tide of hatred. They knew she was not evil.

Juniper pulled herself out of bed on an overcast morning. Reid stood at the washing basin. He had taken off his shirt to wash. Silver scars crisscrossed his muscular bronze back. As a knight, he kept his body strong. While not excessively handsome, Juniper enjoyed looking at him—particularly without a shirt.

Reid turned and caught her staring. He hadn't shaved in the past few days, and a shadow of brown hair graced his jaw.

For a moment, they only stared at one another.

"You look remarkably like your uncle when you don't shave." Juniper pulled her legs up and leaned onto her knees.

He blinked as if he didn't understand her. He turned away, pressed a towel to his face, and then reached for his shirt.

"How do you think they're doing in Rusdasin?" she asked.

He pulled a heavier shirt over the first. Their clothes were gifts from Jarek and Ingrid, and most were plain, old, and in dull browns, dark greens, and beige. Not that she complained. She hadn't brought any beyond the clothes she had stolen on her way out of Delphine. The druids' clothing was also woolen and warm.

He reached for his boots, and she took that to mean he didn't want to answer. She shoved the thick wool blanket off her legs and set her socked feet on the floor. The cool winter air seeped the warmth from her skin in an instant.

"I wish I could say," Reid said at last. He buckled his sword belt.

"I'm worried." Juniper knew Reid was too. His uncle and aunt were in Rusdasin, as were his friends from the Order, and Prince Adrian. Adrian and Reid had grown up close as brothers.

Reid met her eye. He didn't have to confirm his worry with words—she saw it in his eyes. She headed for the washing basin, Reid headed for the door, and he gave her a light squeeze on the shoulder as he passed.

The affection was minimal, but sufficient.

She washed, dressed, and headed toward the smell of breakfast. Ingrid stood over a pot of stew, Reid stood at the table, and Jarek was pulling a cloak over his broad shoulders.

"It's a mess," Jarek said. Dark circles hung under his eyes. "We don't have the timber or stone for repairs. This winter won't be pleasant."

Ingrid sighed.

Juniper made it halfway down the stairs when Lilianna burst through Jarek's door. She doubled over, panting.

"What's the meaning of this?" Jarek demanded.

"What's wrong?" Ingrid asked on the heels of her husband's words.

Lilianna gulped several breaths. "Scouts…heading this way."

"What?" Jarek asked, softer but no less demanding.

"My Shadows." Lilianna straightened and met her chief's eye. "My Shadows saw scouts heading this way. Not very many, but they were being sneaky. About an hour's walk from the village, to the north. They're mages, I think."

"Mages?" Juniper's stomach dropped into her groin.

Jarek cursed, and Juniper raced down the stairs and out the door before he could say anything more. She ran all the way to the northern battlement, one of two still standing, and climbed the wooden ladder two rungs at a time. The sentries didn't try and stop her, though they glared more than necessary.

She squinted into the northern distance. She didn't see anything but the Wylds, deadened trees and brush.

Footsteps sounded on the battlement behind her.

"Mages?" Reid appeared beside her, scowling at the north.

"Why?" Juniper asked no one in particular.

Lilianna appeared on her other side. "I don't know how many. It's not an army, but it's more than a few. They are sneaking and harboring violence."

Jarek joined them on the battlements. The sentries shed their scowls and straightened their shoulders.

"Ready yourselves for battle," Jarek barked.

Those words rang over the battlements. The sentries scrambled, and their quiet panic spread over the wall and into the village below. Warriors scrambled for armor and weapons.

Juniper spat a curse. "They could only be Nexon's mindless followers. How did they find us?"

"The wellspring," Lilianna whispered. "It pulsed. I felt it in my magic."

"I did too," Juniper said. "And it's possible Nexon felt something, or one of his followers or someone within range of it."

"They could have come from Baxion," Reid said flatly. His fingers tightened on the hilt of his Mage's Bane. "It was supposed to be north of the Dead City, and if my direction is correct, the Dead City is somewhere to the northeast of here."

"The Dead City is a real place?" Juniper asked.

Reid frowned, and he looked more like his old self. "Of course it is."

"I thought it was just a legend."

"What is the Dead City?" Lilianna asked.

Reid hesitated, looking between the two of them, then his gaze returned northward. "The previous royal city of Collatia. It was abandoned after the civil war. The survivors fled south."

Juniper hummed a note. "So...no one lives there? It's completely empty?"

"Yes," Reid said. "Why?"

"Just wondering." Juniper tore her eye from the northern distance and met Reid's suspicious gaze. "What?"

His scowl deepened. "What are you thinking?"

She grinned at him, hoping he would return it. He didn't.

"Are you all right?" she whispered.

His face didn't change. "I'll be fine. We don't have time to worry about things like that with a threat approaching."

"I disagree," she said. "There's nothing like an imminent threat to pull out those things one shouldn't put off, should the worst happen."

Reid sighed through his nose. His eyes hardened. "I have nothing that needs said."

His harsh tone and his words hurt. Juniper waited for him to realize it, to apologize, to do something—his gaze returned to the Wylds. Every bit a knight awaiting battle.

And rather than stay and wait for her heart to break further, she turned to Lilianna. "How far can you send your Shadows and how fast?"

Lilianna considered those words, then understanding darkened her expression. "Far enough, and fast."

"Send me with one," Juniper said. "I want a better look at these scouts."

That snagged Reid's attention. His empty gaze met hers. She knew the look—he wanted to argue, but he didn't. She wanted to think he held his tongue because he knew she would go anyway, and that she could defend herself against a few mages, but she didn't know.

"Are you sure?" Lilianna asked.

"Yes."

Lilianna didn't present an argument. If anything, she seemed happy about the idea.

Despite everything that had happened, Juniper still had a realm to save and a monster of a man to rid the world of. Having something immediate to worry about helped her push the dread of Reid's predicament down. Helped her pretend he was fine. As she made her way down the battlement and to the northern gates, she focused her harsh feelings and anxiety on the scouts and Nexon, who had caused it all to happen.

If not for Nexon, her friends wouldn't be hiding in the Undercity, she and Reid wouldn't have gone to Delphine or the Wylds, and Reid wouldn't have fallen and come back broken.

It was all Nexon's fault, and Juniper would make sure he felt it tenfold.

Juniper approached the northern gates. Druids in ramshackle armor and well-used weapons had assembled, led by Sein and Asher. They stood brave-faced and ready to meet the incoming threat. They wore stoic masks Reid would be proud of, impassive and unfeeling and ruthless.

Juniper marched through the northern gates. Lilianna summoned a sleek Shadow of shimmering blackish emerald. The creature bounced to Juniper, circled her once, and nosed her stomach.

A few druids stumbled away from the Shadow, though a few held their ground. As Reid marched through the gates and to Juniper's side, the druids shook their visible fear. Sein and Asher approached, though they paused a step behind Reid. Both had schooled their fearful expression into a knight's mask. The Shadow warbled, and Juniper climbed onto its back. The magic holding it together sizzled and thrummed under her touch. The skin felt light as air yet sturdy as leather, warm as a summer breeze. Juniper flattened against the Shadow's back, and with a yip of warning, it took off through the Wylds.

The Shadow bounded over the thick roots, between the gnarled trees, and over the cracks in the stone without trouble. Juniper barely felt the motion—the Shadow seemed to be gliding. It bounded to the north, as if it already knew of the scouts—another marvel of Lilianna's magic. It climbed through the towering trees, jumped between the thick branches, until they rose far above the forest floor. Juniper clutched the Shadow's strange skin with white-knuckles. She trusted Lilianna, but the fear of falling prickled along her back and neck, down to her bones.

As they neared the scouts, the Shadow slowed. It slunk along a tree branch, and it didn't take Juniper long to see the scouts. They moved slowly through the Wylds. They were mages—they burned brambles out of their way, smoothed jagged stones, and formed bridges over cracks in the earth. They were no travelers. They carried minimal supplies, and not everyone wore a satchel. They marched over the roots and through the brambles like snakes. They were marching toward Sinjon with purpose.

Nexon knew where they were, or his followers did.

The Shadow snorted.

"I don't like them either," Juniper whispered. "But I have a plan. They aren't going to make it to Sinjon."

The Shadow warbled in agreement.

"Take me lower. We've got the element of surprise." Juniper patted the Shadow's side.

She held on tight as the Shadow navigated the tree limbs like a cat. It dropped onto a bough that jutted above the scouts. She slid from the Shadow's back and to the hardened bark. The Shadow leaned closer to the branch, and Juniper tiptoed as far as she could, then crouched.

As the scouts came into better view, she counted five mages and a thrall. The thrall walked behind the mages, his face blank and devoid of all emotion. He wore plain iron armor, dented and discolored. Thankfully, they were all strangers.

She waited until the scouts came closer, and then summoned a wave of glittering blue ice. It crashed into the ground with a thunderous clatter of clinking ice, snapping brambles and thorns like old thread. Fireballs and chunks of stone crashed into her ice, but the scouts were no match for an archmage. Her ice knocked the mages off their feet and smothered them, ending the confrontation before it began.

All but for one. The thrall.

Juniper wrapped tendrils of ice around his waist and hoisted him into the air with enough force to send his sword clattering to the ground. She curled her ice around the two of them, blocking the Wylds from sight, so all the thrall could see was her. She brought him closer and an icy hand forced his eyes to meet her own. His heavy-lidded eyes were dull brown.

"I know you're in there somewhere, Nexon," Juniper hissed.

It took a moment, and she feared it wouldn't work, but then the thrall's eyes shifted into blue—the cold, vicious blue of Nexon's eyes.

"Congratulations, you found me." Juniper cocked a grin. "But you're not looking for me, are you?" She held up her left hand and wiggled the moonstone ring. Nexon's gaze focused on it with a hunger that made her nauseous. She pushed past it, and in a haughty voice, she said, "You're looking for this. I've got a matching brooch too."

Nexon's gaze snapped to her face. "You—"

"I'll be waiting in the Dead City," she spat. "Come and get it."

With a flourish of her wrist, her ice twisted the thrall's neck. The body crashed onto the forest floor.

CHAPTER 9

Juniper went over her plan at Jarek's table. She spread her stolen map of Collatia over the table and held it in place with stones. The Wylds had been drawn with gashes for cursed trees and peaks for mountains. To the northeast, a ruined castle represented the Dead City.

"Nexon will come for me and the moonstones," Juniper explained. "The Dead City is empty, and no one else will get hurt."

"Are you sure about this?" Jarek asked. He hadn't been too enthused when she'd revealed the truth of her mission, though he didn't look surprised either.

"You'd rather face Nexon and his horde of mages and monsters here?" She motioned toward his house.

"She's right," Enna added. "Sinjon won't withstand the next storm, let alone a battle."

Jarek didn't offer an argument.

"I have a proposition." Enna looked at Jarek.

The chief lifted his dire gaze from the map and looked at Enna.

"Since Sinjon is sundered, and we lack the time and supplies to properly repair it, I say we all go to the Dead City."

Jarek straightened. "Abandon our home?"

"Our home is a pile of rubble," Enna said flatly. "And the Dead City is made of stone and likely would provide better accommodations."

"You are asking me to send my entire village into the line of fire?" Jarek asked.

"The Dead City is a large place." Enna tapped her dirty fingernail against the map. "And you know as well as I do that there aren't enough resources here to sustain life for much longer. We would have to leave or die, and I prefer to leave. This is a grand opportunity."

Jarek stepped away from the table and began to pace.

"And," Enna said carefully, "We could reestablish a druid community. We could send word to our lost neighbors and reestablish lines of communication. We could rejoin the rest of the world. Now that the Shadows are under control and the wellspring no longer threatens us, we are free to do as we please. But we can't wait for the forest to regrow."

"It would be an undertaking," Ingrid added, neither agreeing nor disagreeing. She watched her husband pace.

"An undertaking," Jarek said with a scoff. He paused his pacing and put a hand to his temple. A dirty bandage hugged his palm and wrist. "But I understand your concerns. I will bring the proposition to the council this evening."

"Either way, you'll need supplies," Enna said to Juniper. "I'll see to the gathering. The journey there will be trying, and I doubt you will find much in the Dead City, other than ghosts."

"I'm going." Lilianna looked at Juniper, not her chief or her grandmother. "I have my Shadows and my magic. It will add to your numbers."

Juniper looked at Reid. He hadn't said a word since she'd returned, and he had taken her account in unreadable silence. Even now, he stared into the hearth.

"We leave as soon as possible," Juniper said. "We need to be in the Dead City and ready for Nexon. We don't know how far Baxion is from there, and I'd rather not trek through the Wylds and walk into a fight exhausted and thirsty."

"We should send word to Rusdasin and Delphine." Reid met her gaze, and a prickle of unease shot down her spine. His expression remained distant.

"We should, but how?" she asked.

"My scouts can take letters," Jarek said proudly. "The roads south lead to Delphine, and undoubtedly your queen has the means to send word onward to Rusdasin."

"You'd sent them to Delphine?" Juniper raised her brow. A challenge.

"The Wylds have calmed," Jarek said. "The roads are safer. The only trouble my scouts would have is the weather and time."

"I will write to His Majesty," Reid said.

"And I will write to Myrisha and Crespin," Juniper said.

"We begin at once," Enna said. She shooed Jarek toward the door. "This can't wait until tonight. Gather the council immediately. We leave as soon as possible. Preferably at dawn."

Juniper packed her few belongings in silence. Reid did the same. She had brought minimal supplies when she had fled Delphine in the middle of the night, and Reid hadn't taken time to pack once he had realized where she had gone. Despite Sinjon not being her home, packing filled her with an uneasy finality. A nervous energy had taken over her senses, and she felt like running until she couldn't anymore.

Reid stood with his back to her, staring out of the window. A winter chill slithered inside, fighting with the heat from the small woodstove. They'd added their last log to it, and Reid hadn't said a word as Juniper carved a rune on the window frame, one to keep out the cold. She'd added one downstairs too, though she'd carved it near the bottom of the doorframe and mostly out of sight.

"What do you think will happen?" she asked.

Reid didn't answer for a long moment. Then he asked, "What do you mean?"

"With the villagers," she clarified. "Do you think they'll come with us or stay here?"

Another long silence.

She didn't care what the druids did. She just hated the stiff silence between herself and Reid. She missed the somber tone of his voice, the warmth of his words.

"Having druids would make things easier," Reid said.

She nodded, though he wasn't looking. "I agree. We could use their affinity for growing food. I doubt the Wylds are friendlier to the north."

The front door opened. Juniper stepped out of the bedroom in time to see Ingrid hanging her heavy cloak beside the door.

"Any news?" Juniper asked.

Ingrid sighed. "Word has gotten around that you are heading north. There are mixed feelings whether we should stay here or leave this place for somewhere else. Jarek is holding a meeting at the Great Hall as we speak."

"What do you think?" Juniper asked.

Ingrid looked longingly around her house, at the pots and pans, at the hearth, at the rack of spices.

"You don't have to go," Juniper said.

"I know," Ingrid said. She sat at the table. "This is my home. It's the only place I've ever known. I've spent my life between the Wylds. Thinking about leaving it makes me nervous, but it's not entirely bad. I know there's more out there, but the idea of exploring it makes me a bit sick."

"I've heard change does that." Juniper understood; she'd gone through enough changes in the past year.

"And I don't know if this change is for the better or not," Ingrid said. "Sinjon is a mess. It would take years to reverse the damage and return to where we were before the storm. It will take several seasons for the Wylds to shed the curse, if they even can. If we were to leave, now would be the time. We can start new somewhere else rather than in the same place."

Footsteps sounded outside. The door opened. Jarek marched inside. He looked at his wife, then Juniper.

"Well?" Ingrid asked.

"It's settled." Jarek frowned. "We're leaving."

Juniper helped Ingrid pack barrels and crates and trunks with anything and everything. Reid helped Jarek in the village, packing wagons and loading things. The evening rang with nervous energy. Juniper stayed out of the main preparations. Word had spread of how Juniper had dealt with the scouts and the witch, and thanks to Rue and Calvex, most had heard of her identity as the lost princess of Collatia. To Juniper's dismay, the sentinels exposed her prophesied role in Nexon's downfall.

Before sunset, Juniper and a few druid hunters returned to the dead scouts. They looted what supplies they could, then buried the dead among the roots of the Wylds. The scouts had little on their person, mostly rations, a few healing tonics, a length of rope, and a few decent blades. They didn't have a map to Baxion, which Juniper had been foolish enough to hope for.

The evening meal was a watery stew. Many gathered at the Great Hall to eat—most had been sleeping in the Great Hall too—and Juniper and Reid joined them. The animosity toward her had calmed, though she felt the tension rise at her presence. They gave her a wide berth, and whispers of princess and prophecy followed her through the hall.

She accepted her bowl of watery stew and sat with Lilianna near the far wall, a safe distance from everyone else. Reid sat on her other side.

Those most willing to go to the Dead City were those whose homes had been destroyed in the tremors. They had lost most of their possessions, and they liked the idea of starting again somewhere else. As expected, others were hesitant to leave their ancestral home. But as one of the elders had mentioned, the Wylds needed time to rejuvenate. It could take years, or it could take decades.

That night, Juniper struggled to fall asleep. By Reid's uneven breathing, he hadn't fallen asleep either. She rolled onto her side, facing him. He lay on his back. In the soft flow of the woodstove, his eyes were dark glints. Staring at the ceiling. He was deathly still, and just when Juniper lifted a hand to touch him, he blinked.

"What are you going to do when we get there?" Reid whispered.

"I don't know," she whispered back. "I thought the Dead City would be better because there wouldn't be many people who might get hurt, but if the whole village goes with us, that plan doesn't matter."

"Nexon won't arrive alone."

She knew that too. "We have the Shadows."

"Lilianna can't control an army's worth."

"We have the sentries and warriors."

"Who have never fought a mage."

Juniper sighed. She wanted to shove him off the bed for being so negative, but…he was right. "I wish we had more knights," she whispered.

Reid glanced at her. Even in the dark, his indifferent stare felt like a dull blade.

And…an idea struck.

"Reid, could you train the druids how to fight magic?"

He frowned.

"You learned, so they could too."

"It takes a knight years to learn how to defend against magic."

"You've got a week," she said sternly. She rolled onto her back.

"It's not that simple."

"They don't need to become knights. They need to be able to not die against a mage. Teach them wards and how to deflect."

Reid sighed through his nose—she imagined his grimace.

Softer, she added, "If anyone could teach them anti-magic, you can."

A beat passed. Then another. Juniper wanted to curl into his side, into his warmth, but a sliver of fear made her pause.

"You're sure?" he whispered.

"Of course." she said. "You're the best knight the Order has ever had."

Reid didn't say anything more.

The day dawned bright and cold, and the druids of Sinjon began their journey north. Juniper walked ahead of the caravan, heavy woolen cloak around her shoulders and scarf tucked around her throat. The elderly and sick rode on wagons or in carts. Everyone else walked. Druid hunters marched alongside the caravan, watching for any threat from the Wylds. Rue and Calvex marched among them.

Lilianna walked with Juniper. Shadows moved ahead of them, slithering through the brambles and brush. They would sense a threat far sooner than anyone else.

They followed an ancient road, the cobbles nearly lost to the Wylds and the weeds and the grayed dirt. With the wagons, livestock, and narrow road, they couldn't travel as fast as Juniper would have liked. Where the road narrowed, hunters hacked at the thick brambles and fallen trees. The withered trees of the

Wylds rose tall on either side, shading the ancient road with their empty branches. When the darkness grew too thick, lanterns were lit.

Juniper summoned a magelight.

"What is that?" Lilianna asked, eyes wide.

"Light," Juniper explained. "You can summon one too."

Lilianna tried, but no light appeared in her palms.

"We will work on it later," Juniper said. "When we have a few moments to rest."

The darkness gave way to dappled sunlight after midday, when the canopy thinned enough to let it through. Lilianna tilted her head toward the light and closed her eyes. The sunlight made her emerald skin glow.

They traveled until dusk. They didn't have time to find a clearing large enough for them all—not that one existed within the cramped Wylds—so they camped where they stopped along the road and pitched their tents on any flat surface they could find. Several campfires sparked to life along the caravan, trailing white and gray smoke toward the canopy.

Juniper collapsed onto a large tangle of tree roots, just out of the circle of a campfire. The air had turned frigid. She took a deep breath of it and allowed it to leech warmth from her skin. It stirred her ice magic, nursed it, caressed it.

Lilianna sat beside her. A Shadow materialized in front of her, small and sleek as a house cat, and bounced along the roots with unnatural grace.

"They patrol as we speak." Lilianna stroked the small Shadow's head. "They haven't come across anything since we left the village. Nothing but a few birds. No other creatures stir within the Wylds."

"Enna said it would take time for the forest to recover," Juniper said.

Lilianna nodded. "She is right. Without game to hunt, we would not have been able to survive here."

A Shadow darted on the other side of the road, within the shades of darkness, barely visible even with Juniper's night sight. Despite the lack of creatures, Juniper felt safer with Shadows on the prowl.

"I'm getting better," Lilianna said. "I'm able to give them more control. They listen to me, but they are more…independent. They have a mind of their own. That's something Angyla told me about, but I didn't understand at the time. The Shadows can think on their own, and it's less demanding on me if I let them."

Juniper didn't understand, but she nodded anyway. "That's good. How about your magic?"

Lilianna summoned a spiral of sage air in her cupped hands. The fresh floral scent of magic filled the air, along with the faint bittersweet hint of silver polish.

Lilianna held the spiral for several moments before it flickered out. She sighed through her nose. "Better."

"It takes time to build up a well of magic," Juniper said.

She felt the prickle of eyes. Glancing up, she met Reid's gaze. He sat with hunters around the closet campfire. His molten eyes pierced her, taking in each word she said. Whether he had taken to teaching them anti-magic or not, she didn't know. He hadn't walked with her, and they hadn't had the chance to speak since they left Sinjon.

"Magic is something you have to work at," she said to Lilianna. "You'll get stronger. You'll learn to control more and more of it. Your well will deepen. It takes time and practice, just like using a sword or playing an instrument."

"Why are you smiling?" Lilianna asked.

Juniper half-laughed. "Ison told me that once, and I hated the advice at the time. Now I'm giving it."

The fires shrank, the Wylds grew dark, and the druids climbed into their tents. Lilianna's Shadows would continue to patrol, even while she slept. When asked about it, Lilianna hadn't been able to provide an answer.

Juniper hesitated before her tent. She had Reid had each brought a tent from Delphine, however she'd given hers to Ingrid to give to someone who needed it. She and Reid would share, she'd said, and Ingrid hadn't argued. Reid approached the tent, and her heart thumped. He paused before it. Within the dimmed firelight, his eyes appeared black.

"I can bunk with Lilianna, if you'd rather not—"

"No," Reid said at once. His words and his face betrayed nothing. He motioned for her to go inside.

Juniper crawled into the tent and Reid came in after. The small tent left little space between them. Not that Juniper minded. With winter's chill, she craved Reid's warmth. The trek had exhausted her, and she doubted it would take long to pass out. She settled onto one side and he on the other. Awkwardness prodded the sliver of space between them. They laid in silence. All around them, the druids were falling asleep, and the Wylds were whispering. Shadows were patrolling.

Juniper felt the tug of sleep. She shut her eyes to welcome it.

Reid exhaled and shifted - he rolled onto his side and draped his arm over her middle. The simple action banished thoughts of sleep, but it brought a deeper sense of comfort she had missed. She snuggled closer into his side.

She had missed him.

CHAPTER 10

Reid dreamed of an ocean. Or, he thought it was an ocean. It seemed far too deep and endless to be anything else. He was sinking deeper and deeper into the depths, and the light above him faded with every moment. The water pushed him down. The deeper he sank, the harder it pushed. It tore at his being, threatening to pull his body apart and crush it at the same time.

Deeper he sank.

He tried to swim up to the light before he drowned, but he couldn't move. Soon, it was too dark to see.

Shapes moved in the dark. They started far away, but as he noticed them, they came closer. Dangerously close. They resembled people, but he couldn't be certain. He instinctively reached for his sword—it was gone.

Unarmed and in danger. His panic rose like bile.

The shapes whispered and hissed. They reached for him, tugging at his being, pushing and pulling. It engulfed him, crushing him into pieces and cobbling him back together. Again, and again, and—

"Reid?"

His eyes snapped open, and his dream evaporated. A hand gently pressed against his bicep. For a frightening moment, confusion reigned. The crushing sensation remained, pulsing with every rapid breath.

He blinked. Canvas arched above him. Darkness pressed against the other side. Winter's chill seethed in the air.

He remembered. The tent, the Wylds, and Juniper.

The feverish panic lessened. The whispering of the dream became the hissing of the wind in the barren trees and Juniper's gentle breathing.

"Reid?" Juniper whispered.

The fear in her voice stirred his own, and the instinctive response to remove whatever frightened her. Her shape barely stood out against the darkness of night, but he felt her eyes on him. Her attention. Sleepy but alert. Her cool fingers rested on his arm, waiting for his response.

Her hand tightened on his arm, for a moment, everything was back to normal. It was Juniper and him, no magic or whispers or confusion.

And then the ocean crashed.

It felt like the world was closing in on him, pressing in from every side, while simultaneously pulling him apart. It pulsed around him like a giant heartbeat, as if the world itself was breathing.

The whispering winds became screams, the earth hummed, and the Wylds growled. It was everywhere, and it knocked the breath from his throat. It was all he knew.

"Reid?"

He sucked in his next breath. Juniper had asked him a question…hadn't she? He couldn't remember what it was. He brought his hand up and rubbed his eyes. The overwhelming heartbeat stole away his capability to notice anything else.

"You were dreaming," Juniper said, stealing back a fraction of his attention. She moved her hand from his bicep and flattened her palm over his heart.

At her touch, the whirlwind inside of him calmed. The coolness of her magic seeped into his skin, into his bones, icy but comforting, familiar. He had felt her magic before, but he had never felt it like this—like it coalesced around him, blocking out the worst of the turbulence.

Juniper remained crouched at his side, searching him for words he couldn't form. He knew what he wanted to say, yet had no means to explain it. Unable to speak, he acted. He pulled Juniper as close as he could. She curled into him as if she knew, though he doubted she understood. How could she?

Gods…he didn't know how much more of this madness he could withstand. If this would be his life, he would have chosen to remain dead.

Morning dawned biting cold. Reid woke with his hand pressed against Juniper's stomach, under her tunic and undershirt, his skin against hers. Despite her icy magic, she was warm to the touch. She slept soundly. After he had woken from the nightmare, he had too.

He'd had the same nightmare every night since he died, since he'd inherited the archmage magic.

It happened again—in a single moment, everything felt normal. He felt like himself again, and then the magic slammed into his being. This time, unlike before, he was more prepared. He worked against the magic; he shoved it down and away. He was a knight, trained to combat magic, not wield it! He could not be a mage or an archmage. The entire idea was absurd.

The magic fought back, and he fought harder. He shoved it, it shoved back. He shoved harder, using all he had learned as a knight. The magic complained but listened. It retreated. The pulsing continued.

He refused to be a mage.

Juniper stirred in his arms. Her sleepy gaze found his. Her auburn hair was messed from sleep, but the rest had smoothed her features. She didn't say anything, but he didn't mind. Between the pushing and pulling and magic threatening to burst from his chest, he had little concentration to spare.

"Best not dally." Juniper groaned as she sat up. She rolled her neck before crawling out of the tent.

Reid followed her.

The day was overcast, and snow threatened to fall. Most of their caravan still slept, but a few druids prepared tea and warm ciders over the rekindled fires. Juniper heated water to wash, and she made rounds throughout the caravan to do the same for the others. Reid accepted a cup of warm cider from a druid woman whose name he didn't know. He drank, then put himself to work. Work helped him not think about the abyss under his feet.

Within an hour, they were moving again. Reid walked with the druid hunters. Juniper and Lilianna led the caravan forward, Shadows patrolling for any sign of threats or danger. Sein and Asher were talking, but Reid couldn't concentrate long enough to follow their conversation. Every other thought fell apart halfway.

Moving forward helped. Doing something helped. When he stilled, the magic threatened to overtake him.

Dinner varied from campfire to campfire, but most had a variant of wild stew or dried meat. While he ate his portion, Reid struggled to shove the magic down and keep it there.

And everything else: Nexon, the Dead City, his mother's confession, this…magic. Too much, too soon. It weighed heavy on his heart and mind, and he didn't know how much more he could take before it tore him apart.

CHAPTER 11

Juniper had lost track of the days. She was tired of sleeping on a bedroll on uneven forest ground. Her feet hurt from walking. The warm tea and cider were good, but the wild stew and unseasoned dried meat had lost its appeal days ago.

Juniper and Lilianna walked ahead of the caravan, far enough not to be overheard. Juniper told Lilianna everything she remembered from her magic lessons with Mason Hobbs and Ison during her few short weeks of instructions.

That night, sitting around a campfire, Juniper dropped Mason's name. Reid tensed at once and went to bed early. Juniper had the horrible feeling of having said something hurtful.

"He hasn't been the same," Lilianna whispered to Juniper.

"He hasn't," Juniper agreed. "Whatever he saw or felt in that cavern bothers him immensely."

"Do you think he's really an archmage?"

"I don't know." Juniper didn't know how it was possible for Reid to have inherited magic, but when she had placed her hand on his chest the night before, she had felt a fathomless magic, chaotic and hazy. A storm.

He had yet to perform any magic.

When Juniper crawled into their tent, Reid made no motion he heard her. She curled into his side nonetheless.

The day came too soon, and after a cup of warm tea, the trek continued. They walked, and walked, and walked. The forest rose and fell over small mountains and rolling hills. The Wylds stretched on forever in every direction. According to her map, the Wylds would fade by the time they reached the Dead City. Juniper both dreaded and looked forward to getting there.

Each evening, Juniper helped Lilianna adjust to her new magic. She showed her tricks she had learned on her own and from the Undercity mages and the Marca, like summoning a magelight and sparking a tiny flame on her thumb. She tried her best to explain natural magic and unnatural magic, though she only confused herself on the topic. Despite Juniper's lack of teaching skills, Lilianna had made considerable progress.

"When did you become an archmage?" Lilianna asked one afternoon.

Juniper realized she had no answer. She thought back over her life, but she didn't remember her magic ever being different. Her magic had always been her magic. It had always been there, a lingering thing in her chest. She had moments where she had felt unstoppable, like she could move entire oceans. Had she always been an archmage?

"I...don't know," Juniper answered.

Lilianna seemed to sense Juniper's unease, and quickly changed the subject. "Can you show me how to draw that rune?"

Juniper spent the rest of the evening teaching Lilianna the runes she had learned, from Ison and from Marca. She drew them in the dirt, and Lilianna copied her.

"Some runes are dependent on what material they are carved into, and others need magic to activate," Juniper explained, tracing a rune for silence in the dirt. "This one was used on doors. Half the rune would be on the door and the other half would be on the wall, so that when the door closed, the rune completed. The Marca used it to make quiet rooms."

"That sounds horrible," Lilianna said. She had been tracing the silent rune, then paused.

"It won't activate in the dirt," Juniper said. "Don't ask me how or why. I don't know, or I wasn't paying attention that day. Something about dirt negating a lot of runes." Juniper shrugged. "Stone is better attuned or something like that."

Before they went to bed, Lilianna summoned her own magelight. The pale green ball sparked in her palm, threaded with lavender. Juniper applauded her— Lilianna was a much better student than she had ever been.

"There is also a forever flame, but don't ask me the difference. I don't know." Juniper shrugged. "I wasn't in the Marca long enough to really learn much."

"Angyla told me that there used to be schools for magic all over the kingdom." Lilianna let her magelight go out.

Juniper went to bed early. Her mind, feet, and body needed rest. She collapsed into the forest-smelling blankets in her tent. How much longer did they have before they reached the Dead City? She thought of the torturously long trek into Galamond and the equally long trek from Galamond. Of course, the map she had stolen didn't specify how far the ruins were from the Wylds.

She was on the brink of sleep when the tent flap opened. She stirred enough to see Reid crawl into the blankets. He curled his body around hers, hugging her close. Winter lingered on his skin. He tucked his cold hand under her tunic and flattened his palm against the skin of her stomach, just below her breasts. His warm breath graced the back of her neck.

ARCHMAGE IN THE RUINS

Reid didn't wake up in the middle of the night, or at least he didn't wake her up in the middle of the night twitching and mumbling.

She hoped it was a good sign of his recovery.

Gradually, the Wylds faded. The towering trees shrank, the underbrush thinned, and the impossible brambles vanished. The tangled, gnarled roots retreated into the earth. The canopy thinned, allowing more and more daylight to slip through. The clouds thinned and then thickened, as if unsure if they wanted to snow or not. She felt it up there, the water ready to return to the earth.

And then, at last, the Wylds ended. Juniper paused just within the stark line that separated the cursed forest from the rest of the kingdom. Behind them, tainted trees and roots and brambles grew wild and tangled. In front of them, the winter-dead forest stretched to the horizon, the barren trees spotted with evergreens.

"It ends," Lilianna whispered. Her golden eyes were wide as she took in the forest before her.

Reid appeared at her side. Asher and Sein followed at his heels, looking as serious as knights.

Juniper took the first step out of the Wylds. It felt no different. The oppression of the curse had faded with every step away from Sinjon, and with every dawn. She hadn't felt it in…weeks, maybe. She had lost track of time. Lilianna followed close behind, taking in the healthy forest with wide eyes and childlike wonder.

The caravan continued behind them. Juniper led the party over small rolling hills, over an ancient bridge that creaked with the weight of the wagons, and between towering evergreens thick with needles and lingering snow.

A few hours past midday, the Shadows signaled a change on the horizon. Juniper's stomach dropped. Had Nexon's forces found them already? Had their pace been that slow? Or had Baxion been much closer than they thought? Juniper ran ahead. Lilianna, Reid, Sein, and Asher followed at her heels. Juniper crested the next hill first, and the sight beyond stole her breath.

The ruins of the once great royal city stretched to the horizon. Stone homes and buildings lay empty and forgotten, a swatch of gray, black, and weathered blue and green. Nature had seeped through the bottom of the city, breaking apart cobblestone streets and stone foundations. Trees had grown through the stone, lifting walls and shattering homes with their branches.

The Dead City, Collatia's ruined royal city. Her birthplace. Even standing at the edge, the whole city felt utterly empty and…dead. Juniper understood the city's forbidding name.

Lilianna paused beside her. "Gods."

"If we continue, we could find shelter before sundown," Juniper said, her tone flat and far too shaky for her liking. She didn't give any of them a chance to point it out. She headed straight into the Dead City.

The caravan followed. The sparse conversations among the druids faded into silence. Only their boots, hooves, and wagon wheels sounded against the broken cobbles. The further into the city they walked, the tighter the streets and closer the buildings. Windows were dark and broken. Everywhere Juniper looked, she spotted evidence of a war long over. Some buildings had been obliterated while others had fallen walls or roofs, while others had been charred black.

Juniper led the caravan through an old square, an intersection of two wide roads. A long-dry fountain sat in the middle. Whatever the marble statue had depicted, it was a pile of rubble now.

"Where are we going?" Lilianna asked.

Juniper glanced behind her. The druids had followed her deeper within. Were they waiting for her to make a decision for them? They had opted to follow her to the Dead City.

"It's a big city," Juniper started. "They can—"

"Druids are a community," Lilianna said firmly. "We aren't splitting up. We are going where you are going. So, where are we going?"

Juniper hadn't made the conscious decision, yet she knew exactly where her feet were taking her. The northern end of the city. Holding herself tall under the gaze of so many druids, she said, "Somewhere dramatic and symbolic and large enough to hold a village."

Lilianna's brows rose, but she asked no questions.

Juniper led them deeper into the Dead City. The daylight began to fade, and as the first stars appeared above, Juniper spotted what she'd been looking for. It loomed in the distance, its turrets and battlements and archer's windows and steeled roofs.

Balendin Castle.

CHAPTER 12

Ison stared at the polished granite of Espone's statue. The goddess of merriment had been artfully carved in theatrical robes, like the actors of old. She wore a joyful expression, lips curved and eyes wide, hair flowing down her shoulders. She held a feather quill in one hand, and a small harp in the other.

The mages of Baxion had erected one massive temple that housed a chamber for each god. According to the priestesses, that was how the temples used to be built—with the gods together. With what might come, he figured the best place to go was to the gods. It had been a while since he had prayed or given an offering. The smoke from his offering rose in a sensual stream toward the temple ceiling.

Someone shifted in the temple. Ison didn't pay attention. People came and went from the temples at all hours, some seeking solace and some seeking penance.

That someone plopped onto the wooden bench beside him. Dark hair flounced around her face, loosened from her short braid. Cera. She wore her scouting leathers, the same Xavier wore, only her left hand was bandaged. Shadows hung under her dark eyes.

"I thought you were scouting," Ison asked. He nodded to her hand. "What happened?"

"Spider bite." She turned her bandaged hand over. The tips of her fingers were swollen. "It might have been poisonous, but I burned the stupid thing to a crisp before I could identify it. So, I took a few potions to negate the poison I might have in my blood, and the healers have pulled me from scouting duty for the next four days. Said it was better for me to pass out in Baxion than somewhere in the woods."

He started to ask what potions she'd ingested, but refrained. No one in Baxion knew he had been the court magician's apprentice or the potions master at Bradburn Castle. They knew him as a stable hand. A stable hand wouldn't know the difference between a health tonic and a glass of milk.

Cera leaned back to look up at Espone. "They say our magic is supposed to correspond with the stars and the gods? I'm a fire mage, but I was born under Espone's stars. One of the old mages here said I'm a *deevi*. It's Iluvin or something. It's when your magic doesn't match your patron."

"I've never heard of that," Ison said. "They didn't talk about that at the Marca."

"Of course not," Cera spat. "Anything remotely Iluvin is tossed out."

"What does that mean? Being a *deevi*?"

She shrugged. "Nothing, apparently. I spent my childhood thinking I was supposed to have been an air mage, not a fire mage, but until I got here, I couldn't safely ask about it." She sighed and brought her gaze back to Ison. "I'm glad I ended up here. Sure, it's not perfect, but nowhere is. This is better than anywhere else I would've ended up."

Ison's guilt twisted. "You're right. This place is far better than I thought it would be."

"Xavier says you're working wonders with those monsters," Cera said. "He talks about you a lot. Don't get me wrong. It's cute. I wish someone thought about me like he thinks about you. Like you matter."

"I'm sure people here think you matter," Ison said.

Cera rolled her eyes. "Yeah, they'd have to find another scout."

She slumped forward.

The motion, the tone—he recognized it. Unhappiness.

"Is everything going all right?" Ison leaned forward to study her expression. Her youthful face bore exhaustion, addled by mysterious potions and maybe-poison. The pinkish tint to her skin, the twitching of her toes, the brightness of her eyes.

"I'm fine…" She motioned to her hand and her chest with her good hand.

"You're having a reaction," he said.

It took a moment for her gaze to focus. "What?"

He stood. "We need to get you a healer before you get worse."

Cera looked at his outstretched hand like he'd gone mad, but she took it. Ison led her out of the temple and into the late evening light. He didn't need a healer—he needed his potion room and a simple base of herbs and minerals. The healers would ask too many questions, so he led Cera to a closed apothecary. Cera didn't say a word as he pulled her into the alley and to the backdoor, or as he negated the security rune on the backdoor and pulled her inside. She sat in a kitchen chair while he readied the potion making equipment. He summoned the smallest forever flame he could and set it inside a tinted flask, giving him just enough light to see the different minerals and herbs.

Every creak and whisper from the street had him dimming his forever flame. If they were caught… No. They wouldn't be caught.

He took the finished potion from the small flame, added a single drop of winter's tears. The pale green potion clouded into milky blue and then cooled into clear green.

"There," Ison said. "Take this."

Cera had gone ghostly pale, and sweat lingered on her brow. She looked into the potion. "I took like ten of these. How is this going to help?"

"You're reacting to something within one of those potions," Ison said firmly. "You're allergic to something. This potion will negate the reaction."

Cera tilted the potion to her lips and drank it in a few gulps.

Ison quickly put everything back where he'd found it. The color returned to Cera's cheeks, and her breathing evened. Ison washed the glass and returned it to the cabinet. The two of the slipped back into the dark alley.

"I feel better," Cera said a few streets later. "I didn't know you were so good with potions."

"I dabbled."

Cera looked sideways at him, the magelight illuminating her doubt.

"I took to it better than anything else," Ison admitted. Shame heated his cheeks. "At the Marca. Spell craft wasn't my strong suit."

"And you lied about it when you got here," she said. "You could have been making potions instead of working with those...things."

He knew that. "I have my reasons."

She didn't argue.

They walked for a while longer in silence. Cera paused at a corner and pulled Ison to a stop. She looked remarkably better, though still exhausted. The pinkish tint had left her skin, her eyes were focused.

"Thank you," she said. "I don't think anyone else would have done that for me."

"You're welcome," Ison said. "I, uh, would appreciate it if no one else found out."

Cera flashed him a genuine smile. "Your secret is safe with me."

Ison stood on the side of the arena as the beasts ran in formation, just like Mercer had demanded. Ison wanted to argue that they were not war horses; they were people, but then he would have to explain how he knew that. Then Mercer might tell Nexon, and Nexon would know exactly who he was. Their plan would be over.

And he couldn't afford that, not now when they were so close.

The beasts ran in formation to one end of the arena, and that was when Ison saw it - a pale furred beast lingering by the door that led to the lower floors. Ison had left the cages open so the beasts could come and go as they pleased, and so that they wouldn't feel trapped. The pale beast had been in the newest batch, but while the others had acclimated to the new dynamics, the pale beast had lingered. It had avoided the others. It had not lashed out, which he took as a good sign. So, Ison left the pale beast to make up its mind first. It would join the others when it was ready.

It watched the other beasts with curious intent. The beast had pale eyes the color of the sky, and as if it felt Ison's stare, he turned that curious stare onto him.

The latest batch had come out remarkably intelligent. They made the beasts Ison had been a part of in Bradburn Castle look like rabid wolves.

"Ison!" Mercer's harsh voice called over the arena.

The beasts stopped their formation, and Ison looked at the mezzanine. Mercer stood overlooking the arena, his dark hair tied back and his leathers spotted with dirt. A woman stood with him, pale haired and sneering. She wore riding leathers and a fur lined cloak. She stood shorter than Mercer, but she held herself proud and tall.

Ison recognized her as the woman Mercer had been talking to that night. She had come and gone from the arena over the past several weeks, but she didn't talk to anyone but Mercer.

"I'm cutting this playdate short," Mercer called.

Ison waved, acknowledging his command. He whistled; it was the easiest way to reach all the beasts at once. They shifted their attention to him. The alpha sauntered a few steps closer.

"Let's head back down," Ison said to the alpha. It started toward the open doors, and the others followed.

The beasts funneled out the arena without fuss. They grumbled and growled, sounds Ison had come to know as them talking to one another. How their language worked, he didn't know.

Ison walked with them to their cells. The other stable hands had cleaned the cells and added fresh water and bedding. The beasts retreated into their little homes, and Ison closed the doors.

With no one but them listening, he said, "It might be sooner than we expected."

A series of growls, either of annoyance or acceptance. He didn't really know. He closed the door to the pale beast's cell, and the beast met his eye again.

"Are you with us?" Ison asked.

The beast hesitated, then let out a small growl. It sounded as much like acceptance as anything else.

Ison retreated to the stairwell, and he found Mercer and the sneering woman waiting for him at the top. At once, his stomach turned over and back again.

"Ison, this is Lora," Mercer said. "Lora, this is the trainer I've told you about. He's got the beasts running in formation."

Lora.

Ison fought to keep his expression neutral. Everyone in Baxion had heard of Lora—she was Nexon's second in command.

"I saw," Lora said. Her voice was somber and vicious. Her gaze raked over Ison, and he prayed she hadn't heard of him from Nexon. If she had, she didn't show it. "Mercer has told me all about the wonderful progress you've made with the beasts. Tell me, boy, how have you managed this when so many others failed?"

Ison swallowed. "I—I don't know. I've always been good with animals."

"I've heard him talking to them," Mercer said to Lora as if Ison wasn't there.

Ison's face burned. He had been so careful when talking to the beasts. He hadn't realized Mercer had heard him. Had anyone else?

"Ah," Lora said, indifferent. "Little is known about the process and the aftereffects of the transformation. Maybe a sliver of humanity remains behind. Who knows? It doesn't matter." She turned her sharp gaze onto Ison. "The time has come to test your mettle. Nexon has spoken to me. There has been a disturbance to the south. Our scouting party was decimated, and Nexon has been challenged. We are heading to the Dead City to stomp out the last of the rebels."

The floor shifted under Ison's feet. He widened his stance to counterbalance.

Lora's brows rose at his silence. Looking down her nose at him, she asked, "Are the beasts ready?"

Ison felt a tremor that seemed to come from below. He imagined all the beasts below stomping in agreement and encouragement, ready.

This was it.

He steeled himself. "Yes, ma'am. We're ready."

CHAPTER 13

Balendin Castle loomed against the amber and plum of dusk. Juniper took the first step over the broken gate and into the overgrown front garden. Once, a stone path had led from the gates to the castle steps, but weeds and war had shattered it. Winter-dead trees, scraggly vines, and bushy weeds grew wild on either side. The castle itself would have been a marvelous sight—its turrets and towers rose high above the city, its steepled domes looked to have once shone like silver, and its gabled roofs had broken stained glass windows taller than a grown man. Blugo had graced the ruined castle in ice, making it seem made of crystal and silver.

Twenty years ago, the castle would have been a wondrous sight. Now, it looked haunted.

Icy fingers wrapped around Juniper's heart and squeezed. Her next breath came shallow. It took more effort to draw a full breath.

Lilianna paused at her side. "We can handle this."

With a graceful wave of her hand and a low hum, the overgrown weeds and vines retreated from the broken stone path. Ingrid appeared on Juniper's other side, humming the same simple song, and commanding the vines further away. Juniper watched as the druids came forward, humming as one, and tamed the garden right before her eyes. The druid song rose in volume, haunting in the dim hour. The dead vines curled away, withered weeds shrank, and the knee-high grass shrank to a much more manageable height.

"There," Ingrid said, looking at the uncovered stone path that now led straight to the castle doors. "Much easier for the wagons."

Despite Juniper's trepidation, she led the caravan over the broken gate and through the garden. The wagons clanked over the broken stones. Juniper couldn't look away from the looming castle. She tried to imagine what it would have looked like twenty years ago when the castle was intact, but her mind couldn't conjure anything other than its ruined state.

Moss bounded around the garden, sniffing at the ground, taking stock of the new surroundings. He sank into a tuft of tall, dead grass, and jumped out of the other side with a playful warble.

The main castle doors had been blasted in, leaving the vestibule open to the elements. Twenty years of rain and snow and wind had turned the once grand space into a nightmare.

Portraits were molded, mildew grew between the stones, and old char had turned into something vile and black in the mortar. Spider webs clung to the ceiling in clumps. The stone walls and pillars that lined the long chamber bore scorch marks and evidence of earth magic. Several pillars had collapsed or been twisted in unnatural positions.

And the silence. It pushed in from every side. Only her own breath sounded, and the pounding of her heart.

For a moment, within the silence, she heard whispering, urgent and fearful. It scratched against her mind and sent a sudden chill over her skin. Before she could listen harder, the druids followed her through the broken doors. Their boots and wagon wheels and horses hushed any other sound. To be honest, she was rather glad for the noise.

At the back of the vestibule, a short but grand staircase led to what once might have been a set of lovely wooden doors, but the wall had collapsed. Now, the stairs led only to rubble. The receiving rooms just off the vestibule had suffered broken windows, and an overgrowth of mold, weeds, and a strange prickly plant grew from the puddles of murky water within. Corridors led away from the vestibule, into dark and damp.

"This will do," came Jarek's booming voice.

Juniper tore her eyes from the rubble and turned. The caravan had stopped. Jarek looked at the vestibule with something frighteningly like optimism.

"It will hold us all," Ingrid added, coming to stand at his side. Every druid in the vestibule watched their chief and his wife. "A little cleaning, and it'll be a nice space. Sturdy."

Jarek then looked to Juniper, as did Ingrid. Expectantly. Others looked to her, and whispers slipped in as more druids entered the vestibule. Juniper spotted Reid among them, flanked by Rue and Calvex, and she waited for a sign from him—he gave none. His expression remained impassive, indifferent. Rue gave Juniper a nod of encouragement.

"This is where we make our stand," Juniper announced. Her tired voice carried over the old stones with far less intimidation and assurance than Jarek's.

No one moved. All eyes remained on her. What else did they expect her to say?

"You heard her," Jarek cut in, his booming voice carrying to every corner. "We make camp here."

The druids began the odious process of unloading and unpacking the wagons and carts, while others tended to the livestock and horses, and others still set about cleaning the vestibule of mold, spiderwebs, dead bugs, overgrowth, and stagnant water. Jarek oversaw it all. He commanded a patrol around the castle at all times, and a group of hunters left for the front garden.

Juniper watched it all from the stairs that led to the crumbled doorway. The druids cleared the floor of grime and dead plants and sparse animal bones. They weaved vines into curtains and hung them over the broken windows, clogged the holes in the wall with packed mud and fibrous paste, and laid rugs over the cracks in the stone floor. They erected a city of tents within the vestibule and its adjoining rooms, and altered the front garden to house the livestock and the horses. Incense burned away the stench of mildew and musty air.

By full dark, the vestibule looked and smelled livable.

Lilianna navigated the crowded vestibule and sat by Juniper on the stairs. "Things are coming alone better than I thought they would."

"That's good," Juniper said.

"Grandmother wants to turn the back garden into an herb garden," Lilianna added, her tone was light, conversational.

"I can only imagine how monstrous it looks."

"It's overgrown," Lilianna confirmed. "Enough that it doesn't look like a garden anymore. But there's no garden druid song can't handle. It won't take long to have herbs and food growing."

Juniper knew what Lilianna said was good news, that they would need food to survive, but her mind couldn't focus on it.

"We need to be ready for Nexon's attack," Juniper said lowly. Because he was coming. There was no way of knowing when he would arrive, or how many mages he would bring. "We need to be ready at all hours."

"The hunters are used to watching for things moving in the dark," Lilianna said, her voice strong and assured. "My Shadows are patrolling further out than the hunters. If anything approaches, man or mosscat or mage, we will know in advance."

"Good," Juniper said. How long would they have?

"Angyla told me about this place once." Lilianna looked at the arched ceiling. Twenty years ago, it might have been painted gold. The weather had dulled it to dismal grays. "How magic made it what it was and then destroyed it."

"Nexon destroyed it," Juniper said firmly. "Not magic itself. He tore this place apart in his rampage for power."

Looking for *her*, the princess who would supposedly stop him.

Lilianna didn't say anything more, and Juniper didn't either. Being inside Balendin Castle felt like an invasion, like she had disturbed something sacred. How many people had died that night? How many souls called this their grave?

Had it been a mistake to bring the druids here?

Doubt crept in as the druids handed out rations. Before they reached her, Juniper stood.

"I'm going to take a walk," she said to Lilianna.

She marched down the closest hall without waiting for an answer. The light from camp faded, and her night sight adjusted. The inky darkness lightened into shades of indigo and charcoal and plum. Juniper tucked her hands into her skirt pockets. The journey had drained her energy, yet she felt little inclination to sleep. Now that they were here, she didn't know what to do. She hadn't planned further than the Dead City. She didn't know how she was going to fight Nexon, especially if he brought an army of apostates.

And all she had was herself.

And a village of druids.

She wandered through empty corridors and ransacked chambers, over spots of mold and stagnant water, and past scorched walls. She wound up crumbling stairwells, through blasted doors, and over shattered glass. She pushed aside drooping spiderwebs with her magic, and stepped around the lingering spiders. The winter wind whistled through the castle, through the broken windows and drafts, and sounded terribly like voices.

She had no goal or intention other than to just…move. She didn't feel like sitting or resting.

This castle had been her home. She was born here. Yet she had never known it. Her parents, King and Queen Balendin, had sent her away because they knew what she was, and that Nexon would come for her. And they were slaughtered not long after. Her entire family had been killed in this castle, while she had survived.

She had spent the majority of her life as a thief and assassin, using people to get what she wanted, and she had grown callous. The Undercity had operated on lies and deceit and favors. She had become one of them, the best of them—the queen of thieves. And yet, being in this place, where an unknown number of people were slaughtered because Nexon had tried to kill her—it hit a nerve she didn't know she had.

The life she might have had ended here. Nexon had ripped it away.

What might have happened had she grown up here as Princess Isolde instead of Juniper Thimble? She would not have inherited the throne; her older brother would have. She had been the youngest. Would she have been a spoiled princess? Magical prodigy? Would she still have become the Archmage of Water?

Juniper meandered and wondered, not minding her direction. With every step she took, the feeling of being followed worsened. More than once she glanced back, expecting Reid or Lilianna, but neither appeared.

It unnerved her. She reasoned that a castle this large and empty likely had animals seeking shelter.

Juniper turned a corner.

"Run!" screamed a shrill female voice, panic and fear etched into her cracking voice.

Juniper sucked in her next break and flattened herself against the wall. She summoned a shield of ice—the corridor was empty. No one ran toward her or away. No footsteps sounded. Silence pushed against her.

She took several deep breaths, willing her heart to slow.

"What?" Juniper whispered to the corridor.

Someone had very clearly screamed.

Yet no one appeared.

Juniper released her shield. She continued down the corridor, and turned a corner into a wider hall. Dim moonlight seeped through the adjoining rooms, illuminating the rubble and puddles and growing vines and moss and mold.

An explosion shook the air and the castle under her feet. For a frightening moment, the air was red and white. Juniper stumbled forward onto a pile of rubble—a yelp escaped her throat. The wall beside her crumbled. She rolled out of the way—the rubble faded and became the pile of rubble she had landed on.

Gasping, Juniper rolled onto her feet.

The corridor was just as it had been. The moonlight hadn't changed. The wall she had seen fall had fallen long ago. Moss grew along its weathered edges and in the cracks between the stones.

Juniper leaned against the smoothest part of the wall and pressed her hands over her eyes. Enna had warned they would find ghosts.

"They're through the gates!" came a panicked male voice.

Juniper looked through her fingers in time to see a translucent man in long pale robes run past her.

CHAPTER 14

Juniper had never seen a ghost, and it took several heartbeats for her mind to realize what she was seeing. The man in pale robes looked no older than thirty. He wore his hair long and braided back. Runes covered his neck and arms and vanished under his collar and his sleeves. Panic and purpose twisted his features.

"Get to the library," said a female voice.

The robed man paused by a set of broken doors. A woman in similar robes ran past him, and ghosts materialized out of the moonlight, varying ages and shapes and colors, and ran into the library. Another explosion shook the castle, and a ghostly stream of fire flashed over one window.

Screams echoed from outside. Thousands of screams. As real as Juniper's pounding heartbeat.

The man vanished into the library, closing ghostly doors. Juniper followed on shaky legs, stepping over the broken and mildewed library doors. For a flash, she saw it as it had been: towering bookshelves of dark wood, cushy alcoves, burning hearths, and magelight. The panicked ghosts were escaping through a secret door hidden behind a bookshelf.

Everyone went through, except the robed man and woman.

"Go," said the robed man.

The woman paused before the hidden door. Fear brightened her eyes.

"I will catch up," said the man, squeezing her hand. "Go before it's too late."

"There are too many of them!" She tugged him closer to the hidden door. "Fire mages too."

He shook his head. Arrogance hardened his expression. "It will take a thousand fire mages to defeat the Archmage of Water." He winked.

The woman hugged him quickly, then vanished into the passage. The man, the archmage, did not follow. He closed the hidden door and used magic to move a large desk back to where it had been, blocking the bookshelf from opening. A crash sounded from within the castle, and the ghost looked toward the door. His dark blue eyes looked through Juniper.

She felt sick. She leaned against a charred bookshelf, and as she fought nausea, the ghostly doors to the library burst open. Fire surged over the books, spiraling up into the second floor and into every alcove. Mages rushed inside. The Archmage of Water stood his ground, face twisted with determination and resolve. Water and ice danced around his hands, frosting the ground at his feet and silencing the flames as they came at him.

A flash of fire, and the library returned to its current state of ruined books and charred shelves and broken furniture. Broken windows had allowed the weather in, and the space reeked of mildew. Under a bookcase, she spotted what looked like bones. Human bones. Looking closer, she spotted several specs of white amid the ash and ruined books.

Her stomach churned. She pushed off the wall and collapsed—she emptied her stomach onto a pile of decade-old ash.

She pushed all her strength into her arms to hold herself up. Her body shook, her mind fogged, and she wanted to lay down and sleep until this horrible feeling went away. But she refused to sleep in his haunted place. Between the books and the dead, she couldn't stand it.

She took several deep breaths and forced herself to stand. The first few steps seemed impossible, yet she made it back to the corridor. On legs that felt like sand and with a mind that felt like lead, she began the long trek back to the camp.

She hadn't expected to find anything. She'd only wanted to get away for a while. She certainly hadn't expected ghosts.

Her balance and stability returned by the time she returned to the druid camp. The warmth of the vestibule graced her skin, making her aware of just how cold she'd become. The druids had transformed the vestibule with campfire, welcoming incense, and simmering stews. Several cooking pots had been erected in one of the chambers.

Juniper meandered alongside the camp, to the main doors, where the wind whispered through the woven vines of the makeshift door. No rune of warmth had yet been carved, and Juniper quickly carved one into the stone with an ice dagger. The druids nearest the door eyed her skeptically, though as the rune took effect and the seething cold halted, relief slipped through their hatred. A few loosened their grip on their woolen cloaks.

Juniper turned—more than half of the druids in the vestibule were looking at her. Golden eyes speckled the hall, blinking unevenly. It might have been her tired mind, but she felt their judgment. Disapproval. Wariness. Blame.

She bristled. How dare they blame her for their predicament. She didn't make anyone come with her. They chose this. This was Enna's idea, not Juniper's.

She stepped outside into the bracing cold. Few torches spotted the front garden, and the overgrowth had been cleared away. Already, a few herbs and root plants poked through the druid-aided soil. Lilianna stood near the broken gates.

Her Shadows were helping uncover the broken gates and using the rubble to construct lookout towers near the fallen battlements. Sentries stood watch, wary of the Shadows they had feared for so long.

Night blanketed the Dead City in shades of deepest indigo and black. She spotted things moving in the darkness, big enough to be Shadows, and others…she didn't know. Animals, she assumed. She heard things, too, scurrying and cawing and chittering. Something out there made a deep mewing sound that chilled her to the bone.

Juniper stood on the castle step, taking it all in.

A shuffle caught her attention.

Reid stood just outside the door, half in shadow, with one hand on the hilt of his Mage's Bane. His dark eyes were looking at her.

"It's odd to see druids and Shadows working together," Juniper said, though it came out uncertain. The bitter chill shook her words.

Reid didn't say anything.

She swallowed. She hated this strange side of Reid. She hated it because she knew it was partly her fault, if not entirely. A quiet voice in her mind said it would have been better to let him pass on, rather than yank his soul back into this world and live a cursed life. A louder voice said it would have been worse to live without him.

"You're pale," Reid said in monotone. His gaze remained on her, boring under her skin, peeling her layers back. "You were gone for a while. Did something happen?"

"This place is big and empty and dark," she said. "I'm sure it was nothing."

The change in his expression was subtle, the narrowing of his eyes and twitching of his scowl. He didn't believe her.

Biting her lip, she looked back to the Shadows. They had successfully unburied the gate, and were propping it up against the battlements.

"Want to take a walk with me?" Juniper asked. "I hear the grounds are lovely this time of year."

She stepped down and offered Reid her hand, like a gentleman would do for a lady. Reid did not smirk. His lips didn't even twitch. He stood still as stone, looking at her hand with the same barely-there scowl of disbelief.

After a long heartbeat, she curled her fingers together and held her hand against her chest. Embarrassment heated her skin and cooled her insides in a devastating flash.

Had something of Reid been left behind in the cavern? Had the wellspring stolen a piece of him? She had been so desperate to keep him. She had poured the magic into his mouth. If he had lost something, she was to blame. She had done this to him.

She took a step back toward the castle, mind on laying in her tent and pretending that everything was fine.

Reid sidestepped, blocking her way into the castle. The sudden movement rattled his silver armor. The torchlight made the scratched across the breastplate seem far deeper.

Juniper jumped—a shiver of fear and instinctive defense surged through her bones, there and then gone.

"There's a hole in the back wall that leads into the Royal Grounds." Reid stepped around her and into the garden, toward the back wall. He took a few steps, and when she did not follow, he turned to look at her. "A walk?"

Juniper took a cautious step toward him, then another. When she reached his side, he continued. She kept a step between them. She…didn't entirely trust him, and she wanted his entire person in her view. Especially the Mage's Bane. She hated herself for it. Losing Reid felt worse than finding ghosts.

CHAPTER 15

Juniper followed Reid through the garden and along a broken stone walkway. Once, it had led through a gated archway. That archway had since collapsed, the gate bent inward and rusted beyond revival. Reid stepped through a hole in the wall beside the archway. Juniper followed his steps through the weeds and dead brush, ignoring the tugs on her trousers.

The other side of the castle was wild and overgrown. The stone walkway continued through the fallen archway, and Juniper used her magic to push the worst of the weeds and winter-dead brush out of their way. Nature didn't listen to her as well as the druids, and she only moved what she had to. Tree roots snaked over and through the stones, belonging to those that had sprouted throughout the grounds. The path wound around the castle, past a derelict stone and rotten wood structure that might have once been a stable, and through a large archway that led into the Royal Grounds.

Reid carried no torch. Juniper had her night sight, yet he didn't seem bothered by the dark. He stepped over brambles and roots and what looked like a rusted, broken blade without hesitation. He wasn't even looking down.

The Royal Grounds stretched over low-rolling hills. Once, they might have been tame and beautiful, but now they were wild and full of unsightly saplings and weeds. The edges of the stone path crumbled and weeds wormed through cracks and seams. It snaked through the overgrown flower beds, their wooden bases weathered gray and cracked. Only the harshest of plants thrived. Without proper tending, weeds, brush, and thick scraggly vines grew in troves. Weeds rose higher than her head in some places, bending over with the weight of themselves, and whispering in the winter's frozen breeze.

It sounded horribly like voices, and she hated it. She saw flashes through the weeds and trees that looked frighteningly like people and flames—ghosts fleeing from the siege. She imagined them running through the Royal Grounds and finding refuge in villages to the north. How many of the survivors had made it to Delphine? The untamed garden shied from the stone path, and the extra space allowed Juniper to walk beside Reid.

Her breath puffed from her lips in white clouds. The same puffed from Reid's, reminding her of his warm breath, of his beating heart. He took in the royal grounds with cautious indifference, as if scanning for threats.

Juniper was looking at him—the toe of her boot hit a tree root, and she tumbled forward. She grabbed Reid's arm to steady herself, and to keep herself from hitting the ground face-first. Reid paused, expression unchanged.

She cleared her throat and straightened. "Mind the roots."

They continued. Juniper glanced at the root she'd tripped over. Reid had stepped right over it.

The flower beds gave way to open forest, barren boughs and gray bark spotted with dark green pines. The trees grew tall, and she imagined the canopy full of lush summer leaves, shading the path on all sides. She imagined moonlight dappling through the forest full of birds, chittering cicadas, crickets, and grasshoppers. She imagined the leaves changing into shades of crimson, copper, and burned orange.

What would it have been like to grow up in this forest, a young Isolde, climbing trees and riding horses and hiding from her older siblings?

That life had ended before it began.

The gentle sound of water punctuated her imagination. She felt the mass of it, all around. She didn't see any—

The trees thinned and then opened, and at first Juniper thought it was a clearing, but her magic said otherwise. It was a lake. The sapphire water reflected the muted moonlight, as still and smooth as glass. Juniper felt the lake, the water within; the edges were shallow, but the center fell deep. She felt…things moving within, swimming while barely moving.

She suppressed a shudder.

The path diverted. One path continued into the forest and vanished from sight. The other wound onto the lake, over an arched stone bridge, and ended at a gazebo; the gazebo sat just off center of the lake, beside the deepest point.

Reid started along the path toward the forest, but Juniper grabbed his hand and pulled him along the path to the gazebo. He gave no resistance.

The gazebo had seen better days. The ivory trimming had dulled and chipped, the stone crumbled, and one of the balusters had fallen to the water below. Winter-dead morning glory and vining roses grew unchecked along the balusters and over much of the roof, dangling off every side.

Juniper stepped over the bridge and into the gazebo. Despite the lack of care, it stood firm.

She felt something—it might have been the water, but it felt different than any other water she'd encountered. It felt…she couldn't describe it.

Reid came to stand beside her.

The clouds shifted across the moon. Juniper caught a glimpse of Blugo's stars, and as the clouds moved, they revealed Bera's smaller constellation. Dread coiled in her gut. The solstice was not far away, meaning Isolde's birthday was approaching. Juniper tore her attention away from the stars. Moonlight graced the forest, the gazebo, and the surface of the lake. The lake glistened as if it were made of real sapphires.

Juniper gasped and pointed to the water. "Oh, Reid, look!"

As moonlight glittered deeper into the water, it glinted off fish with opalescent scales. They varied in color and size, making it look as if the lake was littered with jewels. A school of topaz and aquamarine swam under the gazebo.

"The jeweled lake," Reid said. "It was supposed to be beautiful."

Juniper tore her eyes from a ruby scaled fish and to him. His distant gaze met hers. "You don't think it's beautiful?"

Reid sucked in a breath as if he would speak, but he didn't.

"Just because there's no grounds keeper to tame the weeds and prune the roses doesn't mean it's not beautiful," she whispered. It felt wrong to speak too loud here. "It's natural. It's…rustic."

His gaze shifted back to the water as a fish with topaz scales swam past. "Reid?"

A heartbeat passed. His gaze returned to her, distant and cold.

"Are you all right?" She whispered the question, fearing the answer.

He remained silent. Several long moments passed.

"I already know the answer, but I was offering you the chance to admit it. Reid, please talk to me." She hadn't meant for it to come out as a plea, but it had.

Reid's gaze bore into hers, worse than any dagger, worse than any hurtful word. It stole her breath and shuddered the next.

Had she truly broken him?

She sucked in her next breath. Guilt and fear and shame imploded within her. The pressure pushed against her eyes and an endless darkness opened within her chest, pulling her down into its cold depths.

Reid studied her face. As she turned her watering eyes away from him, his callused hand cupped her cheek. The touch surprised her, and a jolt radiated through her entire body. Reid pulled her gaze back to him.

"What's wrong?" he asked.

She wanted to hit him for even having to ask.

"You," she whispered. "I'm afraid I did this to you."

His brows came together. Confusion drifted over his cold gaze.

"Reid…" Her voice cracked. "I felt your heart stop. I saw the life leave your eyes. You were gone. And now…you won't speak to me, or anyone, and I'm afraid I did something to break you. Fate took you, I took you back, and I'm afraid you're not you."

She feared fate had played a cruel joke by giving him back, taunting her with what she couldn't have. How dare Juniper believe she could have love? That a man as good as Reid could possibly love her for her?

"Why would you think that?" he asked.

"When you look at me, you look like you're planning my death in the most gruesome way possible."

Reid blinked, and something faintly like confusion passed over his features.

"You've done nothing." The husky words sounded more like him than any had. "I don't… I don't know what happened to me. I don't understand it, and I don't know how to start. I…." He huffed. His stoic mask shattered—fear and panic replaced it. His fingers twitched on her cheek. "I don't know how to explain it."

Juniper pressed her hands against his chest, against the scratched owl and chain of his armor. "Try," she whispered. "There's no one else here. It's just me and you."

The fear, confusion, and insignificance in his eyes made him appear like a boy, despite the several days' worth of scruffy chestnut hair along his jaw and the dirty hair on his head.

"You can tell me anything," she told him, and she meant it.

She reached for his hand and folded her fingers around his. He was freezing, as was she. At once, his hand tightened around hers.

"It feels…like the world is about to crush me." His eyes drifted to the lake. His gaze turned unfocused and distant. "I feel everything. It's everywhere and constant. It never stops. I can barely breathe. It…doesn't stop. I can't sleep. I can only fight it for so long. It's…consuming me. If I lower my guard, I fear this…magic will devour me."

"Reid," she whispered lovingly, soothingly. His gaze met hers, panicked and fearful. "I'll be here, no matter what, and I always will be. Mage or not. Nothing will devour you on my watch."

He took in those words, each one. His hand squeezed hers.

"Your anxiety is understandable," she said. "You grew up hating magic. You've spent most of your life working toward becoming a knight, being against magic and mages. The Order fell, and now you're a mage. You have every right to be a nervous wreck. You've had the ground ripped out from under your feet several times, and that you haven't completely lost your mind is a feat. If it were me, I'd have gone mad by now."

She held his hand between them.

He stilled.

"I'm no expert on magic," she said. "But maybe what you're feeling is your magic trying to surface and your instincts as a knight pushing them down. Your magic and your dire sense of justice are battling."

"What do I do?" he whispered.

Honestly, she had no idea. "See if you can use your magic. Make something. Uh, do that thing where you gather your magic in your palm."

She demonstrated in her free hand. Her icy blue magic formed an orb above her palm.

Reid looked at her magic, then lifted his hand parallel to hers. For a long moment, nothing happened. And then, among the bitter scents of the forest and the moist scents of the lake, a floral aroma wafted. Juniper recognized it at once as magic. Reid inhaled, held it, and as he exhaled, bright gold light appeared above his palm.

Energy. It pulsed with his breaths, a heartbeat of its own. It was the color of molten evening sunlight, of cinnamon and amber, rich with warmth. It brightened the gazebo like a miniature setting sun.

Reid gasped—his energy trembled.

"It's your magic," Juniper said. "It listens to you."

His grip on her hand began to shake. He tightened his grip enough it hurt. In any other situation, she would have complained or wiggled her fingers out of his steel grip, but right now, Reid needed her. She could put up with a little pain, and surely Enna or someone could heal a broken finger.

The golden light warmed his face, highlighting his fearful expression and concentration.

The energy elongated into a blade, though Reid could not hold the shape solid. The energy flickered and swirled like smoke, trying to escape his control. Reid's gaze intensified, and the blade grew in size. The larger the blade grew, the more unsteady the magic.

The blade shattered into a million pieces of light. Juniper gasped and squeezed her eyes closed as the energy peppered her face and neck. It didn't hurt—it felt like bits of warm water.

"Jun?" Reid gasped.

She opened her eyes to see him studying her face—looking for injuries.

"I'm okay," she assured him.

Reid touched her face to make sure. His thumb traced her cheekbone.

"I couldn't control my magic either, remember? But look at me now. You'll learn to control it. You'll rise above this struggle."

"You seem sure of that." His tone implied he wasn't.

"Of course I am," Juniper said. "I haven't a doubt. You are remarkably strong, Reid, and not just in body. You have a powerful mind. I know you can and will. Just like you made that ward when you didn't think you could."

His gaze softened. "Thank you."

"You're not alone in this." She folded her fingers through his. "You never will be. Not as long as I breathe."

"Nor will you," he said, and those words sent a feathery warmth up her spine. "We should get back. We both need rest. Gods only know what tomorrow will bring."

CHAPTER 16

Juniper and Reid walked back to the castle with their fingers laced. Juniper considered telling him about the ghosts, but she didn't want to burden him with her problems on top of his own. He had plenty for one person. She would handle her own worries. Besides, they were just ghosts.

The druids had readied for the night. Many had already retreated into their tents. Teams had searched through parts of the castle and found more candles and lanterns and musty-smelling blankets. It made the castle feel less like a campsite and more like...something else. A village.

Juniper went into the designated washing room—a room divided by woven vine partitions and bowls of water. Despite the campfires and runes, the chamber retained a winter chill. She quickly washed the grime and sweat off her skin, then dried herself with magic. She redressed and returned to the vestibule, braiding her hair over her shoulder.

A druid song drifted over the camp, a tune that spoke of deep forests and lost valleys. Juniper crawled into her tent, and a short moment later, Reid joined her. He had removed his armor and washed, though the scruff on his jaw remained. He relaxed beside her, and she curled into his side.

Ghosts filtered through her dreams, as did a comforting, molten warmth.

The horn sounded after dawn. Most of the village had sat to eat breakfast stew, and the horn sliced through the sleepy murmurs and left a vicious, fearful silence in its wake.

"Already?" Juniper cast a panicked look at Reid and Lilianna. Both shared her worry.

Abandoning her breakfast, Juniper ran outside. She skidded to a halt at the base of the watchtower. The druid hunter leaned over the edge, horn in hand. Reid and Lilianna were right behind, followed closely by Jarek.

"What's happening?" Juniper called.

"Ask him." The sentry pointed to the Shadow perked on the edge of the watch tower. The sunlight glittered off the smoky skin, and only the eyes remained steady. He let out a short, sharp bark.

Lilianna rushed forward, and the Shadow met her on the ground. She bent down, stroked his snout, and then stood. The color paled from her green skin.

"Well?" Jarek barked.

"Approaching from the north," Lilianna said. "He didn't get a good estimate of how many. He ran back here as soon as he saw them. Enough they aren't bothering to hide."

Juniper didn't wait for further talk. She rushed back to the castle and climbed along the weathered stone. Higher and higher, to the tallest tower. The wind picked up, hissing between the fractured stones. To the north, between the winter-dead trees, evergreens, and abandoned field, a dark mass marched toward them. Judging by the distance, they had maybe an hour before the army arrived.

"Shit," she breathed into the frigid air.

This had been her plan, but seeing an army approaching made her stomach drop and her lungs shatter. Nexon had an army of trained and violent mages. She had a village of sheltered druids and a handful of half-trained hunters.

Juniper returned to the ground with shaky hands and legs. Lilianna, Reid, Jarek, and a handful of hunters were waiting for her. By their dire faces and the three new Shadows talking to Lilianna, they already knew what Juniper had to tell them.

"I need a Shadow," Juniper said breathlessly.

Lilianna shook her head. "There are too many of them for you to take them out by yourself."

"I know," Juniper said quickly, not that she wouldn't have tried. She gathered what strength she had and steeled her shoulders and expression. "I want a better look at what we're up against."

"Depending on their numbers, our strategy will change," added Reid, in the strong voice of a knight. He sounded like his old self, commanding and ready for anything. "We can use their numbers against them and use the terrain to our advantage. We'll need trickery and stealth."

At that, Juniper felt a prickling of hope. She met Reid's gaze, and he didn't object.

A sleek Shadow materialized beside Juniper. Its dark green skin flickered like sunlight through a dense canopy. She climbed onto its back and held on—it darted over the outer wall and rushed through the ruined streets. It seemed to glide over the rubble, over fallen walls, and around trees that had sprouted through the cobblestone. It darted through the outskirts, past what had once been farms and ranches.

The ruins gave way to forest. The Shadow climbed into the trees, hopping from branch to branch, and finally paused. A low warble of warning gurgled in its throat.

They had arrived.

ARCHMAGE IN THE RUINS

The army marched through the wild field, stomping the weeds and burning the dead grass from their path. Few wore armor. More wore painted runes on their cheeks, foreheads, and throats. Mages. Juniper spotted a few thralls, but she was too high to see if they were indeed thralls or just dumb-looking mages. She didn't know which she'd rather face.

But it wasn't the mages or the thralls that gave her pause or made her chest squeeze and her breath hitch—it was the beasts.

Hundreds of beasts marched with the mages. They stalked behind the mages, patchy fur and taut leather hides identical to the abominations Nexon had created in the bowels of Bradburn Castle.

Cold, slippery dread curled against her insides. How the hell were they to win against those monsters?

The Shadow let out a low growl of dislike.

"I know," Juniper whispered. She stroked its head. "They're as bad as they look."

It snorted.

"Let's get back and give the others the good news."

The Shadow slid through the forest and the outskirts and ruins with such urgency that Juniper feared it would throw her off. Somehow, she held on—by the time they skidded to a halt in the front garden, her knuckles ached. Jarek and Reid were waiting for her, and the hunters were passing out ramshackle armor and weaponry. Despite the odds, each held themselves stoic and proud. Sounds fluttered from the vestibule, organized panic of a village readying for a siege.

At the thought of another castle siege, her heart sank.

"Well?" Jarek demanded.

"Mages, a few thralls. More than before," Juniper said in a single breath.

"How many more?" Reid's molten eyes bore into hers.

She bit her lip. Reid's frown deepened.

"Several hundred more," she said.

Jarek spat a curse, and Reid's expression turned even more dire.

"We don't have the men," Jarek whispered.

"Or the experience," Reid added.

"I am well aware of our disadvantages," Juniper said. She swallowed against the lump in her throat and turned to Reid. "And, not to add to them, but the mages also have beasts."

"How many?" Reid demanded.

"At least a hundred," Juniper said. "I didn't stick around to count heads."

Reid's face darkened. His grip on his Mage's Bane turned white-knuckled. He could take one beast, but a hundred of them?

"We have Shadows," Lilianna said. "They will fight for us, and if one falls another will take its place."

That logic didn't settle well with Juniper, even knowing that Shadows didn't die; they returned to Lilianna. It would take a massive toll on her fledgling magic. By the stern and proud gleam in her golden eyes, Lilianna understood.

"We prepare for battle." Reid's strong voice commanded the entire garden, a knight's. It riddled through the panic in Juniper's chest. Her Reid was still in there.

The druid hunters gathered in the garden. They looked at Reid with fear and determination, desperate for guidance, for someone to tell them how to win an impossible battle. Reid marched along the front line, hand on his pommel, shoulders back, silver armor gleaming into early daylight, breath puffing in the freezing air—this was what Reid knew, what he excelled at, and seeing it before her eyes gave Juniper a chill. It also set her blood on fire. She adored this side of him.

Not even Hiada could take Reid's warrior spirit.

"We cannot take them head on," Reid said. "There are too many, and they will be using offensive magic. We will use diversion and stealth statics. We went over this briefly. There is no time to practice. We fight here, we fight now, or we die."

The druids did not balk.

As Reid began to bark orders—sounding far too much like his uncle— Juniper and Lilianna rode Shadows to the northern edge of the city. They paused before an overgrown field of winter-dead grass. Juniper sucked in a cold breath—this was where they would face Nexon's forces. She would either succeed or die.

"Do we have a plan?" Lilianna asked.

Juniper half-laughed. "If you mean do I have some ingenious battle strategy designed for this exact playing field, the answer is no. My plan is much simpler."

Lilianna frowned.

"If I play this right, the fighting will be minimal. If we're lucky, the fighting won't make it to the castle," Juniper said. "All I have to do is get to Nexon as quickly as possible. Kill him or maim him or in some way incapacitate him from leading."

Lilianna's brows rose. "But what if his followers continue to fight?"

"For what? Their great leader is gone, and we have the other four archmages on our side," Juniper reasoned.

Lilianna's frown deepened. "There are far too many holes in that plan."

"Yes, yes, I'm no strategist," Juniper said. "I thought we'd have a bit more time to gather ourselves before Nexon charged in." She heaved a sigh. "I need you to cover me while I look for Nexon. Then, I end him in any way possible." Like twisting his neck until it snapped, or shattering his bones to bits, or freezing him to death. She'd had plenty of time to think of ways to kill Nexon.

Lilianna nodded. Her green cheeks had gone rosy in the cold.

"And...do your best," Juniper said as kindly as she could. "I know I've put a heavy burden on your shoulders. You and your Shadows will be invaluable in this fight, and any that come after."

If they survived.

Lilianna didn't argue the claim. Her dire expression mirrored Juniper's.

CHAPTER 17

Juniper and a small army of Shadows advanced to greet the first wave of mages. Lilianna lingered back. Both girls rode Shadows, better to weave in and out to find Nexon. Without Lilianna there, Juniper let her panic show. Her hands shook. Her gut trembled. Sweat gathered under her hair and along her spine despite the chill.

Her original plan hadn't involved a village of druids hiding in the castle. It was supposed to be her and her alone. Now, she had other people to worry about. If she failed, the mages would not show them mercy. If she died, everyone in the Dead City would too.

It only made her dread tighten and liquefy.

The Shadows formed a line. The darkness mass of mages and monsters marched closer. All too soon, the figures sharpened into faces. She cleansed her face of panic or worry. She could not afford it. Juniper Thimble did not cower.

The first wave of mages halted. Beasts made their way to the front lines, growling and snorting and pawing at the ground. The Shadows hissed and snarled.

For a long moment, no one moved. Juniper waited for Nexon to appear, to make himself known with some grand and arrogant speech. She scanned the mages marching into the field behind the first wave, but Nexon was not among them. She spotted several fair-skinned blond men, but not the one she wanted.

There—a wagon rose above the rest near the middle of the field. A commander center, or something like it. Someone important would be inside. Watching the battle unfold.

It felt all too obvious, but Nexon had stopped being inconspicuous when he took Bradburn Castle.

Juniper had a target, and her panic subsided. So, rather than wait another agonizing minute for the other side to strike first, she let her archmage magic go.

Ice surged at her command, rushing through the field, overwhelming the first wave of mages. Shadows rushed behind it. Juniper cast her ice up in a tidal wave, and with all eyes on the field looking up, she allowed slits within the ice for the Shadows to pour through near the bottom.

And the fight began.

Juniper and her Shadow rushed into the fray. Her ice preceded her, knocking mages off their feet, snapping necks, slashing skin. Shadows went for the beasts, and their howls and growls and snapping jaws filled the air. Magic surged in every direction; flames, stones, and gusts of wind battered against her ice. She felt it like heavy rain, beating against her.

She pushed past and fought her way deeper onto the field. Her ice moved around her, a raging blizzard of freezing water and ice daggers, catching throats and chests and anything made of flesh. Magic surged against her, pushing and pushing and pushing.

She made it halfway to the tent.

Flames burst through a weak point in her ice, searing against her hand. She flinched and stumbled to get out of the way. And her ice shuddered in response.

For a terrifying moment, she stood vulnerable in a sea of pissed-off mages. She met the eyes of the mages closest to her, and she acted—daggers of ice appeared in both of her hands, and a dozen more circled her. Her daggers sliced through the mage's flames and found his throat.

Another mage appeared at her back, and something hard struck her between the shoulder blades.

She went down—as she fell, something cold and heavy washed over her skin. It pressed against her magic, submerging her mind like smoke. She recognized the feeling. The mage had hit her with an anti-magic rune. Her panic returned tenfold.

She held onto her ice daggers, and it hurt. The rune pulsed against her magic, shoving it down, out of her grasp. Her ice trembled. Screaming, Juniper slashed at the mage who had used the rune on her, slicing his head nearly off his shoulders.

The moment her magic vanished, she would be crushed or burned or shattered into bloodied bits. Her magic spasmed. One of her daggers vanished.

She reached for the steel at her side, a habit she was glad for. Ice in one hand and steel in the other, she lashed out at the nearest mage. Steel cut in his shoulder, then ice slit his throat.

Flames burst behind her, searing the cold air with undulating heat, and Juniper reached for her ice—it did not listen.

Panic flared as the heat licked her skin. She shifted her weight into a defensive stance, and as she brought her arms to guard her face, a Shadow jumped between her and the flames. The Shadow absorbed the fire, turning its greenish-black skin a sizzling crimson, then a frightening yellow as the flames dissolved the creature. Another Shadow leaped from behind the fire mage and fastened its teeth around his head. The mage barely had time to scream before the Shadow wrenched its jaw, twisting the mage's neck with a meaty crack.

Shadows slithered around Juniper, guarding her. Juniper composed herself and let her ice go. She grabbed a dagger off a fallen mage. It was heavier than she would like, and didn't look very sharp, but it would have to do. As the next mage started forward, whips of air around his arms, Juniper and the Shadows attacked in tandem. The Shadows circled her, taking the brunt of magical attacks while Juniper fought with steel.

Juniper didn't hesitate, and neither did the Shadows. They snapped and bit with a viciousness she didn't know Lilianna possessed. Juniper pushed the druid girl out of her mind; she couldn't worry about her right now, with blood splattering her own hands and mages cursing her name, or it would be her own blood on the ground. She lashed at the next mage as a Shadow absorbed a force of hot air, slitting the throat without looking at the mage's face. And the next.

Blood splattered her hands, her arms, her face, her clothes. It froze in the cold, and an uncomfortable chill worked its way into her bones.

Without her magic, it would take hours to reach the tent.

And she wouldn't last that long.

Mages circled the Shadows that protected her, pelting them with earth and air and boiling water and flames—the Shadows seemed to appear as quickly as they dissolved.

But Lilianna couldn't keep it up for long.

Panic wormed its way into Juniper's heart. Her bravado shattered like her ice.

How could she have thought this would work?

She felt the rune on her back. If she allowed one of the fire mages to sear the skin, would it cancel out the rune?

She was scanning the mages for flames when one of the beasts let out a vicious, mind-shattering howl. The sound tore through her panic and obliterated her focus. The battlefield blurred and the sound of magic and Shadows dulled behind a shrill ringing. Juniper fell forward. Her hands smacked into the bloodied, stomped grass.

As the battlefield sharpened and the ringing vanished, a mage came at Juniper with twin hammers of stone. She brought her steel to block—

A beast jumped over her head and tackled the earth mage, ripping his throat out before they smacked the ground.

Juniper staggered to her feet. The best spat blood and sinew onto the ground, and in the same motion, leaped for the next mage. By the angry, shocked expression on his face, that wasn't supposed to happen.

"What are you—" The mage screamed as the beast tackled him.

The ringing subsided, and Juniper heard the difference. The howls and hisses had ceased, and panicked screams filled the air. Magic surged all over the field. Two beasts and a Shadow circled her, but none were looking at her. They were protecting her.

And she suspected she had either died and was a ghost, or some god had taken a very large mercy on her. Her body was not laying on the grass at her feet, or anywhere, and her body ached and her head pounded from the beast's cry. Alive, then.

She glanced up to the crystalline sky, to where Bera's small constellation had been the night before. She whispered a thank you, just in case Bera had turned the beasts away from her.

Beasts attacked the mages. Bodies spotted the ground, blood soaking into the dead grass and hardened dirt. The Shadows were few. Those remaining stayed close to Juniper.

The beasts looked the same as those from Bradburn Castle, taut skin and patchy fur, yet their eyes were sharper. They were…thinking, she realized with a sinking feeling. Strategizing. Attacking in formation. Protecting each others' flanks. They were no less vicious as they tore Nexon's forces apart.

The mages were as confused as she was. Some ran into the woods or back the way they had come, either cowards or the smart ones.

The beasts and Shadows fought together, slaughtering the mages faster than Juniper could have.

The anti-magic rune was wearing off. She summoned an ice dagger and let the cheap steel fall to the ground. No mage had been able to cross the beasts and Shadows circling her, but it made her feel better.

Juniper started toward the tent, and the beasts and Shadows moved with her. The air reeked of floral magic and blood. The sounds clawed at her insides, ripping her dread into painful, nauseating threads. Magic sizzled; earth ripped and crunched; air hissed and howled; water rushed and drowned; and beasts and Shadows shrieked and roared.

They closed in on the tent. A woman shoved her way through the flaps, and her cold gaze settled on Juniper.

"You bitch," the woman spat. "What have you done?"

"I didn't do anything." Juniper meandered a step closer.

Two beasts stepped between Juniper and the woman. Their bloodshot eyes looked at her, but they were not vicious or bloodthirsty; they were…cautious.

A shiver of panic threaded around her spine. "Let me through, please."

The beasts, to her utter surprise, parted.

Juniper sauntered through and stopped a safe distance from the woman. The tent behind her was otherwise empty. Its guards were dead or had fled. The battle raged around them, and by the sounds, the mages were losing.

"Where's Nexon?" Juniper demanded.

The woman sneered. "He won't belittle himself with the likes of you."

"Look around you," Juniper spat. "You've lost this battle."

The woman's sneer didn't change. She took half a step closer to Juniper, and cerulean energy magic circled her hands. "You have something that belongs to my master."

Juniper feigned innocence "Oh, you mean this?" She wiggled her moonstone ring, then smirked. "Come and get it."

The woman half laughed. "I'll pluck it from your corpse."

They rushed each other—her clear blue ice collided with cerulean energy. Juniper stumbled back a back, digging her heels to keep from falling.

"All that fighting must have been exhausting," the woman taunted. "You've been fighting so hard. I haven't."

"True," Juniper said, straining to keep her voice even as she pushed against the woman's energy. "But I'm stronger than you."

The woman chuckled. "Few are stronger than me."

"You're not an archmage," Juniper taunted. It sounded pompous, but at that moment she didn't care.

Surprise rippled through the woman's magic, and Juniper took full advantage. She pushed everything she had, ripping through her energy with ice, slicing down the beam of energy and to the woman. The ice dulled before it hit flesh, and rather than ripping her in two, it knocked her off her feet and threw her into the tent. The material collapsed and the woman fell to the ground with a grunt.

The beasts encircled the crumpled tent, and Juniper strutted in. The woman staggered ungracefully to her feet.

"You've lost," Juniper spat.

The battle had lost momentum. The sound of tearing flesh and screams had faded. The woman glared at Juniper from within the tangle of broken poles and canvas. A beast stalked to Juniper's side, and she took her eyes off the woman. Within that moment, a surge of energy rushed from the ground. Juniper's ice barely formed a shield in time. The heat of the energy brushed her cold skin. The woman started to rise—Juniper sharpened her shield into an ax and brought it down.

"Wait!"

As the ax came down, a grayish wind caught it mid-swing. It stopped a hand's width from the woman's head.

Juniper released the ax. She *knew* that voice.

Ison appeared between her and the woman. His dark brown hair had grown into a mess of curls, his gray eyes were wide, and his ashen skin had turned pink with the cold. He wore the same leathers and wools as the mages whose bodies littered the field. He held his empty hands in front of her.

"Ison?" Juniper gasped.

"We can use her," Ison said breathlessly.

He turned. Grayish tendrils of air wrapped around the woman and lifted her into the air.

"This is Lora." In a single breath, he added, "She's Nexon second in command, and she had information we could use."

Realization struck Lora at what Ison had done, and it settled as only bone-deep betrayal could.

"What have you done?" Lora screamed at Ison.

Ison ignored her.

Juniper took a ragged breath. Her head spun, her chest heaved, and her magic throbbed from the use and the rune. She took another, steadier breath, taking it all in. The battle was over. They'd won. She wasn't dead. Ison was alive and standing right in front of her. Joy trembled through her bones. "Gods, Ison, I worried the worst."

"Really?" Ison's brows rose. "You didn't think we could do it?"

Lora started to speak, but Ison wrapped a tendril of gray air around her mouth. Her muffled threats continued despite it.

Juniper could hardly believe it—Ison, here. Without the panic of looming death, she took another look at him. Ison's ashy skin had warmed under the sun, and faint brown hair graced his jawline and chin. He looked thinner. She didn't remember his cheekbones or his throat being so pronounced. A few scars dotted his hands and one on his cheek. From Baxion, she assumed.

One of the beasts nudged Ison's shoulder. He gave the beast a gentle pat on the cleanest patch of fur he could reach.

"You did great," Ison said to the beast.

Juniper looked between the beast and Ison. "What did you do?"

Ison flashed her a mischievous smile. "The beasts don't listen to Lora. They listen to me. Or, they listened to my suggestions to turn on Nexon and join the forces against him."

Several of the beasts snorted in agreement.

The beast beside Ison eyed Juniper. It had startlingly intelligent eyes.

"I told them about you," Ison said to Juniper. "I told them you were going to stop Nexon, and they agreed to help. I didn't tell them to save you. They acted on their own."

Juniper didn't know how she felt about intelligent beasts, however they had saved her and by extension, the druids in the dead city. The beast blinked at Juniper, tilting its head not unlike a wolf.

A Shadow tiptoed to Juniper's side, white eyes pinned on the beast. It let out a weary warble.

"What are those things?" Ison nodded toward a Shadow.

Juniper half laughed and stroked the velvet snout of the Shadow. "We have a lot to catch up on."

CHAPTER 18

Juniper climbed onto the back of a Shadow, and the beasts offered the same to Ison. As they started for the Dead City, Juniper saw the extent of the battle. Because of Ison's betrayal, Lora's forces were decimated. Bodies littered the field, some in several pieces, others unrecognizable. Blood had turned the dead grass a putrid red.

Juniper felt numb. Unreal. She barely registered the sizzling of the magic of the Shadow underneath her. Ahead, the ruin of Balendin Castle loomed. The sight did little to alleviate her numbness. Her eyes were on the castle; she didn't notice others approaching until they rode beside her.

"You look worse for wear," came a cold, clear man's voice.

A panic slithered over her skin, but it soon evaporated.

"Xavier," she gasped.

Her brother rode on a beast, his dark skin spotted with dirt and blood. His leathers and wools resembled the mages, dotted with nicks and scratches, but he looked otherwise unharmed. A wary, welcoming grin stretched his lips. "Nice to see you alive too, Sister."

Mabyl rode on his other side, blonde hair tied back into a short bun with hairs too short falling around her neck and face. Fearless as ever, she flashed Juniper a knowing grin despite the blood splattering her face. None looked like her own. Finn and Bois rode another beast. Bois held onto Finn's middle, her blind, glassy eyes unfocused. Juniper felt a tingle of Bois's air magic as the girl mapped the world around her.

But, to her utter surprise, they weren't the only ones. Fifty or so mages had joined them.

"Defectors," Ison explained. "I tried to find as many mages along the way who might be willing to see reason."

Juniper cocked a brow. Proud and surprised. "And no one found out about your plan in the process or tattled?"

Ison shrugged. "Everyone was nervous about the attack. And, when the beasts turned on Nexon, I told those I could what we were doing—"

"He shouted above the battle for any to hear," Xavier added, grinning. "That Nexon had fooled them and led them to their slaughter for his own gains, and those who wanted to survive should turn on him before he killed them."

Juniper glanced back at Ison with raised brows.

Ison's already pink cheeks flushed. "It was a spur of the moment."

"And we made all these new friends!" Mabyl said, though she lacked enthusiasm. "How have you been?"

Juniper tried to give her a smile, but her entire body felt like falling apart. "I'll explain everything once we get back to the castle. There's...a lot."

Juniper led the pack of Shadows, beasts, and defecting mages toward Balendin Castle. Ison's wind carried Lora behind them, wrapped from her knees to her mouth. To say Juniper anticipated Reid's face was an understatement, unless that fighting spirit of his old self had vanished since she'd been away. Hopefully, Lilianna's Shadows wouldn't ruin the surprise.

As they marched through the fields, the party funneled behind her. Ison rode on one side, Xavier on the other.

Reid and the druid warriors met her on the outskirts. To Juniper's delight, Reid's brows rose and his mask slipped as he took in the beasts, Ison and the mages, and their prisoner. Sein openly gawked.

Lilianna pushed through the warriors, breathless and pale. She took on the beasts, then her gaze settled on Juniper. "What happened?"

Juniper motioned to the army behind her, and said with enthusiasm she didn't feel, "Look who I found!"

Neither Reid nor Lilianna mirrored her grin.

"Does this castle come with a dungeon?" Xavier motioned to Lora with a dagger made of his charcoal energy.

Reid's gaze snapped to the dagger—Xavier noticed. He flipped the dagger up and caught it effortlessly.

"Enough talking," Juniper said. "I need a bath, and I'm sure our new friends could use a rest."

"We did set a grueling pace," Xavier added.

The druid warriors parted, and Juniper led the party into the Dead City. Back in the city, a fierce exhaustion settled on her bones. By the time the castle came into view, she felt like lying down for a very long time.

Uncertainty and fear hung heavy in the air. Green faces watched her approach from the gates and from the watchtowers. She lifted her hand in greeting, and to let the druids know she had returned—they had not lost.

Realization rippled across the castle courtyard, and a feverish thrill of victory thrummed. She paused on the street just outside the gates.

"Tell Jarek we've won," Juniper called to the sentries. Several pairs of feet rushed into the castle.

The next few hours passed in a strange and calm blur. Lilianna saw to her Shadows, Ison saw to the beasts, and Juniper saw to herself. She washed herself several times. Once to rid herself of the blood and whatever else, a second time just to make sure, and a third to feel the warmth of water against her skin. Dry, she made her way through the vestibule and to her tent. She fell asleep almost instantly.

She woke to her name being called.

Sitting up, she blinked the heavy sleep from her eyes and met Ison's gray stare. He knelt in front of the tent. Since the battle, he had washed, shaved, and found clean clothes. He looked so different from the timid apprentice who had once brought her healing tonics with downcast eyes and soft words. Ison had grown since then.

Before she could formulate a response, music drifted in. Flutes and strings. By the thumping of feet on stone, people were dancing. Food was cooking too. Gods, it smells delicious.

"Think you're up to a war meeting?" Ison asked.

She groaned. "There had better be food and wine."

"The druids made up some winter-berry juice. Tastes enough like wine."

She decided that was good enough, and she crawled out of the tent.

The druids were celebrating. Campfires flickered in the garden, and they danced around the flames. Others played wooden flutes and stringed instruments, others still stomped and clapped, filling the twilight with a sense of magic. Juniper felt like she had stumbled upon something sacred, a woodland ceremony, known only to the secluded druids. Laughter and song prompted a sense of fearlessness and joy—Juniper had never seen the druids so happy or carefree.

Maybe her imagination had gone a bit wild with the battle.

Ison led her away from the vestibule and into a corridor previously cold and decrepit. Magelights hovered near the ceiling, illuminating the patched stone walls and floor.

"The druids have done wonders making this place livable again," Ison said. "Our earth mages are busy with plans to repair and rebuild. Or they were, before the dancing started."

Juniper followed him into a chamber lit with magelight. A stone table stood in the middle of the chamber, with stone chairs to match. Reid, Lilianna, Xavier, Bois, Mabyl, and Finn were already there. Whatever conversation they'd been having ended when Ison and Juniper entered.

"There she is! The guest of honor! Come, sit, enjoy dreary talk." Mabyl reached for a cloudy bottle and poured a healthy amount of dark red liquid into an earthen cup. She set it next to the empty chair beside her. "Drink."

Juniper sat between Mabyl and Reid. She sipped the winter-berry juice. It definitely tasted like berries, sweet with a tang of fermentation, but not enough to get properly drunk. She took another sip.

"We've secured a large building outside the gates for the beasts," Ison said, sitting. "The mages fixed it up as best they could with the time and resources. The mages are staying in a house across the street from the beasts."

"The beasts caught the game we're having for supper," Lilianna added.

"Is that what smells so good?" Juniper asked.

Lilianna nodded. "We haven't had good game in…I can't remember."

"You live in the Wylds?" Ison asked.

"I used to," Lilianna said in her calm, somber tone. "I live here now, I suppose."

They busied themselves by retelling their journeys since parting ways in Rusdasin. It took several bottles of winter-berry wine. Ison and Xavier took turns detailing their encounter with the scouts from Baxion, and then how Ison had gotten pushed into the training ring and had managed to talk his way out. Reid remained silent, and so Juniper told them what had happened when they arrived in Delphine, met with Delmont, and snuck out to the Wylds to find the Archmage of Air.

"You snuck out?" Ison asked, brow raised.

Xavier wore a conspirator's grin.

"Yes." Juniper cleared her throat. "Myrisha told the council who I was, and they refused to let me leave."

"Because you were a thief?" Lilianna asked.

"Because she's the lost heir to the Collatian throne," Xavier said plainly.

Lilianna's lips straightened, and she glanced at Juniper. "Is that true? The heir? I thought you were just a princess."

Juniper hesitated. "Heir is a strong word."

Mabyl nudged Lilianna's arm and whispered loudly, "She's really Princess Isolde Balendin, and her parents sent her away before Nexon could kill her, because there's this old prophecy that says she'll defeat him."

"Is that true?" Lilianna asked Juniper, eyes wide.

"Some of that…might be somewhat true," Juniper said. And hearing it again only made her feel like she'd eaten something heavy.

"So this is your castle," Lilianna said.

Juniper didn't answer.

Ison did. "It is."

"It is *our* castle right now," Juniper corrected. "And we have bigger things to worry about, like how we can't fight Nexon the way we thought we could."

Her plan worked—the atmosphere changed.

Juniper took advantage of the silence to explain what she had learned from Angyla, and the ghostly scene of Nexon's previous defeat.

"The archmages ripped his magic into pieces, and in the process destroyed the forest and created the Wylds. If we did that again, it would decimate anything and everything around. And, it wouldn't even kill him. He can't die unless he has the last two pieces of his power."

Ison frowned. "So, until he is restored to full strength, he's immortal."

Xavier sighed and said wistfully, "What a conundrum to be at partial power, but to live forever."

Juniper looked into the dark dregs of her berry wine. "Nexon feels the absence of his magic. He needs it back. He craves it. That's why he sent such a force to reclaim them. He won't feel complete until he has them."

Because she had divided her magic to save her friends, and she had felt the obsessive need to get those pieces of magic back. She could not imagine having felt that absence for one thousand years. No wonder he had gone mad.

She banished that thought. It did not excuse what Nexon had done.

"And when he learns his army was destroyed, he'll have no choice but to come and confront me himself," Juniper said, though she said it with more assurance than she felt.

"Are you sure?" Mabyl asked, brows raised. "If he shows up with a bigger army, what chance do we have? Sure, we've got beasts and Shadows and druids, but that's all we've got. He has thousands of brainwashed mages, thralls, and likely more beasts."

Juniper sighed dramatically. "Thank you for your uplifting attitude."

Mabyl shrugged. "Not that I'm not looking forward to seeing the show. I'd just like my chances of survival to be a bit higher."

"Gods," Ison said at last, rubbing his face. "What about the other archmages? Can they help us out at all?"

Juniper half laughed. "We've got three in this room."

A beat of silence passed.

And another.

"Three?" Ison repeated.

"Me," Juniper started, pointing at herself. "And Lilianna became the Archmage of Air when Angyla died."

"Who is the third?" Xavier asked carefully, leaning forward.

Juniper looked at Reid. He had kept his eyes on the table for the most part, and he hadn't touched his berry wine. He wore his impenetrable mask, and his eyes had gone dark and cold.

Ison followed her eyes to Reid, as did Xavier.

"Reid?" Ison asked.

He didn't respond.

A heavy silence settled, full of disbelief and shock.

"Is that why you've so moody?" Xavier asked.

"But…how?" Ison asked.

Reid shifted his empty gaze to Ison. "My great-grandfather was Mason Hobbs. And Nexon has wiped out most of the energy line."

Another beat of harsh silence.

"And…*you* are an archmage?" Mabyl barked a laugh. "A knight, an archmage! Can I see some magic?"

Reid only glared at her.

Ison paled. "If you're the archmage, then Mason is…"

"Gone," Reid confirmed. "Killed by Nexon in an attempt to find the location of a piece of his magic."

Ison leaned back, remorse pulling at his features.

Juniper quickly explained what had happened in Sinjon—Angyla, the wellspring, the Shadows. Lilianna helped.

"Sinjon took a lot of damage, so they decided to come with us," Juniper said.

"I'm glad they did," Xavier said, finishing off another cup of berry wine. "This is delicious."

A cheer filtered down the corridor, and Juniper reminded herself of their victory.

"Nexon will come at us again." Juniper stood, punctuating the staring match between Mabyl and Reid. "We have to be ready. We need a better plan and a strategy. But, let's save all that for tomorrow. I'm exhausted and hungry, and you all look ready to pass out."

"We did spend the last few days marching through the woods," Xavier said.

"I could use a long nap," Ison agreed.

"Then it's agreed," Juniper said, clapping. "We start planning tomorrow."

Just like that, their meeting ended. They drifted back toward the vestibule where the druids had begun serving whatever their wild game stew. Juniper eagerly accepted a bowl and started to eat. Many still celebrated in the front garden. Juniper chose to enjoy this moment of peace and joy while it lasted. She feared they would have precious little of either in the days to come.

CHAPTER 19

Blythe looked down over what had once been Rusdasin's busiest market, filled with colorful carts and stalls of goods, textiles, clothes, and food. It had been in that once bustling market where Amery had taught her how to appear innocent and fragile while cutting the strings of a rich man's coin purse. Nexon's takeover had initially turned the market into a barren street of forgotten stalls, but business had slowly crawled back. Vendors had returned to their stalls over the past few months, and new shops had popped up in the places of others.

Many of the new stalls sold magic things. Without the Marca or the Order to regulate the magical trades, enchanted things sold like fresh bread. Mages sold spells, scrolls, and jewelry engraved with runes that promised to do all manner of things, from making the wearer appear more attractive or lucky to guarding against lies and preventing disease. A few sold enchanted clothes, like boots that stayed warm in the snow.

Blythe wouldn't mind a pair of warm boots. A fresh blanket of snow had fallen over Rusdasin in the night, and the steely sky promised more. She crouched on the roof of a bakery. New owners had taken over, and sweet scents of butter, sugar, and cinnamon wafted upward. The remains of Blythe's sugar bun dotted her dark pants. She had spent the afternoon weaving through the bustling market crowd, and a few coin purses jostled in her many hidden pockets. She had rewarded herself with a sugar bun—and had paid for it.

She thought about snagging a few other things before calling it a day, but she didn't want to press her luck. It had been a good day. No guards had chased her. Fewer guards patrolled, and most stalls had their own bodyguards. Blythe had been careful—she didn't want to test which runes actually warded against thieves and which were for show.

She should have left the market with her sugar bun, but she had spotted a familiar face in the crowd. He stood at a stall with bolts of leather and wool, leather pouches and sheaths in an array of styles. She had chosen to stalk him from the roof of the bakery.

He was tall and lean with umber skin and short brown hair. He looked just like Blythe remembered. Unlike her, he had inherited their mother's charming smile.

"The finest leather from the eastern farms," her brother said sweetly as customers passed.

He had sold a few bolts of wool and several leather goods while Blythe watched. It was good for any shopkeeper, however their father wouldn't be pleased unless he sold every item he had brought to market.

Blythe watched until her brother packed up his goods into a large backpack. Curious, she followed, keeping out of his line of sight.

She hadn't seen or heard of her family since the day her father had sold her to pay off his debts, and despite how much she didn't care to see him, she wanted to know how her family had fared since her departure and Nexon's takeover.

She followed him three blocks, and then a group of mages surrounded him.

"Oh, look what we've got here," said one of the mages in a nasally voice. He eyed the pack on her brother's shoulders. "Looks like you're carrying a heavy load there. Why don't you give some of it over?"

Her brother gripped the blade hidden under his shirt. Their father had always done the same.

A tendril of orange magic shot out from the mage and slapped her brother's hand, and the dagger clattered to the cobblestones.

"You think steel is going to protect you?"

A gaggle of stupid laughter followed, and her brother shrank.

Blythe had seen countless mages taking the chance to bully. Most mages had blended in with the recovering city. Some played the role of bodyguard to shopkeepers or nobles, others had formed guilds of their own in abandoned houses, and others still lorded their magic over those without. Normally, she ignored the bullies.

"Get away." Her brother had a deep voice like their father, only threaded with fear. "I don't have anything you want, only leather and wool."

"And coin," said another mage. "Unless you're selling them for free?"

The mage laughed, as though she'd made a brilliant joke. Blythe rolled her eyes.

"Give us the coin you made," said the first mage. "And you can live."

Her brother swallowed. Like her father, and like Blythe, he was stubborn. And yet, he started to remove the pack from his shoulders.

"Please," her brother started. "My mother is sick. I need to buy her medicine."

Blythe didn't know if those words were true or not, but it gave her the last bit of motivation. She blew out a breath, steeled herself like Amery had said.

Fire danced around the mage's fingertips. "Come on, I don't have all day."

Blythe jumped from the rooftop. In her graceful fall, she pulled twin daggers from her back. Maddox had gifted her the blades a few weeks after the Marca collapsed. The dark blue steel was feathered with red—Mage's Bane. How Maddox had acquired such daggers, she hadn't asked.

Blythe landed on the shoulders of the fire mage, and her dagger sliced into the space between the shoulder and the neck. The fire vanished from his hand, and pitiful yelp escaped his throat.

As the mage gurgled and stumbled, Blythe flexed her legs and ended the second mage before he could send his prepared stone fists at her.

"Shit!" screamed the third mage. She stumbled backward. Her hands on the pack slipped, and her brother yanked it back. The mage started to gather water, but Blythe threw one of her daggers—it sank into her gut.

The Bane seeped into the mage's blood, and the water she had called from canteens splattered onto the cobblestones. Blythe straightened and stalked to where the water mage lay, feebly trying to grasp the dagger sticking out of her gut. Blythe reached down and unapologetically yanked the dagger free. She then buried it in the mage's neck.

"That was unnecessary," her brother said, his voice shaky. "She was already dying."

Blythe turned and looked her eldest brother in the eye. He blinked, and realization erased any other emotion on his face. He mouthed her name.

"I didn't want to take the chance," Blythe said plainly. "I ended her suffering."

"With Mage's Bane," her brother whispered, nodding to the bloodied blades.

"Is Mother really sick?" Blythe hated how pitiful she sounded, but if she didn't ask, she'd always wonder.

"No," he said. "I thought it might buy their sympathy."

"They don't have sympathy unless you've got magic," Blythe said, a warning. "I recommend you stay out of Rusdasin for a while, unless you want to risk this happening again. They might be part of a guild. I won't always be around to help you."

His expression wrinkled. In that moment, he reminded her of their father, too stubborn and proud to accept help.

Blythe wiped her daggers clean on the dead mage's robes, then returned them to the hidden sheaths on her back. She turned to leave.

"Thank you," her brother said.

"You almost sounded sincere." Blythe glanced over her shoulder at him. He wore the same stubborn expression. "But you're welcome."

She headed down the closest alley, then another, and another. She didn't stop until she had put sufficient distance between herself and her brother. The snowy daylight had faded enough to douse the city in shadows. Magelights dotted the main streets and the districts the mages had claimed, but most of the city would remain dark.

Blythe leaned against the alley wall and allowed herself to breathe. The daggers on her back hadn't felt as heavy before.

She hated killing people.

She hated how it felt when the blade went in, when it hit bone and tore through the insides. She hated the sound and the smell.

Xavier had warned her how it would feel, like she had taken a ghost dagger and thrust it into her own stomach, like she would throw up, like she would never be able to sleep again, like her hands would never stop shaking. He warned it would take a long time to get better.

Why had she intervened? She could have let her brother return home empty handed. None of her siblings had tried to save her when their father sold her like livestock. No one had sought her out. She had thought about seeking them out more than a few times. Just to see.

She had wanted to let them know she was alive, that she was okay. Now they would know, unless her brother neglected to mention her.

Footsteps stomped through the alley behind her. The stench of florals made her nose wrinkle. Magic. Blythe grabbed onto the uneven stones of the building behind her and hoisted herself up to the rooftop. She rolled out of sight as the mages marched into the alley below.

Blythe stilled and held her breath. The Undercity mages had crafted vanishing runes—Blythe wore one on a necklace. When she remained totally still, the rune hid her. So far, it had worked.

Despite the rune, her heart hammered. She steeled herself, thinking of how Xavier would react, and waited for the mages to pass.

"Little bitch can't have gone far," spat one of the mages.

A thud sounded an alley away, like someone slipping and falling to the ground.

The mages ran toward it. Blythe dared not move until their footsteps faded.

She took several long, deep breaths. Her anxiety didn't alleviate. It remained in the bottom of her stomach and in her bones, making her feel too heavy and too light at once. Hiding from mages made her feel the fear and fragility that she had heard so many others talking about since Nexon took over. She didn't have magic to defend herself with, and most mages had height and weight on her eleven years and slight frame.

She didn't want anyone to see her like this, so she stayed on the rooftop until her heart returned to normal and she didn't feel like the world would shatter if she stepped wrong.

She returned to the southern districts where the rebels had maintained a sense of safety. A lot of people had flocked there, abandoning their homes in the northern districts where Nexon and his mages had staked their claim. The Undercity mages had etched runes in alleyways and doorways, meant to cause anyone with ill-intent to forget what they were doing or turn the other way. It was a complicated rune from what Blythe had heard, and she didn't care to learn more.

Blythe neared the runed barrier, and her heart skipped a beat. She passed through—it sizzled on her skin. She feared that one day it would not let her pass.

Slipping through the alleys and backstreets on her way to the Undercity, few residents have her more than a passing glance. People stood around burning barrels, the fires kept alive by magical means, drinking and laughing and being as normal as they could, huddling under layers of clothing.

She had overheard Captain Grave and Maddox talking about trading routes and economy, but her attention had wavered. They had been able to keep goods coming and going, mostly food and clothing and the basics.

She passed a window and glanced at the family within. The father, mother, and their four children sat around a smokeless fire. The father was speaking, telling a story by the animated motion of his hands and the expressions on his face. Again Blythe wondered what would have been had her own family wanted her. But, her father hadn't wanted her. She had been the expendable child, so when offered gold, he had pushed her into the hands of slavers without a second thought.

"Oh, look who's back," came a voice much too close.

Blythe jumped and pulled a steel dagger from her thigh. Ven jumped out of dagger range, grinning stupidly. He had two and a half years on her, and several inches. His sandy blond hair had grown out, and he tied it behind his head. The summer spent scouting topside had tanned his pale skin.

Ven crossed his arms. "Looks like I'm getting better, or you're getting worse."

"I knew you were there," Blythe snapped. She pushed her dagger back into the sheath.

She started toward Amery's manor. Ven stayed at her side, his footsteps near silent. He had gotten quieter, and it irked her. Most things about Ven irked her, especially the way he always managed to find her.

"Hear anything good this morning?" Ven asked. "The east side of town was boring."

She huffed. She didn't feel like talking with Ven. "I might have. I'm on my way to talk to Amery now."

"Ah, well, let's not waste time," Ven said, taking a few jogs ahead of her. "Let's go."

Blythe wanted to protest, but what she had overheard that morning while she lounged on the roof of a magic shop sounded important.

CHAPTER 20

The morning dawned bright, clear, and frigid. Juniper wrapped a sage colored wool shawl around her shoulders. Despite the runes' heat, winter persisted its assault on the Dead City. She accepted a cup of tea from Ingrid, and sipped it as work began in the castle and its surrounding areas. The celebration had lasted into the night, and though tired and hungover, druids and mages rose with the sun.

Jarek divided the druid warriors into patrols around the castle, and Lilianna guided her Shadows through the battlefield, looting the dead and bringing supplies back to the castle. Mages assisted her, burning the dead and burying their ashes. Air mages kept the smoke from filtering into the city.

Juniper watched it from one of the watchtowers. The druid sentry said nothing. He kept his golden brown eyes on the battlefield.

"Hey, Jun," came Ison's call.

She turned to the front garden. Ison and Xavier stood below.

Ison waved her down. "Come here. Walk with us."

Juniper felt like finding a quiet spot and stealing enough snow for a hot bath, but she also felt like hiding in the darkest corner of the castle she could find. She did neither of those things. She climbed down the steep watchtower steps to where her friends beckoned.

"What is it?" Juniper asked.

"Feel like an interrogation this morning?" Xavier asked, his voice filled with an assassin's dark humor.

"No, but might as well," Juniper said.

Ison and Xavier led her back into the castle. Halfway across the vestibule, Reid appeared at her side, clutching the hilt of his Mage's Bane. Juniper had a thought to warn him about being too close to his own blade, though she reasoned that his hand was the safest for it.

She and Reid followed Ison and Xavier into a windowless corridor deep within the castle. Finn, an earth mage, had crafted a makeshift cell for Lora from the collapsed remains of a room. Stone pillars formed the bars, and two beasts stood guard on either side, looking like they would rather rip Lora into pieces than guard her.

As Ison approached the cell, the reddish beast whined in greeting.

"Hey there," Ison said casually. He scratched the beast under the chin. "Has she caused you any trouble?"

The other beast snorted.

Juniper thought it sounded like bitter laughter.

Lora had been chained to the wall with stone cuffs. A rune on her throat silenced her magic. It looked to have been drawn in blood. Juniper hated such runes, but she saw the need.

Juniper and Ison stood before the door. Reid and Xavier lingered a step behind.

"Not looking so hot now," Juniper said.

Lora turned her seething glare at Juniper. "Nexon is right about you," Lora said haughtily. "He told me you may look like a princess, but you talk like trash."

Juniper knew Lora was trying to worm her way under her skin. Unfortunately, Juniper had slept soundly, eaten a warm breakfast, and grown up in the Undercity among bullies and thugs.

"I'm not sure that's a bad thing." Juniper shrugged. "Look, let's not drag this out. You know things I want to know."

"Such as?"

"Nexon is coming to find me himself," Juniper stated. "How long do we have?"

"I can't say," Lora said. She hummed, and her vicious eyes glittered.

Juniper didn't swallow her yawn. She could have slept longer. When Lora didn't offer anything else, she glanced over her shoulder at Finn. "Can we just let them in and be done with it?" She motioned to the beasts.

The beast bared its teeth at Lora.

Finn started to move, and Lora paled.

"He will know something happened when I don't check in with him," she stammered. "Will he march at once or wait a day? I don't know. I have long since stopped trying to figure out how his mind works. You might have a few weeks. When I last spoke to him, on the dawn of the battle, he did not disclose his location to me, but I suspect him closer to Rusdasin."

"Should we trust her?" Juniper asked Ison.

"No," Xavier answered. "We should anticipate Nexon in half the time she says."

The arrogance on Lora's face cracked further, and Juniper relished in the power her friends had brought to the interrogation.

"When you say, 'check in,' what do you mean?" Juniper asked, more so out of curiosity. "Does he break into your mind like he does everyone else?"

"He can, but it's tiresome this far away," Lora said. "It takes much of his energy, and he knows I will follow his orders. He knows he doesn't have to watch me. Besides, there are better ways to communicate over distance, but I'm sure the Order would frown on them."

Lora's gaze slid over Juniper's shoulder and settled on Reid, on the owl and chain on his breastplate. Reid gave no indication of being bothered by it; his face remained steady and cold.

"My magic knowledge is a bit rusty," Juniper said, leaning against the bars. "What type of communication?"

Lora only sneered. "I'll tell you, but not for free. How about we make a deal?"

"No," Juniper said flatly. "I don't want to know that bad."

Lora's sneer flickered but held. "You don't even know what I was going to ask."

"And I don't care," Juniper said. "I'd rather leave you down here to starve and rot than make a deal of any kind. I'm not the desperate one here. You are. If anyone is going to offer a deal, it will be me. Not you. You're not in charge anymore. Your army was decimated. You failed your master. And now you're hanging in the enemy's dungeon. Or, soon-to-be dungeon."

"There's a small goblin problem in the real dungeons," Xavier added. He looked down his nose at Lora. "Be glad you're up here and not down there with those little nuisances. They pinch."

Lora's sneer became a frown.

Juniper hadn't gone to see the infestation herself. According to the druids, goblins were nasty little creatures that lurked in deep caves and sunless ruins. They collected trash and slept in their own filth. It would take years to get the stench of them out of the dungeons. Which, she supposed, was an appropriate stench for a dungeon.

"Then what else would you like to know?" Lora spat. "I'm not talking if there's nothing in it for me."

"Your well-being is in it for you." Juniper summoned an ice arrow and sent it flying. It sank into the stone beside Lora's thigh, nicking the material of her pants. "Why follow Nexon so earnestly? You've likely seen how he treats his lackeys."

Lora's sneer returned. "Because I want to see magic rise, and Nexon has promised that I will become the next Archmage of Energy. I will be his equal in power, and we will bring in the new Imperium to this realm."

A thick silence stretched over the corridor, save for the heavy breathing of the beasts. Juniper glanced at Ison, and he cast her a knowing look.

Lora's sneer faded. Her declaration hadn't had the effect she assumed it would. Several long moments passed in silence, and then Juniper gasped in pretend surprise. Lora's frown fell into a scowl. "The *next* archmage," Juniper repeated. "How could Nexon promise something like that?"

"He has spent centuries eliminating the competition," Lora spat. "He has cut down the Iluvin who destroyed him, and he has made sure no mage could rise to power without his blessing."

Nexon had worked from within the Order to disband organized magic and eliminate the Iluvin people and the once great civilization. He had forced mages into the Marca where he could eliminate archmages before they realized their power, and he could cut down possible inheritors with his knights.

Juniper and Ison came to the conclusion at the same time.

"He has killed any energy mage who has not stood with him," Ison whispered. "That explains why they were so few in the Marca, and why so many were pulled by the Order."

Reid's hand tightened on the hilt of his Mage's Bane, and he glared at Lora with a mixture of pity and disgust. Juniper's heart hurt for him. Lora had given him more evidence that the Order hadn't been what he believed it to be.

"Nexon has killed anyone in line before me, leaving me the only logical inheritor of the magic," Lora said matter-of-factly. "He has made sure no energy mage stood between me and the title."

Juniper glanced at Xavier, who watched Lora with a calm scrutiny. He shrugged.

"I'm not complaining," he said. "We all know I wouldn't do well with power. I think the magic chose wisely."

"Chose?" Lora's frown deepened. She looked between Xavier and Juniper, panic rising. "What do you know?"

"You know what they say," Juniper said. "Magic has its own set of rules." She relished the dramatic pause, Lora's rising panic, the tension in the air. "The energy magic has already chosen a new archmage, and it's not you."

"Liar," Lora spat.

The sneering arrogance flashed into wild rage, and the rune on Lora's throat began to glow. The rune cracked, cerulean energy flickered to life and shot toward Juniper. Before her own ice could respond, a golden disc of energy solidified in front of her. Lora's magic smashed into it, shattering like glass and disintegrated into dust before hitting the ground. Juniper stared at the disc. It was solid yet translucent as amber. Through it, Lora's eyes widened and the color drained from her face.

Reid stood a step behind Juniper, hand outstretched toward the disc. His hand trembled, and he looked more shocked than anyone else. The golden energy disc lasted a moment more, then dissolved. Reid released a shuddering breath. Pulling his hand back to his chest, the color in his cheeks paled.

"Damn. I was starting to doubt your story," Xavier said, brows raised.

Lora's shock shattered into rage. Her wide eyes narrowed with a murderous madness. "No! It's not possible. How could the magic choose *you* over me? A *knight* as an archmage? It's absurd! You can't even control it. It's mine! It is rightfully mine! It will be mine. I will carve it out of your chest. I will—"

A thin dagger of ice sank into the stone beside Lora's calf, slicing open the skin. Lora's tirade ended in a bloodied shriek.

"You won't live long enough," Juniper spat.

The beast on Juniper's left snarled in agreement.

A horn sounded. The blare echoed through the corridors, and it sent a wave of cold panic over Juniper's skin.

"What does that mean?" Ison asked, the same panic mirrored in his eyes.

"The midday meal is ready." Reid spoke in his calm, stoic coldness. His face mirrored his voice.

Juniper released a breath. Just food. Not an incoming army.

"Soon," Lora spat. "Nexon will paint the earth with your blood."

Juniper waved dismissively toward the cell and started back toward camp. She could use something warm to eat, and some sunlight. These dank and dark corridors were grating on her nerves.

CHAPTER 21

Juniper fell into step beside Reid on the trek back through the lonely corridors. Ison and Xavier walked ahead. Reid gave little indication that he noticed her. He kept twitching his hand, the one he'd summoned the energy shield with.

"That was impressive," she whispered.

"It was instinctive." He glanced at his hand. "I saw the attack, and I thought to protect you. I acted. I…knew I could. The magic…listened."

"It does that," Juniper said. "When we brought the Marca down, Carol whisked embers at me. I felt these hot pin pricks on my face, and I panicked, and my ice just acted. It made a thin layer of ice over my skin, healed me, and snuffed out the embers. I didn't know magic could do that."

"It bothers me that magic can do so much, and yet we don't know a fraction of it." Reid curled his fingers into a fist. "So much knowledge of magic has been lost because of Nexon."

"So much of everything is his fault," Juniper said. "He's trampled anyone and everything in his path to power. He destroyed the Order from the inside, has slaughtered countless mages to get them out of his way, and caused the Collatian civil war to kill an infant. After we get rid of Nexon, we can discover all the things magic can do. It will give us something to work toward."

Reid looked at her. His eyes held a spark of his old warmth, even as his silence returned. Juniper took it as a sign that her Reid was still in there.

Mabyl plopped down beside Juniper during the midday meal. "I have a proposition for you."

Juniper brought another spoonful of warm, flavorful wild stew to her mouth. With the now empty spoon, she motioned for Mabyl to continue.

"I want to explore more of the castle," Mabyl said proudly. "I'll take a few earth mages and start the restoration."

Juniper blinked. "Restoration?"

Mabyl pretended to be horrified. "Of course the restoration! We can't squat in the vestibule while there's an entire castle above our heads. We've got hundreds of rooms! Entire wings!"

Juniper took her time with another spoonful. Then she asked, "Why ask my permission?"

"Because it's your castle," Mabyl said, like it was obvious.

"It was abandoned."

Mabyl rolled her eyes. "It's still rude to rifle through someone else's abandoned home without their knowledge or blessing. And," —she lowered her voice— "you didn't exactly get a say in the matter. So, as far as anyone here is concerned, this castle belongs to you."

Juniper sighed. She didn't want a castle. Especially one her family was murdered in, especially a *haunted* castle.

The old Juniper would have loved it.

"It will take a while," Mabyl said, looking around. "But we don't have anything else to do, and I'm tired of sleeping on the hard floor. Have I mentioned that Finn snores? Like thunder."

"Fine." Juniper knew she wouldn't win. Mabyl would keep it up until she caved. Sighing, she said, "Let's go see what we can find."

Mabyl's entire face brightened. "Thank the gods. If we stay here, the druids are going to keep handing me chores. I'm not washing anyone else's dirty underwear."

After the meal, Juniper, Mabyl, Finn, and two earth mages they'd recruited from Baxion set off for a preliminary exploration. Juniper led the party, magelight in hand. The idea of finding more ghosts made her stomach clench and twist, but Mabyl was right. They couldn't continue squatting in the vestibule. The druids would find more and more chores, and with the added mages, people were walking on each other's toes. They needed more space.

Juniper needed that dark corner to hide in.

They wandered slowly through the castle, allowing the earth mages to uncover fallen rooms, rearrange the broken stones of walls and ceilings, patch drafts, and restructure ceilings and doorways. Juniper and Mabyl worked together to dry the stagnant water and clean out any lingering mold and plant life. The combination left the corridors reeking of magic and ash.

Chamber after chamber, corridor after corridor, stairwell after stairwell, they explored. The sun eased across the sky.

The parts of the castle closest to the vestibule had sustained the most damage. The further in they explored, the lesser the destruction. However, the mustiness had permeated everywhere, and animals had nested and left their stench behind. Rats scurried through the dark, bird nests filled the exposed rafters of a domed chamber, and something had died years ago and left behind a massive pile of bones with dried tendons barely holding it together in what might have been a parlor.

Mabyl gagged and scorched the entire room, leaving only the bones behind.

It took most of the afternoon, and as they climbed another stairwell and found themselves in a corridor lined with tall, narrow windows, the sun had streaked the sky in plum and persimmon. Juniper lingered by the window. She could see for leagues. The ruins of the Dead City spread far, and beyond it to the south, the Wylds shadowed the horizon.

"Look at this!" one of the earth mages shouted.

Juniper panicked and spun. An earth mage had moved a collapsed pillar to its original upright position against the wall, revealing an intact door. Another mage carefully opened it, stone spear in hand—they had encountered far too many creatures to not be prepared. It was a closet. Within that closet were stacks of linens, towels, and hardened cleaning supplies. Mabyl stepped around him and grabbed one of the linens.

"They smell like they've been sitting in a dank castle for ages, but they look fine," she said. "The door's been blocked so none of the rodents could get in."

"We can use these," said Finn.

"Take some down to the camp," Juniper said. "They could use them right now."

The two earth mages grabbed as many blankets as they could carry and started back through the castle.

"You want to head back or keep going?" Mabyl asked Juniper. "We've got a few hours before the dinner horn sounds."

"Let's keep going." Juniper had little desire to go back. She didn't want the druids' never-ending list of chores either. "We might find more supplies."

Juniper, Mabyl, and Finn trudged onward through the darkening twilight, fixing fallen stones and clearing nests—until they entered the upper level of the castle's northern wing. Two grand doors had been smashed aside and burned. Even before they passed through the doorway, Juniper felt a horrible pitting in her stomach.

It felt like walking into a tomb.

They passed empty chambers full of smashed and charred furniture and grand hearths. Juniper entered one at random. The door had been blasted inward and left to rot. A grand hearth took up much of one wall, the stone pale blue and etched with images of stars and trees in full bloom. Beyond the door, the worst of the destruction seemed to linger on one side of the sitting room. The other side seemed relatively untouched. The furniture looked to be in moderate condition, despite the time and disuse. Whoever had burst in hadn't bothered with the rest of the room, only the one side. By the dark stain on the stones underneath the char and dust, whoever had been in this room had died by the door.

Juniper's gut quivered. Who had it been?

The bedroom held a grand bed with four thick posts with moth-eaten curtains, and another hearth, a smaller version of the other room. The leaded glass windows were intact.

The bathing room had been left nearly untouched, including the towels and soaps. The closet held a young man's wardrobe. Juniper lifted one of the fine shirts. Whoever had worn these had been tall and lean, and a fan of plum. He had far too many plum shirts in a variety of patterns. Within a small chest of drawers, she found a silver star-shaped pendant on a thick silver chain. A topaz rested in the center of the star.

Juniper could not explain, but she wanted the necklace. So she tucked it into her pocket. Its weight tumbled against her, cold but pleasant.

"Oh, shit." Mabyl's voice echoed down the corridor.

First, Juniper thought of goblins. Then she thought of Nexon. She rushed out of the empty chamber and into the corridor. Mabyl had gone into another chamber down the way, whose doors had been blown off with enough force to crack the stone on either side. Juniper skidded to a halt just inside, ready to attack—and within a moment, she realized why Mabyl looked bloodless and nervous.

Maybe it was the scorch marks on the bookshelf, or the large bloodstain on the floor, or the moldy portrait that had long ago fallen from the wall. Though molded and discolored, the portrait showed King and Queen Balendin. With them were two sons and a daughter. The oldest son looked no older than thirteen, his brother looked no older than ten, and the daughter couldn't have been older than four or five. Each had been painted in royal attire, deep plums and gray fur. The eldest son wore the topaz pendant.

The painting did not show the infant daughter.

"These are the royal chambers," Juniper announced. She tore her gaze from the painting, only for it to snag on the bloodstain.

This was where her father had been murdered. Her father, the man she had only met in the realm between life and death.

A thick silence settled over the room. Mabyl looked at her, ashen-faced. She had no clever words to offer, and Juniper wasn't sure if she was glad for the silence or not.

Juniper stepped over the bloodstain. If she stood still any longer, she would collapse. Her gut warned her to retreat, but she knew if she left, she would not be able to return. No, this was a demon she needed to face as soon as possible. She meandered into the adjoining chamber with wooden legs. The bedroom. Another bloodstain marred the floor by the vanity. Her mother.

Juniper forced her breath even. In and out.

Beyond the bloodstains, her parents' chamber looked as untouched as her brother's. The furniture remained whole. The attackers had come only to kill, not destroy. Because that was all Nexon had cared about. The linens and clothes in the closet remained. The jewels in her mother's closet had been taken, and hatred burned in Juniper's chest—she took a deep breath and reminded herself that she didn't need jewels. She didn't need fine jewelry. And, they had been taken after a siege.

The thief within her whispered, *Finders keepers.*

She had told herself those words in the early days of her thieving career, when the thought of taking something from someone else made her sick. She had repeated those words over and over again, until they had numbed, until she had numbed.

She had stayed numb for so long, but in the past year, something had cracked. Friends and affection had whittled away that numbness, but in that moment, she wanted it back.

Juniper ran her hand along her mother's dresses. She had so many, each beautiful and regal. Back in the bedroom, Juniper ran her fingers over the quilted bedspread. She pulled a dark strand of hair from the pillow, and something cold sliced through her heart.

Footsteps entered the sitting room. The heavy sound of moving stone filled the corridor, followed by the floral and silvery stench of magic. It overtook the mold, at least.

"You know, this place isn't in the worst condition," Finn said. "We could fix it up in a few days and make it livable again. There's a closet with a servant's entrance in the corridor too, behind that old tapestry. Something's nested in it, and the passage is full of cobwebs and rat droppings, but it might lead to the laundry or maybe the kitchen."

"That's an adventure for tomorrow," Mabyl said pointedly.

"If we start early, we could have people moving back in tomorrow night," Finn added, oblivious to Mabyl's tone. The hope in his own made Juniper feel like throwing up. "If we started right now, we might have this place good enough for tonight."

A pause. Slow footsteps entered the bedroom.

"Juniper," said Mabyl. "What do you think?"

Juniper let the dark hair flutter back onto the bed. Mabyl stood in the bedroom doorway, eyes fixed on her. Finn stood in the sitting room, eyeing Juniper with wary interest and unease—he must have figured out whose bedroom this had once been, who had died here.

To give herself some time to think, Juniper meandered back into the sitting room. Mabyl and Finn gave her a wide berth. She tried not to notice the bloodstain at her feet, or that she stood exactly where her father had stood in the moments before his death. She tried not to think about how this was where her family would have grown up, had Nexon not interfered.

Her heart felt close to bursting out of her chest and smashing itself on the floor. She pushed the feeling down; she thought of nothing, of that abyss of non-feeling.

It was harder to find than it was before. Her mind kept going back to her parents' spirits within the Spirit Pool, how alive they had looked, how lovingly they had looked upon their youngest daughter.

It took a moment for her to realize that Mabyl was talking.

"…Juniper in this suite, of course," said Mabyl. "It's only fitting."

"What?" Juniper asked.

The conversation ended.

"We were just saying how you should get the largest chamber in the royal chambers," Mabyl said carefully. She watched Juniper warily.

Because it was *her castle*. Because she was *Princess Isolde*.

But the very idea of taking her parents' chamber as her own twisted dread and a sense of invasion into her gut. Their blood still stained the stones. Their clothes still hung in the closet. Her mother's hair still clung to the pillow.

Mabyl threw her hands between Juniper and the room, and quickly said, "But that can all wait. There's still a lot of cleaning up to do."

"It's fine," Juniper lied. She stormed out of the royal suite, out of the royal chambers, and just…away. She needed to get away.

She didn't want to see the bloodstains or feel the death that lingered in the air.

CHAPTER 22

Crown Prince Adrian Bradburn walked behind his father, King Bradburn, on their way back from a morning meeting of the Undercity leaders. Adrian had tried his best to pay attention, but nothing new had been discussed between his father, Josephine—leader of the mages, and Maddox Hawk—leader of the thieves and criminals.

The king's house—as dubbed by the people of the Undercity—came into view. While relieved at being back, a part of Adrian felt stifled—not unlike the feeling of being underground. He'd gotten used to the reddish and gray stone of the Undercity, yet he missed the castle. He missed the windows, sunlight, and oils and candles. He missed his bed.

He missed…not having servants. Many servants lived in the Undercity, but the dynamic had changed. A trusted few served in the king's house, however most worked to better the Undercity and keep things running. It wasn't like living in the castle where servants tended to everything too trivial for a prince. Adrian had even washed dishes when no one else could.

His father and Captain Sandpiper went up the stairs to the meeting room on the top floor, but Adrian didn't follow. He'd had enough meetings.

Feminine voices sounded from the back of the house, from the kitchen. Glenda Sandpiper emerged, followed by Captain Tinnly's wife, Lily, who waddled with one hand resting on her swollen belly.

"Bed rest is what you need," Glenda said. "Stay off those feet. If the swelling doesn't go down, send one of the girls to fetch me or Josephine."

Lily frowned. "I don't want to take any potion. What if it…does something to the baby?"

"If it's between losing one or both of you and taking a potion, what would you choose?" Glenda paused in the main room. Her gaze fell on Adrian. "Oh, Your Highness. That means the meeting is over."

"And another is beginning upstairs." Adrian nodded toward the stairs. "I am delaying the inevitable. Hopefully, my absence will go unnoticed."

"I doubt it," Glenda said. A motherly grin warmed her entire face. "I am walking Lily home. I'll be back shortly to start something to eat. Don't start snacking."

"I would never dream of such a thing." Adrian bowed his head and placed his hand over his heart. He stepped away from the door. "Good evening to you both."

Glenda and Lily departed, and a guard fell in step behind them.

Adrian meandered into his bedroom. If forced between taking a potion and dying, he would take the potion. Captain Tinnly, Adrian had discovered, remained wary of magic and everything to do with it. Before the curtain swished closed behind him, he tugged the ties of his tunic undone.

"Bad meeting?" came the sleepy and seductive voice of Roslyn Derean, his betrothed. She lay in their narrow bed, raven-black hair a mess around her shoulders, canary nightdress off one shoulder. She pushed herself onto her elbows and fixed her brown eyes on him, as effortlessly seductive as her voice.

"If you mean bad as in boring, then yes." Adrian undid his belt and flung it over the back of the old wooden chair at the foot of the bed, over which Roslyn had flung the dress she'd worn the day before.

Back at the castle, a servant would have whisked his laundry away in a heartbeat. Now he carried it to the washing house himself. Well, he and his armed escort.

Adrian collapsed onto his side of the bed. Roslyn propped herself on an elbow, looking at him. His father would not have allowed Adrian and Roslyn to share a room or a bed before being properly married, but with the current situation, propriety was left behind.

"Everything is going well," Adrian reported, like he did after every meeting Roslyn did not attend. She and his mother stayed busy with keeping order over the market stalls and its many vendors. Several former Undercity shopkeepers had returned, and they had brought their shady tendencies with them.

"And yet it bothers you?"

"Oh, no, it doesn't bother me that everything is fine," Adrian said. "I'd much rather sit through a meeting of supply reports, mages' training, and armory reports from the Order than a meeting of panic and impending doom."

He had a feeling those would come.

"Then what's bothering you?" Roslyn draped her arm across his chest. Her body curled into his, warm and soft and perfect.

Adrian felt several things. A few he would discuss only with Roslyn. A few he would have rather discussed with Reid, but his oldest friend had gone to Delphine to find archmages.

"My father," Adrian started. "He...is a great man."

Roslyn didn't say anything. She didn't sigh or flutter her eyes or offer advice. She listened.

"He loves his people and his kingdom, and his people and his kingdom love him in return," he continued. "He has the experience of a warrior and the mind of a king. The people look up to him, even Maddox and his horde, with awe and respect. I don't think people will ever look at me the same way."

"Of course they won't," Roslyn said.

Adrian frowned. "That's not the response I expected."

She smiled. "You aren't your father. You can't be your father because you are you. Your mind and your spirit aren't your father's. He has his own mind and spirit. But that doesn't mean your people won't love and respect you. They already love you and have reasons to respect you. Right now, you are within the shadow of your father's rule. You will lead one day, and your people will love you all the same. But they will love you because you are you, not your father."

"I love you," Adrian said. The heaviness weighing on his heart eased. "At least one of us has a mind for these things. We'll be unstoppable."

"We'll be something." Roslyn nudged him with her chin. "Is that all? That meeting was awfully long, and you were looking awfully mournful when you walked in."

Adrian sighed. "My father wants me to look after the knights."

"Oh?"

"I…" He didn't know how to explain it.

Roslyn waited for his reasons, his thoughts, patient as stone. She made him feel as though he could lay his soul bare without judgment.

"My father has never put me in charge of anything," he said at last. "I've never held that kind of power. My father has carried it all himself, and I feel as though he is slowly trying to shoulder his responsibilities to me. I knew it would happen one day, I just didn't think it would happen like this."

"What does he want you to do for the knights? They seem capable of handling themselves."

"I agree, but Father thinks it would be good for me to take charge over something," Adrian said with a sigh. "I'm to meet with Henry tomorrow and discuss their progress over lunch. Would you like to go?"

Roslyn hummed a note. "I believe your mother and I have plans with Josephine, but that was yesterday. Things change quickly down here. And to be honest, your meetings sound dreadfully boring."

Adrian sighed. "I agree."

A beat of silence passed.

"I miss not having to make decisions," Adrian whispered. "I miss being the prince everyone else looked after."

"Ah."

He turned toward her. She wore a knowing look. "What?"

"You're growing up," she said, patting his chest.

"I'm not a fan of it," he said, as the root of his troubles hooked under his ribs like a finger, forcing them painfully upward. "I can't be that prince anymore. The people need me to be more than that."

He couldn't hide in his castle anymore.

He hadn't realized he had been hiding until he wasn't.

"And I will be there with you." Roslyn kissed his cheek. "You're doing a marvelous job so far."

"At least one of us thinks so."

The following day, Adrian headed toward the Undercity house the knights had claimed as theirs. His armed escort walked on either side of him, though none of them wore the gold and black doublets of the Royal Guard. Some wore their bronze armor, but most wore a mixture of iron and steel, whatever the Undercity blacksmiths could forge. Jax walked on his right, shoulders back and eyes alert. He had been part of Adrian's previous personal guard, added after that assassin—Xavier—killed his guard.

That was another grievance forgotten about in the name of unity and circumstance. Regardless, Adrian was glad to have Jax's familiar face among so much change.

The knights had taken a large building near the center of the Undercity. The squires standing guard at the entrance bowed to Adrian. Earth mages had carved out the first floor to make room for training—many had flocked to the Order to learn to fight, children driven out of their homes, castle servants, and even a few of Maddox's criminals. The Order turned none away. Nexon had the advantage of numbers and magic, and if they were to retake Bradburn Castle, they needed a stronger fighting force. It smelled like the barracks, but also like the knights' hall: sweat, leather, steel, and armor polish.

Knights and guards lingered about the room in various states of training. Proficient knights fought with dulled blades while others taught defense. Sir Henry Julian stood among a group of young boys and girls, teaching them how to hold a sword.

Henry had grown up in the castle, and he and Adrian had known each other most of their lives. Henry had earned his knighthood on a quest to save Adrian's life, alongside Reid and Juniper. To say that Adrian felt an overwhelming sense of gratitude would be an understatement. Henry, like Adrian's father and Reid, had already done great and selfless things.

Adrian strolled to where Henry instructed.

"Stance is as important as grip." Henry demonstrated, and the children mimicked. "A wrong grip will break your wrist or drop your sword. A wrong stance will hurt your knees and make it easy to lose your balance. Either will get you killed. Go watch the knights fight. Study how they move and how they hold their weapons."

The children rushed to where two knights practiced combat.

Henry eyed Adrian, and then his eyes fell on the space beside him—Adrian hoped for a quick moment that Roslyn had changed her mind and come with, but as he turned his heart dropped. A young woman with shoulder-length black hair, pale olive skin, ink-dark eyes, and sly grin stood beside him.

Adrian blinked. "How long have you been here?"

"About as long as you," Amery said in her sweet but dangerous voice. "I assume the king wants you to spy on the knights too."

"You're spying?" Adrian frowned.

Amery shrugged, a non-answer. "Maddox likes to know what's going on, and despite what everyone seems to think, he is not all-seeing."

He just had an army of spies and thieves.

Henry didn't look surprised. He motioned the two of them toward the door. "Let's see about that lunch. I'm starving."

The three of them—along with Adrian's guard—made their way into the Commons, the central point of the Undercity, and neutral ground. Adrian steered them toward a food counter run by former castle servants. The food and drink smelled like the castle, and it reminded Adrian of home, of safety. They sat, and his guard fanned out.

"I see the training is going well," Amery said. "It warms my heart to see little girls learning to use a sword."

Henry shrugged. "Traditionally, knights are men, but we won't turn down a good sword arm and a fighting spirit. Besides, the old Order is gone. We're building it anew."

"Women included," Amery said, her grin a bit mad.

Henry nodded. "I'll be honest, I didn't think I'd like a woman in armor. Turns out I do."

Amery chuckled.

"We have more people coming in every day to learn how to fight," Henry reported, mostly to Adrian, though Amery listened. "They are eager. We have promoted close to a hundred into pledge status, and a few talented warriors into squire status. The smiths are busting themselves to produce enough armor and weapons, and most of the knights have conquered mental resistance."

Adrian still shivered at those words. The knights had learned mental resistance—resistance to magical invasion of the mind—in order to stop Nexon's followers from possessing them and turning them into thralls.

Everyone in the Undercity had been encouraged to learn mental resistance. Adrian had tried and failed. He had hated every minute of it, that strange pricking feeling at his thoughts, a foggy warmth sliding over his mind. He would rather wash a hundred dirty tankards or even a hangover than feel a strange presence inside his head.

He shivered.

A young girl appeared beside Amery in the midnight clothes of a thief. Daggers and lockpicks hung on a leather belt from shoulder to hip, and a deep hood shadowed her dark face. Her clever eyes quickly looked Adrian and Henry over.

"Blythe?" Amery asked, a note of surprise on her voice.

"I have news. Maddox said to tell the king at once." Blythe's eyes shifted to Adrian.

Adrian felt a prickle along his spine. "I'm not the king."

"But you're close enough," Amery said. "Go on, Blythe."

Blythe's eyes bore into Adrian. "Nexon has left Rusdasin. He's heading east. He's taken a thousand mages with him, and he's put Fowler in charge."

CHAPTER 23

Juniper hadn't planned on going back to the vestibule; she hadn't planned on going anywhere. She just wanted away from the bloodstained royal suite, from her siblings' clothing, from Isolde.

Just…away.

She walked, not minding where she was going, until she entered a dark, dank, quiet corridor untouched by the earth mages and the druids. Without them, the castle felt as it should—empty. A tomb.

She doubled over and took several deep breaths, trying to calm her furious heartbeat and trembling hands.

Boots passed in her peripheral. They did not disturb the puddle of greenish water gathering in a dip in the stones. She straightened in time to see the ghost vanish through a broken door thick with cobwebs. Though the idea of finding another ghostly massacre twisted her stomach, she followed.

The door led into a closet. The closet held linens and towels and twenty years of dust, sagging cobwebs, and petrified mouse droppings. The ghost blinked into existence, and with him, the closet appeared as it once had—as if a servant had just stacked freshly washed linens. Juniper thought she caught the scent of lemongrass and something sweet, but the stench of a sodden castle overtook it. The ghost pressed his hand to the back wall, and a rune flared. A secret door swung inward, the ghost walked through, the rune faded, and the secret door closed.

Juniper blinked, and the vision vanished. She stood alone in the closet.

Heart thumping, she pressed her hand to the stones where the ghost had. The old rune glowed faintly, and for a moment she didn't think the magic would work, but then the stone door swung inward with creaking stone and rusted metal. The stone door stuttered to a halt halfway open.

Wide stone stairs spiraled down into darkness. Juniper took each step carefully, half expecting the steps to flatten and sending her sliding into a pit of long dead snakes or rusted spikes. The ghost didn't reappear. She could have summoned a magelight, but with only her, her night sight would do—she had been using her night sight all her life, and being in the dark made her feel safe. It made her feel like Juniper Thimble, not Isolde.

The stairs wound down, down, and further down. She hadn't realized how high in the castle she'd been. Unless, like Bradburn Castle, her own went deep into the ground.

The ghost stood at the bottom with a flickering magelight in his hand. He stood with his back to her, facing a seemingly solid stone wall. He performed the same trick—he touched a part of the stone, a rune glowed, and a door opened.

Juniper followed the ghost's path and opened the second door. It opened a little more than halfway and led into a dark chamber filled with strange shadows and floor-to-ceiling shelving and cabinets.

It took a moment to realize the odd shapes as ovens—the kitchens.

For a moment, a phantasmal clatter of pots and pans and voices sounded. It faded as quickly as it came.

Juniper meandered through the rows of cold ovens, long-dried and shriveled herbs, sacks of what might have been rice and flour—bugs and mice had long since riddled through them. She made her way into an adjacent room filled with washing tubs and empty buckets. Dirty dishes piled in several of them, and cleaned dishes stacked on drying racks and shelves. Broken dishes scattered on the floor, the pieces smothered in dust and dirt. The silver had long tarnished and dulled, the china was clotted with dust and cobwebs.

In the next room, a row of tables once held plants. The plants were dead and shriveled and unrecognizable. Moonlight flooded in through the wall of windows, fractured by the overgrown weeds that had snaked through broken glass. Moss crawled along the far window and halfway down the wall. What looked like an old bee nest hung from the ceiling.

Seeing the moonlight calmed something within her. It called, and she followed. An old but intact wooden door in the next room led into the garden. Juniper forced it open with a squeal of rusted hinges, ripping weeds that had grown high on the other side. A path had once led from the door and through the garden, but weeds and thorny roses had stolen it. She forced her way through, pushing the thorns and weeds out of her way with icy tendrils.

The path met the one she and Reid had taken. The castle loomed behind her. It still looked haunted and empty, and not at all like it housed a small army of mages and druids.

And now she knew exactly where she was and how to get back to the vestibule. A part of her deflated at knowing where she was, while another rejoiced. Granted, she'd meant to get lost. It…made the castle feel smaller.

She didn't want to return. Not yet. She started along the path toward the lake, where the gazebo sat in silence over the Jeweled Lake. The moon vanished behind a cloud, muting the light and brightening the stars. She didn't mean to, but her eyes found Bera's stars.

Soon, the solstice would be upon them.

Juniper leaned onto the stone railing of the gazebo. The fish glimmered and glinted, easing through the water like coins dropped in a fountain. It made her think of buried treasure. More than a few times she had daydreamed of finding lost pirate treasure and escaping the Undercity. It all seemed like another life.

The water barely rippled as the fish swam closer to the surface, fracturing the moonlight.

She felt it again, that presence deep within the lake. It felt familiar, yet unknown. She didn't see anything within the water, only dark depths. Her magic sank into the water like ink, spilling to every corner. She felt the fish swimming about, the rocks littering the bottom, and...something else. Something alive.

She reached out to it with her magic, and, as if spurred by her awareness of it, it moved. It glided through the water with little effort. The fish did not skitter away or dart out of its path. It moved with a fish's grace, curling in on itself as it slowly came closer. Like smoke, like magic.

Juniper pulled her magic back. Her immediate thought was to run back to shore, but something held her firmly. Despite the fear bubbling under her skin, she didn't feel threatened.

Something dark and blurred appeared within the depths of the cerulean lake. It swam closer to the surface with every graceful swish of its elongated body. At first, Juniper thought it was a massive fish. Scales of jade and sapphire covered its sleek body. It had a blunt snout and large black eyes that glittered up at Juniper from under the water. It had four feet tucked against its pale green belly, and a long tail lined with curved fins of emerald green. It curved back and forth, as if performing, before it stuck its head above the water.

Juniper could only stare. She had never seen anything like it. She had read about sea monsters, dragons, and merfolk, but nothing fit the description of this creature.

And its eyes sparkled as if it knew.

"You have returned," it said in a whispering, harmonious voice. "Alone this time."

A prickle of unease spider-walked down her scalp. It had been watching her and Reid? It could speak?

"I have been alone in this lake for so long, waiting for a new master to come," it said. "And here you are."

"A new master?" Juniper asked weakly. She didn't like those words. Swallowing, she found her voice. "I'm not anyone's master."

"But you are," it said, and it didn't sound upset by it. It sounded intrigued. Glad, even. "My previous master told me the next would come to me here in this lake. His friend, the seer, saw it."

"And you've just been waiting here?"

"It hasn't been too long," it said. "I died when the castle burned, and it takes years to regain myself. Though, I can't say how many years have passed. Tell me, how many years has it been since the enemies breached the gates?"

"Nineteen," Juniper said. "I'm assuming you mean the civil war."

"I am." The creature twirled under the water and resurfaced, glistening scales. "Nineteen years. How time flies."

She dared not take her eyes off the thing. "And you…died?"

It swam in a graceful circle, scales glittering like wet gemstones. "I did. I put up a fight. I killed hundreds before they took me."

"And…" Juniper started, mind grappling with the concept. "You're here. Alive?"

It clicked its tongue at her. Still, its dark eyes glittered.

She leaned closer to the railing and asked, "What happened to your previous master?"

"He died shortly after the castle burned," the creature said in a sigh. "I didn't see it, but I felt it. We are connected, you see. And now *we* are connected. You and I."

Something tugged within her chest, like a string was tied around her lungs. She put a hand against her sternum. The creature let out a rumble of a laugh.

"You can feel that?" Juniper asked before she could think better of it. The creature swam in a figure eight. "What are you?"

The creature paused and raised its head above the water. "You don't yet know?"

"If I knew, I wouldn't've asked."

It laughed. It sounded human but also inhuman. Juniper had the sinking, sickening feeling she had heard the laugh before.

"Surely you have an inkling. Tell me, young archmage, what do you think I am?"

She swallowed. "How do you know that?"

"It is one of the many things I can sense about you," it said. It rose higher. Silvery fur lined the underside of its neck, and the hard fins on its head resembled horns. "I will give you a hint. I have four siblings. We were gifts, helpers and friends, weapons and guards. We must obey our master, but only our master."

And…she knew what it was.

"A wechun," she whispered.

"Ah, you do know! And yet you say the name with fear. You have had a negative experience with one of my siblings."

She half-laughed. "That is putting it lightly. A wechun tried to kill me. Several times."

It didn't seem surprised. "Which one?"

"Earth," she said. "Nexon's wechun. You don't look anything like that one. It was horrible. We all thought it was a demon. You're..." She paused, unsure how to phrase it.

It tilted its head, awaiting her words.

"More appealing to the eyes," she said.

"What I become depends on you," said the wechun. "Wechun are dependent on their master. When you command me, I listen. If you are filled with malice and darkness, I reflect such. If you are filled with love and kindness, I reflect such."

"I could make you more beautiful?" Juniper asked.

It laughed. "Yes, you can. Our appearance depends on our master's intentions. It was a way to expose an archmage if they had been corrupted by their gods-given power. By your words, I imagine the Archmage of Earth was filled with dark intentions, fueled by hate and greed."

She nodded. "He is."

"I have missed much in these years," said the wechun. "Will you fill me in?"

"I don't know much more than you," Juniper said.

"Have you been sleeping in a lake for nineteen years?"

"No, but..." Her breath caught in her throat. "If you are so ancient, then you know a lot more than me."

"I might know more of some things," it said. "But of these past few years, I know only things that have occurred in this lake."

"Then you know of the Iluvin," she whispered. It seemed too good to be true.

"I know much of them."

"And you know of magic."

"I am partly made of magic."

Juniper laughed.

It paused its swimming and tilted its head. "I said no joke. Did I?"

"No," Juniper said, relief bright in her chest.

Juniper sat on the floor of the gazebo and told the creature all she knew about what had happened after Nexon had invaded Balendin Castle, how he had killed the royal family looking for her, how the city had been abandoned, how Delphine was the new capital. The wechun reclined in the water, listening. When her tongue felt heavy and her throat dry, she stopped.

The wechun hummed. "And you wish to know more about the Iluvin?"

"Yes."

"It has been a thousand years since I lived among the Iluvin," it said. "My memories have faded with time, I'm afraid. There were libraries as large as Balendin Castle, filled with books and scholars and teachers of every school of magic. I could regale you with memories, however it is late. Your friends are likely worried over your prolonged absence, even your grumpy Archmage of Energy."

"You can tell that about him?" Juniper asked.

"He…radiates magic," it said. "He's not very good at holding it in. It just goes everywhere."

"He's new to being a mage," Juniper said. Then, the thought struck, and she gasped, "He has a wechun too?"

"Indeed, though I don't know where it has gone. I haven't seen any of my siblings in several centuries. They will sense their new master only when they are close enough, and some spend years searching the realm. But, enough of this talking. You may be the Archmage of Water, but you are not invulnerable to frostbite. You are also exhausted."

"I'm fine," Juniper said, rubbing the chill out of her arms. "I'm not that tired."

"Our special bond allows a certain awareness of your state," the wechun explained a bit sternly. "Now, go inside before you fall asleep out here."

"I thought I was supposed to command you?"

It laughed. "You are still young and uncertain. When you command me, you must mean it. When you command anything, you must mean it. Now, until next we meet. Farewell."

The wechun curled backward and swam back to the depths. Juniper lingered until she could no longer see it. She could feel it, waiting and listening, lingering within her awareness. Its magic was tied to her own.

Far too much had happened, and it was right. She needed rest.

CHAPTER 24

The Undercity leaders packed the tavern. King Bradburn, Captain Sandpiper, and Adrian sat on one side of the large center table; Maddox Hawk and Amery sat on another; and Josephine sat on the shorter side. Even the new council of knights had come for this meeting, Sirs Darvel, Willard, Tegard, and Monlen, if Adrian remembered their names correctly. Isaac had gone to Delphine with Juniper and Reid.

Silence fell as Blythe told her tale in her small but sharp voice. She had gone topside to scout on Maddox's orders, and she had overheard mages talking about Nexon.

"They said Nexon left in a fury." Despite her lack of volume, Blythe's voice filled the tavern's silence. "Something had enraged him, but they didn't know what. He took a large number of his mages and thralls with him, and these mages were mad he didn't take them too. They were left behind to mind the castle, they said."

The silence turned deadly, as if each person held their own, waiting for the first to shatter this revelation.

"They are marching to war," said King Bradburn, his tone heavy and commanding.

"It certainly seems like it," Maddox agreed. "One doesn't march with a thousand mages for nothing. My spies tell me another wave is set to leave in the coming days."

No one argued. Maddox's spies scattered the city and beyond.

"They were heading east," Josephine repeated. She motioned to the map they had spread on the table. "I think it is safe to assume or at least speculate Nexon is heading toward Juniper."

"That would imply he knows where she is," Maddox added. He set his unreadable gaze on Josephine, then her map.

"Magic is a strange thing," Josephine said. "It would be no small matter to set Nexon off in a rage enough to march an army across a kingdom."

Adrian fought the urge to slump in his comfortable wooden chair. He wished they had gathered instead to talk about supply lines. He held his stare on the little person-shaped figures on the map, their feet pointed east. Did Juniper know an army was marching toward her? How could she possibly know something like that? Unless...

"Juniper might have spurred him on purpose," Adrian mused.

Whatever Maddox had been saying, he paused. His dark eyes pinned on Adrian. Something sparked back, that gleam of knowing what others did not. "I am inclined to agree, Your Highness."

King Bradburn glanced at his son, expression masked. "We cannot worry over what our allies in the east are doing. Not with this opportunity before us." He straightened, commanding the attention of the room. "Nexon has left the castle exposed. We have the advantage. Now is the time to retake the castle, so he has nowhere to return to."

"Are our soldiers ready?" Maddox asked, though if Amery had been spying on them, he already knew the answer.

The king didn't answer, and Adrian realized he waited for his son to. Something slimy slithered down his spine and pooled in his gut. Steeling himself under the gaze of Maddox Hawk and his father, he said, "Henry assures me the knights are training hard, as are their new pledges and squires."

"We are as ready as we can be," Captain Sandpiper said dryly.

"Our knights are trained in anti-magic, our mages are trained in combat, and we have all received mental resistance training," said the king. "Now is the time to strike, while the enemy's back is turned and we have the advantage."

Adrian fixed his eyes on the map, on the drawn castle. Could they retake the castle? The idea of a siege made him sick, but it couldn't be avoided. They couldn't hide in the Undercity forever. They couldn't wait for Juniper to fix everything. Still, it worried him. What would they do after they had retaken the castle? What if Nexon came back for it with his mages? What if Juniper failed?

No, he couldn't think like that.

"Then it is agreed," said the king. "We begin preparation immediately."

A strong hum of agreement resounded.

Adrian stood with his father and marched back into the Undercity's magical sunlight. Stones fell into his gut, and he forced himself to match his father's pace and not empty his stomach onto the ground.

A strange chaotic rhythm came over the Undercity in the following days. Smiths hammered out new armor and fresh blades. Healers crafted as many healing potions and tonics as their supplies allowed. Routes were planned into the castle. Teams were sorted. Supplies were passed out.

Adrian headed to Josephine's for his daily lesson on mental resistance. It seemed as though everyone else had grasped it, yet it still eluded him. He walked with two guards instead of his full retinue, including Jax. There was far too much work to be done for guards to follow the prince about.

He and his guards walked through the ward surrounding Josephine's house with ease, and at once the bustle and chaos of mages preparing for battle met his ears. Potions brewed in the workroom, defensive runes were being sewn onto clothing, and offensive magic was being taught in the front lawn. The young mages looked positively terrified yet determined. If only Adrian could muster that same determination.

He let himself into the first floor parlor where all of his other sessions had taken place and plopped into one of the well-used armchairs.

Josephine appeared after a long few moments, as calm as if they weren't about to lay siege to a castle. His castle. His home.

"I didn't know if you would come today." She shut the parlor doors, and the runes carved into the wood cut into the wood muted the sounds beyond. She sat in the chair across from him and draped her arm across her lap. Her other sleeve hung straight from her shoulder, empty. Adrian had never asked how she had lost it, but rumor suggested it had been removed to save herself from Mage's Bane in her younger years.

"Why wouldn't I come?"

"There is much to do."

Guilt pooled in his stomach. "Should I leave? I don't mean to be a nuisance."

"Oh, not at all. It is important you know mental resistance. Are you ready?"

Adrian inhaled, held it, and released it. No, he wasn't, but he never was. He nodded.

Josephine's gaze intensified. Adrian felt the pressure first, a pinching on his mind. Then, a warmth slid down his thoughts. It felt…easy. He could just lean back.

"Adrian," Josephine said.

He snapped back. The warmth vanished.

Josephine looked at him with pity. He'd failed. "Once more. Ready yourself. Push against me."

Adrian nodded. He still didn't understand what that meant, but he'd try.

His mind pinched. His thoughts turned to warm honey. This time, he was aware of the invasion, and he tried not to give in to the ease, to the painless darkness. He pushed back; Josephine pushed harder.

It didn't last. Adrian failed and fell under.

Again. And again. And again.

"Adrian," Josephine said, pulling him back into awareness.

He released a sigh of defeat and slumped onto his knees. A sheen of sweat had gathered on his face and neck, sticking the hair to his neck. "I'm sorry."

Josephine didn't say anything for a long moment. "Your focus is off today."

Adrian rubbed his face and ran a hand through his sweaty hair. "Let's try again."

The pinching sensation didn't come. Josephine remained still. Her motherly gaze did not relent. "Your lack of focus could be due to an excess of nerves or fear—"

"Of course I'm nervous and afraid," Adrian spat. All his agitation burst. "My kingdom is on the cusp of annihilation, I'm living underground, and my friends are scattered over the realm trying to do something while I'm squatting underground because I can't do anything to help them."

Josephine's brows rose, though she did not speak.

Shame flushed through him. "I—I'm sorry. I didn't mean to shout."

"No, go on." Josephine waved her hand toward him.

Adrian heaved a sigh and leaned back into the chair. He felt like drinking until he couldn't feel his bones. "I'm useless," he said at last. "I'm terrible with a blade, I can't do magic, I've no mind for scheming, and while my friends are preparing to fight for their lives, I'm…" He gestured for the words he couldn't find. "I'm still here."

"Here?"

"Trying to learn mental resistance," Adrian said darkly. "Everyone else seems to get it."

"Most others here have more experience with magic," Josephine said plainly. "The knights and mages have a deeper understanding due to their training and very nature, whereas you have little experience. It is normal to struggle with a new concept."

She was right. He had learned little about magic in his studies. The knights learned how magic smelled and felt, and the mages had magic in their blood. Adrian had had minimal contact with magic in any form.

"I have a suggestion," Josephine said. "Spend more time with the mages or with the knights. Expose yourself to magic. See how it feels. It will do you good to get experience."

Adrian could do that. It was better than this, failing over and over. "I will," he said, standing. "Thank you."

CHAPTER 25

Over the next several days, everyone worked. The druids had tamed the front garden and the bailey and had started on the royal grounds. Because of the restoration, their camp had spread into several corridors of the castle. The earth mages fixed the royal wing, and Juniper hadn't been able to tell them not to. It seemed silly to refuse them, given the dire situation.

Juniper went to see the wechun every afternoon. She wanted to know about the Iluvin, and it wanted to know about her and the situation she had found herself in. She didn't see the harm, so she answered every question honestly.

Reid trained with the druids, and a few of the mages had joined them. From what Xavier had told Juniper, Reid hadn't been himself.

"He's a bit…distracted," Xavier had said.

Everyone knew something had happened to Reid, and Juniper didn't know how to explain it. The change was obvious in the way he acted and the way he spoke, and the predatory way he held himself. Like a panicked animal. Juniper hadn't seen him much. She stayed busy, as did he. They saw each other only at night when they collapsed from exhaustion in the same tent.

One afternoon, while Juniper stood in the gazebo speaking to the wechun, the clouds thickened into steely grays.

"Can you feel that?" the wechun asked. "A storm is coming. Snow is on the way."

She could. She felt it thick in the sky. It toyed with her magic and made her feel like she stood within an abyss.

"One of my previous masters once told me that standing in a snowstorm felt like being submerged in the ocean," the wechun whispered.

"I have never seen it," Juniper said.

The wechun *tsked*. "That is an easy fix. Wander south long enough, you will find it. Perhaps, if we both survive this war, we can see it. I would like to swim in the salt once again."

Juniper turned the offer over in her mind. Yes, she would like to see the ocean. To feel salt water on her skin, to know if it tasted as nasty as the books said, to know if it really made you see things that weren't there.

"We can talk of the ocean another day," the wechun said. "You have grown tired, and you need to eat something."

"I'm fine," she said.

"Yes, but you are too skinny," the wechun mused. "Go. I will be here."

It slithered back into the depths. Juniper sighed, knowing the conversation was over for the day. Standing, she brushed off the druid-made woolen dress and started back toward the castle.

The druids had cleared the back gardens of the castle of the winter-brown weeds and overgrown roses. The process had revealed old planter boxes which now held freshly turned soil and sprouting greens, a feat accomplished with druid magic. Instead of decay and winter, the gardens smelled like spring soil and herbs.

Juniper entered the garden's door that led into the kitchen. The druids and mages had been hard at work turning the cluttered kitchens into a usable space. They had scrubbed the nasty dishes and cleaned out the cobwebs and dead mice and gods knew what else. They had cooked several days' worth of meals, and the savory scents lingered in the air.

As she passed a row of cleaned and warm ovens, Ison came around the other corner. His gray eyes met hers, and a tired smile came over his face. Someone had trimmed his wild curls, and the several days of warm meals and rest had brought life back into his face.

"Jun, there you are," he said.

"Were you looking for me?"

"No, but now that you're here, I want to show you something." He motioned her into a side room that had been cleaned and repaired. Ancient potion making equipment lined two long tables, flasks and burners and steamers. One wall held floor to ceiling cabinets and shelves, and jars of all sizes and material had been stacked.

"I found all of this here." Ison motioned toward the potion-making equipment. "It's in decent shape."

"That's good," Juniper said.

"We'll have potions in no time," he said, hands on his hips. "And the druids are growing herbs faster than I thought possible. I had no idea they had such talent with plants."

It was good news, and it should have made her happy. Yet she couldn't muster the effort to smile. "Is everyone getting along?"

"So far, yes," Ison said, though he looked away when he said it.

She frowned.

"Well, all things considered, yes. The mages are skittish of the druids, the druids are skittish of the mages, and everyone is skittish of the beasts. Save the Shadows." Ison folded his arms over his dusty shirt. "Everyone is keeping to themselves, though they work together when asked."

"That's all we can really ask for right now," she said. "Everyone here has left someplace behind. They've all been misplaced, and the world is shifting around them."

Ison blinked at her.

"What?"

"That's very worldly."

"Why are you surprised? I can be worldly." Even though the wechun had been the one to say those words first.

Ison smiled, though cautiously. "It seems so."

A horn sounded, signaling dinner. Ison and Juniper headed through the castle and to the room designated as the dining hall. It might have been a small ballroom once, but now stone tables and benches lined the long room. It had easy access to the kitchens, making the designation as dining hall simple. Druids and mages filed in from all over the room, and chatter filled the air. Several large stew pots dotted the tables, and piles of mismatching bowls and wooden spoons set around.

They sat down with Xavier, Bois, Mabyl, Finn, and a few other mages Juniper had seen around. She looked around and spotted Reid. He sat with the druid warriors. Lilianna sat with Sein and Asher and a few druids she knew by face but not name.

"You're looking a bit pasty." Mabyl wagged her spoon at Juniper.

Juniper set her gaze on her bowl. "It's been a long few weeks."

No one argued.

Dishes went into baskets, and druids took those baskets back to the kitchens to be washed and stored.

Ison tugged Juniper aside as the others filed out of the dining hall.

"Walk with me," Ison said. "I want to show you something."

She had nowhere else to be, so she agreed.

The castle had lost the harsh edge of its abandonment. With so many calling it a home now, sound murmured through the halls and magelights dotted the ceilings. It smelled better too, like magic and herbs. Ison led the way, and it took a few corridors for her to realize that he was steering her toward the royal wing. Her heart thudded. She'd been avoiding the royal wing.

Magic had healed the stones, straightened the walls and evened the floors. The shattered doors were gone and replaced with woven curtains of fibers. The floral scents of magic had replaced the dust and dank.

"We stopped here on our way to Baxion," Ison said. "I couldn't sleep, so I wandered. I found something. It's not morbid, I promise."

Juniper trusted her friend, so when he guided her into the king's chambers, she followed. Darkness pulsed at the edges of her vision. Whatever Ison said next, she didn't catch it.

Magic had fixed the walls and floors, and a fire burned in the hearth. It smelled like rosemary and roses. The fallen portrait had been hung, and someone had done what they could to remove the soot and dust from the painting itself.

Her eyes caught on the clean stones on the floor. The bloodstains were gone. The stones were clean.

Ison slipped his hand into hers and led her into the adjoining study. It too had been cleaned and freshened. Another fire burned in the hearth, though smaller than the other. He led her across the study and into a tower with curved walls etched with a sprawling family tree. Ison stood aside while she took a lap of the space, eyeing the names, the lines connecting them, the iron stairs in the middle, and the five names at the very top.

It didn't take Juniper long to realize what it was. An Iluvin heritage map, starting with the first archmages. She followed the lines to her parents, and then to her—Isolde Balendin. Her name was circled in gold, just as every archmage.

Her name was the final name. The mapping had ended with the civil war.

"There is Mason Hobbs," Juniper said, pointing to his name on the wall. Ison came to her side. She dropped her finger to the name below Mason's. "He had a son, but whoever kept this tree didn't know about Reid's mother or Reid."

"I can't believe Reid is an archmage," Ison said. "I can't believe you are either, but you being one is more believable."

"I know," she said. "Reid can't believe it either."

"Is that why he's so…different?"

Juniper bit her lip. Ison noticed.

Ison nodded toward the door, then led her into the bedroom. They had fixed it too. New linens covered the bed. The moldy curtains had been replaced with simpler white curtains and tied with hemp cord. Woven shutters hung over the windows.

And…Juniper's satchel, which she had left in her tent in the vestibule, sat at the foot of the bed. As did Reid's.

"They are determined to make me sleep in my parents' bed." Juniper sighed through her nose. "And occupy the room where they were murdered."

Ison sat on the bed and patted the bed beside him. "Want to talk?"

She sank onto the bed beside him and leaned onto her knees. "The bed is softer than I thought it would be."

"It's not the same mattress or blankets," Ison said. "The druids and mages have been working tirelessly to fix this place up."

"It still feels…" She sighed and buried her hand in her hands. With her eyes closed, she told him about the ghosts.

"I've not heard anyone else mention ghosts," Ison said. "But it might be because of your connection to the place and to the people who died here."

"That's unfair," she whispered. "If I have to witness the misery of the siege and the last memories of those who died here, other people should too. If no other reason than to share in my misery."

Ison offered her a sympathetic smile. "What about Reid? You were going to say something else."

She glanced toward the sitting room, just in case Reid had snuck in when her eyes had been closed. He hadn't.

"When he fell, I…" Panic and shame ricocheted up her spine. She took a calming breath. "When we were in Delphine, I stole a bottle of this magic water from what they called a Spirit Gate. It was this portal thing under a singing tree where I spoke to my parents."

Ison's brows rose, but he didn't interrupt.

"And when Reid fell, I poured that magic into his mouth." Her voice thinned to a whisper. "I was desperate to keep him, and I'm afraid I did this to him. What if the magic I poured into his mouth somehow made the archmage magic come to him? What if it wrenched him out of the hands of death and death is trying to take him back?"

Ison's gaze went unreadable. "Have you told Reid about it?"

She shook her head. "I'm afraid of what he'll think. I don't want him to blame me for what happened, and I don't want him to push me away any more than he already has."

Ison leaned forward to look her in the eye. "Are you doing all right?"

She hesitated. "I…I'll be fine. I just… He's colder than he has ever been, and I can feel his panic and fear. I don't want to add my problems on top of his." Her voice dropped to a whisper. "I don't like the distance between us, and I'm afraid I'm the one who put it there."

Ison didn't offer any advice, but she didn't know what she expected to hear. Regardless, it was nice to speak to someone, to have someone listen to this madness, who understood why she felt like she did. The wechun listened, but Ison listened differently. Talking with Ison felt more like relieving herself of a burden. It made her feel less alone.

"And…you're all right?" Ison asked again.

"I'm breathing, so that's a win," she said. He heaved a sigh and tried to laugh it off. It felt hollow. "I'm as fine as I can be with the threat of war hanging over our heads. Every time I pass a window, I fear I'll see an incoming army. I hate waiting. I know we need to train and fortify and prepare, but…gods, I hate it."

Voices drifted in from the corridor.

"Xavier and I are staying across the hall," Ison said. "If you need someone to talk to, find me. But…uh, knock first."

She raised her brow.

A small smile stretched his lips. "It's a fair warning."

"And I thank you for it."

Ison stood. "Now, would you like a small tour of the repairs we've managed so far? It's impressive."

"I suppose. I'll just be moping and brooding in here otherwise."

Arm in arm, Ison showed Juniper the corridors they had fixed. Woven shutters and curtains had replaced the broken glass and doors, the walls had been fixed, the floors were smooth, the ceilings repaired and a few even had designs in the stone similar to those in other chambers. Every hearth had a roaring fire, and the winter chill had been banished from the royal wing. Magelights dotted the ceilings and shaded the space in various shades of blue and yellow. Runes had been added for warmth, protection, and scents.

"Scents?" Juniper's brows rose at one such rune that emitted lemongrass.

"These are some of the forbidden runes the Marca forbade," Ison said. "Gods forbid we dabble in perfumes." Ison rolled his eyes. "Some of the more useful runes I've found have been forbidden. Most are harmless."

"Can you make a rune that smells like lavender and honeysuckle?"

"I don't see why not. I didn't carve these, though." Ison glanced at the scent rune. "They're particular, all these little things indicate different scents. It's quite complicated. But, I will look into it for you."

"I would appreciate it," Juniper said. Odd how just the idea of a smell could warm her chest. It made her think of the home she thought she'd had, the home she had dreamed about in those long nights in the Undercity, and even as a captive in Bradburn Castle. Despite that home being a farce, the nostalgia for the scents of it remained. "But don't take the mages away from other work. It's not a priority."

Ison nodded, and she hoped he'd listen to that last part. She didn't want the mages thinking her needy or frivolous while they slept on bedrolls in the dirt or hard stone.

They continued their tour of repaired corridors and woven curtains and pleasant scents. If she closed her eyes, she could imagine being in Bradburn Castle, ignorant of Nexon and his plans, of her birth and family. They passed mages working to rearrange fallen stones without bringing the corridor down on their heads. They worked together, with air mages and fire mages to catch the stones if they fell and burn away the cobwebs and dust and sweep it out the window.

"We're working on other wings as we speak," Ison explained. "At this pace, this entire castle will be livable in a few months."

Her heart thudded hard. A few months. "Do you plan on us being here that long?"

His gray gaze went pensive. "Do you want to return to Rusdasin?"

She didn't have an answer to give. She didn't know. Yes, because it was the only home she'd known, and Reid's family was there. She had friends there. No, because she didn't have a home to return to. The Undercity wasn't home; Bradburn Castle wasn't home; Delphine wasn't home. She didn't have a home. She had Reid. If Reid returned to Rusdasin, then she would follow.

"You don't have to go back," Ison said. "You could stay here. Start over. Start something new. Do what Nexon told people he was doing: make a place where mages can go."

She didn't answer, but she thought about his suggestion. She thought about it after they had parted ways and she washed up in the royal suite, in the bathing room recently scrubbed with lavender oil and scented with winterberries. She didn't call for water; she magicked it from the gently falling snow outside and heated it to steam in the massive tub of smoothed marble.

She could start over. She could stay here.

And the more she thought about it, the more she didn't know what she wanted.

CHAPTER 26

Reid circled the druids as they sparred. A space had been carved out of the back gardens for them, and it led into what had once been the castle barracks. The mages were busy renovating, and many of the druid warriors had moved into the new space. It felt oddly familiar; Reid had spent much of his time in the barracks of Bradburn Castle, sparring with the Royal Guard or his fellow squires.

The druids sparred in teams, and Reid kept his guidance to a minimum. It was not that they were not making mistakes, but Reid could barely focus. With so much movement, his attention was being pulled in every direction. Between the druids and the tangled grounds, he couldn't focus on a single pair of warriors long enough to see what they were doing wrong.

It was beyond tiring.

The druids had come a long way from where they had started, but they still had a long way to go. They wouldn't stand a chance against Nexon's army. They would need months, if not years, of a knight's training against magic. Nexon's mages would slaughter them.

But he trained them. If for no other reason than to give himself something to do, to give them a sliver of a chance to survive.

Reid noticed the beast a heartbeat before it snarled. It patrolled the other side of the hedge the druids had erected around the training grounds. The beast's ears stuck up over the top, and it moved with near silence, but Reid felt it. Sensed it.

He could not explain it. Everything…pulsed with a strange awareness, an energy, and it reacted with the cursed magic within him. He had been taught to sense magic as a squire, and he had spent so long waiting for a glimpse of magic, yearning to prove himself to the Order, that being submerged in it threatened to drown him. He couldn't stop sensing the ocean of magic around him. It yawned under his feet like a grave, and it hung over his head like a noose.

One wrong move, one distracting thought, and it would crush him.

Reid started to pace again. It helped.

Asher hit the ground in front of him. He scrambled to his feet, eyes on Reid, ready for advice and correction.

"Try again," was all Reid could think to offer.

Foolish words. His uncle would never have said those words to him. He would have offered a misstep, a misjudgment, the angle of the sword—Reid cursed himself for not paying better attention to these warriors. Guilt and shame twisted in his chest. They looked to him for guidance, and he could not give it.

He started around the sparring ring. Halfway back to where he had been, Xavier appeared beside him, silence as death. A beat within the grand scheme of pulsing, crushing awareness.

"It's going well?" Xavier asked, his voice a steady confident slither.

"Yes."

"Jun asked you to teach them how to be knights. They don't look like knights to me."

Reid frowned. He had tried to teach them how to be knights, but *how*? He had spent years learning the ways of the sword before he had learned anything about anti-magic defenses or suppression techniques.

Xavier crooned, "And how will *you* fight?"

Reid glared at Xavier. He still didn't trust him, regardless of how much others did. He had spent too much of his life lying and sneaking.

"I will fight the same," Reid answered simply.

"With your sword?" Xavier nodded to the blade at Reid's side.

Reid frowned. "Of course."

Xavier's brows rose. "You realize your sword is Mage's Bane? You are a mage now. One wrong move, and you'll kill yourself with that thing."

His hand tightened around the pommel. He had received his Mage's Bane sword upon his knighthood. It symbolized his achievement and the power granted to him by the Order and His Majesty. Not that it mattered now. However, Mage's Bane had always been a symbol of safety and protection. A blade at his side and in his hand brought him a sense of stability. Yet, being a mage, he carried the deadliest poison at his side.

"You know," Xavier said, a small smile on his face, "the Iluvin thought all mages of an element were family. That would make you the patriarch of the Energy family."

Reid released a slow sigh. Of all the things he'd wanted to be, a mage patriarch had never been one of them.

Thick clouds bubbled to the northeast. The kind that promised snowfall. A few bright stars already twinkled in the late afternoon. Soon, dark would be upon them, and the frigid and unforgiving cold of night.

"They look cold," Xavier said with a frown.

Reid followed his gaze to the druids. Indeed, their green cheeks and noses had gone rosy with the cold, and their breaths puffed white. Reid blinked. He hadn't been focused on the cold—they stood outside in the middle of winter. In ragged, well-worn clothes and mismatched leathers. The cold seeped through the steel of Reid's armor and through the seams of his clothes, icing the surface of his skin. He felt the chill in his own face.

How had he not noticed before?

"All right," Reid said above the clatter of steel and blast of magic. At once, the commotion ended. The druid warriors and the mages looked at him. Expectantly. Like he had something worth hearing. "It's late. Get some sleep. We reconvene tomorrow morning."

No one complained. They lowered their arms and retreated into the castle. Xavier took a step in front of Reid, blocking his direct path into the barracks.

"Is it odd for you to see magic this way?" Xavier asked. "For warriors, druids, and mages to be on the same side?"

Reid didn't answer. He had thought it odd, months ago, but the reality of it had settled. Not all magic was bad, and they needed magic on their side if they were to stand a chance against Nexon and his army.

"Hard decisions must be made during war, I suppose," Xavier said.

The last druid marched into the barracks, leaving the garden empty save for Reid and Xavier.

Xavier turned his lithe frame toward Reid. His blue-gray eyes pierced him, but glittered with dark humor. "Can you feel it?" Xavier asked lowly.

By his slithering tone, Reid wasn't sure what the assassin meant, so he didn't respond. All the while, Xavier's stare bore into his.

"If you don't control it, it feels like you're drowning," he whispered. "Like all the magic in the world is about to brush your bones, but it never does. It just pushes and pushes."

"How do I stop it?" Reid hated how desperate he sounded. No one else had even started to understand, but he had met so few energy mages.

Xavier didn't balk at his tone or desperation. He remained as serious as death. He summoned a dagger of charcoal energy. Solid as any steel. Xavier tossed the dagger up and caught it by the hilt.

"You don't stop it," he said. "Energy isn't like the other elements. It isn't connected to the sun or the moon or seasons. It's everywhere. It's magic in its purest form. It's neutral. At least, that is what Josephine told me when I complained about feeling everything. Especially with so many mages in the Undercity. It sometimes felt like walking through water."

Reid hung on those words. It did.

"It's not all the time," Xavier said. "Only sometimes, when I'm not on my toes. My advice to you is to use your magic rather than shoving it down because you don't want it. You saw how that worked out for Jun. It won't work for you either. You're a mage now, like it or not. You can mope, or you can use it to decimate the other mages who are likely marching this way to slaughter us all."

"I will consider your advice," Reid said.

"Consider it now." Xavier brandished a second charcoal dagger. He shifted into an offensive position.

Reid tensed. "You want to fight?"

"I want to prove my point. Surely a knight like you isn't sweating over someone like me."

Reid reached for his Mage's Bane.

"No steel," Xavier said. "Magic only. Show me what you can do."

Reid's fingers tightened on the hilt of his sword. "...I can't."

"Of course you can," Xavier said, brows high. "I saw that shield you threw up in front of Jun. You were thinking about her, right? You were acting on instinct. Act the same. Consider this the first lesson. Don't worry. No one is here to watch. It is just you and me."

Reid released his Mage's Bane. He tried, but no sword appeared in his hand.

"Don't push it down," Xavier said. "Focus it out, not in."

It took several long moments, but a flickering golden blade appeared in his hand. The light illuminated the faint flurries that had started to fall.

Xavier came at him. Reid raised his blade in defense and met the attack. Charcoal energy slammed into his own and shattered it. Bits of gold fluttered among the snowfall. Xavier came at him again, and panic flooded under Reid's skin. Instinct took over. An opponent, he knew. A fight, he knew. The golden blade reformed in his hand and halted Xavier's.

The golden blade held for a heartbeat, then shattered. Xavier sidestepped, crouched, and aimed low. Reid dodged and formed the blade anew—only to have Xavier shatter it once again.

Back and forth, Xavier's charcoal energy shattered Reid's golden blades. One after another. Until Xavier had pushed Reid into the far side of the ring. His heel struck the mounded edge, and he stumbled backward. His back smacked the hard earth. Xavier pounced. Reid saw the charcoal blade poised for a lethal strike, saw the murderous intent in the assassin's eyes.

And he reacted.

He threw his shield arm between them, and a golden disc appeared on his arm. The charcoal blade crashed into the shield with a dull thud, but the shield held. Xavier let out a low laugh and bounced back to his feet. With the threat gone, Reid's shield fractured and shattered. Xavier stood above him. He let his charcoal blades dissolve into the night, and the two of them were alone in the snowy dark. The snowfall had thickened. A faint white mist shrouded the royal grounds and the castle.

Xavier grinned. "What you did just now, that's the way to do it. You have to focus. You have to channel that focus, not let it go everywhere. Control it, don't let it control you."

Xavier held a hand down to him.

Reid took it.

"I'd like you to consider another piece of advice as well," Xavier said as he helped Reid to his feet. Xavier's grip tightened, and his eyes turned vicious. "Jun needs you right now. She won't say it, but I've known her longer than you and I see it. She is fucking stressed. She has an army of ruthless mages coming to kill her and nothing but a tiny army of terrified mages and half-wit druids depending on her to tell them what to do, all the while she is staying in the castle her family was murdered in."

"She's strong," Reid said. The strongest woman he knew.

"She is acting strong so no one will know how terrified she feels," Xavier countered on the heels of his words.

Reid pulled his hand out of Xavier's and started toward the castle. He'd had a long day, and he didn't want this conversation. Xavier fell into step beside him anyway.

"During our first meeting, she kept looking at you for approval, and you just sat there with a dead look on your face," Xavier said.

Had she? Reid hadn't noticed.

They approached the doors, and Xavier stepped in Reid's way. He hissed, "She needs you, and I'm willing to bet that you need her while you are going through whatever it is you think you're going through." He sighed. "I don't understand why men like you think you have to do everything alone."

Reid inhaled and held it. He'd disliked Xavier from the first moment they had met, but he had never wanted to hit him more.

But…he was right.

Xavier, seemingly aware, smoothed the contempt and frustration from his features. "I am thinking about my sister, and to an extent, you. If you plan on becoming my brother, that is."

With that, Xavier sauntered across the garden and to the kitchen door. Reid stood outside for a few moments longer. The snowfall thickened, as did the silence. The snow blurred the grounds around him, feeling far too similar to the abyss he felt all around him.

He didn't want to listen to the advice of an assassin, but Xavier knew more about energy than Reid. So, with no one looking, he focused.

He focused on that damned magic inside of him. He thought of a blade, he pictured it, he felt it—a blade materialized in his hand. The golden hue reflected in each snowflake and gently hummed against his skin. It was a true extension of himself; he felt it in a way that steel could not be felt. The hilt felt as real as any other, the blade was solid, yet it felt as light as air.

An owl hooted from somewhere above, and Reid's focus shattered. The blade vanished.

Still, he had done something. He returned to the barracks feeling marginally better than he had before.

CHAPTER 27

Juniper returned to the royal wing in better spirits. A wash in cool water helped clear her head. While she washed, someone built a fire in the bedroom hearth. Muted moonlight glowed between the woven shutters. Someone had shined the brassy mirror of the vanity too. She glimpsed her reflection as she passed it—bags hung under her eyes, her skin was pale, and her face seemed thinner. Gaunt, even. What an ugly word.

A knock sounded against the woven door that served as the main chamber door.

Juniper ignored it.

The knock sounded again, this time accompanied by a sweet female voice that said, "Miss Juniper?"

Sighing, she trudged through the chamber and to the door. A young mage in tattered robes stood on the other side, a wooden tray in her hands. Resting on the tray was a porcelain teapot and cup. Steam trailed from the spout.

"I—I brought you tea." The teacup rattled in her grip.

Juniper blinked. In her moment of hesitation, the girl's smile flipped into something like fear. It happened too fast, as if the girl feared a reprimand, or worse.

"Oh, uh, thank you," Juniper said, but the damage was done.

The girl's lips stretched into an awkward smile. "Shall I bring it in?"

Juniper stepped out of the doorway. The girl hurried in and set the tea on the sitting room table. She nervously bowed to Juniper, then scurried back into the corridor. Juniper lingered at the door. Had she missed something? Had she asked for tea and forgotten about it? Had someone else sent it?

She made herself a cup of tea. Her magic didn't detect anything within that shouldn't be there. The druids had planted tea on the first day, and that they already had tea was an astounding feat. In still moments, snippets of druid song floated through the castle drafts. Honey would have been nice, but they would have none without bees, and what hives they'd had were still in Sinjon.

Juniper sipped her tea and paced the bedroom. Her feet took her into the closet. She'd been avoiding the space and her dead parents' clothes—she'd thought about burning them—but that seemed wasteful. She had a limited supply of clothing, as did Reid, and the druids had only what they had brought with them. Her siblings' closets had been raided, though most of the clothing was too small for adults. The material had been repurposed and sewn into new clothing.

Juniper hated the idea of someone else going through her parents' things, and she knew she would have to be the one to do it. Her parents didn't need the clothing, and the druids and mages still living did. She'd been putting it off, secretly hoping someone else would disregard her words and do it anyway.

No one had. Her parents' closet had been left untouched.

Juniper eyed the dresses on her mother's side, and the doublets and trousers on her father's. Shelves underneath held boots and heels and slippers. In a tall chest of drawers on her mother's side, she found silken under garments and corsets and stockings. She pulled out a silken sleeping gown in a deep emerald green. Delicate threading along the sleeves mimicked leaves.

She took the sleeping gown and a pair of woolen socks into the bedroom and changed. The silk slid over her skin, and a strange feeling came over her.

Her mother had once worn this gown. She had stood in this very room. She had died here.

She had died by the vanity, where the stones had been cleaned.

Juniper sat at the vanity. The brass had been cleaned by magic, and the silver polish and floral scents lingered. As did the subtle scents of lavender and honeysuckle. Someone had added the specific runes to the chambers while she hadn't been looking.

A duplicitous sensation of gratitude and shame coursed through her bones. What hadn't been done while the mages saw to her selfish request?

She sipped her tea and imagined her mother sitting in the same spot, painting her face, brushing her hair, and talking to her father while he sat at his desk, reading. Or would he have read in the study?

What would they have talked about?

Her eyes drifted over where her mother's blood had stained the stones.

Such a strange place to die, while her father had died in the sitting room. As if he had gone to meet the intruders while her mother had not.

That didn't sit well with Juniper. The mother she had met in Delphine hadn't seemed like a coward. She hadn't seemed the type of woman to let her husband die for her without even trying to save him. Why had she gone the opposite way he had? Why hide by the vanity?

Unless she hadn't been hiding.

Juniper set her tea down and stood in the place where her mother had died. Where her blood had splattered against the wall.

The *wall.* A prickle ran down Juniper's scalp and into her toes. Her magic felt along the seemingly plain stones between the closet and the sitting room. She felt it, barely there. A rune. A secret.

Juniper pressed her hand against it, and a feverish sense of adventure tingled over her skin.

Nothing happened. The feeling dissipated.

She pressed her hand to another stone, and then another, but the secret door did not open for her.

A yawn hinged her jaw—she would have to think about her mother's secret tomorrow. She brought her tea to her lips. The warmth within surged into her limbs.

She sat on the bedside. The hearth flickered and popped. The flames threw shadows over the walls.

Is this how the castle had felt before the war?

Footsteps sounded in the corridor. She didn't think much about them. People had been skittering all over the castle for days. The footsteps slowed, then paused at her door. She waited for another knock, but none came. Instead, her visitor let themselves into the sitting room.

Cautious, precise steps sounded across the sitting room. Boots. Armor shifted with the wearer.

Relief spread over her. She knew those sounds.

Reid stepped into the bedroom. His molten eyes took in the cleaned space before settling on her. He took in her attire, her face. His expression never changed. He hadn't shaved since they'd left Sinjon, and chestnut hair grew thick on his jaw. It gave him a rugged, wild look.

"Someone brought tea." Juniper gestured to the cup in her hands. "They only brought one cup. You can share mine if you'd like."

Reid stepped closer to her and accepted her offered cup. He took a sip.

"There's more in the pot." She laced her fingers and meandered to the closet. "Let me find you something softer to wear to sleep."

He didn't answer. He walked to the teapot and poured himself another cup.

Juniper sorted through her father's chest of drawers until she found a handsome sleeping shirt and pants. She brought Reid a pair of woolen socks too. She braided her hair at the vanity while he unbuckled and set his armor on the stand, another thing that had appeared without her noticing.

He kept his back to her while he dressed. She had seen Reid bare before, but her eyes strayed to his sculpted back and legs, the muscles of his arms.

He turned, and she averted her gaze into the hearth. "The druids are making this place feel less haunted."

The fire flickered off the angles of his silver armor.

"You picked this room?" he asked.

"I didn't," Juniper said. "Everyone else insisted that I take this room because it was the biggest. Mabyl thinks this is my castle, and I think she's told all the mages the same. Like this tea. I didn't ask for tea. A girl brought it to my door."

Reid sat on the bed.

"It's not the same mattress or linens," Juniper said, though it didn't make much difference. It was still her parents' bed. She set her brush down. She didn't know if it had once been her mother's or not, and she didn't want to think about it. She stood, pulled the screen over the hearth to mute the light, and meandered to the bed.

The barely-there light warmed Reid's face yet shadowed it at the same time. His gaze focused on her with a predator's intent.

"Someone added runes by the windows to keep in the heat," she said, rambling. "And someone brought up a pitcher of clean water."

It sat underneath the old washing basin.

Juniper climbed into bed opposite Reid. Whoever had dressed the bed had added several layers of blankets, and she wondered if everyone else received as many, or if someone had given her special treatment again. Was someone else shivering tonight?

She asked Reid.

"They have enough," he said. He pulled the blankets over his legs. "No one will be cold tonight."

She took his word for it and settled into the pillow. This bed, this room…it was much larger than the tent. It was larger than the room in Sinjon, than her chambers in the Summer Palace, than her chambers in Bradburn Castle. She had slept in worse places, on more uncomfortable beds, in worse company, and in far more danger—yet a shiver wormed through her gut. She feared ghosts appearing in the night. She feared watching apparitions of her dead siblings or her parents. She feared watching them die.

She…couldn't.

Reid shifted and rolled onto his side. The muted firelight glinted in his open eyes.

"Jun?" he whispered.

She swallowed. Reid had watched his parents die. He had witnessed their murders. It would be foolish for her to complain about her own.

"If I close my eyes, I can imagine being back in Bradburn Castle," she said. "Pretending to be a lady whose biggest concern was what she would wear that day, and dealing with a grumpy squire."

"Is that all?"

The question caught her off guard.

"Yes," she lied. "It's been a long day, and we've got another ahead of us. We need our rest."

He didn't argue or call her bluff. Instead, he lifted his arm and motioned for her. She settled into his body. Reid wrapped his arm around her and pulled her closer.

Her anxiety didn't go away, but Reid made her worry about it a little less.

CHAPTER 28

Sleep didn't stay. Juniper woke up countless times as apparitions slipped out of sight. Finally, she gave up and slipped out of bed, quiet as a shadow. The hearth had burned low, and the cooler air of the dark bedroom chilled her skin. Reid slept on his back, arm over his eyes, still as stone. His chest rose and fell. A warm, gentle breath escaped his lips.

Alive, she told herself.

Satisfied, she tiptoed across the room and to the window. The tightly woven vines of the shutters blocked out almost all the moonlight, save a sliver between the panes. She pushed one shutter aside. A thick snowfall blurred the sky in misty darkness and shrouded the royal grounds in white.

She loved the way the snow muted sound. She heard only the crackle of the hearth, and she could imagine being in the middle of nowhere, isolated and hidden and safe.

She could feel it too—every snowflake.

Is this what being an archmage was?

All those moments of endless magic, fathomless power... Was that her archmage magic? She didn't know how long she had been an archmage. According to the wechun, the previous archmage had died during Nexon's siege on Balendin Castle. Juniper would have been halfway to Rusdasin by then. She would have been too small to remember.

Despite how much she wanted to deny it, her being an archmage—and the odd twist of fate of Reid's being one, too—gave the prophecy credence.

She still didn't know what she was supposed to do against Nexon. He had a thousand years of training his magic, of honing his battle strategy and tactics, and she had a few months. Lilianna had a fraction of that, and Reid... She didn't know what to think about Reid.

Despite the runes of warmth carved into the walls, cold air seeped through the shutters. The snow did not come inside. It floated toward the window then floated away, deterred. It continued its free fall to the ground.

Reid sighed and rolled onto his side, facing her. His eyes remained closed. His arm fell back to his side. His fingers spread over the blanket, as if searching for her body beside his. He stilled, his breathing evened, and he remained asleep.

He looked like he belonged in the grand bed. Though the original curtains had been removed, she could imagine thick velvet in plum and cream, tied with golden cords. Reid had always had an air of regal authority. It came from his stoic demeanor and his stern sense of justice. He'd always been a bit…kingly.

Unlike her.

Using her night sight, she pulled one of her mother's cloaks over her shoulders and tiptoed into the corridor. Magelights hovered near the high ceiling, dim for the night. They shaded everything in pale off-white, almost green.

The earth mages had done a marvelous job with the repairs. The corridors she meandered down looked as though no war had happened. The windows wore woven shutters, the drafts had been clogged, and the fallen stones had been set upright. Still, she could feel the snow just beyond the castle walls, churning gently against the many runes protecting the castle. She felt the cold, the night, the darkness. The snow flowed like water against stone, gently and easily. The cold would persist. Over time, the snow would wear down the runes.

Like she would. She would persist. She would defeat Nexon…somehow.

She came to the courtyard attached to the royal chambers. In a blink, she saw the doors as they had been nineteen years ago: dark wood carved with artistic whorls of flowers and stars. Then, the doors vanished. The wooden doors lay open, the hinges broken, the whorls cracked and weathered. Runes had been carved on either side of the door, shielding the interior from the cold and falling snow.

She stepped through the doorway and into the courtyard. The cold engulfed her and tangled with her ice magic. It needled against the warmth in her skin, but it didn't hurt.

The courtyard consisted of a wooden pergola. Years of neglect had sent one of the four supports to the snow-covered winter-dead grass. The others looked one strong wind away from collapsing. The snow gathered on the weathered beams, yet the structure held. Large ceramic pots held the withered remains of unidentifiable flowers.

In a brief flash, she saw the courtyard as it had been: climbing roses with petals of velvet red and deepest violet strung along the pergola's supports and its beams and along a wide trellis. Wooden chairs circled a delicate table, on which sat a steaming teapot and matching cups. Stars twinkled above the summer-lush royal grounds. Pots of jasmine scented the humid air, and thick grass carpeted the courtyard.

And then, as quickly as she saw it, the past vanished. The snow and broken stone returned.

And it pained her heart a little more.

Why did the castle insist on showing her what could have been?

She started into the courtyard. Her first step melted the light snow on the dead grass, as did her second, but each step faded a little more, until the snow did not melt. It showed the indentation of her foot, but the ice remained. She made her way through the courtyard's dead grass, passed where the seating had been, through where the trellis had stood, and onto the balcony.

The snowstorm churned above, the mass of water and ice and cold in the winter's night. She felt the entirety of it, and for a moment, she lost herself in it. An owl hooted, and she returned to the balcony. The storm would continue into the morning, maybe longer. The storm had plenty of water to give. It pulsed with it. It surrounded the castle, surrounded her.

She could move it along if she wanted. She could command the snow to fall faster or not fall at all.

She did neither. She allowed the snow to fall as it wanted, to let nature do as it pleased. It graced her loose hair, her brow, her cloak, her nose and cheeks. It kissed her eyelids. Cold air slithered under her collar, under the silken nightdress. It swirled around her, as if it knew what she was.

She stood in the snow until it had covered her shoulders and her toes, until it had frozen the sleeplessness she'd felt. The snow did not melt. It settled against her.

Another flash—a woman stood beside her. Dark hair cascaded down her back, and a dark velvet cloak hung off her shoulders. Juniper touched the pale gray fur that lined her own cloak, the same that the ghostly woman wore.

"Mom?" Juniper whispered.

"You're not very sneaky, love," said Queen Lenora Balendin. She sounded just like she had in the Spirit Gate, warm and gentle yet powerful.

Juniper's blood ran cold. Her mother couldn't possibly be talking to her. Her mother was dead, murdered. Her heart thumped in a desperate hope that this was some stretch of the spirit world into their own, that her mother had somehow found a way to reach out to her.

Queen Balendin turned, eyes on the doorway. Under her cloak, she wore a dress of silver and blue. Jade hung in her ears.

Juniper's heart fell. Her mother was not looking at her, but at a little girl in the courtyard doorway. She looked no older than five, with round cheeks and dark blue eyes. Auburn hair hung in two braids down her back. Her little chubby hands clenched fistfuls of her long-sleeved nightdress.

Juniper had seen the little girl before, in the portrait of the royal family. Her sister.

"Alma, it's far too late for you to be wandering about," her mother said.

"Isolde was crying again," Alma whined.

"Is she still crying?"

"No."

"What else is bothering you?" Her mother hummed a calming note. "If your sister is no longer crying."

Juniper stood transfixed as her sister ran to the railing to stand beside their mother. The railing came up to her chin. "Father is pacing."

"Ah." Her mother glanced through the open door and into the castle, then turned her attention to the grounds. "He has a lot on his mind."

"Like the man that tried to sneak in yesterday?" Alma asked.

Her mother frowned. "I see gossip has spread. Who told you about that?"

"The guards were talking about it this morning," Alma said innocently. "They said the man was trying to get into the royal wing. They said he was trying to kill Isolde."

Juniper swallowed. Her sister didn't sound very upset about it, only confused. Her mother, however, looked angry.

"Forget about that man, Alma," said her mother. She bent down and took her sister's miniature hands. "Remember what we talked about? That some people are no good and only want to cause you harm?"

Alma nodded. "He was no good?"

"I'm afraid so," said her mother. "Your father is worried about more people like him. You know that little door in the back of your closet? The one that locks?"

"You said not to go in there, because—"

"Unless it is an emergency," her mother interrupted, her tone a gentle correction. "I want you to go there if you feel afraid, okay? If you hear odd sounds at night and you can't get to me or your father. I want you to go there and hide, okay? If you get too scared, follow the passage. It will lead into catacombs. You remember the way to Sina? To Treva's house?"

Alma nodded. "Follow the moons."

"That's my girl," their mother said, cupping Alma's chubby cheek. "Everything will be all right."

Her mother said something else, but the courtyard shifted.

"No," Juniper pleaded, but she again stood alone. She took a deep gulp of the frozen air and gripped the railing. She searched her memory for those names—Sina and Treva. She had never heard of them before. She tried to recall the map of Collatia, but there were hundreds of little towns marked on it.

Of all the ghosts to see, why had it been her mother and sister? Her walk through the castle had done the opposite of calming her down.

CHAPTER 29

Juniper re-entered the castle in a sullen mood. She passed through the rune barrier, and at once, warmth assaulted her, stinging over her frigid skin. She cast the snow from her skin and clothes, leaving her dry, and started back toward the royal suite. With every step, the warmth trapped within the castle sank deeper into her bones.

She kept to the shadows. Halfway to the suite, she realized she didn't have to. There were no guards to sneak past, no druids to question her presence, or mages to attack.

This was...her castle.

She slid between the woven vines of the royal suite and into the bedroom. She undid the clasp of her velvet cloak.

"You look like a ghost," came Reid's husky whisper.

She jumped and turned.

Reid sat on the pelt before the hearth. The hearth had faded into a dusky glow, and it turned his eyes into molten darkness. He stared at her like a predator eyeing a potential threat. That look stopped her dead where she stood.

She fought past the unsettling feeling and continued into the room. As she returned her cloak to the closet, she asked, "Did I wake you?"

"No."

But he had woken up and she hadn't been there. Again.

She meandered to the empty bed. Reid's gaze had returned to the muted fire. "I couldn't sleep. I took a walk."

Reid continued to stare into the hearth, expressionless and distant.

"It's snowing." She took a cautious step toward the hearth.

Reid glanced at the shuttered window, then her. His gaze didn't change. He looked threatened, like a dire wolf pushed into a corner. Juniper chanced a step closer. He didn't move, so she took another, then another. She sat on the pelt and left a safe space between them.

She ran her fingers over the pelt's dark brown fur. It hadn't been there before. It looked to have come from a bear. She would have to thank the druids for it.

"I keep having these dreams," Reid whispered, eyes on the fire. "I keep seeing... I don't know what it means. It..."

"It scares you," she finished.

He didn't openly disagree, but he didn't openly agree either. Guilt darkened his expression.

"That's nothing to feel ashamed of," she said.

"Knights are trained to face any threat," he said bitterly. His hands curled into fists.

"Being a knight doesn't make you immune to fear." She took a gamble and set her hand on top of his closed fist. The warmth of his skin surprised her. She hadn't realized how cold she had become.

His eyes snapped to her hand. A shiver of panic seared underneath her skin and her instincts told her to get back. She steeled herself. This was not some wild beast. This was Reid, her Reid.

"Reid, so much has changed so quickly, if you didn't feel fear, I would be worried," she whispered. "You lost your home, you lost the Order, and *you died.* Just one of those things would terrify anyone. On top of all that, you're an archmage. You have every right to be afraid."

"I'm not…" He pulled the rest of his words back in a sharp inhale.

"You're not what?" She leaned forward to see into his burning eyes. Stubbornness looked back at her. "You're not human? You're above such things? Such foolish feelings are beneath a knight?"

He turned his wild, angry gaze on her.

She wanted to snatch back those words as soon as they left her lips.

"I'm not a lot of things," he said with a growl.

Her hand twitched, and she shrank back at his tone.

Reid closed his eyes and released a slow breath. He rubbed his face with his free hand, scratching at his beard. Shakily, he said, "I'm sorry, I just… I can't keep up with this."

"You're a knight," Juniper argued. "Trained to counter any situation and withstand any disaster with steel or your mind, whichever is called for. You will overcome this. You'll be all right."

His eyes met her again. The agitation faded into exhaustion. "You believe that?"

"Firmly." She adjusted her hand so that her fingers lined up with his. "Because you are you, and you are far too strong and stubborn to let anything get in your way. Who says you can't be a knight and a mage? Just because there hasn't been a mage-knight doesn't mean one can't exist. Once, knights didn't exist. With the Order redesigning itself, you can change the rules."

Reid's lips twitched into a soft smile.

"There he is," Juniper said. "I knew you were under that sulky wild man somewhere."

"Is that what you've been thinking? What are you thinking now?"

She hesitated for dramatic effect as she searched his eyes. "To be honest, I'm thinking about how I haven't gotten to run my hands through your beard yet."

It had crossed her mind more than a few times.

The corner of his lips twitched in a soft smile. "You had several opportunities on the way here. We shared a tent."

"With everyone watching and you being so sulky and moody? Not to mention those tents have thin walls. Everyone would have heard."

He frowned, but it lacked the mania of before. He looked more like his old self, the grumpy squire with a hard-to-get-to playful side.

"And if everyone slept as well as I did on the way here, then you know they were all awake," she said. "Gods only know what Ingrid would have said the next morning."

Reid lifted their laced hands and placed a tender kiss to her knuckles.

And her Reid returned—warmth and steel and strength. A glimmer of that feeling of security returned, the same she had felt in Bradburn Castle when she woke from the poisoned sleep and saw Reid at the bedside. She had known everything would be all right. She had felt safe. She felt safe now, sitting by him, like she had a home and a future.

As Reid lowered her hand from his mouth, she kissed him. He hesitated, then kissed her back. She ran her fingers though the coarse hair on his jaw, mapping his face anew, even as it tickled her chin and lips. The kiss had the tenderness and passion she had missed, that they had lacked.

His hands traced up and down the silk of her nightdress. He pressed his palms against her spine, pulling her closer. She climbed onto his lap and he wrapped his arms around her. She broke this kiss to look him in the eye—the cold, wild man had retreated further. Her Reid looked back at her, molten eyes lighting the familiar sensation of heat, desire, and belonging.

Gods, she had missed him.

She covered his mouth with hers. His magic reached out to hers, tentatively and unsure, as if Reid didn't quite have a grasp on it. Her magic touched his— warm and golden, like a sunrise—strength and renewal.

His hands tightened on her back, taking fistfuls of her nightdress.

"Can you feel that?" Reid whispered. Uncertainty shined in his eyes.

"Depends on what you mean." She grinned wickedly.

His uncertainty twitched into a small smile. "You know what I mean, the magic. Can you feel it?"

"I can," she said.

She kissed his magic with her own. By his sudden intake of breath, he felt it. It felt far more intimate than a kiss on the lips, like her very being touched his. His clenched fists tightened, and his knuckles pressed hard into her skin.

"Do that again," he breathed.

She did, and kissed him while their magic mingled and twined. She ran a hand through his hair. It had grown out enough she could capture locks between her fingers. He kissed her again. And again.

She slid off his lap and pulled him to his feet and toward the bed. They would have at least one more romantic night before the world came crashing down. They fell atop the blankets. Straddling his hips, she kissed him hard, pushing him onto his back. His callused hands roamed her thighs, her hips, her waist, her breasts, pushing the silk higher and higher, until he pulled it over her head. It landed with a *ploosh* on the other side of the bed.

She moved against his hips as his hands wandered. The cool air graced her back and chest, eliciting a chill over her skin. Reid's warm hands hooked on her hips, and his hungry eyes took in every inch of exposed skin. She pushed her hips into his again, and yet his body hadn't responded. His hands tightened on her hips, almost painfully, and she ground her hips into his again. Reid let out an exasperated, frustrated huff. In a deft move, he flipped her onto her back and pressed himself over her.

She tugged his silken shirt up his muscled torso, dragging her nails along his skin. Gooseflesh erupted in her wake. He growled into her neck. She couldn't tell if it came from desire or frustration.

She told herself it came from desire. She nipped at his ear, tugged at his hair, and thrust her hips up into his.

And yet, Reid's desire hadn't manifested.

"Damn it," Reid spat. He rolled off of her and threw his legs over the bedside. He sat with his back to her, and heaved a shuddering breath. He tore his hands through his hair.

"Reid?"

"I'm sorry," he said, standing. He grabbed his shirt and pulled it over his head. "I just...can't right now. I need some air."

He stuffed his feet into his boots and left.

Juniper sat up, alone and naked where he'd tossed her aside. A chill raked over her skin that had nothing to do with the cold. She pulled the blankets over her bare shoulders. Never had she felt so exposed, as if he had flayed her open. Never had rejection felt as bitter and cold.

CHAPTER 30

Reid stood in a breezeway lined with stone arches. Like everything else in Balendin Castle, the breezeway had been left to the elements. Must and murk had whittled away the stone accents, leaving it weathered and barren. The breezeway overlooked the vast and snowy royal grounds. The snowfall blanketed everything in sight and turned the world into a silvery haze. He couldn't see the jeweled lake, but he imagined the royals of old had planned it that way. The mystical lake remained a secret among the dense, misty wood.

He leaned against the stone, letting the frigid air suck the feeling from his face and hands. Gods... He'd never had trouble with intimacy. Especially with Juniper. Even in the first days he had known her, her voice had warmed his blood and her touch had set his skin on fire.

He was too unfocused. Xavier was right—Reid needed Juniper. When he held her, the overwhelming sensation of being crushed faded. It was manageable. When she told him he would be all right, he believed her. He wanted her, but his body couldn't focus. The pressure of the world overwhelmed him.

He felt someone approaching before he heard footsteps before he saw the shadow. He knew the swagger, the slithering presence.

Xavier leaned against the railing beside him.

"I'm assuming you're sulking out here because you can't sleep," Xavier drawled. He shifted his blue-gray eyes to Reid. "There's no other reason to be out here when it's this fucking cold."

Reid didn't have an answer for the assassin.

"Nightmares?" Xavier's nonchalant tone gritted against Reid's foul mood. "Your shifty expression suggests guilt." He leaned forward to see Reid's face better. Reid turned away, but Xavier added, "Shame?"

Reid sighed through his nose. "It's nothing that concerns you."

"If it concerns Jun, it concerns me." Xavier turned his back to the grounds, leaning against the stone. He crossed his arms lazily. "Unless it's bedroom things."

Reid's face flushed, and as Xavier's brows rose, he realized that Xavier hadn't meant it seriously. But it was too late to take it back.

"Is that so?" Xavier asked, surprise genuine. It turned into curiosity. "May I ask what happened?"

Reid sighed through his nose.

"Hmmm…" Xavier tapped his fingers against his arm. "Let me guess—you can't focus with everything bombarding you? Trouble pitching the tent?"

Reid blinked. Xavier didn't speak in taunts or pity. He spoke with understanding.

"I've had those moments," Xavier said with a sigh. "Not so many in the past few years, but early on, though, I did. I learned to focus my magic."

"I've been trying," Reid said.

"And you are more coherent," Xavier said, studying Reid's face. "You aren't staring murderously into the distance. You are speaking in full sentences and with more than three words. Do you need another lesson?"

"No," Reid said at once. Though, as the word left his lips, he regretted it.

Xavier continued to wait for his answer, as if he knew.

"Perhaps," Reid whispered.

Xavier grinned. "Look at you, the big strong pigheaded knight lowering himself to train with the likes of a lowly assassin. You're learning humility. It's admirable."

Reid huffed.

Xavier's grin stretched. He started down the corridor. "All right, my ward, follow me. We'll need somewhere with space."

Xavier led Reid into a dark corridor and then summoned a magelight of charcoal light. They wandered down a stairwell and finally into a large empty room without vines for shutters and runes for warmth. Xavier added runes on each wall, and Reid felt an immediate change.

"First, I propose a trade," Xavier said haughtily.

Reid held his ground, neither agreeing nor disagreeing.

"I want to learn how to make a ward."

"Why?"

Xavier frowned. "What do you mean why? It's a shield that deflects magic. Why wouldn't I want to learn how? So, deal? You teach me how to cast a ward, and I'll teach you to be an energy mage. Sounds far too fair if you ask me."

Reid readied himself. He didn't see any other option. "All right. I accept those terms."

"Right, ward first. Show me that hand thing you do." Xavier drew his fingers toward his chest and pushed them outward in a pitiful mimicry of the proper technique.

"It took me years to summon a ward," Reid said. He drew his hand toward his chest, gathering his strength into a palpable shield. He took a deep breath, then pushed outward, extending his fingers and expelling the shield outward.

Summoning the ward came far easier than it ever had, and the shimmering shield now glowed golden.

Xavier's gawked, lips parted and eyes wide. "Correct me if I'm wrong, but has it always looked like that?"

Reid stared at the ward in disbelief. No, it had not. Every ward he had ever seen, including his own, had been clear and shimmery, a distortion in the air. Of course, only knights had ever created a ward. Not only had the color changed, but his ward was thicker and lighter, connected to him in the same way the blades had been. An extension of himself.

"Look at that," Xavier said, tilting his head. "Not only is your ward bigger, but it's a different color. The same color as your energy. Clearly, it's charged with your magic. All right, show me how."

Xavier tried to mimic the hand movements, but no ward appeared. Reid tried his best to explain how he summoned a ward, the techniques behind it, the strategy—Xavier was as impatient to learn as Reid was patient to teach.

Finally, after several curses, glares, and threats, Xavier summoned a charcoal ward half the size of Reid's.

"Why is yours bigger?" Xavier scowled.

"Practice," Reid said. "I've been honing my skills for years. You've had an hour at most."

"Can you teach those druids how to cast a ward?"

Reid hesitated to answer.

"Think about it," Xavier said, grinning. "We're about to face an army of mages who know an ungodly amount of black magic and have no qualms about slaughtering us all. We need every advantage we can get, and if we can teach our little army how to withstand magic, we'll have slightly more of a chance not to die."

"Juniper suggested the same," Reid said.

"Because she sees the practicality in knowing how to fight magic with anti-magic." Xavier cast another ward. It wobbled, but held.

"Keep your fingers evenly spaced," Reid said, motioning to Xavier's trembling fingers. "Like you're holding a real shield against your hand."

The ward evened and straightened.

Reid was breaking countless laws of the Order by showing him the technique, but he reminded himself that the Order had fallen. If the Order ever returned, it would be a different organization. Better.

He didn't know how he felt about it.

Archmage in the Ruins

Reid returned to the royal suite exhausted like he hadn't been in years. It reminded him of those days before he met Juniper, when he spent every spare moment practicing the sword or learning the knights' anti-magic techniques. He had pulled himself into the barracks every night thoroughly exhausted—mentally and physically.

This time, his exhaustion was heavier, deeper. His entire being felt wrung out. Even that strange new place with him, where his magic resided, was quiet. It frightened him. He had never felt such exhaustion before.

Is this what it felt like to hold magic? He remembered how deeply Juniper had slept after expending her magic. He needed that deep, rejuvenating slumber.

Juniper was asleep. Her green nightdress remained on the floor where he'd thrown it. In sleep, worry vanished from her features. Reid picked up her nightdress and laid it over the vanity chair. He undid his boots, removed his shirt, and crawled into bed beside her. Her eyes fluttered open, and as he settled into the bed, she curled into his side, cool against his warmth. He folded his arm around her and held her close.

The overwhelming awareness remained. He felt everything—the flicker of the dying fire, the snow against the shutters, the waning rune—but it was manageable. Constant but gentle, like a river current. When he held Juniper close, he felt her magic. Everything calmed as her magic came between him and the world, a comforting cool breeze, clear and blue, the color of the sky on a frozen winter morning.

CHAPTER 31

Adrian made his way into the mage's sector. He had gone to see Henry at the knight's hall first, but a pledge told him that Henry had gone to help train mages. Adrian wanted to talk to Henry about magic exposure, not dive headfirst into training with a mage he didn't know. He definitely didn't want to admit this failure at mental resistance to everyone.

The mage district smelled of magic, like overpowering floral perfume, only sweeter and less stringent. It reminded him of the rooftop courtyards of his castle, of the flowers and bushes and fruit trees during spring and summer. It wasn't exactly the same, but it was the closest thing he had.

With the help of a kind young mage who blushed when Adrian asked her for directions, he made his way to the training arena. The earth mages had carved the space from stone, large enough for mages to practice safely.

Inside, the floral stench overpowered his senses. The underlying metallic twinge, like silver polish and wet iron, stole his breath and brought water to his eyes. He stumbled over his own feet, and Jax took hold of his elbow to keep him from falling and making a fool of himself. He lingered by the entrance and let the nausea pass and his senses adjust.

Luckily, no one in the room paid any attention to him. They were far too busy cradling flames in their hands and swirling water above their heads or shaping stone into different shapes. Adrian spotted Henry standing beside Abrielle, one of the mages they had rescued from the Marca. She instructed a group of young water mages while behind pledges standing behind Henry observed. Henry noticed Adrian first and waved him over. Adrian paused a safe distance behind them.

"Be mindful of wards," Abrielle said. "The thralls know how to cast one, and a ward has the capability of rebounding onto the mages."

Abrielle motioned to Henry. He summoned a ward—the air in front of him shimmered and distorted outward from his palm, and as his arm and fingers extended, the ward widened into a shield. Abrielle gathered a fistful of raw magic—a pale blue—and cast it at Henry's ward. The magic hit the ward and fizzled into nothingness. The ward shimmered as it absorbed the magic—it glowed a faint blue where Abrielle's magic struck it, then faded back to its clear color.

Abrielle staggered. "It feels a bit like being stunned when your magic hits a ward, but it's not too bad. You will need to know how it feels and how to shake it off quickly. Who wants to go first?"

None of the students seemed overly eager, but they formed a line.

"All right, Lex," Henry said to the first pledge. "Just as we practiced. Control your fears. It will show in the ward."

Lex took the first step forward. The other pledges lined up behind him, looking as terrified as the mages. Lex adjusted his stance, took a deep breath, and erased the emotion from his face. He pulled his right hand to his chest, tucked his fingers toward his palm, and then slowly opened his hand. As his fingers opened, a shimmering ward appeared in front of him.

The first mage summoned a ball of rose-colored magic and threw it at the ward. It struck. Lex's stoic mask flickered upon impact, as did the ward.

"Focus," Henry advised.

Lex blew out a breath, and the ward strengthened. It turned rosy where the magic had struck, then returned to its original clarity. The mage staggered backward as if struck. Abrielle put her hand on her shoulder. The mage retreated to the back of the line.

"Nicely done," Henry said, patting the pledge on the shoulder. "You're progressing well."

Lex beamed. The next pledge and the next mage stepped forward—magic against ward. Abrielle offered advice to her mages, and Henry did the same to the pledges.

"Exciting to watch, isn't it?"

Adrian jumped. Amery stood beside him, dark hair pulled away from her face in a series of braids. She flashed her white teeth at him, a sly grin of a girl who knew she'd surprised him.

"You should wear a bell," Adrian said, schooling his face.

"Just a bell?" Amery winked.

Adrian chuckled and put a hand over his heart. "Apologies. I am a taken man."

"Shame," Amery said, though her grin stretched.

"Rumor has it that you are too," Adrian said.

She made a sound between a laugh and a scoff, though she did not deny it.

A burst of vibrant orange magic crashed into a ward, and the blond pledge let out a squeal of surprise. The ward dissolved and the pledge fell backward. Two others quickly caught him.

"Try again," Henry said.

"Does it bother you that mages are learning to fight?" she asked.

"Not at all," Adrian said.

Amery arched a brow.

"Magic is dangerous, but it is also useful. It is better to have a knowledgeable mage than an ignorant mage. Magic exists regardless of how skillful a mage is, so might as well be skillful."

She hummed a pleasant note. "I like that point of view."

The training continued until each mage had attacked a ward twice, then Abrielle dismissed them. Henry likewise dismissed the pledges. They filed out of the house, gawking at Adrian.

"Adrian," Henry said in greeting. He frowned at Amery. "I said no."

Amery set her hands on her hips. "What, I don't get a friendly hello?"

"Not when I know you're here to complain."

Amery pouted. "I come with a better offer."

"I'm not accepting *offers*." Henry crossed his arms. "It's not up for debate."

Adrian looked between the two. "What have I missed?"

Henry let out a grievous sigh. "Maddox wants explosive runes for his people to take into the siege. I've said no. Twice."

Amery frowned. "He's used to getting what he wants."

"He's not dealt with the Order before," Henry said. "We're not common street thugs to be bargained with."

Amery pretended to be insulted, but Adrian saw the playful spark in her eye. "Are you referring to me as a common street thug?"

Henry didn't balk. "To an extent. You are acting as Maddox's thug."

Amery sighed then started to speak—

"No."

"Adrian," Amery whined. "Help me make this fool see reason."

"Or be the voice of reason," Henry said.

A pause—Adrian realized they were waiting for his input. "Remind me," Adrian delayed, "what is an explosive rune?"

"A stone engraved with a rune that explodes when activated," Abrielle explained. "One of the runes forbidden by the Order."

"Luckily, the Undercity mages knew about it," Henry deadpanned.

"A controlled, small explosion," Amery added. "It could be a distraction or a weapon. Given the upcoming siege, they would be dead useful, especially considering us non-magic folk who will be going against mages."

"It's too dangerous," said Henry. "They're hard to craft, and one wrong stroke and our mages will explode themselves. This is why the Order monitored runesmithing. They're also dangerous to use."

"I think it's brilliant." Amery grinned. "It would be more power for our little army."

Henry looked at Adrian with desperation.

Adrian hesitated. "It's times like these I wish I knew more about magic."

Amery let out an annoyed groan. "Of course you'll agree with the Order. Because magic is only an evil, horrible thing."

"That's not what I—" Adrian tried to speak.

"I'd *love* to be a mage," Amery said, her playful tone turning spiteful. "I'd love to whisk my hand through the air and set fire and—" Amery whisked her hand through the air, and a burst of yellow sparks surged from the motion. The sparks arcs and fizzled within the span of a heartbeat.

A steep silence sank into the room. Henry gawked at Amery, who stared at her own hand as if she had never seen it before.

A strong twinge of silver polish filled the air—the stench of unnatural magic.

"I thought you weren't a mage," Abrielle asked, her voice several pitches higher.

"I'm not," Amery said, still shocked. A long moment passed, then a furrow appeared between her brows. She glared at Henry. "But you're not mage either. What is a ward if not magic?"

"I'm a knight," said Henry, his expression stony.

"A knight is not a mage."

Henry started to say something else but stopped himself.

Amery sauntered a step closer. Her shock diminished with every passing heartbeat, and a vicious fascination took its place. "*Is* a knight a mage?"

Henry didn't speak, but he wore the answer all over his face.

No, they weren't.

"Hmm…" Amery wiggled her fingers through the air. Nothing more happened. "I've never been a mage or able to use magic, however I've never been in magic this thick before. Now suddenly I can use magic? And a knight can summon a ward, which is basically magic, which means it doesn't matter."

"I don't understand," Adrian said. "If you're not a mage, how can you use magic?"

Henry looked as if he had eaten something very dry. His dark skin had paled. He inhaled, stoic mask intact, and then he sighed and succumbed to exasperation. He looked more like the goofy kid Adrian had grown up with than the stoic knight.

"I guess it doesn't matter anymore. The Order's gone to shit anyway," Henry mumbled. He rubbed his face.

"Am I right?" Amery squealed.

Adrian felt the truth bubble up his throat and prickle his skin—fear and excitement for what it meant, and anger that the Order had kept something else secret.

Amery let out a lady's laugh. "If I can use unnatural magic…"

"Anyone can," Henry finished. Betrayal weighed on his shoulders. He deflated, his shoulders slumped and his posture abandoned.

"Anyone can use unnatural magic," Adrian repeated.

"How and why, we don't know," Henry said. "The Order was very secretive when it came to the specifics and workings of magic. Little is known about non-mages using unnatural magic. Those who have been caught…tend to vanish." He heaved a sigh. "So, now you know just as much about it as I do."

"The knights have been taught magic?" Adrian asked.

Henry shrugged. "Yes. The wards, detection, disruption… It's all magic, just a different kind. It's unnatural magic."

Adrian felt something in his chest tighten and uncurl at the same time. It did not dwell well with his anxiety.

Amery's grin turned vicious and a bit mad. "Anyone! Why does everyone look so glum? Don't you fools know what this means?"

No one answered. Henry looked as though he had done something very wrong. Adrian felt like he had eaten stones and his stomach was about to vomit them back up.

"Our rebels can use magic," Amery whispered.

"It's not that simple," Henry said. "It takes a knight years of intense study to safely manipulate unnatural magic."

Adrian felt lightheaded. Jax stepped closer as if he suspected, and in turn made Adrian feel worse.

"Enough talk," Amery said, her grin growing madder with every passing heartbeat. "Show me how to set shit on fire."

CHAPTER 32

Cera marched down the corridor toward Lora's cell for her turn at guard duty. As she came around the corner, the beast's ears twitched up, followed by its wolf-like head. Beady black eyes watched her approach, as if trying to decide if and when to rip her apart. It sniffed in her direction, then returned its head to where it had been on the floor. Tanner, the air mage currently on guard duty, looked exhausted and annoyed.

Before defecting, Cera had never met Tanner. She'd never been good at making or keeping friends, yet defecting from Nexon had somehow solidified her place among the outcasts. Her odd friendship with Ison somehow gained her a foothold with all the other mages, who looked up at him with a starry-eyed awe.

"I'm your relief," Cera said without enthusiasm.

Tanner flashed her a grateful smile. "Thank the gods. This woman makes me want to stick daggers in my ears." He started away. "See you later."

Cera did not take the guard's position beside the cell bars. She leaned against the wall opposite the bars, crossed her arms, and stared into Lora's cell. She looked awful. Her hair was matted and greasy, her face unwashed, and the cell reeked of urine. Despite that, Lora retained that vicious glint in her eyes.

"Ah, the new guard," Lora taunted. "Another turncoat."

Cera had made peace with that. When Ison had declared his betrayal of Nexon, Cera was sure that he would be dead, but then the beasts joined his call and turned on Lora's forces. A beast had turned its vicious gaze on Cera, and an instinctual fear that it would rip her apart flashed through her bones—it hesitated. Waiting for her decision. Cera didn't want to get eaten and left on a forsaken field, but she turned on Nexon too.

She'd rather be a traitor than dead.

"You were always the haughty one," Lora said. Her eyes reflected her soured outside. "Is this considered a demotion?"

"From scout to guard?" Cera deadpanned. "It's more of a lateral career move."

Lora was baiting her, but she would rather play a game than stand in silence for three hours until the next guard arrived. Cera had little to lose by talking. She knew nothing of Ison's plan or Juniper's plan. She hadn't even seen Juniper save for a few glimpses during meals.

Cera shrugged. "The food's better here."

It wasn't untrue. The druids knew how to season wild meat. The venison stew they'd had the other night had been among the most delicious meals she'd ever tasted. Not to mention that berry wine. It wasn't really wine, not the get-drunk kind, but Cera wouldn't turn it down.

The beast snorted at Lora, then curled up like a wolf, its leathery haunches folded inward.

"You should be honored," Lora said. "Ison trusts you enough to watch me."

"Or because no one else wanted this job," Cera said. "We decided shifts by dice. I rolled a three, so I got the third shift."

The beast eventually began to snore. Cera's attention wavered. Lora stopped talking for the most part, though she tried several times to bait Cera into getting mad. Cera ignored her and focused instead on digging the dirt out from under her nails. This was going to be a long shift.

Cera should be honored, she supposed, that Ison had asked her to be among the mages to guard Lora. It meant he trusted her more than others. Still, she'd rather be scouting, even if it was so cold she couldn't feel her face. The Dead City was a treasure trove of abandoned houses and banks and hotels. Already, scouting teams had brought back supplies and treasures. The city had endless adventure, whereas guarding Lora had endless boredom.

Cera was in her own mind, thinking about treasure hunting, and she assumed the hissing came from the sleeping beast.

Snap—Cera looked up in time to see the rune on Lora's throat disintegrate into ash. Lora's face gleamed with madness. The air sizzled and charged like the moment before lightning struck. Primal, visceral fear coursed underneath Cera's skin, flashing freezing cold and scorching hot. She sent a burst of magic into the magelight just as Lora's energy exploded.

CHAPTER 33

Juniper returned to the bedroom after a quick wash to find Reid standing by the window, flexing golden energy in his palm. He focused on the magic, on forming solid spheres and short swords. He stretched his arm out, and his energy grew into a sword not unlike his Mage's Bane. He held it for several moments before it flickered and shattered.

He noticed her stare.

"You're getting it," Juniper said. A spike of hope seared through her chest.

"I…" Guilt drifted over his face. "Xavier is trying to help."

"It looks like he's done a good job so far." She sauntered further into the room. "Although, I'm not sure if he's a good teacher or not. I'd certainly not sign up for any of his classes. He's not—what's the word?—nurturing."

Reid nodded, though he didn't say anything. He brought a sphere of energy to life in his palm and struggled to keep the surface solid. The floral perfume of magic hung heavy in the air as the sphere undulated in his control. He shifted his stance, and sunlight struck the sphere. It gleamed like liquid gold.

"It helps," he said, his voice strained with concentration. "I taught Xavier how to summon a ward."

"Oh?"

"He told me I should be teaching the druids and the mages the same."

"It's not a bad idea," Juniper said. "Fighting magic with anti-magic."

"That's what he said." Reid's golden sphere grew, it rose into the air, then returned to his palm. "I will try. Today."

"Should I schedule time to come watch?" Juniper meandered into the closet and ran her fingertips along her mother's dresses. Someone had snatched her dirty clothes from the bathing room, and she had no choice but to go naked or wear one. She pulled a gown of plum and rose and had just tied the front laces when a furious and panicked knocking sounded at the chamber door.

Reid got there first, and Juniper rushed into the sitting room just as Finn half-fell through the door, panting.

Sweat glistened on his brow despite the chill in the air. Behind him, the magelights in the corridor glowed a dangerous amber.

Dread and panic thumped together, one pulling her up and the other yanking her down.

"What's happened?" Juniper asked.

"Lora," Finn said between gasps. "She's escaped."

160

Juniper stood in front of what had been Lora's cell. Blood and black ash spattered the corridor. A lot of it. The stone bars had been blasted to pieces.

Reid stepped into the cell. "She blasted her way out. She used a considerable amount of magic in a short time."

"Cera's been taken to the infirmary." Ison frowned. "She was on guard when Lora escaped. The earth mages and the healers are working to remove pieces of stone without doing more harm. The odds aren't very good."

"She has better odds with our healers than with anyone else," Lilianna countered. Ison didn't offer an argument.

"According to Kell, he was going to repaint the silencing rune after breakfast," Xavier said distastefully. "It should have been done last night."

"It's too late to throw blame," Juniper said.

"It's never too late to throw blame," Xavier added darkly. "And I choose Kell."

"We have to find Lora," Ison said. "She'll tell Nexon everything the first chance she gets."

Juniper was looking at the bloodied bits of black ash. The beast had taken the brunt of the blow, sparing Cera's life and giving up its own. When Ison had told her about it, she hadn't at first believed the beasts were capable of such selfless acts. Had it not, Cera would be dead. Blown to bits like the bars.

It took a moment to realize the others were waiting for her. She blinked. They were all watching her, waiting.

"What?" Juniper asked. "I agree, we should find Lora."

"Give the order," Xavier whispered, though everyone heard. "*Your Highness.*"

She scowled at him. "I'm not going to *order* anything. Any one of you can go tell the warriors what's happened here."

Xavier started to protest, but Reid stepped up and commanded, "We seal the castle exits. Prevent her from escaping. Shadows and beasts will tighten their patrol of the perimeter."

Ison and Lilianna took the order and left, to inform their separate packs of scouts. Xavier trotted off after them.

Juniper sighed and started toward the vestibule. The news of Lora's escape preceded her. Jarek had taken control over the druids, commanding scouts and warriors to various points of the castle. Lilianna sent out her Shadows alongside them. Ison had gone to the beasts.

The next several hours passed in a hectic blur. Beasts and Shadows scoured the corridors and chambers, hunting their lost prisoner. Others hunted through the forest and city ruins just in case she had managed to slip through. The druid warriors and mages took up guard posts in the populated wings of the castle.

As the sun began to set and the smell of dinner wafted through the mess hall, Lora had yet to be found.

Juniper and the others took their dinner in a meeting room. Finn had created a little stone model of the castle, and as Ison and Lilianna reported where their respective creatures had searched, Finn removed that part of the castle.

"There are too many hiding places," Ison said, exhausted, looking at the remaining castle.

"And many are uninhabitable," Lilianna added.

"She might be counting on us thinking that," Xavier added. "It would be too much to hope she gets bitten by a poisonous spider and dies, isn't it? Or eaten by goblins?"

Juniper sat back and let the meeting happen. The stew sat warm on her stomach, and she wanted a long bath and a longer nap. Doubtful that she would get either.

"There is uncertainty among the warriors," Reid added.

His voice brought Juniper out of her stupor. Reid had remained silent in so many other meetings, and to hear his voice warmed her, though differently. Xavier met her eye, and his lips twitched upward.

"I think it is a good idea to keep you under guard until we find Lora," Ison said to Juniper.

Juniper barked a laugh. No one else did.

"I told you she wouldn't like it," Mabyl said. She turned to Juniper. "I said it was a stupid idea."

"Thank you," Juniper said. "At least someone doesn't think I'm incapable of taking care of myself."

"This isn't about taking care of yourself," Ison argued. "Lora's goal was to kill you. That's what Nexon wants. She's been disgraced by losing that battle, and he won't be happy. She'll see it as a way to gain his favor."

"By giving him your head," Xavier said.

Juniper huffed. "Lora doesn't have a chance against me."

"In a straight out fight, no she doesn't," Ison said. "And she knows that."

"She'll try to get to you any way she can," Xavier added. "And since she can't do it where you can see her, she'll sneak up on you. She'll wait until your back is turned and your guard is down, when you don't expect it."

"I'll just have to be on my toes," Juniper said. "That doesn't mean I need a guard."

"What about when you're asleep?" Xavier said, brows high. "Or when you bathe? Or when you take that spare moment to breathe so you won't lose your mind?"

She scowled at him. As an assassin, Xavier knew all the tricks to kill someone without anyone ever knowing.

"I agree," Reid said, his voice slicing through the argument.

"Reid," she said, meant to dismiss his input.

He met her gaze. "Xavier is right. There are moments when you aren't watching your back. You can't be alert constantly. It will be too much."

She held his gaze, and knew he wouldn't back down. And…she had lost the argument. Sighing, she slumped and said, "Fine."

"We'll assign guards," Ison started.

"I volunteer," Mabyl said.

"As do I," Xavier said, though he sounded like he had a thousand other things he'd rather be doing. Juniper knew her brother too well to think so; if he didn't want to help, he wouldn't have volunteered.

"We start immediately," Ison said. "I'll assign a beast to stand guard outside your chamber."

"I will keep Shadows close by," Lilianna said.

And Juniper had been outvoted. She finished the dregs of her stew while the others divided the day into shifts. She'd rather hunt down Lora herself than wait for her to come to her.

CHAPTER 34

Uncertainty hung heavy as night settled over Balendin Castle. Mabyl took the first shift as Juniper's babysitter, and the two girls ended up helping the mages clean a few of the chambers. It had been Mabyl's idea, and not until she and Xavier had switched for the night did Juniper wonder if Mabyl had planned it—Juniper had been surrounded by other mages all evening.

"Ah, ready for a riveting night?" Xavier asked as he strolled into the bedroom. He plopped down in the vanity chair.

"Of me sleeping and you staring at me?"

Xavier shrugged. "Feel free to pretend like I'm not even here."

"Are you expecting Reid and I to give some grand show of affection?"

He shrugged. "Wouldn't be the first time."

She frowned.

"Not you, specifically," Xavier clarified. "People are notoriously easy to sneak up on after a round or two of passion."

Juniper gawked, though she didn't put it past him. One didn't become the best assassin in the Undercity without skill.

"I let them finish," Xavier reasoned, as if it changed everything.

She half laughed. "Don't get your hopes up. I don't think I could do that with you watching."

"I could turn around."

"Wouldn't that defeat the purpose of babysitting me?"

"I'm guarding," he said. "Not babysitting. If I were babysitting, I'd have locked you in one of the empty chambers."

She had a retort on her tongue when the chamber door opened. Reid marched into the bedroom. He didn't look at all upset or surprised to see Xavier lounging in their room.

"The beasts still haven't found her," Reid reported. "And there are Shadows watching every part of the corridor and the roof."

"I feel remarkably safe," Juniper deadpanned. She did feel safe, however she also felt smothered. She changed into her nightdress in the closet where Xavier couldn't see her, then crawled into bed. Reid went into the closet to change.

Juniper glanced at Xavier. "How did you convince Maddox to let you come all this way?"

Xavier gave her a no-nonsense stare, his eyes cold as any assassin's. "I told him I was going to Baxion, and that I was willing to climb over his corpse to do so. He didn't argue. Even wished me luck. He told me to write, but I haven't found the time. Not to mention a courier."

Juniper's brows rose. Few in the keep had the gull to threaten Maddox, and that Xavier was still breathing suggested Maddox took the threat seriously. Of course, with Xavier being a mage, he could have killed Maddox easily.

"I heard a curious thing today," Xavier said as Reid exited the closet in his sleeping clothes. He climbed into the bed beside Juniper. "The druids say the solstice is approaching."

"As it does every year," she said.

"But this year it's also your birthday."

She groaned. "It's not…"

"But it is," Xavier said, leaning back in the chair and throwing his leg over the side. "Princess Isolde was born on the solstice. On Bera's night."

She frowned. "Yes, I'm aware."

Xavier's eyes glittered. "Are you planning anything? It's not every day a girl turns nineteen. And I missed your last birthday."

"If we survive Nexon, we'll throw a ball," Juniper said, though she meant it entirely sarcastically.

Xavier huffed a laugh. "I'll take that. Now, go to sleep. I can't guard you with you distracting me."

Juniper silenced the magelight, leaving only the hearth's soft glow. She tried to sleep. She couldn't feel Xavier's presence, but she knew he was there. Anyone else would have been making noises, swishing clothes or breathing or twitching. Xavier could have been a ghost for all the sound he didn't make.

And it bothered her.

It always had, even though she admired it.

Lora did not appear in the night to end her. Juniper woke to Xavier standing by the window and Reid sleeping soundly at her side, arm slung over her middle. When she stirred, he stirred. His arm tightened, his breath blew against her neck, and his eyes fluttered open. She wanted to stay there, in his warmth and company, and pretend nothing at all was wrong.

Reid, however, had other thoughts. He kissed her temple and climbed out of bed.

Sighing, Juniper peeled herself out of bed and washed in lukewarm water. She could have heated it, but she knew others would be washing in cold water. By the time she returned to the bedroom, Reid had gone.

"He's got a day of training planned for the druids," Xavier said. "He's going to be teaching them how to fight magic."

Juniper chose a dress of sunshine yellow and maroon. Not her best colors, but it had a short front-tie corset rather than the odious long ones. Xavier followed her into the corridor, a silent shadow.

The castle smelled much better than it had on that first day. Magic scented the air in florals and sweet metallics, and the scented runes flavored every corridor a little differently. Bowls of jasmine water and dried rosemary added an earthy scent. Magelights spotted the ceiling in shades of green, blue, and orange. Woven vines shuttered windows and curtained doorways. The corridors looked as if they had never been sundered.

It looked…homey. As if the druids had always lived here.

Juniper made it to the dining hall, where hearty scents of breakfast wafted through the adjoining corridors. As she entered, a hush fell over a group of druid women. Juniper met the golden eyes of one druid, and she knew they had been talking about *her*.

The druid bowed her head to Juniper and said quickly, "Good morning."

"Morning," Juniper said dryly. She continued to one of the stew pots for her portion of whatever porridge-like concoction the druids had made.

Xavier fell in step beside her.

"Strange," Juniper whispered.

"What? Saying good morning? Just because you're not a morning person doesn't mean others aren't."

She frowned at him.

Standing in line for porridge, Juniper felt the air shift. Eyes all over the dining hall were looking in her direction, and whispers seethed like the winter's wind. She did her best to ignore it. The server ladled a larger serving into Juniper's chipped bowl than the others, and she almost said something, but the line moved along too quickly. She took a cup of tea and sat. Xavier said beside her with his own porridge.

The stares and whispers continued while she ate. She felt the odd attentiveness of the room as a prickle on her scalp. Keeping her eyes on her bowl, she forced the grainy porridge down. The strange air had diminished her appetite.

A flash of blonde plopped down on her other side.

"So, we've been talking," Mabyl said casually. She took a loud sip of tea.

"About me?" Juniper asked dryly.

Mabyl chuckled. "Everyone's been talking about you. Tonight is the solstice, you know."

Juniper bit down hard on her spoon. *Tonight?* No, no, it couldn't possibly have come so soon. Could it? They had been here that long? Her heart sped up.

"And it just happens to be your birthday," Mabyl said in that tone that always meant more to follow. "And we've been talking about throwing a party."

"No."

Mabyl grinned. "For you, but also for the victory. A solstice celebration."

Juniper sighed, blowing the steam off her porridge.

"The druids are already planning a cake for you, and more berry wine," Mabyl said.

"We don't have time for a party," Juniper said. "What if Nexon shows up while we're busy dancing? Or hungover tomorrow? We need to be on our toes."

And she didn't want to celebrate Isolde's birthday. The birthday she had celebrated since she could remember was more than a month away. And…it solidified her place in this mess, that she wasn't really Juniper but Isolde.

And it opened a pit in her stomach.

Despite Juniper's protests, her friends, the druids, and the mages started planning the solstice celebration. The druids had traditions of their own, and Juniper was glad to see them. She didn't like the idea of the celebration being solely about Isolde. She hated it, actually.

Xavier and Mabyl switched guard duty, and Juniper spent the morning outside near the barracks, watching Reid teach anti-magic to druids and mages. By midday, a handful of them could summon wards, though none were stable.

"Have mages throw some magic at those wards," Mabyl suggested to Reid as they filed into the castle for the midday meal. "I bet they'd learned a hell of a lot faster."

The druids looked terrified of the idea, though Reid considered it.

Juniper sat at the farthest table during the midday meal. Everyone kept staring at her like she was some spectacle.

She wanted to spend the afternoon with her wechun, but she didn't want to take Mabyl there. She didn't want to reveal it or explain it. So she wandered the castle—she visited Ison in his potion room, and helped the mages clean out the upper chambers in the east wing and the library. She didn't see any ghosts, and without the ash and bones, the library looked far better. The shelves had been cleared of ruined books, and she imagined the space filled with new tomes.

Her eyes hooked on the desk, on the secret passage.

As the winter sun set and the first stars glittered, dinner wafted through the lower parts of the castle.

With Xavier as her guard, they headed to the dining hall. They had been busy since midday. Garlands of thick green and red flowers hung between the pillars, bowls of cinnamon water and cloves flavored the air, and magelights in an assortment of colors hovered near the ceiling. Eyes turned to Juniper as she entered, as she made her way to the nearest stewpot. Whispers surged and conversations turned hush. A titter started, excited and childlike.

The druids poured a little more in her bowl than Xavier's. A few of the mages even bowed as she passed.

She plopped down at the table, mood soured.

Xavier sat on her other side. "It seems they're finally taking notice of you." She scowled.

"What?" He chuckled. "Don't tell me a part of you doesn't love the attention. The old Juniper would have loved it. Is this Isolde finally coming out?"

She stared into her stew. "I don't know."

Her sullen tone shushed Xavier's next comment, and his playful grin. They ate in silence. Mabyl, Ison, and Lilianna joined them. To Juniper's surprise, so did Cera. She limped and wore bandages around her arms, but she was whole.

"Hello," Cera said awkwardly.

"How are you feeling?" Juniper asked.

"Like I was peppered with rocks and sewn back together with druid weeds."

Juniper chuckled. She eyed the tiny red lines on Cera's face. They would fade. "Did that beast really jump in front of you?"

"It did." Cera nodded, though she looked uncertain. As if the selfless behavior unsettled her as much as it had Juniper.

The talk turned to the beasts, the Shadows, and the persistent goblin problem in the dungeons. No one mentioned Isolde or the solstice. With her friends, it was easier to ignore the stares and whispers.

"What's bothering you?" Lilianna asked as they left the dining hall. She had taken over guard duty. Moss followed close behind. He'd been thrilled to see Juniper again.

Juniper waited until they were out of earshot. "Everyone is treating me differently, like I'm..."

"Like you're the person they believe will save them from Nexon," Lilianna said calmly. "I have heard the mages talking, or my Shadows have. They left Nexon's side to come to yours, and many believe you will defeat him. Without you, no one will stand between Nexon and his conquest, and they know what he will do to turncoats. You are their protection. You also happen to be a princess and an archmage."

Juniper groaned inwardly. Lilianna was right. Still, she didn't like the pressure to become someone worth extra blankets and a larger heaping of stew. Isolde wasn't a real person. Juniper was, and she wasn't worthy of any of it. She didn't know how to become that person or even if she could.

"It wasn't supposed to happen this way," Juniper whispered.

Lilianna remained silent, waiting for her to continue.

"I was supposed to come here by myself and fight Nexon. I didn't want anyone else to be involved. No one else was supposed to be in danger."

"But, had you fallen, Nexon would have stormed through the rest of the realm, and we would have fallen anyway," Lilianna said. "And the Wylds would have swallowed Sinjon, and eventually the rest of the kingdom. The beasts would have ravaged the cities and towns. Nexon would have gone unstopped."

"And now we stand a chance," Juniper finished. "I know, I know."

They continued for another corridor. They had no destination; they merely walked.

"I must confess something," Lilianna said.

"Yes?"

"I was told to distract you tonight and take you to the vestibule." Lilianna held Juniper's gaze, unflinching and unafraid.

Dread coiled in her gut. "Why?"

"It is a surprise, they said."

Juniper groaned and rubbed her face. "I hate surprises."

Lilianna offered no condolences. She shrugged. "We should head back."

Juniper wanted to refuse and hide in her bedroom until the sunrise, but her friends would not relent. Might as well get it over with. She motioned for Lilianna to take the lead, and they meandered back the way they had come. With every corridor, her stomach clenched a little tighter. Her dread coiled higher, choking every other breath and making her hands shake.

They reached the vines separating the corridor from the vestibule. Voices rang on the other side, a gentle clatter. A lot of them. Juniper took a deep breath and walked through.

The murmur hushed, and the several hundred pairs of eyes turned to her. Jarek and Ingrid stood with the druids, Reid stood with the druid warriors, and Ison and Xavier stood with the mages. It seemed that everyone had packed into the vestibule.

It all made Juniper feel like throwing up. She should have picked a nicer dress.

The crowd parted, and it didn't take long for her to see what they had done. They had fixed the back wall of the vestibule, righted the collapsed doorway and its flanking pillars, so that it led into the receiving room. Magelights glowed on the other side. Juniper fought to keep her steps steady and her breaths even, to keep the panic from her features, as she made her way through the parted crowd and up the smooth stone steps into the receiving room.

Wreaths and garland hung on the pillars. A woven rug ran the length of the hall. Jasmine water scented the cold air. But it wasn't the decorations that bothered her. It was the mages standing on the far side of the room, beside tightly woven fibers that hung where doors would have once stood.

Juniper didn't like this at all.

A hand landed gently on her back.

She jumped—Reid stood beside her. His molten eyes met hers, and he gave her a little push forward.

Reid knew what it was. She saw it on his face. But his presence gave her the reassurance she needed to force her legs across the room. She reached the curtains with Reid at her side, and the mages bowed in unison. She pushed through the woven door.

The room waiting on the other side stole her breath and forced her dread into her throat.

It was the throne room.

CHAPTER 35

Juniper stood in a stupor. Magic had fixed the shattered stone walls, reassembled the flying buttresses and carved pillars of the arcade, and erased the cracks in the marble stonework of the floor. Magelights shone near the ceiling, clear as pure sunlight. Potted ferns, jasmine, and pointed red flowers lined the arcade in earthen pots. Vines formed banners and hung from the arcade, each spotted with blue flowers. On the far end of the rectangular room was the dais. Above it, on the stone, were the remains of an ancient mural that depicted the stars of the gods and the bones of men, woven together in harmony.

Below the mural sat an elaborate stone throne. A sage green woolen blanket had been thrown over the bare stone, and a shiny silver pelt rested over it.

Rue and Calvex stood on either side of the throne, their Sentinel armor gleaming, looking stoic and impassive.

And everyone in the throne room was looking at her.

Juniper couldn't breathe. This—this was what she did *not* want.

She was not a princess or a queen or any kind of ruler. She was a thief, lowly criminal scum of Rusdasin, and she... She didn't want to be queen. She didn't want to be in charge. She didn't want to be Isolde.

The world tilted sideways.

No. No. No.

"Juniper?" Lilianna asked, her name a tentative question.

"I need some air." Juniper turned and marched out of the throne room. Her words had come out weak and desperate, not at all like someone worthy of a throne.

She ran out of the throne room, through the receiving room and vestibule, through the confused crowd within, and ran into the first corridor—she had no destination, she only ran. She ignored the calls of her name. She ran, pushing down the dread and panic, every step feeling like she might empty her stomach.

She kept going, not minding where she went. Why hadn't anyone listened? She had told everyone from the beginning that she didn't want to be Isolde. She didn't want to be anything more than she already was. Why had everyone pushed and pushed her into being Isolde? She missed living in the shadows, doing what she wanted, going where she wanted, and taking care only of herself.

Juniper paused in a quiet corridor. She hadn't been minding where she'd gone, and her feet had taken her back to the royal wing. It was quiet, save for the crackle of hearth fire.

Everyone had gone to the celebration. The royal wing was gloriously empty.

She retreated into her chambers and magicked snow into the sink. She heated it until it steamed.

Lilianna had not followed. No one had.

No footsteps rushed after her in the corridor.

She was alone.

She washed the panic and shame from her face with druid-made soap that smelled like lavender and winter berries. It helped. The loneliness ebbed her racing heart.

Juniper took a deep breath. She could face the odd looks at her hasty retreat. The embarrassment didn't bother her. That would come later. Right now, she wanted to be alone for a while longer.

Or...she could take these worries to the wechun.

She made her decision. She took a servant's passage to the kitchens. A few druids lingered near the sinks, chatting about her hasty retreat as they washed, and Juniper easily slipped past them. Despite the winter chill, the kitchens were hot from the ovens and steaming soapy water. By the time Juniper slipped into Ison's workshop, sweat gathered along her hairline. She eased through the bubbling, hissing positions in varying stages of progress, and into the quiet, dark, snowy grounds.

The darkness of the grounds had never felt more welcoming. She took a deep breath, inhaling the flowers and herbs kept alive and lush with druid magic, and the snowfall in the pines. She started along the stone path, straightened by magic to the edge of the garden. She continued along the broken part of the path toward the lake. Even the walk outside the castle had helped. She just...needed a few moments to herself, by herself, without anyone expecting more of her.

Creak. Tap.

Juniper heaved a sigh and paused her walk. Of course, someone had followed. She'd had her moment alone. Who would it be? Lilianna? Xavier? Reid? What reprimand did they have prepared?

A gentle step behind her, and a swish.

Juniper readied her excuse for not returning to the party. She started to turn, she started to speak.

A shadow came at her. She barely saw the glint.

Something sharp seared against her upper arm. Juniper flinched and threw herself backward. Her heel struck an uneven stone, and she hit the ground ungracefully. Panic flared, and something instinctual took over—she rolled onto her feet. Pain throbbed down her pain, and warmth seeped into her sleeve. Hot and sticky, reeking of iron.

Lora stood on the path, bloodied dagger in her hand, madness in her eyes. Stringy hair framed her dirty face, and mud and blood splattered her clothes.

Juniper summoned twin daggers of ice. Pain flared from the wound in her arm, twisting under the skin like fire. She lashed at Lora. Their daggers collided with a vicious clank of ice and metal. Juniper's ice melted onto Lora's steel, ripping it out of her hand. It landed somewhere in the underbrush.

Lora ran into the forest.

"You're not getting away," Juniper spat. She gave chase.

Gods, her arm stung. With every step, every jostle, every swish of torn fabric against her torn skin, it burned and ached and throbbed. Pain reached from the wound and into her fingers and up her neck.

Lora laughed as she ran between trees, over brambles, and jumped over frozen streams. "Run, run, little princess," she taunted.

Sluggishness followed in the wake of the burning pain. Juniper stumbled over an unseen root and careened into a tree trunk. Lora laughed. Her figure in the forest doubled and blurred. Foolishness washed over Juniper—she'd been poisoned. It burned on her skin and through her blood, crawling under her skin. It yanked at her legs, slowing her down and giving Lora the advantage.

"Shit," Juniper spat. She pushed away from the tree, sliding her hand against the rough bark. She wouldn't let Lora get away with such a dirty move.

With every step, Lora got further away.

Juniper's magic seized, deep and twisting. Her vision blurred, her legs gave out, and her arm went limp at her side. The ice dagger in that hand vanished. She hit a patch of dead grass and tree roots.

Lora appeared in her vision, doubled at first, then tripled. Juniper struggled to focus. A dagger gleamed in Lora's hand, thrice over. Juniper summoned a shield of clear blue ice between them. It distorted Lora into the monster she really was.

"Feeling a little tired?" Lora asked, her tone grating.

Juniper had no clever response. Whatever poison Lora had dipped her dagger in slugged her thoughts and slowed her heartbeat.

Lora slashed at the ice shield. It chipped.

"Feeling lightheaded?" Lora slashed at the ice. Her grin widened. "A little confused? Like you could just lie down and never get back up?"

Juniper tried to stand, but her legs wouldn't move.

"I will serve your head to him," Lora seethed. "And I will carve every traitorous mage, delusional druid, and that boy of yours into pieces."

ARCHMAGE IN THE RUINS

Lora slammed her dagger into the ice. It cracked. She slammed it again, spreading the cracks. Juniper tried to strengthen the shield, but her magic wavered and trembled and curled inward. Lora chipped away at the ice, one strike at a time, until Juniper's hold fracture. The ice shattered. Lora grinned with madness and victory. She brought her blade up for the killing blow.

Lora's eyes shifted over Juniper. Her grin faded into confusion, and then twisted into fear. A terrible, high-pitched roar rent the night, rattling the darkness and the stars. Its maker thundered through the forest, graceful over the brush and through the winter-dead weeds.

A blur of emerald and indigo rushed over Juniper. It brought with it the smell of lake water and magic. Lora screamed, but the shrill sound ended abruptly.

Juniper felt cold, but not the cold she knew. This was a dangerous, foreign cold.

She blinked. When she opened her eyes again, the wechun stood at her side. In the moonlight, its emerald and jade and indigo scales glittered. It had traded its fins for limbs that looked too long for its body. It sniffed, then growled.

The wechun scooped her up into its long arms, and they began to move.

"You're poisoned," it said, nostrils flaring. "It smells like winter hemlock. It is not conducive to magic. It is an ingredient in Mage's Bane. I will take you back to the druids. They have planted herbs that will make an antidote. I watched them."

Juniper barely heard the words. She must have fallen asleep. One moment, darkness graced the other side of her eyelids, and then the glow of magelights. Voices. Clattering pots and pans.

"Juniper?" asked a panicked voice she knew, yet she could not place the speaker. "What happened? What...is that?"

The wechun spoke, the tone low and somber.

"I'm all right," Juniper managed to say, or so she thought. A hand touched her cool cheek.

They had returned to the castle. Juniper's cold panic receded, and she gave into the tug of darkness.

CHAPTER 36

Adrian had never felt magic so close. It hung in the air like the heavy summer days when the sky threatened rain, when his clothes stuck to his skin. He sat in a small room in the knight's hall with a handful of others, including Amery, Blythe, and a thief-boy whose name Adrian couldn't remember. Henry had invited them for a lesson on magic.

Sir Darvel stood by the door, watching with the disdain of a senior knight. The remaining Order had not been happy to hear their best kept secret had been exposed. By Amery, no less.

Abrielle stood beside Henry at the front of the room, looking like she would rather be anywhere else than in the Order's hall. Amery sat beside Blythe, looking utterly delighted.

"All right," Henry started. "Normally, it would take months to master control and awareness, but this is a crash course."

"We have castles to siege," Amery chimed.

Henry took a deep breath and blew it out slowly. He glared at Amery. "Let's start with the basics. Natural magic exists within a mage. It manifests differently for each mage. This is also called raw magic."

Abrielle summoned a ribbon of blue magic that circled her fingers. A bright floral scent filled the air.

"It is a force that a mage manipulates. Smell that? Like flowers? That smell belongs to the magic essence that is released by the use of raw magic," Henry continued. "The more magic Abrielle uses, the more essence she releases. That essence is what you will be attempting to manipulate. The knights use the essence to detect magic and perform detection and disruption techniques. This type of spellwork doesn't come as easy to someone without magic in their blood, like Abrielle. A knight endures years of tireless training and rigorous study to do what we do."

"So we're not setting things on fire today?" Amery frowned.

Henry leveled his glare on her. "If you manage to set something on fire, I will personally deliver a dozen explosive runes to your doorstep."

Amery's grin turned wicked.

"Unfortunately, we don't have a lot of time," Darvel interrupted. "Let's get started."

Henry instructed them on how to feel the magic essence rather than smell it, and how to reach for that magic. How to pull it, how to knead it, how to shape it to the user's will.

Several long hours passed. Henry gave them the task of moving an object by magic. Sweat beaded on Adrian's forehead and on the back of his neck. His head hurt from trying to coax the unseen flowery magic into pushing the pebble across the wooden tabletop. His hadn't moved at all. Amery had moved hers a fraction, and the thief-boy had moved his a bit more. Blythe struggled, and at the sight of her unmoving stone, the thief-boy stuck his tongue out at her. She looked like she wanted to cut it out of his head.

Trying to use magic essence poked that same spot in his head that hurt when Josephine tried to teach him mental resistance.

Adrian took a deep breath and tried harder, cursing silently at the unyielding magic. He coaxed it toward him. It resisted. He could feel it resisting him, denying him the use. He tried again to contort it into a solid force to push the rock, but the magic just folded over. It had a will of its own, like wet sand.

"This is a start," Henry said dismissively.

Abrielle disbanded her ribbon of magic. She'd used it to continuously feed the room with magic essence.

"Rest up and keep practicing. We'll meet again tomorrow."

Adrian left with a steep sense of disappointment. Jax followed at his heels. On the way out, Henry set his hand on Adrian's shoulder, looking relieved that the class was over.

"We've released a monster, you know that?" Henry said.

Adrian nodded, jostling that pounding in his head. "That's what the Order is for, right? To keep the monster on a leash?"

"It will be." Henry steeled his expression, looking far too knightly for Adrian's liking.

Adrian headed back toward the king's house. How many others would be able to pick up magic as easily as Amery? How many would use it for ill rather than good? By the time the king's house came into view, Adrian wanted nothing more than a stiff drink and a dark room to lie in.

An attractive blonde waited for him in the front room.

"You're the prince," she said, her red lips curving in a courtesan's smile.

Adrian blinked at her. She looked familiar, but he couldn't place her. It had been more than a year since he had visited her type of establishment. Ever since he met Roslyn. "Yes, I am. You are?"

"Helena Thimble. Juniper asked me to help out, and I've got something for you." She undid a stained leather sheath hidden in the folds of her skirt. She handed it to him. "This is something I've been playing with for a while. Finally got it right."

Adrian had a horrible apprehension for accepting strange daggers.

"It's laced with Mage's Bane," Helena whispered.

"It's…what?"

"I dabble in poison, and I have a knack of poison that clings to steel. I finally developed a recipe that is toxic to magic, and Juniper asked me to help out, and I'm giving it to you."

"Why?"

"Because you're not very good at magic, and you might need the extra protection. I don't know how much poison the blade has though. Likely one or two toxic hits." Helena wiggled the dagger.

"And you don't want this?" Adrian asked.

"I made myself one." Her eyes glittered. "And Juniper likes you, so I'm extending a gift of goodwill."

He took the dagger. It felt no different than any other.

"Farewell, Your Highness." Helena curtsied with grace to rival any courtier, then departed.

Adrian fingered a dark stain on the leather sheath. He pulled the dagger out halfway—a dark substance coated the edge.

A clatter came from the back of the house. Adrian sheathed the blade and tucked it into his pocket.

He found Roslyn in the kitchen, sorting out a box of supplies. It contained soap, bottles of wine, salt, and other things distributed from the commons. Roslyn looked like a dream in a creamy yellow dress. It was simple, but it fit her curves like a glove.

Relief pushed through his chest, and he was ready to spill his worries while laying in his lover's arms.

She caught his eye, and that playful gleam brightened in brown eyes. She started to speak, but a panicked shriek cut through the air. Her expression fell and her eyes widened. A second shriek followed.

Roslyn abandoned the box of supplies and rushed into the street. Adrian followed at her heels, and Jax and Roslyn's guard followed. Another shriek sounded—coming from Captain Tinnly's house beside the king's. Roslyn rushed forward, but before she reached the door, a girl burst out of it, panic all over her face and trembling hands.

"Marcy, what's happened?" Roslyn demanded.

"The baby is coming," Marcy said, her voice several pitches too high. "I—I've never delivered, I—I don't know—"

"Go get Nera," Roslyn ordered, and the girl's frightened demeanor shifted. "She'll be at Josephine's or the mage's hall. Go."

Marcy bolted toward Josephine's district. Roslyn rushed inside. Her guard, Adrian, and Jax followed. Adrian and Jax paused just inside the main room. Roslyn and her guard rushed down the short hall and into one of the bedrooms. As Roslyn pushed aside the curtain that served as a door, a pained, desperate cry filled the house. It sent gooseflesh over his arms and neck, and it made his blood run cold.

Adrian dared not enter the birthing room—despite living in the Undercity and drinking the same ale as criminals, he would uphold the tradition of no men allowed.

"Adrian!" Roslyn shouted, her tone stern and commanding.

The color drained from his face. She couldn't mean—

"We need help!" Roslyn demanded.

Another painful shriek followed.

Adrian looked to Jax for help, but his young, unmarried guard looked nearly sick. Adrian took one step closer to the bedroom, then another. As he reached for the curtain, Roslyn shoved it aside. She wore determination and held a knife.

She pointed at Adrian's chest. "You, warm water in a basin. Big enough for a baby. You" —she pointed at Jax— "towels."

Adrian caught a glimpse of the room. Tinnly's wife reclined against a mound of blankets and pillows, her knees bent and spread, her hands clutching her swollen belly, her face red and twisted in pain. Her eyes brimmed with tears.

"At once, ma'am," Jax said in a single breath. He darted deeper into the house, duty to Adrian forgotten.

Adrian fumbled his way through the kitchen looking for a basin. What constituted a basin? A large bowl? How large were newborns? How warm did the water need to be? He stumbled across a basin in the bathing room. With shaking hands, he held it under the tap. The water gurgled and spat into the basin. Cold. "Damn it," Adrian breathed. His heart raced, his heartbeat thundered in his ears, and he couldn't even complete one stupid task.

Useless. Useless. Useless.

Desperate, he set his hands on either side of the basin, willing the water to heat. He imagined steam. He imagined Juniper doing the same in a sliver of the time he took him to draw a breath. Distantly, he heard Roslyn talking and Mrs. Tinnly whimpering and grunting.

The water remained cool.

It would have to do. Adrian carried the basin to the birthing room. A step before the door, Marcy and Nera rushed into the house, out of breath and red-faced. Nera raced toward him, snatched the basin of water, and as she turned to go through the curtain that Marcy helped open, the water began to steam. Jax appeared a moment later, and Marcy snatched the towels out of his arms.

The curtain swung closed.

Jax glanced at Adrian.

"What do we do?" Jax whispered.

"We can't do anything," Adrian said. He returned to the front room and stuffed his hands into his pockets. "We wait and pray the gods be merciful."

Unable to sit or stand still, Adrian paced. The *sounds* coming out of the birthing room were terrifying. Between Roslyn's commands and encouragements and Mrs. Tinnly's shrieks of pain and tearful screams, Adrian couldn't form thoughts.

Then, a strange pocket of silence descended. Adrian's heart skipped a beat, Jax paled, and then the pitched cries of a newborn filled the house. Adrian fell into the nearest chair. Jax leaned against the wall, hand on his heart. He still looked like he might vomit.

The baby continued to cry, and the girls continued to chatter. Adrian leaned forward and rubbed his face.

It was done.

And then it wasn't.

Roslyn's tone turned stern once again, urgent and commanding, talking about blood. Too much blood. More water. Towels. Adrian sat up as Roslyn skirted through the door with a tiny bundle in her hands. Blood splattered her yellow dress. She handed the bundle of blankets to Adrian.

"Cradle the head, don't drop him," she ordered, then vanished back into the birthing room, where Marcy was talking to Mrs. Tinnly, and the floral scent of magic wafted out.

"Stay with me," Roslyn said, her voice softer yet no less stern.

The baby whined. Adrian didn't know what to do. He had never held a child, let alone one fresh from the womb. The blanket covered everything but the red, blotchy, wrinkled face. The eyes were shut tight. The tiny mouth bent in an unhappy grimace. An unhappy grunt, the tiniest sound he had ever heard, emitted from its puckered lips.

"Yes, I know," Adrian said to the newborn. He brought the babe closer to his chest. "You were so cozy and warm, now you're out here where it's bright and cold and miserable."

It struck him that while magic could do wondrous things and cast fancy illusions, it could not create life. The life he held had been crafted in the womb, stitched together by the gods' design, not by man or magic.

"She'll be all right," came Roslyn's tired voice.

Adrian looked up. Bloodstained and exhausted, she was still the most beautiful woman he'd ever seen. She looked at him and the babe in his arms with softened eyes.

"I didn't know you knew how to deliver," Adrian said.

"Most of the Galamond villages are so remote from each other, there isn't time to go find a healer or a midwife. It's just…something I've picked up." She slid her arms into his and scooped the infant from his hold. "I was fourteen when I helped deliver the first one. I was terrified..I threw up after. Thankfully, Nera was here, or this could have gone much worse."

The door to the house burst open, and Captain Tinnly half-fell into the room, breathless and panting and a frightening shade of white.

In any other situation, Adrian would have laughed at the man.

And then the captain laid eyes on the bundle in Roslyn's arms, and he looked like he might break into tears.

"Glad you made it," Roslyn said kindly. "Momma's doing fine. We had some bleeding, but Nera saw to that. She'll need bed rest for a while. Here, meet your son."

Captain Tinnly took the baby into his arms like it might shatter. He mouthed the words, *my son*. The baby began to fuss, mousy little sounds at first, but those little mews grew into high-pitched cries.

Nera appeared in the curtain to the birthing room, equally covered in blood, and held it open for the captain to come through. "He sounds hungry."

Captain Tinnly carried the baby into the birthing room, and Nera let the curtain fall closed.

Roslyn released a sigh and nudged Adrian. "Let's go. I need a bath."

They returned to the king's house, arms linked. Not wanting to be alone, Adrian followed her into the bathing room. He sat by the door while she reclined in the bath, washing the blood and gods-only-know-what-else from her olive skin.

"Well?" Roslyn asked after a while. "Is that your first baby?"

"Yes." Adrian tilted his head toward her. "I had no idea how horrible the birth process was. I mean, all of that just to bring someone into the world. For every human that has ever existed, a mother has had to go through that."

Roslyn nodded. "Indeed."

"It's so…horrible." And bloody and painful.

"Horrible?"

"So much pain and risk just to bring someone into existence." Adrian gave his future wife a mischievous, albeit haunted smile. "I mean, the first step of making a child is still my favorite. It's far more enjoyable for both parties."

At this, Roslyn laughed, filling the stone chamber with her charming laugh. "My mother told me that being a mother is the hardest and most rewarding thing a woman can do."

"I should buy my mother flowers," Adrian mused. "And compliment her."

"Every day."

CHAPTER 37

Ison magically increased the heat under the old flask, easier and more precise than using the tea lights or oil lanterns the Marca demanded they use. It filled the air with a faint scent of silver polish, but he didn't mind, and no one could tattle on him to the knights. The druids used magic freely, and from what he had learned and witnessed, their magic didn't operate quite the same as his own.

It was fascinating. According to the Marca, druids had vanished ages ago from the realm. Some had theorized their magic connected to the Iluvin, but now Ison knew the truth. They had thrived in the forest that became the Blackwood Wylds, and that forest either drove them away or devoured them. Now, Ison worked beside druids to grow herbs and spices and rare leaves. The gardens outside his workshop were bursting with life, despite the dead of winter, thanks to their haunting song.

Even as he sat in the workshop, he could hear a few of the druids in the gardens, singing as they tended to the herbs. He had watched lavender shoots and roses shake frost and bloom within a single refrain as Ingrid sang.

Absolutely breathtaking.

The castle smelled of flowers and herbs and magic, and he loved it. It felt like a place he could stay.

Ison lessened the flame under the flask, and the potion of healing went from sage to bright green in a few seconds. He set it aside and got to work on the second part of the potion. He set a new flask of darkened glass and added the tinderroot to mint water, as instructed by the wechun.

He felt a shadow at his side, and this time he didn't jump.

"It asked me to bring you this," Xavier said, his voice dry. He held a little leather pouch by the strings, and if it held poison. "I didn't ask what it was."

Ison took the pouch and opened it. Inside were narrow, crisp leaves of dark blue. The wechun had already removed the stem, leaving only what Ison needed.

"Leaves from the mallow bark," Ison said. "He called them Ander leaves."

Xavier's brows rose.

"It...told me it would gather some for me," Ison said.

Ison waited for the potion to heat, then added the leaves. They dissolved instantly. The potion turned a pale blue and filled the workroom with a minty scent. It reminded Ison of frozen earth, of a snowstorm.

Xavier lingered, leaning against the wall where he could see both the door and the shuttered window.

"Who's with Juniper?" Ison asked.

"Reid is there, and Mabyl is standing outside. That…fish-dragon *thing* is also with her."

Ison chuckled, though Xavier's description fit the creature. Ison had nearly fainted when that monster appeared in the kitchen, carrying a bleeding and unconscious Juniper in its long arms, declaring that she had been poisoned, her attacker was dead, and she needed attention. It had carried her to her chamber and one of the fire mages had seen to cleaning and wrapping the wound. All the while, the monster had watched.

It had offered no explanation of its presence until Reid had asked, "What are you?"

"Juniper tells me you are cunning," it had said in its wispy, somber voice. "Does your knights' instinct not already know what I am?"

Juniper, being an archmage, was in command of a wechun. The very idea made Ison nauseous.

"What are you thinking?" Xavier asked.

"I'm thinking that until Jun wakes up and confirms that thing's story, I'm not believing it," Ison said.

"Yet you are crafting the potion as prescribed by it."

"I've heard of all these ingredients before," Ison said. "Some, like Ander leaves, are so rare that the merchants in Rusdasin can't stock them. They grow only in winter and require the dark and cold."

"Are they deadly?"

"No," Ison said, shaking his head.

Xavier raised a brow.

Ison turned sheepish. "The wechun told me to look in the old potion books if I doubted him. And…I did. These leaves are in there. They are used for healing, particularly for mages. It works well with magic. They counteract witchroot and hemlock, both of which happen to be ingredients in Mage's Bane."

Xavier's gray-blue eyes slid to the bookshelf Ison had spent an afternoon arranging. Most of the books had been left untouched, unlike the library which had been torched. The books were old and some were outdated, but some had been hand-written by generations of potion makers. Each was a well of knowledge.

He had planned on going through each and rewriting them on fresh paper, before time took the knowledge completely.

Ison's eyes snagged on a piece of red among the drab grays and browns of the workroom—Xavier wore a red scarf around his neck. The scarf that Ison had given him, the scarf that had been given to him because he had shown an old man compassion and kindness.

Xavier's gaze met his. "What? It's still drafty in here."

A few months ago, Ison would have left the conversation at that, but he had gotten used to the subtle flickers in Xavier's impassive gaze. Ison turned away from the potion, keeping his gaze on Xavier's, and crossed the space between them. He'd also learned that Xavier rarely made the first move.

Ison pushed him against the wall and flattened his body against his. Their lips hadn't met but for a moment when a knock sounded at the door.

Xavier let out a gruff chuckle.

Ison lingered a moment, then answered the door. Xavier quickly recomposed himself into the careful, emotionless assassin.

Bois stood at the door, holding a satchel over her shoulder. Her air magic swept over the room, over Ison and Xavier, the potion equipment, the shelves. Mapping the room.

"Yes?" Ison asked.

"The mages requested that you look at these items," she said in her soft, feminine tone. She held out the satchel. "Things recovered from the battle."

"Why me?" Ison took the satchel and set it on a stool by the window. It wasn't heavy; there was not much inside.

"These are things the others don't know what to do with," Bois explained. "The items are magical in nature or enchanted, and you are the more experienced mage."

Ison sighed through his nose. He would have never considered himself the more experienced mage, but admittedly, among the apostates who hadn't grown up in the Marca or hiding with their nose in a book, he was.

"I'll take a look." Ison opened the satchel carefully and pulled out a double-ended blade. Tiny runes had been engraved into each blade, different ones. A plain stone rested in the middle of the leather-wrapped grip.

"Thank you," Bois said. She left. Her magic-net went with her.

As Xavier shut the door behind her, he shut out the sounds of the kitchens.

Ison gently touched one side of the blade to his sleeve. The plain stone glowed blue. He tried the same with the other side. The stone glowed orange.

"Each end does something," Ison said. "What, I'm not willing to try on myself."

"Too bad the wechun ate Lora," Xavier said flatly. "Save that for if we have prisoners."

184

The wechun hadn't eaten her. Lilianna's Shadows had arrived first, and she had given Ison the report. Lora's throat had been torn out, nearly severing her head. Ison hadn't asked how quickly she had died. He didn't want to know those things.

"You think we'll have prisoners?" Ison asked.

Xavier shrugged. "It never hurts to be prepared. Besides, I'm not entirely convinced all those mages are on our side. They just didn't want to die."

Ison believed the same.

He set the double-sided dagger on the windowsill, and reached back into the satchel. He pulled out a marble of clear glass. Little dents and nicks spotted the surface. As he held it, a fog appeared in the middle. It turned a grayish green, then grayish blue, then somewhere in the middle. The fog swirled like wind.

"That looks like magic," Ison said. "My magic."

Xavier plucked the marble from his hand. Immediately, the grayish wind died and an orb of charcoal replaced it.

"It's showing us magic," Ison said. "I've heard about these. They are rare and nearly impossible to craft. Only a master smith could have successfully done it."

"What is it?"

"It's a device used by the Order to show a mage's magic," Ison said. "They were used in the past to denote a mage, so that a mage could not hide."

"But how?"

Ison shrugged, too in awe by the thing to think about it. "I don't know. No one knows how they're made. Those in existence are ancient."

He set the marble on the windowsill beside the dagger, in a little indentation in the stone to keep it from rolling away. Such a stone would be worth a king's treasury.

Next, he pulled out what appeared to be a worn, leather-bound diary. The pages were stained by time and light, faded and dulled. The leather bore a few nicks and stains. Ison undid the leather string and opened it to the first page, fully expecting to have found a dead mage's diary.

The pages were blank.

Every single one.

"Odd," Xavier said. "Why bring a blank book?"

Ison ran his fingers along the pages. The pages bore the indentation of a nib. He tilted the book in the light, and he saw the lines made by letters. The lines overlapped each other, like someone had written over the page a hundred times.

When he showed that to Xavier, he frowned.

"Odd," he repeated, darkly. "In a bad way."

Ison grabbed an inkwell and pen from his desk.

"Are you sure that's wise?"

"I'll not write any of my secrets," Ison said. A part of him knew it was a mistake, but his curiosity won out.

"You didn't used to be so rash or reckless," Xavier said, though he smiled.

"Blame it on my friends," Ison said, laughing.

Ison sat and wrote a simple line: *It's snowing. The lavender is shriveling.*

The words sat on the heavy parchment, ink drying. The words did not sink into the page as Ison had expected.

"Hmmm," Xavier hummed.

Ison started to say something, but then more ink appeared on the page, below his own.

Curious that the lavender is in a state to shrivel.

Ison blinked at the words. The ink appeared a letter at a time, as if in time as it was written. The slanted penmanship was not Ison's.

Before they could speak, more words appeared.

I take your prolonged silence as good news.

Ison swallowed and glanced at Xavier.

"They didn't say where on the battlefield this was found, did they?" Ison asked.

Xavier shook his head.

Ison dipped his nib into the ink. He wrote underneath the slanted words, *Of course.*

For a long while, no more words appeared.

"I don't like it," Xavier said.

"I agree." Ison set aside his pen and shut the book. Out of curiosity, he opened it—the words had vanished, leaving only new indentations.

"Ah, the answer." Xavier said.

Ison didn't set the book on the sill with the other enchanted items. He set it on his desk, underneath a heavy candle. He didn't want whatever was inside the book to get out.

"We'll worry about that later. First, I need to finish Jun's potion." Ison turned to the cooling Ander leaf potion. It had turned an icy shade of blue, almost white, like freshly fallen snow. He added it to the simple healing potion. As the two met, fog hissing and spilling over the sides of the glass, turning a dull shade of yellow as it touched the wooden table.

"I'm sure that's fine," Xavier mumbled.

A thick layer of fog remained on top of the potion, churning as the two potions combined, and it filled the workroom with a wintry scent of snowfall.

CHAPTER 38

Juniper dreamed of warm hearths, towering bookshelves, and summer forests thick with leaves. Laughter drifted in and out of the trees. Shadows darted between the massive trunks. Then, the forest shriveled. The boughs blackened, the leaves withered and fell, and decay matted the ground.

"Juniper," came a somber, warm voice. "Look at me."

The dream vanished. A hand touched her cold cheek, and she fought to open her eyes. Her body yearned for more rest. Reid came into focus. Behind him, light flickered over the walls and ceiling of the royal bedchamber.

Reid slid his arm under her shoulders and helped her into a sitting position. He cradled her limp body with his.

"You need to drink," came the deep, rhythmic voice of the wechun.

The wechun approached the bedside with the hearth fire glittering off its emerald and sapphire scales.

Reid held a foggy drink to her lips.

"It will negate the poison," said the wechun. "Drink."

Reid pressed the glass to her bottom lip and tilted it. The fog tickled her nose, and the potion was cool against her lips. She took a small sip. It tasted like snow and citrus. She took another small sip, then another. Reid raised the glass as she drank.

It took a while, but she drank the entire potion. Reid took the empty glass from her lips.

She felt it easing through the sluggishness, the weakness, the shattering thoughts. It lessened her desire for rest. It soothed the burning coil that was her magic.

She remembered. Lora had poisoned her, and the wechun had saved her.

And the wechun now stood in her bedroom. Its glittering black eyes were watching her.

"Ah, it is working," it said.

Ison stood on the other side of the bed, holding the now empty glass. His face was unreadable.

All three were watching her.

After several long, deep breaths, she managed to whisper, "I'm okay."

"I disagree," said the wechun.

Reid glanced at the wechun, his expression masked.

"It will take time for the Ander leaves to negate the poison fully," said the wechun. "Bed rest and tea will do you well. I am sure Reid will see to that."

Reid's hand on her shoulder flinched. She doubted anyone else noticed.

Juniper closed her eyes, just for a moment. When she opened them, the sun had set, the bedroom was dark, and the hearth burned behind a screen, muting the glow. The wechun was curled in front of the window, the moonlight glinting off its scales.

Reid was asleep beside her. He lay on his side, facing her.

How long had it been?

As she shifted, the pain and stiffness became apparent. Whatever Lora had done to her, she'd punctuated her magic. She felt it curling in her bones. Struggling to come back. She vaguely remembered the wechun mentioning hemlock and Mage's Bane.

Reid's fingers grazed her arm. His eyes fluttered open. Upon seeing her awake, sleep vanished from his gaze.

For a long moment, they only looked at one another.

"I'm sorry," she whispered.

His brow furrowed.

"I shouldn't have left," she said. Then Lora wouldn't have gotten that cheap shot, she wouldn't have run into the woods, and the wechun wouldn't have been forced to reveal itself.

"I'm sorry," he whispered. "I should have gone after you. I almost did, but I told myself you needed to be alone. If I had, I would have been there. I would have stopped this."

His fingers curled around hers. His magic felt along hers, tentative and gentle. Her magic reached out in return, weak and limp as a wet weed.

"What happened?" she asked.

"You left the throne room," Reid said, and at the mention of that place her chest squeezed. "And then the wechun carried you into the kitchens. He told Ison to make you a potion. You've been resting since."

"How long?"

"About a day."

She sighed, closing her eyes. A day. She had expected much worse.

A day, meaning the solstice had passed. She had turned nineteen in her sleep.

"Jun," Reid whispered. Her name dripped with worry and questions.

"I'll be okay," she said.

A pause, then, "Are you sure?"

No. Not even a little.

"Talk to me," he whispered, almost a plea.

She took a shuddering breath.

"Everyone's relying on me," she whispered. "Everyone expects me to succeed, to defeat Nexon. If I fail, we're all dead. If I fail, Nexon will slaughter every mage and druid in this castle. Who knows what will happen to the rest of the realm. He will kill anyone who helped me." She couldn't bring herself to list their names. "Everyone is counting on me to save them, and I don't know what I'm going to do. I can't run away from this."

She started to cry. She couldn't stop it. Everything she had been shoving down came flooding forward, in front of Reid.

She covered her eyes with her hands, pressing her palms into her watery eyes.

"Juniper."

His fingers grazed her arm, then pulled her hand away from her eyes. His molten gaze remained steady and stoic, yet worried.

"I'm sorry," she said, her voice weak and waterlogged. "I didn't mean to bother you. I know you have your own problems. I don't want to add to them."

Reid let out a quick breath, then pulled her into his arms. He said, breath hot against her temple, "Don't be ridiculous. I am here for you. I always will be."

She let out a shuddering breath and curled into him as much as her body would allow.

Reid held her close. "I'm sorry. I've been preoccupied with myself while you've been suffering. Jun, I love you, and I forbid you from suffering alone. When you hurt, I will be there for you."

She chuckled at the command. "I love you, Reid. I can't imagine a world without you. I…promise to tell you about all of my problems."

He placed a tender kiss on her temple.

This was her Reid. He was underneath the wild man, the untamed archmage, and she would fight even the god of death to keep him.

CHAPTER 39

Juniper woke to a warm pot of herbal tea. After a cup, Reid helped her into the bathing room. He stood guard while she washed the forest and grime from her skin, telling her of the progress the druids and mages had made, and how he had taught Xavier to cast a ward. After the bath, Reid helped her into a soft night dress and back into the bedroom.

She relaxed into the mound of pillows that had appeared since Lora's attack. The shutters were opened, and cool sunlight draped inside. The wechun had retreated under the bed, saying it preferred darkness over daylight.

It gave her a strange sense of comfort to have a monster under her bed.

Reid had gone to train with the druids, Lilianna patrolled with her Shadows, and Mabyl and Xavier had gone with the mages to better organize them.

They deemed the wechun enough for her protection, and she agreed.

Besides, Lora was dead and they would see an incoming army hours before it arrived. Their only true threat came from the mages. Ison didn't fully trust them. He had gone with the main goal of organizing and job assignments, but he had also gone to root out any turncoats. Xavier had gone with him, which made her feel better about the process. Xavier had an eye for those things.

Juniper sighed. Her magic had unfurled a bit, but the wechun had warned her not to use her magic; it would make the healing process worse.

And…she was bored.

She understood how useful it would be for her injuries to transfer to someone else, someone who didn't have to worry about an army marching toward them. King Bradburn didn't seem as villainous now. She had been the expendable one, and Adrian needed to live. It had been a logical choice, a practical one. Of course, she wouldn't force anyone into the role of protector; she would take volunteers. Then again, if she needed a spare body, the dungeons would be the first place she'd go.

And…she could hardly blame King Bradburn.

Because of him, she had ended up here.

What would have happened if Amery had been caught that night instead of her? Would fate have changed and made Amery the archmage instead? She knew, deep down, that it wouldn't have worked that way. Juniper would still have been the archmage and Isolde, even if she hadn't been caught that night.

Still, it was fun to daydream.

Juniper woke without knowing when she fell asleep. She blinked several times, then sat up. The stiffness in her bones had retreated a bit more.

The wechun slithered out from under the bed. It stretched like a cat, and sapphire and emerald fur unfurled along its back where scales had once been. The soft fur on its belly had grown an icy green. Its snout was elongated. Its ears had lengthened. The few remaining scales had hardened into plates. Gone were its fins, and its feet had flattened into paws. It looked less like a fish or a dragon and more like a dire wolf.

She opened her mouth to question it, and then a horn sounded. The single note ended, and another followed. Silence descended, and a third horn blew. The tone filled the castle, ringing through the corridors and doors, and silencing all inside. Even the hearth seemed to still.

Three horns.

An incoming *something*.

Icy dread slithered from her scalp. The scale-like plates along the wechun's back shifted closer together like armor, and a low growl rolled up its throat.

"No," she begged.

Nexon couldn't attack now! Not with her magic dwindling. Damn it! Lora had planned it this way. She knew when Nexon would be attacking, and she had made sure Juniper would be weakened.

Juniper fumbled to get out of bed. Her side still hurt, but it didn't matter anymore. She couldn't wait.

The time was now.

Whatever was going to happen would happen.

Her weak legs gave out and she tumbled forward—the wechun caught her before she hit the ground. It did not protest as she pulled her night dress over her head and pulled on the first dress she grabbed. She stuffed her feet into her boots and loosely tied up the short corset. Thank the gods the short corsets had been fashionable in her mother's time. She marched into the sitting room, each step a bit sturdier than the last.

She paused before the woven doors.

The wechun draped a woolen cloak over her shoulders. She waited for it to offer some words of wisdom or encouragement. She'd even take false praise.

The wechun offered no words. Did it assume she would die?

She steeled herself and started through the castle. With every painful step, her resolve solidified. She didn't think about anything but putting one foot in front of the other, of facing Nexon with as much dignity as she could muster.

Her wechun fell onto all fours and kept pace beside her. After a few awkward steps, it looked as though it belonged that way.

It jogged a step in front of her. "I can get you there faster."

She blinked. "Are you sure?"

It flicked its thick tail. "If I wasn't, I would not have offered."

She climbed ungracefully onto its back, and it bounded down the corridor far faster than she could have.

The castle had gone frighteningly quiet. Druids and mages lingered in the vestibule with fear on their faces and in their silence. The wechun navigated the vestibule with ease and leaped through the main castle doors. It landed in the morning-bright front garden.

A few gasps of surprise and a handful of shrieks greeted them. Her entrance had gotten everyone's attention, druid warriors and mages. Reid and Lilianna stood at the gates, neither looking surprised. Reid looked dire as ever. Moss crouched behind Lilianna, eyeing the wechun with wary interest.

Juniper climbed off the wechun's back.

"Incoming forces from the south," Lilianna said.

"South?" Juniper felt her stomach give out. The pain in her bones hadn't seemed as heavy before.

Why would Nexon be coming from the south? Rusdasin was to the west, and Baxion was to the north. Unless he had sacked Delphine first.

"My Shadows have not detected ill-intent," Lilianna said. Moss blinked, tilting his head at the wechun. It warbled with uncertainty. "They are unsure but steadfast."

"How many?" Juniper demanded.

Lilianna glanced at Reid, and her mask slipped.

Reid said, "Twice as many as before."

"At least," Lilianna added darkly.

Juniper's breath stammered. No, no, no. It wasn't supposed to be like this. Yet, something about it all didn't settle well.

Why the south?

"I need to see it better," Juniper spat. She took a few quick steps toward the gate, then stumbled. She clutched at the pain in her side.

"No," Reid said.

"There's a secret passage in the library, behind the desk," Juniper said. "Get as many people out of here as possible. I'll buy time."

"What?" Lilianna gasped.

"Absolutely not." Reid stepped closer, panic in his eyes. "Juniper, you can't be serious."

"What other plan do we have? I'm useless, and we're unprepared."

"Not entirely," said Sein. He held himself tall. Asher stood beside him, looking like a real knight. "I refuse to run."

Affirmation went through the warriors and the mages. Their panic had dissolved, and a will to fight replaced it.

"We're outnumbered," Juniper said.

"We hold the high ground and the advantage of terrain," Reid said. "This is what we have been training for. We are ready."

A bark of agreement went through the courtyard.

Juniper's dread curled inward. "Fine, but I'm still going ahead."

The wechun pranced before her. It lowered itself, allowing her better leverage to climb onto its back. Juniper didn't hesitate. No one tried to stop her. The wechun took off through the gates, running south through the empty streets of the dead city. The mages had been hard at work—streets had been smoothed, buildings erected to their former glory, debris cleared. The streets reeked like an overgrown flower garden.

Then they came to where the restoration had ended. The wechun never slowed. It jumped over fallen walls and pillars, tree roots, and holes in the cobblestones. Each bound jabbed at her wounded side. Each street curled her dread, tighter and tighter, until she thought her heart would burst.

She had no plan. She couldn't use her magic to the full extent.

They wouldn't win.

They would perish. Nexon would kill her, then march on the castle. Reid, the druids, Lilianna—they would stand and fall. She only hoped some of them took her advice and escaped through the library's secret passage.

The wechun approached the southern edge of the Dead City, and rather than continue on the street level, it jumped onto a building and then onto the tree that had grown out of it, and onto the roof on a three-story building.

Her breath left her throat.

An army approached from the south. They marched in practiced rows, and banners of gold and white glimmered in the sun. The soldiers wore matching armor in shades of gold and silver with slashes of crimson. Horses and supply trains marched behind and between.

Juniper's heart thumped hard against her chest, and then her breath tumbled out of her chest somewhere between a laugh and a gasp.

A Shadow slunk alongside the wechun, looking up at Juniper with wide, white eyes.

"They're not enemies," Juniper said to the Shadow, and in extension, Lilianna.

The wechun snorted.

"Take me closer," Juniper said.

"Are you serious?" The wechun snorted.

Juniper slid ungracefully to the ground between the wechun and the Shadow. She nearly fell, but managed to keep her balance. She stood at the edge and watched the army marching closer.

"I want to go to the ground," Juniper said to the wechun, that promptly sat. "I thought you were supposed to listen to me?"

It snorted. "You have not commanded me."

She frowned, but then she thought of Nexon's monstrous wechun. She didn't want it to turn into that. She wanted her wechun to remain the snarky, intelligent beauty that it was.

The Shadow warbled at her side.

Juniper climbed onto its back, and it easily pranced the path the wechun had taken to the roof. It took her to the center of the wide street. Several more Shadows appeared on either side—a show of force.

The army had reached the outskirts. Because of the narrower space, the march had thinned.

A soldier in dark silver armor led the march on a handsome chestnut horse. A crimson plume rose from his helmet, fluttering with each hoof beat. As they approached, he signaled for a halt. A horn sounded, and a heartbeat later another sounded father behind. The army halted.

Juniper held her ground. Behind her, the Shadows stilled.

The army's commander slid from his horse and sauntered closer. He paused within a stone's toss.

She recognized the stylized emblem on his breastplate, a stylized circle with half being the moon and half the sun, surrounded by laurel leaves. The commander lifted the helmet from his head. Underneath was a man of umber skin, red hair, and a superior grin.

It was Delmont Thacket, Archmage of Fire.

Juniper couldn't stop the laugh that escaped her throat, spilling her curled anxiety and vicious dread from her lungs.

"That is not the welcome I expected," Delmont said, his voice deep and pleasant and well-articulated with a noble's education and a gentleman's timbre.

"You are not the enemy I feared," Juniper breathed. Or the painful death she feared for herself and those behind her.

CHAPTER 40

Juniper rode beside Delmont as they approached the castle, he on his warhorse and she on the Shadow. The army from Delphine marched behind them. Her wechun remained unseen. She could feel its presence, its closeness. Her magic tied her to it, and she felt it as she had within the lake.

She gave Delmont a condensed account of what had happened since they last saw each other. He remained silent. He took in the city with a forlorn expression. She assumed it came from seeing the city in such a state. Delmont was old enough to have known the city before the civil war, when it was a bustling civilization. Juniper imagined what it would be like to return to Rusdasin and find it in ruins.

They paused before the castle gates. Delmont's forces paused behind them. The druid warriors and mages gathered on the watchtowers, gawking at the army filling the streets.

"Gods," Delmont said at last, taking in the castle. "You have done wonders with the place. The last I remember, the entire castle seemed to be burning."

"There was quite a bit of ash to sweep," she said. "Not to mention the mold, mice droppings, wasp nests, and the goblins in the dungeons."

Delmont did not smile or laugh. His eyes ran over the turrets and towers and battlements, the gates and shutters of vines.

"I would like to see Castle Balendin returned to its splendor," Delmont said as the gates opened. They did not open as steel or iron, but as if an invisible hand had curled them back. They rode through. "It is fitting that you've returned to claim it."

"I haven't claimed anything."

"Yet this sight suggests otherwise," Delmont said, glancing at her with that playful, superior air of his. "And people have followed you here. Druids, too. I didn't think any of them still existed on this continent. Historically, druids have been fickle toward mages and have shied away from us. This sight is more than a little impressive."

They halted in the courtyard, where Lilianna and Reid waited. The druids, despite their steadfastness a few moments ago, look relieved. Moss stood protectively around Lilianna, and warbled as he eyed Delmont.

"And it seems we have much yet to discuss," Delmont said, eyeing the Shadows, beasts, druid knights, and mages, all of which had been ready to fight.

Juniper slid from the Shadow. Reid watched her every movement, looking for injuries. She held herself tall despite the ache in her bones and searing pain at her side.

"Yes, but let's talk over something to drink," Juniper said.

"That would be wonderful," Delmont said.

One of the younger mages rushed into the vestibule, so fast she tripped on the stairs.

Delmont glanced between where the druid had been standing and Juniper, brows raised. "Already giving commands without actually giving commands? *Very* impressive."

Juniper scowled, though she recounted her wording. She hadn't given an order, had she?

While Rue, Calvex, and Ison helped Collatia's royal army to settle—some would be staying in the castle and some would be staying in the city—Juniper, Delmont, Reid, and Lilianna took one of the parlors in the royal wing for a meeting. Tea was brought quickly, along with lavender jam and dark bread.

"Her Majesty, Queen Myrisha, received your letter," Delmont announced, holding his gaze on Juniper. He wore a dire seriousness that she didn't remember him having before. "She has sent a number of battlemages, sentinels, and foot soldiers, as well as supplies and her good wishes."

"And we have nothing but gratitude," Juniper said. She had seen the supply wagons. They would likely contain food and goods.

"We are not great in number, but the battlemages and sentinels are a valuable asset to any war," Delmont said formally. A recitation.

"I agree," Juniper said.

She would not complain about the numbers, though she knew others would. Myrisha had given what she could, and for that, Juniper felt immensely grateful.

They were family, after all, as strange as that thought was.

"Now," Delmont said, leaning back in his chair. His leisurely self returned. "I suppose you have more to explain? You left quite a few gaps in your story."

Over tea and jam, they told him what had happened. Delmont sat quiet through it all, taking in every detail.

"So, we're waiting for Nexon to arrive," Juniper said at last. Giving her story words somehow made it smaller, though it felt far larger in her mind.

If their story worried Delmont, he didn't show it. He asked, "Any plans?"

"If we take Nexon out as soon as possible, it will minimize casualties," Juniper said, which she knew wasn't a real plan, but it was all she had.

"Yes," Delmont said, tentatively.

"And when I made that plan, I didn't think I'd have three other archmages," she said defensively. "I haven't had the time to think of something new."

Delmont considered his tea and the earthenware cup. "Nexon has a thousand years of battle strategy, an unknown number of brainwashed followers, and black magic. We have two archmages" —he motioned to himself and Juniper— "and two archmages barely out of infancy." He motioned to Reid and Lilianna.

"I have been teaching the druid warriors anti-magic," Reid said. "They are not as trained as the knights or sentinels, but it is more than nothing."

Delmont nodded in approval. "I would like to see how they are progressing. I propose we ask the sentinels to assist with their training and for the battlemages to assist in training the defected mages. We need all the able bodies we can afford."

"It gives us more time to find Nexon and end him before the casualties stack too high," Juniper said.

Because there would be casualties. Denying it would be foolish.

"And these…Shadows… They are yours?" Delmont asked Lilianna. "They listen to your command and report back to you?"

"They are an extension of my magic," Lilianna said with much more confidence than before.

"And the one with wings?" Delmont's brows rose. "It is different than the others."

"Moss has always been different. He's more sentient than the others. He doesn't blindly follow my orders."

"That is interesting," Delmont said. "And how long have you known Moss?"

Lilianna blinked. "Years. He was in Angyla's care before mine, and…" Her eyes widened.

"I speculate he's not a Shadow, but a wechun," Delmont said. "Juniper has found hers hiding in the lake, and you found yours hiding in the woods."

"Do you have one?" Juniper asked.

Delmont shook his head. "I've never managed to find it. My uncle before me hadn't been able to find it either. I suspect it went with the archmage before him across the seas to the south. He died and the next archmage was born, and the wechun hasn't found its way back to this continent. Knowing the ways of magic, it's likely hiding in the heart of a volcano. I have no desire to go swimming in lava to find it."

Juniper glanced at Reid. He would have a wechun too. By the subtle shift of his masked expression, he had come to that conclusion as well.

"Nexon doesn't have his wechun," Juniper told Delmont. "I killed it."

"Before you knew what it was or what Nexon was." Delmont tipped his tea to Juniper. "That is luck."

The meeting ended, and their plans began in earnest. Reid went with Delmont to speak with the sentinels and battlemages.

Juniper retreated to a tower that overlooked the front garden and the main street of the Dead City. Delmont's forces had taken the buildings outside the gates, next to the mages. Soldiers and druids and mages helped carry supplies into the castle and into the house. The main streets bustled with people. It felt...normal. To see the city alive.

She imagined how it would have looked twenty years before, or fifty, or even one hundred, the homes bright with magelight, the shops decorated with banners and streamers, people coming and coming.

A light snow began to fall, unopposed by the still winds.

"Well?" Lilianna came to stand beside Juniper.

"It feels like hope," she said. "And yet I know we are still horribly outmatched. I have a feeling this hope I'm feeling now will wither into dread when Nexon arrives."

Juniper leaned away from the balcony's edge. The snowfall thickened. She felt it in the air, in the sky, gathering on roof edges and windowsill.

"I want to show you something," Lilianna said. "My Shadows found something in the royal grounds during their patrol last night."

"Is it another army?" Juniper half-laughed. "I'd even take a goblin army. Nip at ankles and jab at kneecaps."

"No. It is not an army."

Juniper waited for Lilianna to elaborate. When she didn't, Juniper conceded. "All right. Lead away."

CHAPTER 41

Lilianna led Juniper through the servant's passage in the royal wing, down through the narrow passages, through the kitchens and into the royal grounds. The fresh snow turned untamed forest crystalline. Druid magic kept the planter boxes free of white. The snow vanished before it came too close, leaving the vibrant herbs to grow as if it were summer. Lilianna led her past the planter boxes and into the dense forest.

"It never snowed within the walls," Lilianna said, speaking of the old druid village. She tilted her face to the sky. Snowflakes peppered her green skin. "We were not allowed into the Wylds when it snowed."

"Galamond, the kingdom to the north, is nothing but snow," Juniper said. As they trekked deeper into the untouched snowy woods, Juniper told her about how she had been overtaken in the blizzard and nearly frozen to death.

"A poetic end," Lilianna added. "You, freezing to death."

Juniper harrumphed. When she faced Nexon, she would most certainly not be freezing to death. He would have something horrible in mind.

Lilianna guided her away from the castle, and soon the icy trees and snowy brush blocked her sight of it. The snow dampened all other sound, and Juniper imagined walking in a never-ending forest of ice and snow, alone and free of impending demise.

The walk ended in a small, snow-covered clearing. A massive tree grew at the base of the clearing, its towering boughs as large as a house and its trunk as thick as a tower. Thick roots weaved in and out of the snowy ground. Tucked at the base of the tree, hugged by roots, was a stone shrine. A light layer of snow graced the surface.

Juniper climbed through the roots to the shrine and brushed snow from the stone. Someone had engraved the stone with Bera's constellation. A wooden figure lay at the base of the shrine, weathered and worn, but unmistakable. It was Bera, in her hooded robes and holding a key. The edges had worn, and the hand holding the key was gone. Juniper sat it upright before the constellation.

Though the depictions of Bera often showed her holding a key, the goddess had held nothing when Juniper met her in the Spirit Gate.

"That is…?" Lilianna knelt over the shrine.

"Bera, goddess of shadow," Juniper said, standing. "Notorious patron to thieves."

"Ah," Lilianna started. "She is your patron. I heard the mages talking of this patron of the shadow. You were born under her stars."

"I was."

"I don't understand your gods," Lilianna said. "There are far too many of them."

"Druids don't have gods?"

"We do, I suppose. Not in the same sense as yours. We see nature as our god, a spirit of what grows. From that spirit, we learned the song of life." Lilianna took careful steps away from the shine and motioned toward the icy trees. "We do not build shrines or worship stone. The spirit of nature is everywhere, under our feet and in our lungs. Constantly and unbidden."

Like *bones*.

The thought stirred a memory, of the temple of the gods at the crown of the world, of the mural of stars and bones.

"Under our feet and over our heads," Juniper whispered. In the space between one heartbeat and the next, it made perfect sense. In the next, it did not.

Juniper stood, unwilling to boggle her already foggy brain with philosophy and theology. If she survived Nexon, she'd ponder the gods.

"I wish I could fight like you," Lilianna said absently. Her golden eyes were forlorn. "I do not want to hide behind my Shadows, but I have little choice. I can't hold a blade and feel my magic at the same time. It...divides my attention."

Juniper gathered the snow from Bera's shrine, tightened it into a ball, and lobbed it at her friend. The snowball hit her cheekbone, shattering into a spray of fresh snow.

Lilianna gasped and jumped back a step, then a greenish wind whisked the snow off her face. She stared at Juniper.

"Your reflexes *have* gotten a bit shabby," Juniper said matter-of-factly.

"Cheap shot," Lilianna said, unable to keep the grin off her face.

"The basics of combat include awareness," Juniper teased. She pulled three more snowballs from the ground by magic. "I learned to fight to survive, then I learned to add magic. Just like you. I integrated magic into what I already knew. I have steel, but I also have ice. You know steel, and now you have air."

Lilianna charmed a breeze to flutter through the clearing, whisking loose snow into graceful arcs.

Juniper hurled one of the snowballs at Lilianna. The druid girl moved, but not fast enough. The snowball burst at her shoulder.

"A cheap shot can kill you just as well as a skilled shot." Juniper plucked another snowball from the ground. It danced around with the other two. "I can count the fights I won because of a cheap shot. Fighting isn't all about honor and glory; it's about surviving."

A knowing smile crept over Lilianna's lips.

"What?"

"You and Reid," Lilianna said. "You have different ideas of winning."

Juniper hurled another snowball, and then a second right after. Lilianna dodged the first one, but the second hit her thigh. Juniper threw the third. Lilianna dodged, rolled, and as she righted herself, threw a snowball at Juniper.

They abandoned the root-infested clearing for the cover of the forest, hurtling snowballs at one another and laughing themselves breathless. The frigid air stung Juniper's throat and her lungs. It leeched the warmth from her skin and chilled her blood. Lilianna's emerald cheeks paled and turned a shade of rose, yet her golden eyes shone with childish fun.

This was what they had needed. Not more strategy, not battle plans, not dread or panic—fun. There had been a steep lack of fun in Juniper's life the past year. Everything had gotten worse and worse, never better. She needed a good laugh and a healthy dose of fun. By the breathless laughter coming from Lilianna, she needed the same.

Juniper took a snowball to the chest, and another to her thigh, then doubled over laughing. She laughed hard enough to empty her lungs. She was laughing so hard, she didn't hear the footsteps approach until a glint of silver caught on her peripheral. Reid stood between two trees, expression unreadable, looking between the two girls.

Juniper straightened. "You missed it."

"A snowball fight?" Reid asked, tone as masked as his face.

Juniper coughed against her dry throat and tried to command her features into seriousness. "Training."

"And if one of you gets frostbite?"

"I won't allow that to happen." Juniper set her hands on her hips. "Did you need something?"

Reid turned his gaze to Lilianna. "Delmont is looking for you. He wants to go over strategies involving your Shadows."

Lilianna sighed, and her girlish delight faded back into seriousness. She waved farewell and started the trek back to the castle. Moss bounded from the forest, covered in a layer of snow, and trailed after.

In her absence, the silence strained between Juniper and Reid. She didn't feel like going back to the castle, not with the snow looking so beautiful and the royal grounds feeling so calm.

"Want to try your hand at besting me?" Juniper taunted, plucking a few snowballs from the falling snow. "I happen to be excellent on the throwing field."

Reid blinked at her, expression unchanged.

Her bravado fractured. She dropped the snowballs; they plodded at her feet. She added softly, "It might help you get a handle on your magic."

"Xavier has been helping." Reid held out his hand. A sword of golden energy manifested. It glowed against Reid's silver armor and glinted off the snowflakes, making each appear as a fleck of gold.

"Oh, well, obviously he has done a good job," Juniper said, motioning to the energy sword. She knew Reid meant her no harm in his words, but it stung. He didn't need her help. He had Xavier.

"Using it helps." Reid turned the sword over, examining the edges. "Xavier said energy is strange. Most mages can bottle their magic and be all right, but energy is the opposite. It builds up and threatens to drown the mage."

"And you're doing better," Juniper said.

He was more coherent and less distant, like the surly squire she had met almost two years ago. The wild and panicked look in his eyes had gone. He was calm, assured, and capable.

"But," Juniper started, taking a step closer, "fighting with one energy mage is one thing. You will be facing mages of all elements. Are you prepared?"

Reid hesitated, and Juniper hurled the snowball she'd been building behind her back. It burst against his temple. He jumped back, his blade flickered, and he looked at her with wide, surprised eyes. Snow clung to his brow and his nose.

She bit her lip to keep from laughing. "You need to work on your reflexes."

Reid blinked, then brushed the snow from his face. A subtle smile appeared on his lips. He adjusted his footing and his grip on his energy blade. In his off-hand, a golden shield appeared.

"Try that again," he said, his voice a rumble.

And the battle began. She hurtled snowball after snowball at him, ducked and dodged, and he blocked them with his shield or caught them in a net of energy and lobbed them back at her. Juniper jumped over frozen creeks, snow covered bushes, and even a frozen pond over which a thick layer of snow had gathered.

She found herself laughing, each breath gasping in the frozen air, puffing white steam. Reid didn't laugh as much, but in those moments when she saw him, he was smiling.

She made to run alongside the frozen pond, but a snowball whizzed past her head. She threw her weight to the side, and landed on the iced-over pond. A thread of panic seared—the ice held. She felt it—the ice ran deep enough to hold her and Reid. She rolled back onto her feet and started across the pond.

"You forfeit your cover?" Reid started onto the ice, testing it with tentative steps. He held his shield high, hiding all but his molten eyes.

"I believe you are forfeiting *your* cover," Juniper said. "We're surrounded by ice. If I were to will it, the ice would open and swallow you whole. I don't know how long it takes for a person to freeze to death in such cold waters."

"You would do that to me?"

She grinned wickedly. "Of course."

His brows rose.

She banished the humor from her face and said matter-of-factly, "Everyone knows that when you're submerged in freezing waters, you must promptly take off your clothes. That includes armor."

Reid's surprise melted into something warmer and darker. He continued to approach, footsteps assured on the ice. Juniper stood her ground. As a playful threat, she gathered the snow into two tendrils and waved them at him. The space between them shrank until she could feel the glow of his energy. His magic nudged her own, the question and desire and apology laid bare. Juniper tugged back, acceptance of all three. She commanded ice up and over them and formed a cloudy blue dome. The snowfall graced the surface and turned the sunlight velvety blue. All else ceased save for the two of them.

Reid's sword and shield evaporated, and he pulled Juniper into a breathless, desperate kiss. Their magic twined together, their very beings threading. Juniper willed the water in the air to steam, yet the surface of the ice and the dome remained solid and frozen. She grasped for the buckles of his armor; he lined her jaw with kisses and tugged at the strings of her corset.

Tendrils of velvet soft energy snaked under the hem of her dress, up her legs, along her thighs, and a gasp escaped her throat—Reid smiled against her lips. Between his magic and his hands, she had no space for thought or breath for words.

Her dress fluttered to the ground, his armor fell away, and they tumbled back in a tangle of magic and limbs. Juniper expected the bite of ice on her bare back, but instead she felt velvet soft warmth—golden energy formed a blanket between her and the ice.

Before she could think any more about it, his lips took hers. His hands tangled in her hair, and he was inside her. In all of their lovemaking, he had never been as wild, leaving her capable of only gasping his name. Stars danced across her vision, and she forgot about the castle or the army marching or anything else that wasn't Reid.

The energy beneath her never wavered, never flickered. It remained strong as steel and soft as cotton. The only flicker came as Reid gasped into her neck; his hot breath sounded faintly like her name.

Juniper, not *Isolde*.

After, he rolled onto his back and she nestled in his arm, resting her chin on his chest.

"Gods," Reid breathed. He absently stroked her hair.

"I am very curious as to what Xavier has been teaching you," she said, grinning. Her own breathlessness surprised her.

Reid laughed, and the sound warmed her entire being. It reminded her of just how long it had been since she'd heard him laugh.

A distant horn sounded.

"That is lunch." Reid sat up, placed a warm kiss against her lips, and then helped her to feet. "As much as I'd rather stay here with you, we will both be missed."

She agreed, on both accounts. They dressed, dismissed their magic, and Juniper tried to make the pond look as though it hadn't hosted them. A small indention remained where the dome had been, but as they started back to the castle arm in arm, she decided not to care.

CHAPTER 42

The next several days passed in a blur. Juniper spent her mornings with Delmont, Ison, and Lilianna, planning and plotting a battle strategy. She spent her afternoons training with Lilianna and the mages. The poison's effect ebbed with each day, each potion she drank. Ison crafted a number of new concoctions, as instructed by the wechun, who said magic needed to be stretched like any other muscle.

"Use it, and you will be strong," the wechun had said. "Hide it, and you will be weak."

That Juniper knew. She had spent her childhood hiding her magic and pretending not to be a mage. When she finally called upon it, she barely summoned enough to protect herself.

She trained with Reid, who improved a little more every day. He had come a long way since waking up in the cavern, yet Delmont insisted he had a long way yet to go. Reid could wield a blade of energy magic as if it were steel. He continued to wear his Mage's Bane, despite not needing it.

The druids and mages could summon wards and cast small deflections and disruptions.

Juniper fell into Reid's arms every night, and he practiced his control of magic on her skin.

Juniper retreated to her courtyard off the royal chambers that overlooked the royal grounds. Below, druids tended the gardens. Their haunting song drifted upward, muted by the snow. The sunset had turned the cloudy sky shades of salmon and lavender. The fading light glittered off the snowy grounds, making it seem as though the forest was made not of earth and wood but of gold and silver.

Reid had gone to train with the sentinels and druid warriors. Lilianna and her Shadows patrolled and ran strategy with Delmont. Ison and Xavier worked with the mages and battlemages.

It offered Juniper a moment of peace. Her wechun remained in the shadows of the awning, so she wasn't really alone.

She waited for her mother's ghost to appear, or her sister, or anyone—no one did. Even the ghosts had gone.

The sun sank further behind the trees. The sky deepened, and the forest turned black and silver. The clouds nearest the western horizon were striped with cornflower blue and pink while the eastern sky had faded into star-studded indigo.

How long had it been since she had been able to watch the sunset?

"You are reminiscing," whispered the wechun. It padded to the edge of the courtyard and peered at the grounds.

"When we went to the edge of the realm," Juniper said, eyes on the bruised clouds. "The mountain trail went above the clouds. It was incredible. The sun shone over them like a blanket of gold. The sky went on forever. It was another world."

"I would rather stay under the clouds," said the wechun.

"There are plenty of shadows up there," Juniper said. "There was a city, completely abandoned. Dire wolves live there."

"Ah," said the wechun in its knowledgeable voice. "The ancient people of the clouds."

Juniper looked over her shoulder. "Do you know about them?"

"I know old legends," it said. "Legends that were ancient and dusty a thousand years ago. Legends of people who once lived high above the world in a stone city. They lived as servants to the gods, as messengers and scouts."

She waited for the rest of the story. When it didn't come, she asked, "What happened to them?"

"It is a mystery lost to time," the wechun said. "Not even the Iluvin scholars knew, and they knew much. Some speculated they simply died out. Others suggest it was the typical human problems such as pride that led to war, disease, or famine."

Juniper sighed. "That's not a very good ending."

"Not all endings can be good."

The sun sank behind the western horizon and took the last of its light with it. Moonlight and darkness sank into the world, and a hush fell over the grounds. The druids retreated into the castle with their baskets full of herbs and spices and fruit. Magelights brightened, sparkling through the woven shutters of the castle. Every night, more and more windows held light. From the courtyard, Juniper couldn't see the glow of the kitchen, but she could imagine it. The druids would be busy with dinner.

"How are you feeling?" whispered the wechun.

"How do you mean?"

"The poison."

"Much better," Juniper said. "I'm still nervous about Nexon, but at least now we have more soldiers and I'm stronger."

"Your friends are also stronger," it said. "I've watched you train."

Juniper tossed it an arrogant smirk. "And you've never seen anyone more intimidating, yes?"

The wechun hesitated. Its ears flattened.

She slumped. "I know, we're struggling."

It didn't comment, so she assumed she'd guessed right.

It padded closer, paws soft on the stone. "I have lived a long time. I have seen tyrants and kings and upstarts clash and vie for scraps of power. I have seen people rise against their rulers. I have seen rebellions and riots. More often than not, the strongest army vanquishes over the smaller, even if the smaller is clever."

Juniper sighed dramatically. "I'm the clever one, I know."

The wechun snorted.

A northern breeze ushered in a frigid chill, and Juniper returned to the castle. The wechun walked behind her. It had remained on four legs, and its features had become even more wolf-like. The fur of its belly had spread down its legs and up its back, shining strands of emerald and sapphire. Its pointed ears twitched toward sounds she didn't hear.

Most others would be wandering down to the dining hall for dinner, but she had no appetite.

She wanted to be Juniper, a no one who could vanish into the shadows.

Someone had cleaned her chambers. The bed linens were straightened. A fire roared in the hearth, licking fresh logs, and a fresh decanter of berry wine set on the vanity. The whole room smelled like the mint oil the druids used to clean, mixed with a fresh floral scent of magic. Underneath it, lavender and honeysuckle.

Just like home.

No, that place hadn't been home. Not really.

Juniper meandered inside, set on a glass of berry wine.

"You haven't sorted the closet," the wechun reminded her. "You said you would."

"I've been busy, and…" She sighed. It didn't matter if she lied, so she didn't. "It feels odd to go through my parents' things. Especially when I'm probably going to die in a few days."

"Ah." The wechun curled under the window. "It will give you something to occupy your mind, other than your impending demise."

She'd mentioned cleaning out the closet when she had been resting off the poison. She'd been bored, and it had been something to think about other than Nexon's inevitable approach. As much as she didn't want to go through her parents' things, she didn't want to think about Nexon either.

She went first to the decanter of berry wine, needing the sweet boost. She poured a generous amount into the crystal goblet and drank deeply. Her gaze drifted to the polished quartz of the vanity, the shined mirror, the intricate metalwork of the mirror's frame. Her gaze drifted to the worn rune on the wall, the one near where her mother had died.

She'd forgotten about it. Juniper gravitated toward it again and pressed her hand against it. Nothing happened.

The wechun crept to her side. It looked at the wall, then her.

"There's a rune here," Juniper explained. She pulled her hand away. "It's too worn."

"Worn or disguised?"

She frowned, "Disguised?"

It tilted its head. "It's a rune in the king's bedroom. You wouldn't want just anyone wandering inside and finding secrets."

"How does one disguise a rune?"

"The Iluvin had a thousand ways to hide a rune," the wechun explained. "The most common was with blood. A drop of blood would seal the rune to all but those with that blood. Other ways needed passwords, a melody, or a series of touches."

"Blood?" Juniper eyed the rune. If her father, or any of her ancestors, had sealed the rune with blood, hers should work.

"It *might* be blood. Blood magic is tricky. The Iluvin were…careful about it."

"Like Nexon's beasts?"

It snorted. "That is bad blood magic."

Juniper summoned a small knife of ice and nicked her forearm. Blood beaded. She wiped the bead of blood with a finger and pressed it against the rune. At first, nothing happened, but then the rune began to glow. It started faint, then it sucked the blood off her finger. Blood filled the grooves of the rune, the design madly intricate, and then the entire thing glowed crimson.

A click sounded from within the stone, and her heart jumped into her throat. The wechun took a step back, and her own apprehension tightened into dread.

The hidden door slid inward, grinding stone on stone. Darkness pooled on the other side.

The wechun hissed in relief.

"Why worried?" She flashed it a smug grin.

"If you hadn't shared blood with whoever had made that rune, you would have been pulled through the door and locked inside, or incinerated, or whatever horrible punishment the rune-making devised," it snapped, a reprimand.

She blinked. "And you couldn't have said that first?"

"You would have tried regardless."

She couldn't argue with that. She would have. She stepped inside and blinked until her night sight adjusted. It was a small room between the bathing room and the sitting room and the study, and until then Juniper hadn't questioned the walls of the space. This space had been cleverly hidden with the walls between. But that worry quickly evaporated. One wall held shelves, and upon those shelves were artifacts, engraved and jeweled, and encrusted with precious metals. Daggers, goblets, plates, brooches—small but priceless treasures.

She was looking at the treasures, and she almost missed the thicker shadow in the corner of the hidden room. A narrow staircase spiraled down through the stone. Juniper took a deep breath, then started down. Her magic led the way. She kept one hand on the smooth walls. The wechun followed a safe step behind.

The stairs led into a dark chamber with no windows or doors.

"Gods," Juniper gasped.

She had stumbled upon a treasure trove. Piles of coins of gold, silver, and bronze; gleaming gemstones the size of her fists; ceremonial armor of centuries past; thick golden chains; brooches and pins; rings and tiaras; and more wealth than she had ever seen. One shelf held a number of curious trinkets, including a plain wooden box. It looked so out of place among the gemstones and jewelry, that it was to the box Juniper gravitated. She lifted it from its resting place. The wood was dark with a silvery hue. It might have once been painted.

She tried to open it, but the lid didn't budge. She gently shook it, and a mechanism rattled.

"It looks like an Iluvin puzzle box," said the wechun. "Think of it as a box with ten thousand possible combinations. In the tradition of the eastern cities, a puzzle box was gifted as a test of strength, intelligence, and ability. They were gifted to anyone who needed to prove themselves, though traditionally they were given as engagement gifts."

"Engagement gifts?"

"A ring or cuff was inside," the wechun said, sniffing the box. "If one could solve the puzzle and retrieve the gift, then the engagement was announced. If not, they would not marry."

"A cuff?"

It tilted his head. "A cuff, for the wrist."

"I know what it is, but who proposed with a cuff?"

"Men wore cuffs rather than rings," the wechun said. "If one proposed marriage to a man, it was done with a cuff, not a ring—though some men wore rings, and some women wore cuffs. Typically of silver or gold, unadorned."

Juniper examined the box. Had one of her parents proposed to the other with his box?

A flash—she saw the same box with the lid open, a silver cuff resting against the lush velvet interior. She blinked, and the image vanished.

"Hmm?" The wechun eyed her curiously.

"I saw…" She hesitated. Had that vision been a ghost? Something else? "Never mind."

"A curious old legend told of one puzzle box given to a young woman of lower society by a prince," it said, swishing its tail. "His parents were against the marriage, for she was just a poor girl. So they stole the ring from within it and replaced it with the finger of a child. It was meant to frighten the girl away, but it backfired. The prince was horrified at what his parents had done, and he and the girl ran away together."

"And they lived happily ever after?" Juniper finished, though she phrased it as a question.

It cocked its head. "That is where the legend ends. Imagine whatever end your heart desires. I said not all stories end well, but some do."

Juniper turned the box over and over. It appeared solid. She saw no latches, switches, or anywhere a combination might go.

The wechun slunk around the chamber, around a pile of gold larger than her bed. It glanced up at the stairwell. "You should return before someone enters your chambers and finds this place. You did leave the door open. Gold makes humans do foolish things."

Juniper, box in hand, headed back to her room. The wechun followed at her heels.

"Did you know this place was here?" Juniper asked as the secret door closed again.

"I might have," it said. It curled up on the bearskin rug. "I have lived many years and served many masters. I have spent a considerable amount of time in these halls. I know many of their secrets."

Her attention perked. "You mean there are more secrets?"

It didn't answer, but it looked like it was grinning.

CHAPTER 43

Ison sat alone in his workshop, scribbling into the strange book. He had never seen or heard of anything like it, and he found the concept of an enchanted book fascinating. He had been careful not to write anything incriminating or telling. In case there was a way to recover anything within it, he didn't want to reveal anything.

He had discovered that he could write within the book as much as he wanted. He didn't have to wait for a response. When he closed the book and opened it again, everything he wrote vanished. He didn't have to write words either. Any ink vanished, accidental splotches, slashes, or dots. The book didn't always respond, but it seemed more apt in the evenings after full dark.

He wrote mostly lists, herbs and spices, potions that needed to be crafted, and books he wished he had.

Every word vanished.

The druids were busy in the kitchens, and the clatter of pots and pans and dishes served as an odd comfort. Ison knew he wasn't alone. If he shouted, someone would hear.

Ison stared at his latest words as the ink dried, and curiosity got the better of him. *Do you exist within the pages?*

A long moment passed, and then words appeared in slanted handwriting, the same that always wrote back: *I do not.*

Ison considered those words. Whoever was writing did not exist within the pages? He leaned closer and scribbled, *Are you a person?*

Of course I am a person.

Ison dipped his nib into the ink. Before he could write another word, the slanted writing appeared.

I assume you are a stranger to not know such a thing.

Ison swallowed. *I am.*

How did you stumble upon my journal's second half?

I found it, Ison wrote. He hesitated, then added, *on a battlefield.*

A long moment passed.

Ison felt a prick of panic, and added, *Everyone was dead. I thought this was a regular book. I meant no disrespect. I am merely curious as to this book's nature.*

An honest, if not ignorant, mistake.

Ison had assumed the book's previous owner dead, but he didn't know who it had been. He wrote, *Who used to have this book?*

A long moment passed, and Ison thought the book had decided not to answer.

Then, the words appeared. *A dear friend of mine.*

Ison wrote the only thing he could, *I'm sorry for your loss.*

It is fine. It is better for this book to be in new hands than to be rotting on a battlefield. Tell me, did you see the battle?

Ison thought about lying, but then how else would he have found the book? *Yes,* he wrote.

Did you fight?

To be honest, he hadn't fought very much. He had signaled the betrayal, and then he had done his best not to die. So he stretched the truth and wrote, *No.*

How did you manage to escape the fighting?

I am not a warrior.

Then what are you?

A simple mage.

Even a simple mage must understand what that battle represented. The loss on that field signaled what mages have been facing for hundreds of years. Persecution.

Ison blinked at those words. What did they think had happened? He started to write back, but then understood. This book had belonged to one of Nexon's followers, who believed strongly in magic's superiority, and whoever wrote in this book believed the same. It was likely another of Nexon's followers.

At Ison's prolonged silence, the slanted handwriting appeared again. *Do you not think so?*

I don't know what I think.

Confused? That is understandable. Mages are given mixed messages from the day they are born. We are told how special and powerful we are, but we are taught to cower and look down. We are pushed down because we are powerful, and the common man fears magic. They fear mages.

Ison sat reading those words—his pen dripped onto the page. The blotch sank into the fibers and dried.

A tear of ink? Of hesitation?

Ison wrote, *Hesitation.*

If you are near the battlefield, you hold a particular position. It is also a dangerous one. You are near the enemy. One arrow from the dark could end this war before it begins. The master would be pleased. He wouldn't be able to deny you a pardon.

Ison swallowed. *Who?*

The girl who claims to be Isolde Balendn. She is a liar, a thief, and a murderer. The world would be better off without her.

Ison set his pen aside. This conversation confirmed his suspicions; he spoke to one of Nexon's followers. He would never kill Juniper, of course, but he didn't know if the other mages felt the same. Luckily, they had given him the book. He couldn't imagine what a suggestion would do in the mind of someone conflicted about their desertion.

He wanted to close the book and be done with it, but if he ended it here, what would the other person think?

He wrote, *I will consider it.*

Stay safe, friend.

Ison waited for the ink to dry, then closed the book. He opened the book to make sure the words had gone, and only blank pages remained.

He pushed it to the other side of the desk and leaned forward, running his hand through his hair. He heard footsteps, and then a soft knock on his workshop door. Before he could acknowledge it, Delmont Thacket let himself in.

"Ah, here is the potion master," Delmont said, shutting the door. He set a small, covered basket on the worktable. "I have been tasked with bringing this to you. Juniper's wechun asked. It is dust from stones that haven't seen the sun in centuries."

Ison sat up straight. "Oh!"

"You sound much more thrilled than I was," Delmont said. "Is this dust that special?"

"It's rare and useful." Ison took the basket and set it in the dark cabinet. He didn't want to ruin the dust by accidentally whisking it too close to the magelight. "Thank you."

Delmont lingered, gazing around the workshop. "It is a bit small in here. You could use an addition. I'm sure the earth mages could move the back wall. It would provide more space for the clutter."

Ison bristled. He hadn't spoken much with Delmont, and he didn't like the way the archmage spoke to others. He held himself tall and proud, and he spoke with superiority. When he spoke to Juniper, he stemmed his arrogance, but to everyone else he came across as unimpressed and bored. As if everyone else was beneath him.

"I'll consider it," Ison said. He didn't bother to be annoyed.

Delmont took a lap of the space, keeping his hands laced behind his back. He walked like a soldier, but with a swagger, like a man who knew his own power. Ison didn't like him. He paused by the table of old flasks and burners, eyeing it skeptically.

"Do you need anything else?" Ison asked.

Delmont glanced at Ison as if he had forgotten he was there, which only made Ison angrier.

"I've work that needs to be done, and you're in the way," Ison said.

"Does my presence bother you?" Delmont straightened.

"Slightly."

Delmont half-laughed. "To be honest, I'm avoiding that blonde girl. She seems a little too eager to sit on my lap. The wechun asked me to deliver this, and I gladly accepted."

Blonde girl... "Mabyl?"

Delmont shrugged. "I haven't gotten her name."

"Yet you're bragging about her wanting you," Ison said. With every word shared between them, he liked Delmont less and less. "Without even knowing her name."

Delmont eyed Ison. "Have I done something to offend?"

Ison steeled himself. "I am no servant, and I request you not speak to me as one. You might be the Archmage of Fire, and used to sitting beside a throne, but you are no better than anyone else here."

Delmont blinked, unashamed. "My apologies. I was unaware of how I was coming across. I did not mean ill by it. I suppose it is something I have gotten used to."

Ison frowned. "You're used to talking down to others?"

Delmont shrugged, and at least he had the decency to look sheepish. "It comes from being an archmage. The power comes with a degree of isolation. I am not part of casual society, and can't be. I will outlive any friends I make, and taking the time to befriend you will be another funeral I'll eventually have to attend. Even among the few other Iluvin, I am different. They separate themselves from me."

Ison didn't want to think about his own funeral, but he supposed he understood. Delmont, as Iluvin Archmage, would live for several centuries.

"I have already attended far too many funerals for my liking," Delmont said. "And, when people know the power I hold, they tend to shy away from speaking to me like a person. It's been a long while since I've..." He motioned for the words.

"Made friends?"

"I suppose that describes it," Delmont said. His lips fell into a straight line.

"But you have Juniper, Lilianna, and Reid, now."

"That I do." Delmont's expression turned a shade happier. "And I would be lying if I said I wasn't glad to have others."

Ison reclined back in his chair.

Delmont's gaze scanned over the desk, and his eyes snagged on the enchanted book. Ison felt a prickle of panic. He didn't say anything at first, but his gaze turned a shade worried.

"What is that?" he asked.

"A book," Ison said too quickly. "Old recipes. I've been going through them."

Delmont came closer and without permission opened the book. He flipped through the empty pages.

"Interesting recipes," Delmont asked.

Ison had the worst feeling of being scolded. He didn't bother to lie. He had been caught, but that didn't mean he had to explain himself. Delmont held no authority over him.

"Do you know what this is?" Delmont asked.

Again, Ison remained silent.

"If it is what I think, that is. I assume you've written in it? Have the words vanished?"

"They vanished when I close it," Ison said.

"Does anyone write back?"

"Yes."

Delmont's gaze darkened. "Where did you find this?"

"It was recovered from the battlefield," Ison said, suddenly feeling foolish.

"Never write in it again," Delmont warned.

Ison started to argue.

"This is no ordinary book," Delmont said. "It is a scribe. The magic within is complex and ancient. I haven't seen one in this condition in…centuries. The Iluvin crafted them, and the art was lost with them."

"What does it do?"

"Scribes are for communication between two points, in this case, between two books." Delmont flipped through the blanket pages. "The Iluvin also used mirrors and plates of sand."

Ison paled. "Are you sure this is a scribe?"

"Yes. I recognize the enchantment. I have a scribe myself. It is a simple hand mirror. The other mirror is in Delphine."

"So you've been keeping Myrisha updated?"

"Yes," Delmont said. "It also allows me to ask for reinforcements should the need arise. It will be much faster than sending a scout."

216

Had Ison been standing, he would have collapsed. Lora had mentioned a way of communication with Nexon, old and complicated, but she had neglected to mention what or how. Ison had thought he had been writing to one of Nexon's followers, but what if he had been speaking to Nexon himself?

Delmont stiffened. "Are you positive you haven't told this book anything?"

Ison now understood Delmont's panic. "No, I've been testing it by writing lists of ingredients and potions. I didn't write names or places. I've been scarce with my words."

"Smart on you," Delmont said, frowning. "Gods only know who is on the other side. I think it is safe to assume the worst: Nexon has read every word."

"That is what I feared," Ison said.

"But that is the worst case," Delmont said. "Unlikely, but also likely. At that, I must take my leave. I have much to do before this battle begins. Farewell, Potion Master Ison."

Delmont's footsteps faded through the kitchen where dishes clanked in the sinks, bread baked, and berries became juice and wine.

Suddenly, Ison didn't want to be alone in his workshop. It reminded him of those afternoons of memory loss, of unexplained fatigue, of sluggishness, when Nexon had used him to create those beasts.

He could only hope he hadn't done something terrible.

CHAPTER 44

Adrian paced in the meeting room of the king's house. It was the top floor, the closest to the Undercity's ceiling, and made him feel as though he were away from the mess happening below. Jax stood outside the meeting room, silent as the death Adrian feared lay ahead of them. The Undercity light gleamed, faded, and gleamed as he paced from window to window. His most recent mental resistance lesson with Josephine had left him with a dull headache, and pacing seemed to help.

Everything had escalated so quickly. The knights were not only teaching their pledges how to wield a sword and shield, but now taught them how to command unnatural magic. The word had spread far faster than the knights would have liked, and mages and commoners alike flocked to learn how to grasp magic.

Adrian feared what this meant for the kingdom after this war was over.

"You're wearing the floor," came Roslyn's voice. She swept inside the meeting room like a huntress, elegant and ready to fight. She sat at the table. Her guard remained outside the room with Jax.

"I can't sit still," Adrian admitted. He returned to his pacing. "I just... Everything is happening too fast. We have no idea how many enemies linger in the castle or how many will have to face. We have few skilled fighters, and fewer still whom I trust not to betray us."

"It's perfectly natural to be nervous, Adrian."

"I'm not just nervous. This... This feels different."

"Different how?"

He paused at the window that overlooked the Commons where criminals, knights, and children shared space and food. "I fear what happens next. I fear there is no coming back from this."

Roslyn started to speak, then drew her words back in. "This isn't just about the siege, is it?"

Adrian ran a hand through his hair, tugging at the strands over the dull headache. "No. I don't know. Maybe."

"Talk to me, love."

He heaved a sigh. "Magic has always been something that could be locked away. I could...pretend it didn't exist. That I didn't have to worry about it or those who could use it. Magic is dangerous and strange, and now that it is so widely available... I don't like this."

Roslyn bit her lip. Her fingers toyed with her sleeve under the table.

He didn't wait for her next question. "Magic was always something that didn't affect me. The knights protected us from it. They made sure only good mages existed. And now, Amery can use magic. Maddox will be teaching magic to all of his thieves, you know it. What can we do against that?"

"Good people are learning magic too," Roslyn said. "The City Watch. The Royal Guard. Common people."

"I don't like how it's suddenly everywhere," Adrian whispered. "I'm not a mage. I can barely understand Josephine's mental resistance lessons. What kind of king am I to become if I can't handle magic?"

Roslyn sat a little straighter. Her eyes, while kind and soft, bore through him. Understanding what he hadn't said. "You worry about what kind of king you are to become. You worry that magic will be a disadvantage for you, that magic will take advantage of you."

He flushed. Her words struck true. "I am."

"When you are king, you will not be alone. Just as you are not alone now. You will have people at your side, watching your back, and making sure that those people—the ones who would take advantage of you—never get close enough to." Her words were stern, but filled with warmth. "Henry. Reid. Me. Juniper. Whomever you appoint as your court magician. Advisers."

He slumped into the chair beside hers. "You're right. As always."

She flashed him a knowing grin. "You knew it, you just needed someone to remind you. Besides, you're not going to be king tomorrow. You have time to adjust. These times are trying on us all, and they will need a leader to get them through it."

"I love you." Adrian laced his fingers with hers, stopping her fidgeting.

"I love you," she said, squeezing his hand.

They leaned toward one another, but before their lips met, a knock sounded at the door. Adrian and Roslyn leaned away as the door opened. Jax entered, hand on his hilt and face barely containing shock.

"A messenger," Jax said. He swallowed. "For the king."

Adrian sat up straight and banished the worry from his posture. "They may enter, though it is just me."

A young man with vibrant green skin and golden eyes stepped into the meeting room. Adrian blinked twice, thinking it must be an effect of a rattled mind, but the green skin remained. The young man wore well-used and mismatched traveling leathers and old, graying wool. He pushed back his hood, and pointed ears jutted out from his messy brown hair.

Adrian didn't hold back his surprise. According to all the history books he had read, druids had died out. Yet he could think of nothing else the green-skinned young man could be.

Two guards stood behind the druid, looking on with skepticism.

Standing, Adrian asked, "Yes?"

The druid bowed his head, but only slightly. "I've been sent from Sinjon with a message for King Bentley Bradburn."

The druid spoke with an accent Adrian had never heard before.

"That is my father," Adrian said. "I can't say where he's gone at the moment."

The druid didn't seem to mind. He remained standing in front of Adrian, expectantly.

"Though, I suppose I could pass on your message," Adrian said. "As long as it's not dire."

Adrian held his posture while the druid told him about this faraway village of druids in the Blackwood Wylds, of how Juniper Thimble and Reid Sandpiper had stopped the spread of dark magic, and of how they had ventured north to the Dead City where they planned on meeting Nexon's forces.

Adrian struggled to maintain his princely posture. At the mention of his friends, alive and well and fighting, his heart swelled. That they were planning to meet Nexon's forces in a ruined city made his knees weak.

When the druid's message ended, a strange silence came over the room. Every pair of eyes looked at Adrian.

"I suppose we now know why Nexon took an army east," Adrian said darkly. "Thank you for bringing this message. Please, take a well-earned rest and something to eat. I will bring this to my father's attention."

The druid nodded and followed the guards down the stairs.

Adrian collapsed onto the chair beside Roslyn. She held herself like royalty, proper and alert, like nothing in the realm could shake her. If only Adrian could mimic his father's steadfastness, his command. Instead, he felt like he might faint if he stood. He knew he shouldn't feel nervous about the news. They had suspected Nexon's motives.

"Jun will be all right," Roslyn said. "She's a tough girl."

Adrian knew that. Everyone who had met Juniper knew that. "But an army of mages?"

Roslyn shrugged. Her lady's mask slipped for a tiny moment, and Adrian saw his worry mirrored underneath. Then it was gone, back underneath that mask. He grabbed Roslyn's hand and held it against his heart.

"We will have to hope and pray that Juniper and Reid know what they're doing," Adrian said. "Now, let's deliver this news to my father."

Adrian and Roslyn left the king's house for the knight's house. His father had gone to meet with the council. As they approached the house, Henry jogged out of it, dressed in his silver armor.

"Well, look who's come to bask in the fun of a meeting," Henry said. That goofy grin of his returned, though not as natural as it had once been. "You already look like you sat through one. Why so glum?"

"I'm looking for my father," Adrian said. "A druid messenger just brought me news of our friends in the west."

Henry's smile flattened.

"The king isn't here," Henry said. "He was, but he left. If he said where he was going, I didn't hear him. He might have gone to see Maddox."

Adrian didn't let it bother him. He didn't mind putting off the meeting a while longer, and the walk with Roslyn had been enjoyable.

"To Maddox's," Adrian said.

"I'll go with you," Henry said, jogging to stand with Jax and Roslyn's guard with one hand on his Mage's Bane. "So you won't be entering dangerous territory with just two guards."

So he wouldn't be entering a territory filled with criminals learning magic.

Adrian led the way through the commons, dodging the crowded streets. Somewhere between the Commons and Maddox's district, Adrian heard the first scream. He glanced around for the source, as did everyone else.

"What's happening now?" Henry asked in exasperation. His hand tightened on his blade.

Magic blasted several streets away, trembling the stony ground. A second scream sounded, of panic and warning.

Jax stepped closer to Adrian and turned his body, the better to protect.

Someone half-ran and half-fell around the far end of the block, flailing their arms as they stumbled. Adrian recognized her from the Commons; she was a former castle servant and helped cook.

Behind her, magic and steel collided in a frenzy.

"Attack!" the girl screamed.

Henry darted forward. She tripped, and Henry caught her before she fell.

"Easy," Henry said, his voice commanding but kind.

"Invasion," the girl said between gasps. "The north end. I—I thought they were knights. They were not! They attacked us! Thralls, sir, and mages behind them."

Henry's expression turned stony. To the girl, he said, "Tell Josephine at once."

The girl stumbled to her feet, then darted past them, her gait steadier than before. A crowd had gathered, and whispers of an attack quickly raged.

Henry drew his Mage's Bane. "You heard her." His voice boomed over the crowd. "We are under attack. Defend your home or find a place to hide."

Though no one on the street wore silver armor, swords were drawn.

"You," Henry pointed at a younger boy. "Run and tell Maddox, then spread the word to every corner of the Undercity. We will not be overtaken!"

The crowd echoed his enthusiasm with thunderous war cries. The sound reverberated in Adrian's bones and stirred the hope that they would be victorious. Beside him, Roslyn reached for the bow she wore everywhere. She pulled her hand from Adrian's to notch an arrow. He doubted she had any idea how attractive she looked.

Jax stepped closer to Adrian, sword drawn. Roslyn's guard moved with his back to hers, fighting back-to-back.

Everyone had a weapon drawn, ready to fight for their lives and their ramshackle homes...except for him. Adrian had nothing to defend himself with. Not even a dagger in his boot—he hated intrusive weight.

A clatter came around the corner—a man in bloodied silver armor marched around the corner with a blank, glassy-eyed expression.

"Thrall!" Henry roared, just as three more thralls marched around the corner. He rushed forward, and the small army on the street rushed alongside him.

They were not the puppet-like thralls Adrian had heard about. These thralls moved with precision and purpose—they were being controlled by someone who knew how to fight.

"Adrian, get back," Jax commanded.

He stumbled back a step, then regained his posture. As much as he wanted to help, he couldn't fight. He would only be in the way. Jax backed up with him, sword on the defensive, until they had cleared the fight.

Jax didn't relax. "I don't know where it's safe."

Adrian opened his mouth to speak, but the ground shifted under his feet. Jax turned on his heels, and in a swift motion, shoved Adrian's chest with all his strength. The wind rushed out of his chest, and he hit the stony ground just as earthen spikes thrust upward from the ground. Adrian scrambled back to his feet. The spikes spread, cutting him off from Jax.

Leaving him defenseless.

A masked mage emerged from an alley, eyes glittering with a vicious glint. In the street behind them, fire and air slammed together in a dizzying display. The mage stalked closer and drew stone from the ground. The stone sharpened into spikes.

"Adrian!" Jax called, desperately trying to find a way through the wall of spikes.

Adrian's heart thumped hard. Useless. He couldn't even defend himself.

The mage stalked closer.

A shadow shifted in the magelight, landing on the mage's shoulders. A swift slice, and the mage fell to the ground. The shadow rolled to her feet—it was the assassin girl, Blythe. She held twin daggers of Mage's Bane, both far too bloodied to have come from the mage's death.

Blythe looked over her shoulder at Adrian, eyes dark and distant.

"Thank you," Adrian said.

"You shouldn't be out here alone," Blythe said. Blood dripped from her daggers onto the ground.

"No, he shouldn't," came Roslyn's voice. She appeared from the opposite alley, Jax on her heels, both looking terrified. Blood splattered Roslyn's dress, but none looked like hers. "We need to move. Now. Your father is here, and he's calling for the siege right now."

Adrian's stomach turned over. "Now?"

"We're pushing back quickly. We hit them while they're reeling." Roslyn wore no fear.

If only Adrian could muster that same strength.

CHAPTER 45

Juniper reclined in bed, fiddling with the puzzle box. She ran her fingers over the edges and sides. She felt invisible seams in the wood, things that might have been notches if moved correctly, and panels that did not give. Occasionally, a part of the box would shift under pressure and her heart would skip. Nothing jingled when she shook the box, and despite its possible emptiness, she saw the box as a bank vault, and she had never let impossible security get in her way.

The wechun had refused to tell her any more secrets until she solved the box.

"Think of the box as a test of your cunning," it had said.

Maybe there was a silver cuff somewhere in the treasure room. Reid had already proposed, but so much had happened since that day. She wanted him to know she loved him and always would, regardless of their circumstances. Besides, he had proposed in order to get her out of the Marca. It had been rushed. He knew it, even if he didn't admit it.

A mage had brought a tray of food up to the room when Juniper hadn't appeared for dinner. The wechun had stolen the puzzle box and scolded her for not eating, and only after she had finished enough to satisfy it, did he give the box back. She had spent the last hour fiddling with it. Every time she thought she had discovered a path through its many moving parts, she hit a dead end.

The panels could slide in every direction, and she imagined the mechanism would only open with the right combination. It would take ages to figure it out.

At least the box had taken her mind off Nexon.

Reid returned late. He set his armor onto the stand, then vanished into the bathing room. He returned with a trimmed beard, wearing only a towel around his waist. Bathwater lingered in the hair on his defined chest. It glistened on his bronze skin as he passed the hearth. Juniper watched shamelessly as he walked to the closet. He dropped the towel and reached for the sleeping shirt he had worn the day before, draped over the chair. He started to pull it over his head, then noticed her stare. He paused.

"Yes?" he asked.

She feigned innocence. "I said nothing. Please, continue."

Reid hesitated, then returned the shirt to the chair. He sauntered into the bedroom without a stitch of clothing on, dark eyes pinned on Juniper.

He climbed onto the bed and took her mouth with his in a slow, passionate kiss. She reached for him with one hand, and with the other tried to set the puzzle box on the bedside table. She trailed her nails down his taut chest and to the defined muscles of his hips.

She missed the table, and the puzzle box clattered to the stone floor.

Reid pulled his mouth from hers. His eyes found the box at once. "What is that?"

"A puzzle box." She fumbled to pick it up. "I found it in the secret vault under our room."

Reid's brow creased.

In as few breaths as possible, she told him about the vault. As she spoke, his hand trailed lazy circles on her thigh.

"It's supposed to take a cunning mind to figure out how to open," she said. His hand circled a little higher. "And I accepted the challenge."

"Yet it's empty?"

"It won't be after I open it," she said. Her voice came out breathless. "And I'll have to hide something tantalizing inside it for the next person."

Reid's hand had gone a little higher with every heartbeat. His playful, husky tone implied he knew exactly what his hand teased. "What would you hide?"

She struggled to find her next thought. "Something pretty, maybe a gemstone or a treasure map that leads nowhere."

"That is a cruel trick," Reid said. His fingers brushed against her sex, and she let out a soft gasp. "For an adventurer to go so far without payoff."

She struggled to form her next thought with his fingers between her legs. He took the puzzle box from her hands and leaned across her to set it on her bedside table, and pressed a hot kiss to her mouth as he did so. He shifted as he maneuvered back onto the bed, situating himself between her knees. He pushed her nightdress to her hips.

"Reid—"

"You still have several things on that list of yours," he said, his tone husky and his eyes dark. "And I have yet to get you something for your birthday."

He paused, giving her the option of what she wanted to cross off that list. Truthfully, she didn't care what they crossed off. She was far too glad to have her Reid back. He could take her any way he pleased.

Reid trailed hot kisses down her inner thigh, all the way to where his fingers gently moved. She gasped as his tongue pressed against her, involuntarily gripping the sheets. She forgot about the puzzle box; she forgot about everything.

ARCHMAGE IN THE RUINS

The horn sounded at dawn. Juniper woke with gummy eyes and foggy thoughts. Reid slept curled around her, his chest pressed against her back. At first, she thought they had overslept, and pleasant thoughts of the night before swan back, of Reid pinning her to the bed, of his hot breath, of the ecstasy that had left her feeling wobbly.

The horn sounded a second time, and that feeling vanished.

Juniper's happiness flashed cold, a vicious cold that even Reid's warmth couldn't dispel. The horn sounded a third time, and her stomach shriveled and fell into her spine. Reid's arm tightened around her. His wide brown eyes met hers.

Three horns.

Something approached.

Without a word, they rose and dressed. Reid donned his armor with a straight face. If she hadn't known him better, she would not have seen through his knight's mask. Panic coursed underneath it, the same coursing through her own.

Ghostly gray light seeped between the shutters. The wechun unfurled itself from under the bed, its fur undulating as if made of water.

They rushed into the corridor just as Ison and Xavier fumbled out of their room, looking equally as panicked. Even Xavier's calm exterior looked shaken. Lilianna exited her chamber with Moss on her heels.

No one spoke a word. They rushed toward the vestibule.

Every corridor seethed with panic as druids and mages woke. Whispers followed, of the horns, of the danger, of the man whose approach they had feared. With every step, Juniper hoped they were wrong.

The vestibule fluttered with anxious activity. The druid warriors had gathered, along with the Sentinels and battlemages who'd taken refuge in the castle. The crowd parted as Juniper marched through. She fought to keep the panic from her features. They did not need to see her as fearful as they were.

She needed to appear strong.

She marched into the front garden. Mages and battlemages had emerged onto the street. Their breaths puffed on their lips. Dawn had broken, yet the city remained under a heavy haze and fresh blanket of snow.

"Report," Reid demanded of the watch tower.

"Approaching forces from the west," shouted the druid in the tower. He didn't bother to hide his nervousness.

Shadows rushed to the west at the silent command of Lilianna.

With every moment that passed, more gathered into the street and the front garden. Delmont cut through the crowd, looking determined. The snow nearest him melted. Jarek followed not far behind.

Whispers surged—that Nexon had arrived. Juniper wanted desperately to believe otherwise. She wanted to think that it was another army marching to their aid, but she knew no help would come from the west. Rusdasin had its own fight to win.

The sun rose imperceptibly, cutting through the lingering clouds and lighting the haze. It made the city appear filled with smoke, and Juniper's heart skipped a beat. Delmont's gaze swept over the city. His fists clenched.

Was this a warning from the gods?

Was the city about to burn a second time?

Reid stood firm at her side, steady and stoic, the epitome of a knight. Juniper tried to steal a bit of his steadfastness, even to pretend in front of those counting on her.

In the time it took for the Shadows to return, the Sentinels, druid and mage warriors, and battlemages had gathered. Everyone awaited the report, and most were looking to Juniper, others to Delmont.

If she failed, Nexon wouldn't show mercy. He would slaughter everyone within the Dead City. The druids who had followed her out of their home in hope of something better, the battlemages and soldiers who had followed their princess into battle, and the mages who had fled one leader in hope of another. They were all here because of her.

She couldn't let them die for her mistakes.

This was her fight with Nexon, not theirs.

The Shadows returned, and a hush fell over the courtyard. Every pair of eyes followed as Lilianna closed the space between herself and Juniper. Reid and Ison took the hint and closed the gap, shielding them from onlookers.

"Is it him?" Juniper asked.

Lilianna's fearful expression gave her the answer, but she nodded anyway. Panic surged through the courtyard, too fast to stop, with Nexon's name hissed and whispered.

"How many?" Delmont demanded.

"Many," Lilianna answered. "Five or six hundred, maybe more. They march in a narrow line."

Delmont spat a curse. "His forces outnumber ours, but he does not out-power us. We—"

Juniper interrupted whatever Delmont was about to say next, "Lilianna, can your Shadows take a message?"

"What sort?"

"I need parchment," Juniper said above the whispers. Her voice did not come out as strong as she would have liked. "And ink."

Someone rushed into the castle. Juniper didn't have the mind to who.

Her reaction did not calm the crowd. Confusion followed. Juniper ignored them. Had they expected some dramatic war cry or stimulating speech promising victory? She didn't have the stomach for either of those.

"You intend to write him a poem?" Delmont asked, his saunter replaced with a general's march. He wore no humor. "I doubt that will work."

"Not exactly," Juniper said. "If we march toward him, it will be a bloodbath. If I can stall him, even a little bit, we can get as many people out of the castle as possible."

Delmont frowned.

Ison stepped to Juniper's side and touched her elbow. In a small, timid voice, he said, "I have a faster way to reach him."

Between them, Ison produced an old leather book.

"Ah, the scribe," Delmont said, sounding calmly surprised.

"Nexon will read whatever you write in it," Ison said, his expression dire and sleepless. "He and Lora used these books to talk."

Juniper took the book from Ison's hands. The pages were blank, scared by thousands of penstrokes.

"We found it on the battlefield," Ison explained.

The druid who had run into the castle appeared again. He carried ink, a pen, and parchment. Juniper took the ink and pen and flattened the book on Ison's back to write. The pen shook in her hand.

"What are you doing?" Reid asked.

"I'm asking for parley," Juniper said as she wrote. She finished her note by singing her name, Juniper Thimble, and adding a little heart. The ink slowly dried into a matte. "I have a plan."

That word—parley—did not go over well with the crowd. It whispered around the garden and into the street, and she didn't look to see how the battlemages reacted. If they shared Delmont's scowl, they weren't happy about it.

"You can't be serious," Delmont said. "You're surrendering?"

"No," Juniper said at once, hushing those whispers before they started. Louder, she said, "We are not surrendering. I am taking a risk."

Reid started to speak, then a slanted handwriting appeared on the page underneath her message. Juniper read it aloud:

I accept your offer, Juniper Thimble. My forces will camp due west of the Dead City. I will allow you and a small escort into our camp.

My mages will not attack unless you raise your weapons. I expect you before sundown.

She quickly wrote, *Thank you.*

"It could be a trap," Reid said.

"Nexon is Iluvin," Delmont said. "If he has a shred of dignity, he will honor his word and the parley. Now, who is going with you?"

Juniper took in her friends and allies. Everyone in the front garden was looking at her, waiting for her to make the next room. She looked at Reid, who stood solid and steady at her side. Ready for anything. Ison stood at her other side, so far from the shy mage she had met at Bradburn Castle. Xavier wore no emotion; her brother would follow her if he saw fit. Lilianna stood at attention, Moss a step behind her, eyeing Juniper cautiously. Moss seemed to be the only one aware of the danger they faced. Mabyl and Finn stood with the mages, wary but ready. Rue and Calvex stood with the Sentinels, armor gleaming.

"I am going to speak to Nexon," Juniper said. "I will not ask any of you to go with me. If you want to, you are welcome."

"I will not let you go alone," Reid said at once.

"If there is a chance to punch Nexon, I'm going," Ison said.

"If I don't go, your odds of walking back out are slimmer," Xavier drawled.

"My Shadows will not be far behind you," Lilianna said. "Just in case."

Juniper hadn't the words to give them. They deserved a braver leader than her, someone like Reid or Delmont. Despite their odds, her friends had chosen to stay at her side. To see it through to the end. How she had found such devoted friends, she didn't understand. In many ways, she still felt like the scrawny thief from the Undercity, stealing for her next meal.

Juniper held her chin higher. That thief had survived the Undercity. That thief had never let the odds dissuade her. She was still that thief—still Juniper.

She cleared her throat and added, "Then let's not waste any more time."

CHAPTER 46

Nexon's army camped in the western forest. Canvas tents spotted the hillsides, arranged however the terrain allowed. Clearings had been turned into cooking stations, blacksmiths and runesmiths operated side by side, chickens clucked, and others carried baskets of laundry downhill toward a half-frozen river. It seemed Nexon had brought a whole village with him.

As Juniper and her party approached the edge of the encampment, two guards blocked her path.

"I am expected," she said.

"The master said you would come," said the first guard, a man with a scar across his nose. "I will take you to him."

The guard escorted them into the camp. The other scowled.

Juniper had brought no weapons, and neither had Xavier. They had only their magic. Reid carried the only weapon: his Mage's Bane. The Sentinels' blacksmith had tried to buff out the dents in Reid's silver armor, and while it looked better, it looked well-worn. They had agreed before leaving Balendin Castle that Nexon did not need to know about Reid's magic. As far as Nexon knew, Reid was a fallen knight.

Magic singed the frigid air in heavy florals and sharp metallics. Juniper held herself tall as the mage led them into the heart of the camp. Her appearance didn't cause the stir she thought it would. Few paid any attention. Most went about their chores as if she didn't exist. She caught guards in her peripheral, watching with sharp cautiousness.

She hoped Delmont was right about Nexon retaining his Iluvin dignity.

The closer she got to the heart of the camp, the bigger the tents and heavier the dread in her stomach. The odds of walking into a trap were high, and the odds of fighting their way out were low. The odds of winning this entire battle were low. She couldn't let that discourage her from trying. The odds had been against her since birth. She couldn't let them get in her way now.

Nexon's tent was larger and grander than the others. Wools draped over the canvas, and two armored thralls stood guard on either side. Their empty eyes watched her approach. Like the thralls she had killed outside Sinjon, their master saw everything they did. Nexon already knew she was there.

The thralls opened the flaps of the tent for her. Juniper ducked through first, fully expecting to meet an attack.

She didn't find one.

A seamless stone hearth burned on the far side, taking the chill out of the air. Nexon sat at a stone desk and matching chair. He wore simple traveling leathers and a pale green wool cloak secured by a golden brooch encrusted with rubies. His blond hair was trimmed and combed back, a bit dirty from traveling. The cold had seeped the color from his pale skin and left his cheekbones and nose pink. He leaned back in his chair and crossed his long legs. His ice-blue eyes glittered.

Juniper pretended that she was strolling into Maddox's office or into a hostile fence's shop. This meeting was no different, she told herself.

"Welcome." Nexon smiled with the warmth of an innkeeper. "What do you think of my camp? Is this the grand force you imagined?"

"It's bigger than I thought," Juniper said calmly. The smoothness of her voice surprised her. "I didn't expect you to bring such a large army just for me."

Nexon chuckled, a handsome sound. "It's not just for you. I like to be prepared, and by the sound of things, I gambled right. You've gathered quite a force of your own."

"Does my handful of druids make you nervous?" Juniper teased.

"My scouts tell me you have battlemages and Sentinels from Delphine," Nexon said matter-of-factly.

"They arrived shortly before you did," Juniper said. She schooled her features into a clever smirk. "They weren't here when you set out, so that tells me you were worried about my little army. That, or you were worried about me and you don't want to admit it."

Nexon half-laughed. "Believe what you wish. Now, what do you wish to speak of? Unless you truly requested parley for no other purpose than small talk."

Swallowing her pride, Juniper reached into her old self—the thief, the liar, the scoundrel—and twisted her pride into something closer to uncertainty and fear. Vulnerability. It wasn't hard. Standing in the middle of Nexon's camp with untold lives resting on her shoulders, she felt hefty amounts of both.

"I came to make an offer," Juniper said, her tone low.

Nexon's brows rose. He leaned forward. "Do tell."

Juniper reached into her pocket and withdrew the moonstone brooch. Nexon's gaze snapped to it, and his calm exterior vanished. A vicious look took over his face. His entire body tensed.

"I have the brooch, and I've hidden the ring." Juniper gripped the brooch hard enough to turn her knuckles white. The metal edges dug into her fingers. "If you agree to fight me, just me, one on one, I will give them to you."

Nexon's manic gaze snapped to hers.

"If I lose, you will leave everyone else be," Juniper said. "You and your army will leave them alone. You will not attack them. You will not set foot in the Dead City."

"And if I lose?"

"Then you'll be dead and it won't matter," Juniper said. "But I will hold the same to your army. I will not hurt them. My people will not attack them."

A beat passed. Nexon stared at her. With every moment, the mania in his eyes lessened. Then he asked, "That's it? We fight and regardless of the winner everyone goes their separate ways?"

She nodded. "No one else has to get hurt."

"And you'll give me the ring and the brooch before this fight?"

She fingered the tarnished edge of the brooch. "I will give you the brooch first, and if you win, the ring is yours."

"And if I demand them both at the start?"

"Your power would trump mine," Juniper said. "The only way to keep the battle fair is to keep one of the pieces."

"You would prefer to win when I am not at my best?"

"I never said I was honorable," Juniper said.

Nexon half-laughed, but it lacked warmth. Any trace of humor vanished from his face. "I want the brooch now as a show of good faith, and then I want the ring at the start of this fight. If you are an archmage, then you would do well to respect the old ways of dueling. We will not throw dirt like common thieves."

She snorted at the jab. "Let's say I give them both to you beforehand. How do I know you won't go back on your word as soon as you have them?"

"We make a deal," Nexon said. "Like the ancient Iluvin. If you give me the remaining pieces of my magic, I will not harm anyone within the Dead City. I will let them be, from the day of my victory into eternity."

Juniper swallowed. It seemed too good to be true.

"You seem surprised." Nexon grinned proudly. "That's right. I will allow the Dead City to remain when I resurrect the Imperium. It will be a sanctuary."

"Agreed," Juniper said. "My forces will do the same to yours. They will be allowed to return to Baxion, and we will leave the city untouched."

"I agree to these terms." Nexon laughed and added, "You're an arrogant fool."

She frowned. "If you're so sure of your victory, why ask for your magic back first?"

"It will be a test of true strength," he said. "A one-on-one of two archmages. We will only attack each other, no one else."

"Afraid of my friends?" Juniper taunted.

Nexon's gaze went to the Mage's Bane at Reid's waist.

"The window is closing," Juniper said. "I give you the brooch now, the ring later. My friends will not attack you or any of your mages, and your mages will not attack me or any of my friends. You will fight me and only me. We fight tomorrow. At midday. This is my final offer. Take it or I'm throwing the ring into the deepest part of the ocean."

"I accept." Nexon stood and sauntered around the desk. Reid and Xavier both adjusted their feet to stand closer to Juniper, easier for a defense. Nexon gave no notice; he looked only at her. He paused a short distance away and extended his hand.

Juniper glanced at his hand, then looked at him. "Excuse me?"

Nexon gave her a pitied smile. "The sealing of the Iluvin deal is a handshake. A common tradition that has transcended the ages. Once the deal is accepted by both parties, they shake. The magic will seal and prevent either party from going back on the deal. I don't trust you not to cheat."

She wanted to look to her friends for confirmation. She wanted to go back to the castle and ask Delmont for his opinion on this deal. But she didn't have time. She didn't have anyone to ask for guidance.

She took Nexon's hand.

Magic zapped through her hand, up her arm, and into her magic. Something went taut between herself and Nexon. By the uncomfortable grimace on Nexon's face, he felt the same. Juniper couldn't release his hand. A powerful force held them as the sensation wormed its way through her entire being.

And then, the force calmed and she released his hand.

"What was that?" she demanded.

"A bargain has been struck," Nexon said, straightening. He shook out his hand. The discomfort vanished from his face, and sheer arrogance replaced it. "We are bound to our word. And, as you said, give me the brooch."

A tremor of unease raged through her body. She rubbed her finger over the faintly glowing moonstone, over the fastening pin. She felt the tug in her core to follow the bargain. Her magic urged her to obey, and underneath it, she felt the threat. She took a small comfort in knowing Nexon would feel the same.

She set the brooch into his hand, moonstone side up. Nexon's grin widened into something close to madness, then he gasped. He yanked his hand away from her. In the sudden movement, the brooch fell—Juniper caught it. The pin had stuck his palm, and fresh blood beaded from the wound. Blood from the pin smeared against Juniper's palm, warm and sticky.

"I'm sorry," Juniper said as earnestly as she could.

Nexon frowned; he didn't believe her. "No matter. It is done."

She held the brooch out in her hand. He snatched it as carefully as he could.

In one quick move, Nexon shattered the brooch. The moonstone burst in a blaze of bright white. The metal backing clanked on the floor by Juniper's boot. In the sudden brightness, Juniper stumbled a step back. Her foot hit the rug, and she fell backward onto her rear.

The light flashed and then absorbed into Nexon's body. The gasp of relief that followed contained more madness than before.

"Finally," Nexon said, grasping at his chest. "Just one more."

Juniper staggered to her feet.

Nexon's madness faded. "Now, you have no other business here. I will see you tomorrow at midday."

Juniper nodded, and she led her party back through the tent's flaps and toward the castle that loomed in the distance.

CHAPTER 47

No one said a word until they reached the Dead City's outskirts. Then it began.

"Are you fucking mad?" Xavier sidestepped in front of her, absolutely livid.

"He was powerful before," Ison said. "He'll be impossible with all of his power."

"He will tear you apart!" Xavier spat.

Juniper huffed. Reid met her eye, and she waited for his objection. As Xavier started to pace and complain, Reid stepped up to her side. He wore his unreadable expression.

Calmly, Reid asked, "Are you sure about this?"

"As much as I can be." She inhaled and added lowly so Ison and Xavier couldn't hear. "I think I have a plan. It just needs fine tuning."

"You don't have a lot of time," Reid said.

"It's…missing a few key pieces," Juniper admitted. She glanced over Reid's shoulder at Balendin Castle. The druids had cleared the climbing ivy and the earth mages had fixed the collapsed and broken walls. It looked…like a real castle. Reid stepped into her view. Worry slipped through his mask, and the morning light turned his brown eyes molten.

"I am well aware of how foolish it sounds," she said.

"It sounds idiotic!" Xavier shouted. He stomped over and pointed a charcoal dagger at her chest. "You're going to die and we're going to be trapped in the Dead City while Nexon destroys the rest of the realm."

Ison grabbed Xavier's arm. Something silent passed between them, and Xavier reeled his anger back in.

They continued toward the castle. Guilt layered on top of Juniper's already impossible dread. She'd never seen Xavier that angry. He had always been able to hold it in. He had always been the cool, level-headed assassin, capable of a cold exterior. For him to have lost it over her actions… She heaved a sigh.

Reid brushed his fingers against hers.

At least someone believed in her. That made one.

They walked in silence through the streets. As they approached the castle gates, silence flushed over the battlemages and Sentinels Juniper did her best to ignore the uncertain silence and stares that followed her. The front garden held another type of silence—anticipation. Near the castle steps, Delmont, Jarek,

Lilianna, and Calvex were talking. As Juniper approached, whatever conversation they'd been having ended.

"Well?" Delmont demanded. "What happened?"

"We met as planned," Juniper said, then hesitated.

"But?" Delmont supplied, brows raised.

She quickly relayed the encounter and the bargain.

"Madness," Jarek spat. "Nothing good can come from a magic deal. Especially with a monster."

Delmont looked like he had a hundred things he wanted to yell at her, but he held them all in. He instead turned on his heel and marched up the steps. He said, "I must send word to Her Majesty."

"And you look like you could use something strong to drink," came Enna's caw of a voice. She stepped up to Juniper's side and motioned toward the castle with her knobby wooden cane. "Won't be good for anyone for you to pass out before you get yourself killed. On with you. Breakfast should be about ready."

Porridge filled the dining hall with the rich scents of butter and herbs. Juniper did not feel remotely like eating. Reid sat beside her as she picked at her bowl. Mabyl sat on her other side and kept up conversation with a mage Juniper didn't know. Despite Mabyl's attempts to sound cheerful, a somber tone settled over the dining hall. Juniper had never heard the dining hall so quiet while so full. It was her fault. She had brought this cloud of despair. At some point, a bottle of berry wine appeared in front of her, and she took a sip of the ice-cold drink.

Delmont did not appear for the meal.

News of her bargain had spread, and the uncertainty had grown. She felt it in the air with every word. When she had eaten all the porridge she could stomach, she trudged through the whispers toward the vestibule. She recognized Reid's armored footsteps behind her.

She passed the vestibule and kept going, until she reached a sunny corridor well away from everyone else. The windows did not wear woven shutters, and no runes had been engraved to keep out the cold. The snow filtered in, drifted against the stone walls.

Reid reached for her elbow. "Juniper?"

"I know." She turned and met his molten eyes. No one else had followed, and she felt her resolve begin to crumble. "It's stupid and foolish and reckless and the odds of me dying tomorrow are high."

"And I don't need to remind you," Reid said.

His tone warmed every bone in her body. He did not speak with reprimand or appraisal. He cupped her cheek, and his magic reached out to hers. His skin was warm and callused, and his magic graced hers with a soothing, reassuring touch. She returned the magic embrace, and as their magic intertwined, she felt what he had not said—he had things he wanted to say, concerns and fears to rival her own.

"Regardless of what I think about your decision," Reid said, his voice even and sturdy. A knight. "I love you. I will stand with you, always."

Those words brought tears to her eyes. She didn't try to stop it, and instead she fell into him. She wrapped her arms around his armored middle, and he laid his arms around her shoulders. She hadn't been able to open the stupid puzzle box, or look for a silver cuff, or plan a sickeningly romantic moment to propose. Thanks to Nexon, she likely never would.

"Thank you," she breathed, the tears making her words watery. She stepped back just enough to look at him. "I love you, and you can't imagine how much you mean to me."

He stroked her cheekbone with his thumb, and her being with his magic.

"When this is done," Reid said, a promise on every word, "we marry."

That promise warmed her as much as it tore through her heart. Knowing full well she might not make it through the next day. Reid knew that; his magic could not hide it. Neither could hers. If she could feel his fears, he could feel hers.

"We'll have to go back to Rusdasin," she said. "Your aunt told me we couldn't elope."

A small smile stretched his lips. "I don't care where."

She refused to let herself daydream of a wedding. She had too much at stake here to even consider such a fantasy.

Reid's magic gave her one last embrace, then released her. "I must see to the warriors. We need to be ready for anything."

She nodded and held up the bottle of berry wine. "I also have scheming to do."

Reid departed with a kiss to her lips. Juniper watched him go, remembering a time when his silver armor made her feel sick. Now, it filled her with warmth. She started to wander, feeling lighter than before, and took a drink of the wine. The sweetness filtered through her entire body.

Scheming, indeed.

Juniper found Delmont in his chamber. The archmage had taken a chamber that overlooked the front gardens and the city beyond. He stood by the window, arms folded behind his back, a contemplative expression as he surveyed those below. Juniper paused in the doorway. The woven door had been left open, yet she didn't want to intrude. So she knocked on the stone doorway.

Delmont gave no surprise. He didn't look away from the window. "I've seen battles in my time, and the dread never gets any easier to manage. They're all so eager and terrified. That never changes. Tomorrow will be different. No one will want to speak. Meals will go untouched. Many won't get out of bed while others will be up before the sun."

"Very optimistic of you," Juniper said.

He glanced over his shoulder at her. "It's an objective statement made by experience."

She huffed. She hadn't come all this way to feel more depressed. "I was hoping to find you. Walk with me?"

Delmont considered her, looking at her like he expected a trick. "I would love a tour."

Juniper guided him into the lesser occupied side of the castle, where the walls remained broken in places, a few cobwebs remained, and mice scurried just out of sight.

"You didn't come down to breakfast," Juniper said.

"I had to report to Her Majesty," Delmont said. "With an event like this morning, she had to know. You said Nexon would leave the Dead City, but that leaves the rest of the world vulnerable. It is not a stretch to assume he would go after your allies first. Delphine would be in the direct line of attack."

Juniper hadn't thought of that. It only worsened her guilt. "I don't like how you speak as if I've already lost."

Delmont gave her a knowing look, but didn't respond.

Juniper steered them into the library. The ashes and ruined books had been removed, the floors had been scrubbed, and the bones had been buried in the royal grounds. They hadn't been able to dig a grave for each; they'd gone into a mass grave. Juniper had instructed Finn to craft a gravestone for them all. She hadn't had the chance to go to the grave and see if he'd finished it yet.

Without the mess of broken and burned furniture, the library was dark and empty. Delmont summoned a bright red flame in his palm, and he took a slow lap around the library. He paused in front of an alcove. Wintry sunlight draped inside.

"I studied here," Delmont said without looking at her. "My teachers often chided me for staring out the window. They moved my desk upstairs, away from any window." He looked to the balcony of the second floor, where more barren bookshelves stood. "I ended up napping instead, which infuriated them further."

"When was that?" She meandered to the window. Below, on the grounds, the druids worked the gardens. Their song fluted up, distant and uncanny.

"Four hundred years ago, perhaps." Delmont strolled to the window and doused his flame. They didn't need it with the sunlight. "Seems longer ago than that, but time works that way. That's part of being an archmage, by the way. Even if you don't have strong Iluvin blood. It comes with the magic. I'd say you have a good thousand years ahead of you, congratulations. Considering what happens tomorrow, of course."

She half-laughed. "I either have a day left or a thousand years?"

Delmont smirked. "Lilianna and Reid will live as long."

Juniper hadn't taken more than a moment to wonder about her own life, but a thousand years to spend with Reid? That was something to fight for.

"I imagine you feel the buff from the winter season," Delmont said, nodding to the window. The trees remained powdered with snow. "I feel the same during the summer months. Like I could set the world on fire. I haven't, of course."

She nodded. "I feel it more at night."

"As makes sense with your affinity for ice," Delmont added.

"Before we brought the Marca down, I went to rescue the City Watch captain. It was a cold and stormy night. I might have been a little too dramatic with the escape. I hadn't realized how much magic I'd used until the depletion settled."

"Ah," Delmont said, as if it all made perfect sense. "On those occasions in which our magic coincides with nature, like with you and cold dark nights and me on hot summer days, it makes the well seem endless. It is easy to expel more than you intend. There's a word for it, but I've forgotten it. It's an Iluvin word."

Juniper sighed and glanced out of the window. She didn't suppose Nexon would agree to fight her at night.

Delmont cleared his throat and turned toward her. His calm expression turned dire. "I must ask you something."

She motioned for him to continue.

"I am sworn to the Balendin throne. If you seek to usurp the throne, we will be enemies. Tell me, Juniper or Isolde, whichever name you chose, do you seek that throne?"

She felt the threat in those words, and the pressure of his magic as he let it into the air around him. The air heated, a reminder of his power, and shimmered with a faint red hue. Sweat gathered along her neck and down her back. The sheer force of it made her heart skip a beat. Still, she reminded herself that she had equal power.

"No," she said firmly. "I do not."

Delmont's gaze didn't change. His fiery magic remained.

"I didn't want the throne before, and I sure as hell don't want it now." Juniper set her hands on her hips. "All these people are relying on me to defeat Nexon and save them. The druids followed me here because their home was destroyed. The mages defected to join me. I hold their lives in my hands. I have tasted the responsibility of leading, and I hate it. I don't want any more of it, and when this nonsense with Nexon is over, I refuse to take any more of it."

"Myrisha seems eager to hand you the crown," Delmont said. "I daresay you only have to ask her for it."

Juniper shook her head. "Nice try, but she already asked me if I wanted to be queen. I said no. My answer has not changed."

His brows rose. "Most girls would kill for the chance to be a princess, let alone a queen. Power, respect, and authority."

"And responsibility, duties, and appeasement," Juniper added bitterly. "I would rather stay in charge of myself and myself only."

Delmont laughed.

"What?"

"Being an archmage comes with its own responsibilities. We are in high demand and short supply."

She rolled her eyes.

"History shows that we often become magical advisers, like myself and Mason Hobbs, and keepers, like Angyla. We are appointed positions of power because we are powerful, and those in power want powerful allies," Delmont said. He gazed around the library. His gaze lingered here and there, but Juniper didn't ask why. When Delmont spoke again, his voice was somber. "We are also targets for people like Nexon. If a kingdom holds an archmage in their court, other kingdoms see that as a threat. They seek to prove themselves stronger despite the archmage. It leads to unnecessary conflict."

"Why?" Juniper asked. "Why bend your knee to the Balendin crown? You could go anywhere. Do anything."

"I could," he agreed. "And I spent the first two hundred years of my life doing just that. I traveled, sold myself as a bodyguard and mercenary. Sailed. Climbed mountains. Learned languages. Hunted pirates and smugglers. Fought trolls just to say that I had. I ended up back here, my home. I…grew up, I suppose. I had a large dose of adventure and danger, and I wanted something calmer."

Juniper wanted to see the world beyond her own, but she understood his desire for peace and quiet. "Don't you ever want to leave?"

"Of course," Delmont said. "And I do occasionally. I travel the kingdom. I scout. I explore. I know a great deal, and that knowledge is valuable. Now, if I didn't think Myrisha was a good ruler, I might not stay. But I promised her mother that I would oversee her children. I promised her I would not let Crespin become his father."

That dark emotion passed over his face again. Juniper felt a rock fall into her stomach. Her voice came out weak as she asked, "You knew them? Before, I mean."

"I did." Delmont's gaze returned to the window. "I knew Sabian and Sebastian when they were boys. I knew their father when he was a boy. I watched your father grow into the king and Sabian into a general. I watched the kingdom slowly fall into turmoil. I…have regrets. I wish I had done more. I might have stopped the war from taking so many lives."

"I think my sister escaped," Juniper whispered.

At that, his eyes flashed to hers.

"I saw…ghosts, I think, but they're not ghosts of the dead. The wechun thinks they are memories because I am connected to this place. I saw my mother talking to my sister. She told her to hide in the secret passage in her closet. She said it led out of the castle, to a place called Sina and someone named Treva. I found the passage. It connects to the same passage that this one does." She motioned to the secret door in the library.

"People escaped through here," Delmont said, his voice barely above a whisper. He stared down at the shelves that hid the passage entrance. His expression shifted between surprise and realization.

"Do you know something?" she demanded. "Is she alive?"

"I didn't believe the rumors," Delmont whispered.

Juniper took a step closer. "Tell me," she begged. "Is my sister alive?"

Delmont swallowed. "There were rumors that Princess Alma did not die that night, that she escaped and lives to the east. Crespin once sent scouts to investigate, but nothing came of it. If your sister is alive, she has kept her identity to herself. Girls who claim to be lost royalty have often met unfortunate ends. I suspect Nexon picked them off, just in case they weren't lying."

Juniper leaned into the wall. Her sister might be alive. Alma. Of course, she would have used another name, just like Isolde. What name did she call herself?

"When this is over," Delmont said. "I can direct you to the village of Sina."

"I would greatly appreciate it," she said.

A beat of silence.

"Is there something else you need me?" Delmont asked. "We both have much to do before midday tomorrow."

Juniper inhaled and steeled herself. "There is something else. Delmont, you know more about magic than any of us. Will you share that knowledge?"

He blinked, then said, "Of course."

She blinked; she'd expected him to be pompous about the whole thing.

"Magic is dangerous and complex," Delmont said. "That is something the Order got right. It's even more dangerous in the hands of a mage who doesn't know what they are doing. Even Nexon knows that, and he did all he could to take magic out of the hands of his enemies. Should we all survive, I will share what I know."

"Thank you," she said, though it reminded her that come midday tomorrow, she might not be around to learn anything.

"There are others who know more than I," he said. "Iluvin who have survived and remained hidden from the rest of the world. Should the gods favor us and we are still standing, I say we do our best to find them. They can return to this city, and we can start rebuilding the Iluvin, including the knowledge we've lost."

That made her heart skip a beat. "Will they come?"

Delmont flashed her a grin. "We're the archmages. We are higher than royalty in Iluvin culture. If word gets out that the five archmages have gathered, the Iluvin will return."

"Let's talk about rebuilding empires after we get rid of Nexon." Juniper swallowed her trepidation and took a step closer to Delmont. "There is one more thing I want to ask you."

CHAPTER 48

Smoke and blood filled the Undercity air. Adrian followed Jax, who engaged any enemy they came across, unless Roslyn sank an arrow into them first. Adrian hated every moment of it. Useless. Useless. Useless.

The fight didn't last as long as Adrian feared it would. As the panic eased, people flocked to the Commons. Many still have their weapons out, most were bloodied. To his horror, bodies lay in the streets. He couldn't tell who they were. He had no desire to get closer.

King Bradburn, Maddox, and Josephine stood in the middle of the Commons, talking. Heatedly, by his father's furrowed brow and reddened face. Even Maddox sported blood on his tunic.

As the crowd thickened, King Bradburn climbed onto a table and thrust his bloodied sword into the air. A fierce victory cry sounded through the Commons, trembling the loose stone and thundering against Adrian's sternum.

"Our enemies have fallen." King Bradburn's voice boomed over the crowd. A commander, a leader, a king. "We hit them while they are reeling from their failure, we lay siege to the castle this very hour!"

A roar sounded at those words.

"Right now?" Adrian gasped, sharing a look with Roslyn.

"Janti forces are camped to the west," King Bradburn announced. "Prince A'Ralen commands five hundred soldiers. My own army lies just to the north, three hundred soldiers ready to march. Today, we take back Rusdasin from that wretched creature."

Adrian's heart lurched. Armies waited above ground? It made him feel better about their odds, but it also made him feel like vomiting. He knew his father was right. They needed to attack now, why morale was high and their enemy was down, but gods, he didn't want to.

Roslyn gripped his arm as if she could feel his indecision.

A cheery thundered through the Undercity, so loud Adrian feared those topside would hear it.

"Prepare yourselves for war," King Bradburn commanded.

Adrian returned to the king's house and promptly emptied his stomach into the chamber pot. Roslyn said nothing. She stroked his back, then handed him a rag to wipe his mouth. He sank against the wall, limbs trembling and weak.

All the stories of war and bloodshed that filled history books had always seemed like another world, another kingdom. Adrian struggled to grasp that his own people stood at the precipice of one such battle, and that armies were marching. Roslyn hadn't reacted to the news with vomiting. She had held her bow steady and cheered with the rest.

The door to the house opened, and armored footsteps rushed inside.

"Adrian?" Henry called.

"We're in here," Roslyn answered.

Henry didn't hesitate to let himself into the bathing room. At the sight of Adrian sitting on the floor with a rag against his mouth, skin ashen, he paused.

"Yes, yes," Adrian said, throwing the rag aside. "I'm aware of how pitiful I look."

Henry wiped any emotion off his face. "The king asked me to make sure you arrived here safely."

Adrian let out a bark of a laugh. "Of course, he did. Why would he think that his son couldn't defend himself?"

Useless, even to his father.

Roslyn and Henry shared an uncertain look. It didn't matter. Adrian had let loose the panic and dread and self-loathing that had been building for months. He stumbled to his feet and reached for the earthen decanter of cheap Undercity wine. He washed the bile out of his mouth and spat it into the chamber pot.

"My father is fighting alongside his soldiers," Adrian said. "I should be too."

"Adrian—" Henry started, his name a warning.

"I know how to hold a blade," Adrian finished. He met Henry's stare and dared him to deny his prince's command. "I will not cower underground while criminals, mages, and knights battle for my kingdom."

Roslyn gripped her bow, and whispered, "Are you certain?"

"As I have ever been," Adrian answered. To Henry, he said, "I will need armor, and a helm to hide my face."

"Don't forget the blade," Roslyn said.

Henry frowned, though he wore a mischievous glint in his eye. "Your father will kill me if he finds out. We'll have to go the long way to the armory."

"Led the way, Sir Julian." Before they left, he grabbed the dagger Helena had given him and tucked it into a boot.

Adrian followed Henry through the alleys and backstreets of the Undercity. The cavernous air buzzed with nervous energy, the preparation of battle.

Criminals, common folk turned soldier, mages, apostates, pledges, squires, and knights—working together, dressed in mismatched iron and steel and leather, working with a single purpose: to knock Nexon out of the castle and return the kingdom to its former glory.

He felt it in his bones. Whether they won or lost, history would be made today.

Written in blood and steel.

Having steel in one hand and a shield in the other did something to Adrian's spirit. His helm hid all but his hazel eyes, and he marched alongside the barely trained common folk and mages as they made their way through the ancient catacombs of Bradburn Castle. Scouts had mapped the course through the winding halls, narrow corridors, and steep staircases. Adrian had only been in the catacombs for emergencies, like when Nexon's monsters had attacked Bala's Ball, and the forgotten structure filled his gut with dread.

No one gave Adrian a second glance. Henry marched close to Adrian, but Roslyn did not. Her presence would give the prince away, and despite her dislike of his plan, she had stayed in the Undercity with Adrian's mother and the captain's wife.

Adrian had pleaded with her to follow him into battle.

"There's no one else I would rather stand with," Adrian had said.

Roslyn had shaken her head, a warm smile on her lips and tears on her lashes. She had placed her hand over her stomach, and said, "I need to stay here. If something happens to you and your father, the line must continue."

Adrian marched with newfound vigor. When he had first made his decision to fight, he had been thinking of himself and his feathered pride. He had feared his own cowardice. Had he known that Roslyn carried their child, he might have made a different decision, but he marched onward. He had committed to this path, and he would see it through.

He would return to Roslyn.

Adrian's party paused. Ahead of them was the back of the portrait that would lead into Bradburn Castle. Adrian didn't know how many portraits led into the catacombs, but he knew that after this battle, they would all be sealed.

And then it began with a furious war cry—they burst through the portrait with steel and magic on the offensive. Adrian surged forward with the others and jumped into the parlor they had entered. By the time he rushed into the corridor, the mages they had surprised were dead.

They didn't pause for the small victory. Adrian and Henry rushed with the others, corridor by corridor, parlor by parlor, and every rooftop courtyard. They passed several other parties, and they heard many more. Steel and magic battled and echoed through the castle, shifting stone and blasting fire and spilling blood.

Adrian's party saw little combat. The more experienced knights and soldiers had led the invasion, with the quickly trained commoners behind them. Still, he had expected more of a fight. A chance to prove himself, if to no one else than himself.

Their party convened with another in a rooftop courtyard, and the bearded man beside Adrian sighed in relief. His blade was clean too.

"Report," Henry ordered.

A knight stepped forward. "Success. The castle appears to be mostly empty. The remaining forces have gone to engage the Janti forces on the western side and the King's Army to the north."

Henry stepped closer to the knight, so that only a few could hear him. "Any sight of Fowler?"

The knight shook his head. "No."

"Where is that old fool hiding? He has to know he's lost," Henry spat.

Adrian didn't have to think long. "The king's cellar."

The knight glared at Adrian for interrupting, then he really looked at him. Recognition widened the knight's eyes and flattened his scowl. "Your Highness?"

"Where is that?" Henry asked, cutting off the knight.

"Hidden between the king's personal chamber and his favorite parlor," Adrian said.

"You know the way?"

Adrian nodded.

"That is our destination," Henry said. To the other knight, he said, "I will take a small force to find Fowler. Continue until no enemy mage or thrall remains."

The knight didn't hesitate. He nodded then barked orders to those behind him. Henry did the same, halving their party. Half joined the knight's team, and the other half followed him back into the castle, toward the Royal Chambers. Adrian fell in step beside Henry.

Everyone in their party knew who he was now, and there was no need to pretend otherwise.

His parents' chambers had survived the worst of the destruction. Nexon had likely claimed the space for himself. Someone had. The sheets were messed, clothes littered the floor, and they had helped themselves to the king's liquor collection. Adrian ignored it all and went straight for the hidden door in his father's study.

Henry charged in first, Mage's Bane ready, and Adrian followed behind, steel angled to slice.

Knight Commander Fowler sat at his father's desk, scowling at the letters strewn atop it. A magelight hovered near the ceiling, glittering pale blue. Two thralls stood on either side of the desk. The thralls started forward, and Henry and Adrian met them. The thralls fought with skill, better skill than most others. Adrian sidestepped to avoid a blade to the side, and he caught Fowler's intense stare—he controlled these thralls, which explained their skill. Fowler knew combat. He himself had been a knight.

Henry defeated his thrall first, and Adrian soon followed.

Fowler didn't look remotely surprised.

The knight commander looked down his crooked nose at the two of them. Adrian had long thought the old man looked a few weeks from death, but he had never looked quite as…sick. His skin had a greenish cast, his eyes were milky, and his posture had shriveled. He looked like a shell of the knight commander Adrian had grown up hearing about.

"Well?" Fowler demanded. "Aren't you going to say something?"

"You betrayed us," Henry spat. "You allowed that monster to destroy the Order and nearly the kingdom."

"I allowed Nexon nothing he hadn't already taken." Fowler took a rattling breath. "By the time I became knight commander, Nexon already had his claws around the Order's throat.

Henry paled, and his fury flattened. "You knew?"

Fowler grimaced. "I suspected foul play within the highest ranks of the Order. I thought I could change things once I became knight commander. I was wrong. Nexon had thralls among the Order, and he watched. He heard. He commanded. I had two choices, obey or join the dead."

"We all know what you chose," Henry said.

"Do you?" Fowler's brows rose.

Henry laughed. "Oh, is this the part where you say you've been on our side this whole time? By sending thralls and mages to kill us?"

Fowler laughed, though the sound rattled like his body might fall apart before their eyes. "I held that monster back as long as I could. When I realized who and what Nexon was, it was too late. I did what I could to negate and prolong his commands. He wanted Juniper Thimble dead, so I had her sent to the Marca. I sent Reid to execute Juniper, because I knew Reid would never follow through with the order. He would see through it, see the Order for what it had become. Fowler wanted them both dead, and I gave them the chance to escape Nexon's clutches. I also exposed him."

Adrian glanced at Henry, who had gone still.

Henry adjusted his grip on his Mage's Bane. "This doesn't mean you get to call yourself a hero."

"I claim no such thing." Fowler coughed. He winced, as if the very motion stole hours from his life. Fowler's gaze landed on Adrian. His eyes were yellowed, and the wrinkles looked deeper than they had before. He looked, to Adrian's horror, like a corpse. "I am glad to see our prince with steel. You were always the quiet, observant boy. What do you think?"

Henry glanced at Adrian, knuckles white on his sword.

"Reid told me about that night," Adrian said. "That execution order is what made him turn from the knighthood. It saved both his and Juniper's lives, as well as exposed the Marca and the Order. Because of Reid's betrayal of the Order, he and Juniper were able to warn my father of the siege, and many escaped."

And they had later saved unsuspecting mages from the Marca, who then joined their side.

Adrian knew what he thought. Fowler had done what he thought was best with what he had to work with.

"I will let you in on a secret of mine," Fowler said. "I am dying. I have been for two decades. When I discovered who Nexon was, he didn't want me telling anyone. He cursed me into his service. Nexon believes his victory is on the horizon, that he can simply pluck his magic out of Juniper Thimble's clutches as if she were a child." Fowler coughed. "He no longer requires my service, and he has lifted his curse to let me die."

"And for your final act of goodwill you've allowed us to live?" Henry frowned.

"You sent the mages west and north," Adrian added. "Right into the path of waiting forces."

Fowler pointed a knobby finger at Adrian. A fragile smile twitched his dry lips. "See? Observant. Yes, I divided the remaining forces and sent them to deal with the Janti forces and the King's Army. I sent a pitiful force to attack the Undercity, letting Bentley know that the castle would be less guarded. He has a soldier's mind. He would not let the opportunity to strike pass. The Janti forces will win, and I suspect the King's Army will prevail as well."

The sounds of fighting within the castle had calmed. Only the crackling of the hearth fire remained, the wind at the windows. It sounded as if the siege had never happened, but it did not sound like it should. It was far too quiet. Silence pressed against the stone, tainted with blood and death and betrayal. No amount of scrubbing would wash it away.

"It doesn't matter if you kill me now or wait until this curse does me in," Fowler said, coughing. Blood dribbled onto his lip. "I would not blame you if you needed the satisfaction of killing me yourself."

"A knight practices patience and temperance," Henry recited. "Regardless of the situation."

Fowler's wrinkled lips twitched upward. "Yes, I remember those words. Among the many the knights are taught. I wish more remembered them as well as you. I admit, I had doubts about you, Henry. I thought you would be among the pledges who dropped out within a year when they discovered that knighthood was not easy to achieve, that it requires a sound mind and body and steady heart. But again, you've surpassed my expectations."

"It's not hard to surpass low expectations," Henry said grimly.

"Indeed." Fowler set his age-spotted hands on the desk. "Tell me, what do you foresee in the future of the Order?"

"It will rise from the ashes," Henry said without a doubt. "Even without you or the hall, we gathered and elected a new council. We followed the king into the Undercity."

"That is good to hear." Fowler closed his eyes. "I had hoped someone would carry on with the Order after Nexon's taint had dissolved." He opened his eyes, and fixed his watery gaze on Henry. "You would be a good knight commander."

"I believe that is the nicest thing you've ever said to me," Henry said, not hiding the disbelief in his words.

"The hard truth frightens the weak and prepares the strong," Fowler said. He coughed, and it left his voice dry and harsh. "You were not frightened to walk away from the Order and do what was right. You have learned from your mistakes and the mistakes of others. You have not fallen to the temptation of power. You have remained true to the values of the Order. What does the prince think?"

"I agree," Adrian said.

Henry frowned.

"You would make a fine knight commander," Adrian said. "If the decision were up to me, I would appoint you."

"I doubt anyone would listen to my recommendation," Fowler said, then coughed. He closed his eyes for a long moment. "My thralls are falling quickly, as are Nexon's mages."

"None will survive the battle," Henry said.

Archmage in the Ruins

Fowler coughed. Blood spotted his lips and dribbled down his chin. He leaned back into the chair, eyes glassy and tired. "Neither will I."

CHAPTER 49

Juniper returned to her royal suite and found it empty. The hearth burned with fresh logs, and someone had refilled her decanter of berry wine. Having drunk half the bottle in her hand, she sank before the hearth. The fire crackled and flickered. The wine had loosened the panic from its tight ball, and now it fluttered freely under her skin, like bugs. She collapsed onto the bearskin rug, soaking in the heat of the hearth and letting the wine loosen her bones.

She felt the wechun slink into the room, though she did not see it.

"Your actions have stirred the castle," it whispered. "Whether for good or ill is yet to be determined. Some truly believe all will perish tomorrow. Others believe they will be celebrating by sunset."

Juniper knew which was more likely. It left her stomach in knots.

The wechun curled around her. The flames reflected in its dark eyes. "The druids worry for themselves and their kind. They worry that if they are killed, druids will cease to exist. The soldiers worry for their homes to the south. The mages worry how Nexon will have them killed. Others worry for you. They believe you handed Nexon the shovel to dig your grave."

Juniper took it all in. The wechun had taken to giving her information from the castle and its new residents. It made her wonder if one of its previous masters had used it for spying.

"They might be right about the shovel," she mused. "Though I doubt Nexon needs one to dig my grave."

"Others have discussed whether or not you have turned this city into a prison."

"They might also be right," she said. "It's better than a slaughter."

Its ears flicked toward her, though its eyes remained on the fire. It looked more like a wolf than it had before. Its scales and spikes slowly shrank, and jewel-toned fur grew longer every day.

"Do you think I've gotten us all killed?" she whispered.

It didn't answer.

Juniper rolled onto her back. Her body protested. All the stress settled into her bones, and she felt like she could sleep for days.

The chamber door opened. Reid's magic graced hers in a loving greeting as his armored footsteps crossed the sitting room and entered the bedroom.

"We're preparing," Reid said, his tone professional and stoic. "We have mages and druids scouting the escape route through the library. Those not fighting are preparing to hide there. The battlemages and Sentinels are readying for battle."

"Hopefully, it won't come to that," she said. "Either way."

"They will march south to prevent Nexon from attacking Delphine."

So she couldn't have saved them anyway.

Reid started over, and the wechun uncurled itself from around her. It returned to its place under the bed. Reid sat beside her.

"We missed you for lunch," he said.

"I wasn't hungry."

A beat passed.

"They all expect me to die." Juniper sighed and looked into the fire. "I fear they're right. Everyone put this burden on my shoulders, and I don't know what they expected. Some epic battle where we defied all odds and triumphed? Laughable."

His magic caressed hers. "Whatever happens tomorrow, I'm with you."

"You don't have to go with me. If I… If I don't come back, these people will need you. They will need a knight to lead them."

"If you don't come back, then I won't either," Reid said assuredly.

"Reid—"

"If you die on the battlefield, so will I." Reid tilted her chin toward him. He gazed into her eyes with that damned knight face, and she knew he meant those words. "I don't want to live in a world without you. Without you… I…" He struggled with his words, and his mask cracked. "I could never find someone after you."

He slid his finger over her cheekbone, then placed a tender kiss on her lips. Juniper fell into his arms.

"Thank you," she said. "For everything. I don't know where I'd be if not for you."

His hot breath met her temple.

Juniper hated goodbyes. Hated them more than anything. She hated the sense of finality, the punctuation. To think she might be saying goodbye to Reid pinched her insides and made her feel like letting Nexon destroy everything, her included.

So she didn't say anything, and neither did he.

Juniper spent the day away from the others. The wechun kept her company. As evening gilded the castle, her hands shook and it felt as if someone had twisted all her bones the wrong way. Reid returned to their chambers and updated her. Their forces were as ready as they could be. The druids were packed and ready to hide come morning, and Lilianna's Shadows reported that Nexon had so far kept his word. His mages hadn't moved. They were preparing for battle the same as they were.

She should have spent what could have been her final day in this realm with her friends, dancing and bedding Reid, but she couldn't. She couldn't face her friends. She didn't want to prompt them for a goodbye. Nexon had stolen the peace from her final hours.

She fell asleep at some point, and woke up when Reid climbed into bed. He had washed, and he smelled of lavender and bergamot. The moon had come out from behind the clouds and set the bedroom in shades of silver. The fire had died down, and the screen turned it into an amber glow. Reid wrapped his arms around her. Neither said a word. She didn't want to fall asleep; she wanted to lay in his arms for as long as she could.

The following day dawned, and Juniper did not want to get up. She and Reid remained in bed as the sun brightened, shading the room in pale yellow. He rubbed her back, and she pressed her forehead against his cheek.

Ingrid disturbed the final moments of peace. Juniper had already missed the morning meal, and there would be no time for a midday meal. She set an old wooden tray on the table. It held two bowls of porridge and two cups of tea. A potion sat on it as well, a bright pink with a foggy top.

"Your friend gave me the potion to give you," Ingrid said, her tone only slightly disgruntled. "He said it would help or some such. He said to make sure you drink the whole thing. So, down it goes. Come on, now."

Juniper reluctantly pulled herself out of Reid's embrace and dragged herself to the table. The potion tasted like winter berries and frost, and she felt it slipping through her bloodstream and stealing away the worst of the panic and dread that had settled deep. It made eating the porridge easier. Reid ate his, kissed her temple, then went to see to the defense.

After she had eaten enough of the porridge to satisfy Ingrid, Juniper meandered to the parlor at the end of the royal chambers. It had a balcony that overlooked the front garden and the street beyond. Her forces had congregated. Buildings had been commandeered for supplies and healing, just in case Nexon had fooled them all with his bargain. Ison's beasts and Lilianna's Shadows would be their first line of offense, guarding the edge of the city. The druid-warriors, battlemages, and Sentinels would come after.

Juniper watched her forces from the balcony. The sun eased far too quickly across the sky.

A knock sounded against the stone. Reid stood in the doorway, dressed in his silver armor and his knight's stoic mask. His Mage's Bane rested at his side.

"It's time," he said.

Juniper had stopped feeling sometime that morning. Either from Ison's strange potion or her own deadened feelings. She didn't mind either way. She would rather not feel anything than feel miserable.

With Reid at her side, she marched through the castle. A deathly silence had replaced the whispers, one of fear and dread. Even the wind had hushed. She marched through the front gardens and into the streets. The gathered forces parted for her, some stony-faced like Reid, others terrified, others still looked a bit sick.

The night had brought a fresh blanket of snow to the city, and Juniper felt it all around. It covered the outskirts and the fields where she and Nexon would do this final battle. Blugo's stars were above them, even if the sun and wintry clouds hid them.

Her forces marched behind her as she made her way down an old path between two snowy fields. Reid walked at her side. Shadows and beasts stalked behind. The Shadows relayed all information to Lilianna, who would give the signal to flee or fight, depending on how the confrontation with Nexon went.

No one spoke. Only their footsteps in the snow sounded.

Nexon approached from the forest. His army of mages and thralls marched behind him. He wore a cloak of vibrant gold and shined leather armor that looked more for decoration and style than practicality. Juniper hadn't donned anything special. The druids had put together leather armor for her. She wore her favorite leather boots, a gift from her time spent in Bradburn Castle. The past two years had been hard on them, leaving them scars with nicks and scrapes and wrinkles.

She paused in the middle of the barren field they had chosen. Her forces stood behind her, giving the battle a wide berth. Only Reid remained at her side.

Nexon strutted forward as if he had already won, full of ancient arrogance. Juniper tried to appear enthused about her chances, about what she was about to attempt, but she had already told herself every hopeful half-truth she could think of. She'd run out of hopeful excuses.

"Well, here we are," Nexon said, looking down his nose. His breath puffed on his lips. "Have you kept your end of the bargain, little princess?"

Juniper lifted her left hand. The moonstone ring glittered in the sun. Nexon's eyes narrowed at the ring. Something fiery cracked through his expression, something dark and bitter and desperate.

"Just a reminder," Juniper said, "you fight me, and I fight you. Neither of us will attack anyone else. That includes you trying to hurt one of my friends to distract me."

"Yes, yes," Nexon said. "We already shook on the bargain. The *ring*."

Juniper steeled herself, cold as ice, and stepped into the field. Reid took a step back. Nexon started toward her. They met at arm's length in the middle. A cloud rolled over the sun, dousing the forest and armies in shadow. The moonstone continued to glitter.

She slid the ring from her finger. Every bone in her body screamed not to give it up, not to give him the final piece of his power, but the irresistible tug to follow through on the bargain twisted in her chest.

She dropped the ring into his open palm.

His long fingers closed around the ring, and with a frightening crack, the moonstone shattered into a blinding light. Nexon let out a mad laugh as the light surged into his body. His expression became one of a crazed animal. At once, the earth rumbled under her feet. Juniper threw herself back and rolled on a sheet of clear blue ice. As she landed, she sent spears of ice at where Nexon had been standing. Two missed him, three crashed into a wall of hardened earth, but one—one that had curved at the last moment—scratched across his upper back.

He spat a curse and knocked the ice aside with a force of magic.

Reid stood on the edge of the clearing, eyes focusing on the battle before him, eyes working through a number of strategies. She had seen the look on his face enough to suspect his thoughts. Reid knew he could not harm Nexon or any of his soldiers.

Nexon threw tendrils of earth at her, pushing her back.

Back and forth they tossed spears and daggers of ice and earth. This, Juniper knew. Her panic and dread evaporated. She knew survival, the fight and footing, the subtle movements before an attack. Juniper knew her way around a fight, though Nexon was clearly better at commanding his magic. However, he hadn't learned to fight in the Undercity. If not for magic, she would've had Nexon on the ground and bleeding out in a few heartbeats.

A gentle snow began to fall. Juniper felt every snowflake, and she peppered them at Nexon's face and eyes.

She spotted Reid in her peripheral, gripping the hilt of his Mage's Bane with white knuckles.

Nexon growled and hurled spikes of stone. She dodged, but not quick enough—a spear of earth struck her upper arm, slicing through the woolen sleeve. Blood gushed into the woolen fabric. She stumbled closer to Reid. She hated that he had to see her wounded, but she had little other choice. As she jumped to her feet, she glanced at him; his molten eyes were fixed on her, on her arm.

Juniper threw herself back into the fray. As she dodged a series of spikes and sent daggers flying from every direction, the pain lessened. She formed tiny daggers in the falling snow and hurtled them continuously at Nexon, who managed to dodge most of them. Blood had appeared on his right thigh and his upper arm.

Nexon meant to knock out her footing, and she used the snow under his feet to do the same to him; they both tumbled onto the ground. She bounced back to her feet sooner. Over Nexon's shoulder, Reid's mask had reformed.

The dance went on, ice daggers and stone spikes, bruises and scratches. Blood spotted the snowy ground.

Juniper whisked up a shield of ice in time to stop spears of stone—one broke through. She dodged, the tip barely missing her throat. She rolled and bounced back to her feet. Nexon's gaze shifted over her shoulder, and he hesitated.

Reid rushed the battlefield, drawing his Mage's Bane. A tremor of uncertainty surged through the crowd. A hungry madness came over Nexon, and he waited to see what Reid would do. If Reid attacked Nexon, the bargain was void. Nexon would not have to keep his word, and everyone in the Dead City would be slaughtered.

Reid knew that.

Everyone knew that.

Still Reid jumped between Juniper and Nexon. Nexon's mad grin stretched, and his guard fell. He was giving Reid a wide opening to attack.

Juniper blasted Nexon back with a wave of ice and snow. She threw her arms out. Nexon's blue eyes widened a fraction, and then Reid twisted his body and plunged his Mage's Bane into Juniper's chest.

CHAPTER 50

Juniper felt a sliver of pain upon impact, the sharp and frigid bite of steel, and then everything else numbed. She felt the blade bury in her chest, felt it tear through skin and muscle, scrape bone and puncture vitals. Her lungs sputtered to a halt. Her heart gave a frightening series of panicked half-beats, then stopped.

Cold flashed over her skin, needling bone deep.

Nexon's icy eyes widened and his mouth fell open. His magic dissolved around him.

Ison screamed—his voice was lost somewhere behind her.

Reid stared at where his Mage's Bane vanished into her chest. He pulled the blade out. It hurt—a searing, burning pain radiated from the wound. The vicious bane seeped into every fiber, turning her magic into poison. Juniper fell forward; Reid caught her. The bloodied Band hit the ruined ground.

"Juniper?" he gasped. Panic, fear, and dread flashed across his features—fear that he had made a terrible mistake.

For a breathless, terrible moment, she did too.

And then her heart gave a tiny beat.

And another, a little stronger. The sting of the bane receded.

"It's working," she whispered.

She started to stand, and Reid helped her to her feet. She didn't think her own legs could have held her weight. She leaned heavily on Reid.

"Absolute madness!" Nexon stood dumbfounded. The snow had gathered on his shoulders and his hair. His cheeks and nose had turned pink from the cold. He half laughed, the breath a white puff. He started to say something, but the words never made it to his lips. He paled. Realization settled on his features, smoothing the confused crease between his eyes and turning his surprise into panic. He flattened his hand against his chest. "You…"

Juniper flashed him a devilish smile. She wanted to laugh, but she couldn't muster the energy.

"No… No!" Nexon screamed. He went ghostly white—because he knew what she had done.

Blood seeped through Nexon's woolen tunic and through the seam of his leathers, spreading through the fibers frightfully fast. Nexon trembled. His rage-filled eyes met hers.

"You bitch," he spat. Blood dribbled down his chin.

"You can feel it," Juniper gasped. "Mage's Bane. It's turning your magic into poison."

With every heartbeat, her wound healed, and Nexon's grew. The Mage's Bane that had entered her system tortured him instead, squeezing his magic and curling it inward, turning it against him, killing him.

Nexon took a staggering step forward. A stone spike shot from the ground, but it crumbled before it crossed half the space between them. He stumbled forward and fell to his knees. Blood seeped down his front and spilled onto the snow. Juniper watched him fade, as the Bane tortured him and stole his magic, as his lungs flooded, as his heart stopped; all the while, her own body slowly stitched itself back together as the worst of her wounds transferred to Nexon.

This time, she would make sure he died.

Nexon turned his bloodless face toward her, full of rage and fear. And then, the light left his eyes and he collapsed.

"No!" A mage scrambled into the circle and fell to her knees beside Nexon. She shook his body to no avail. Her scream echoed over the field. Tears lined her eyes. She staggered to her feet, and spikes of earth shot from her feet toward Juniper.

A ward of golden energy appeared between Juniper and the mage. The earth hit the ward with a thunderous bang, then fell to the ground. The mage sent another spike—a grayish wind knocked the mage off her feet.

Ison appeared at Juniper's side. "You're finished," he said loud enough for those closest to hear.

Xavier marched to Nexon's body and knelt. He pressed his fingers to his neck. A moment later, he stood. "He's dead."

"Your master is dead," Ison repeated, louder.

"You cheated!" the crying earth mage screamed, tears running down her cheeks.

A fireball hurled from the left. Ison smacked it aside with a gale, and the fireball crashed into the snow with a powerful hiss.

Cries filled the air, and feet thundered on the battlefield.

"No," Juniper gasped as mages surged and beasts growled and Shadows pounced.

"Get her out of here," Xavier shouted at Reid, a charcoal dagger in each hand. He blocked a fist of stone with a shield of energy, and then brought it down on Nexon's throat. His head rolled into the snow. Blackish blood, poisoned from the Bane, spilled onto the snow.

Reid hoisted Juniper into his arms and climbed onto the back of a Shadow. It shot through the unfurling battle. Reid held her close. Between sluggish blinks, she saw the Shadows running alongside them, magic shooting into the sky, and then the castle loomed in the distance. Snow fluttered despite it all.

They slowed. Juniper opened her eyes. They had entered the Dead City, and the sounds of the battle had faded. Reid held her against him. She shut her eyes again, and when she opened them next, they had paused outside of a stone building remodeled with reedy shutters and magelights. Voices murmured from within.

Reid dismounted and rushed through the woven door.

"A healer," Reid said, his tone commanding and strong.

A mage wearing a sash decorated with the Balendin crest met them immediately. She somehow managed to scowl and look frightened at the same time. The healer ushered them into one of the rooms, and Reid set Juniper onto the stone slab. The healer set to work cutting off the ruined leather cuirass and tunic. Reid remained firmly at Juniper's side.

As the clothing peeled away from the wound, Juniper winced. Reid's hand touched her bare arm. He had aimed between her breasts and run her through, leaving a wound straight through her chest. The healer set about cleaning it, and Juniper focused on her breaths. She felt the wound, but it was a fraction of the lethal wound Reid had inflicted. Everything hurt. Her blood had dried against her skin and tugged at the raw flesh that had begun to stitch itself back together. The healer lathered it with bitter-smelling ointments that numbed the sting and stopped the bleeding.

Only then did the healer speak. "I take your return to be good news?"

Juniper's thoughts snagged on that word—return. "Nexon is dead," she stammered.

The healer's entire expression shifted.

"We saw one of our own sever his head for good measure," Reid added.

"Dead," the healer repeated. A small smile stretched her lips. "All right, let's make sure you don't go the same way."

The healer held her hands over Juniper's wound, and a pale orange glow emitted from her palms. The magic spread over the broken skin and through the wound, healing bone and muscle and everything else the blade had severed. Juniper recognized the itching sensation that followed; she kept her hands firmly at her sides.

While the healer worked, several more healers rushed outside. Wounded were carried inside. Casualties of the battle.

Her heart sank. This was what she had tried to avoid.

The healer did all her magic allowed in a single sitting. She had stopped the bleeding and stitched together the vitals. After slathering the sound with a minty ointment, she wrapped it tight and forced Juniper to drink a tonic that tasted like grass. Finished, the healer scurried away to help with the other wounded.

Juniper scooted to the edge of the bed. Dizziness overtook her.

"Easy," Reid said softly. "You just survived a fatal blow. Give yourself a few breaths."

"Someone else will need this bed," she reasoned.

The dizziness abated. Most of the house looked to have come from Delphine. Bottles of tonics and jars of salves lined the stone shelves. It smelled like a healer's room, stringent and cold.

Reid sat beside her. The panic had vanished from his features, but he wore something she couldn't readily identify.

"Are you all right?" he asked.

"I'm alive," she said, her voice strained. "Which is considerably better than I thought I would be."

"When did you…" Reid sighed and rubbed his face. He leaned onto his knees. "That was a binding spell, wasn't it? How did you do that?"

She couldn't help the sly smile. It had been a brilliant idea on her part. "After the parley. When I gave Nexon the brooch, I opened the back and stuck him with the pin. Some of his blood got on me, and I pretended to trip so I could take the pin. I went to Delmont and asked if he could write a binding spell. He warned me that he had little experience and that the wounds might not transfer cleanly."

"And it didn't."

"I'm lucky it transferred at all." Her heart was beating, her lungs pumping. It would take a few weeks to heal the rest of the way.

"Why didn't you tell me about it?" Reid asked.

"Because I didn't know if it would work," Juniper said. "My original idea was to let Nexon get a few hits on me, and if the wounds transferred, I'd pretend to slip in the snow or something and he'd go for the killing blow. *You* figured it out first."

Reid blew out a breath. "I've never been so terrified."

She reached for him; he took her hand.

"They could use us out there," Juniper said.

"You need rest," Reid said at once, and she knew by his tone there would be no arguing.

As much as she hated the idea of her friends fighting her battle, Reid was right. She wouldn't be much help in her current condition. The tonic was working its magic through her system, and a grogginess overrode her other senses. Another batch of wounded arrived at the healer's door. The coppery scent of blood mixed with the floral stench of magic and burned flesh.

Juniper squeezed Reid's hand. "I don't want to stay here."

"Where do you want to go?" he asked.

"Somewhere that doesn't smell like blood and death," she said.

Reid helped her off the stone slab. No one stopped them from leaving; there were too many other wounds to tend.

The snowfall had thickened. She wore nothing on her upper half but the linens wrapping her chest, but the cold did not bother her. It turned the sky gray and the city silver and white. They started toward the castle. It loomed in the snowy distance, resilient and strong. It had survived yet another storm, another attempt at annihilation. And she had again survived.

She couldn't see the battle for the city and snow, but she heard an echo of it. Magic burst, steel clashed, and screams filtered into the air. The sky above the battlefield flashed with colors like a lightning storm. Florals and metallics scented the air.

Reid steered her toward the castle. The front garden was empty, save for a few druid lookouts. They gawked at her, but none left their stations.

Lilianna stood on the front steps. She didn't look surprised at all. If anything, she looked relieved. Juniper wanted to ask her about the battle, but by the exhaustion that lined the druid girl's face, she decided against it.

Despite the healing, Juniper couldn't move very fast. By the time they reached the royal suite, her body felt like wet sand. Painful wet sand. She had never been happier to see the overly large bed and its woolen blankets, or the burning hearth and bearskin rug. Reid helped her into the bed, took off her boots and bloodied trousers, and pulled the blankets over her.

Before she had shut her eyes, Lilianna burst into the bedroom, hair messed.

"What is it?" Reid demanded.

"They're retreating," Lilianna gasped.

"Thank the gods," Reid breathed. He set his hand on Juniper's shoulder. "We've done it."

Juniper hadn't the mind to reply. Lilianna's message had erased the lingering panic. Her exhaustion surged, and she fell into a dreamless sleep.

CHAPTER 51

The snow continued into the evening, blocking out the light in a ghostly silver haze. Juniper sat in the parlor of the royal wing, reclining on a wicker chaise padded with wools and leathers. A fire burned in the hearth, and runes kept the snow from entering the open balcony doors. She still felt terrible, but a weight had been lifted from her shoulders.

They had won.

She had survived, and so had a large chunk of her forces.

There had been casualties. Scouts had come and gone from the parlor since she'd woken, relaying news of every corner of her forces. The battle had gone on into the later afternoon. Nexon's defeat had caused discontent through his followers, which had given hers an advantage. She had yet to ask for details of the battle itself. She partially didn't want to know.

She took each breath as it came, flexing her magic through the snowfall.

Footsteps approached, quiet and measured, too quick and light to be Reid's. Ison appeared at her side and set a wooden tray onto the table.

"I've brought you a tonic." He set the earthen cup of pale green liquid in her hand. It was still warm. "The druids have done wonders in the garden. It's like summer there all the time. I can't imagine what it will look like a year from now."

Juniper let herself imagine it—planter boxes, fresh soil, and flowering trees. She took a drink. The herbal taste warmed her tongue and her insides; the imagery of the royal gardens became a bit clearer.

"Xavier is still mad at you," Ison admitted sheepishly. "He refused to come up here."

She chuckled. "He's stubborn."

Ison nodded. He wandered to the balcony. Ison, by the grace of the gods, hadn't been hurt more than a few burns and scratches. A bandage wrapped his left upper arm, though his clean robes hid it. Juniper only knew because she had asked the scout about her friends.

"I still can't believe you actually used a binding spell on him," Ison said, grinning ear to ear. He laughed. "It's remarkable. Though, I would have liked to punch him before you killed him. I suppose the look on his face when he realized what you'd done will have to do."

She finished off the tonic in a large gulp. She doubted she would forget it either. The shock and surprise and rage.

"How are you feeling?" Ison asked, taking the glass. He set it back on the tray.

"Better," Juniper said. "Between the herbs the druids have grown and whatever the hell the wechun brought back from the grounds has worked."

Her wechun had disappeared into the untamed royal grounds and returned with a fistful of rare and hard-to-grow silvery nettles that had taken the pain from her body and left her feeling light as air. Ison had brought the potion to her, and she had been more thrilled to see her friend unharmed than the potion.

Ison picked up the tray. "I need to go. I've got potions brewing. There's..." He bit his lip, and his eyes darted quickly to her. "A lot that needs to be done."

"I will see you later," she said, and he left as quickly and quietly as he'd come.

She knew what he'd nearly said. There were a lot of wounded who needed healing potions and tonics and salves. She took a deep breath. She'd known there would be wounded and deaths. Still, it bothered her not knowing how many and who.

With Ison gone, silence returned. The snowfall muted the sounds of the city below.

She had nearly fallen asleep when a presence at her side stirred her from it. Blinking, she saw Delmont standing beside the chaise. He had changed into clean trousers, simple tunic, and a woolen cloak. His red hair had been freshly washed and left down to dry. He sat on the end of the chaise.

"Myrisha sends her love," Delmont said. "Crespin sends congratulations. They hope to be able to celebrate Nexon's defeat soon. She has sent a messenger to Rusdasin."

"Has she heard anything?" Juniper asked a bit more desperately than she would have liked.

Delmont shook his head.

They sat for a while in silence.

"It's peaceful up here." Delmont sighed. "But I must return before the battlemages start looking for me. Is there anything you wish to say to Her Majesty?"

Juniper considered it. "I would like to tell her that I am sorry for leaving the way I did. I was thinking of myself. It was a selfish decision, made recklessly. She should also expect a wedding invitation soon, seeing as how Reid and I both survived the battle."

Delmont chuckled and reached into his cloak and retrieved a beautiful silver hand mirror. Into the shined surface, he said, "Did you hear all of that?"

"I did," came a slightly distorted feminine voice. Delmont turned the mirror to Juniper, and within the glassy surface, an auburn-haired young woman with pale golden skin smiled back at her.

Juniper blinked. "You…you're in Delphine?"

Myrisha nodded. "I am. I am glad to see you alive and well. Crespin thinks the same, though he wouldn't say it as nicely."

"I expect him at the wedding," Juniper said.

Myrisha's smile widened. "I will see that he's there. Until I see you in person, Juniper. Or Isolde."

"Until then," Juniper said, returning her smile.

The mirror rippled, then Juniper's reflection looked back at her. Delmont tucked the mirror back into his cloak, then stood. "I will speak to you later, Your Highness."

How she would love to have a mirror to speak to Adrian, or Roslyn, or even Amery.

Delmont left, and Juniper was again left to relish the peace and quiet. Of course, she wasn't alone—Sentinels stood outside the parlor door to deter possible spies or assassins from finishing Nexon's wishes. So far, none had tried. At least she didn't know if any had.

The hazy light gradually faded into dark gray. The snow continued, piling up a hand's height on the balcony railing.

The snow shifted outside the balcony. She didn't need her magic to find out what it was. She felt it. The wechun slunk onto the balcony from the roof, its fur silvery with snow. It sauntered in and shook the snow from its emerald-and-sapphire fur.

"There you are," Juniper said. "That tonic worked wonders."

"You are absolutely mad," it said.

"You didn't believe in me," she said plainly.

"I had more reasons not to."

"Well, now you have a reason," she said. "In your defense, I didn't fully believe in me either."

"Your man is on his way," the wechun said, curling up before the fire. "He looked dire."

"That's how he looks all the time," Juniper said. She hadn't seen much of Reid since he had carried her into the castle.

She waited for the sound of his armored footsteps, but those she heard were not armored. Her heart deflated a little, thinking a scout had come to give more news or someone else needed to inform her of whatever they thought important. She sighed as the Sentinels opened the woven door and her visitor entered.

Calm and assured footsteps approached her chaise, and then Reid sat on the side. He carried a tray, on which sat an earthen bowl of steaming stew.

"Reid?" she said, his name a question.

He did not wear his silver armor. He wore clean trousers and a heavy woolen tunic. He looked beyond exhausted. Dark circles hung under his eyes, his bronze skin had paled, and he looked…utterly dire.

"Is everything all right?" she said at once.

"As much as it came be." He motioned to her with the tray and then set it on her lap. "Ingrid told me to tell you that you need to eat. She said you've lost weight and you're too skinny."

Juniper harrumphed. "Not every day a girl gets told she's too skinny."

She didn't have an appetite, but the stew smelled amazing. She took a spoonful, then another, and another. Reid remained at her side. His gaze had wandered out the balcony doors and into the snowy night.

"Are you sure you're all right?" she asked again.

"I will be," he said softly. He turned his forlorn expression to her, then to his hands. "There is just so much to do after a battle. I've never experienced a battle of this size, and it's…"

She reached for him. Rather than let her move, he scooted closer and took her hand in his.

"A good heart never gets used to battle," the wechun said. "It is an old Iluvin saying, and though it doesn't translate as poetically, the meaning is there."

"Thank you," Reid said. He ran his thumb across Juniper's knuckles.

Reid did not wear his Mage's Bane. He wore no sword at his waist. Not even a dagger. She didn't mind. She could still picture the blade covered in her blood.

Juniper ate as much stew as she could, then Reid carried her back into their bedroom. The hearth burned warm and bright. Reid set her down in the bed and pulled the blankets to her chin. He pulled the screen over the hearth, then joined her.

"Do you have plans after this?" Reid asked.

"Nothing big," she said. "I have a wedding to plan. I daresay your aunt will want to be involved. I've already invited Myrisha and Crespin."

A small smile broke through his dire expression. "When you are well, we need to travel back to Rusdasin."

"Agreed," she said. A beat passed. "Oh, and I also promised Blugo that I'd end the slave trade in Janti, but only after I took out Nexon."

Reid sat up, eyes wide. "You what?"

She half laughed, or as much as she could with her wounded chest. "When we were traveling to Galamond, I was kidnapped by slavers. I asked Blugo for help, and I promised that if he got me out of that mess, I'd end the slave trade in Janti. Then a dire wolf showed up and…well, you know, ate the slavers."

Reid continued to stare at her. "You're serious?"

"I didn't specify a time limit," she said. "Only that I needed to take care of Nexon first."

"It won't be easy." Reid sighed and reclined. "There are a lot of powerful and wealthy people in Janti with hands in the trade."

"Little I do is easy," Juniper quipped. "I would be disappointed otherwise. I'll have to plan and do research and all of that nonsense, which I don't feel like doing anytime soon. So, before that, maybe I'll take a vacation somewhere warm and sandy with my husband."

Reid chuckled. "We will rest up before we travel anywhere."

"Of course." A beat passed with only the crackling of the fire. "Reid? If I am indeed a princess, would that not make you a prince by marriage?"

"I could handle being a prince," Reid mused. "However, that is assuming you are going to accept your birthright. You will have to return to Delphine."

Juniper sighed through her nose. "I know. Without having an evil archmage to defeat, it doesn't sound so bad. I could get used to living in a palace and having servants to draw my baths and bring whatever food I requested."

"I thought you didn't want to be a princess?" Reid's brow furrowed.

She sighed through her nose and closed her eyes. The herbal concoction was working through her bones. "I'll think about it. I could use a few years of lounging in scented baths and letting others make decisions for me."

Reid smiled, and she loved the sight.

She fell asleep with the sight stained on her eyelids. She woke to him fastening one of her father's cloaks around his shoulders.

"Rest." Reid crossed the space and kissed her temple. "You need it. I'll return before lunch."

"Where are you going?"

"Someone has to make sure things are going smoothly, and since you are on bed rest, everyone seems to think I'm the one they should go to."

"You *are* the better half," Juniper said, closing her eyes. She sighed dramatically. "It only makes sense they would seek your advice and counsel."

"I can send them up here instead," Reid said. "Most would be thrilled to speak to the princess who defeated Nexon not by force but by wit."

"Is that what they're saying?" She cracked one eye open. "What else are they saying?"

Reid grinned. "Rest. I'll tell you after."

She sat up a little taller, and the effort pulled at her wound. "Tell me now."

He held firm, and his smile wilted. "At lunch. I'll have something brought up for you, and we can eat in the sitting room."

She wanted to demand the stories, but she knew she wouldn't get anywhere. She reclined, hiding her grimace from the tug on her wound. "Fine. I expect stories with my food."

Reid laughed. "Commanded like a royal."

The wechun snorted.

Reid left, and Juniper sank back into the pillows. She thought about trying to rest, but her thoughts drifted to the little wooden box on her bedside table. She reached for it.

"Would you do me a favor?"

The wechun unfurled itself, stretching its hind legs, then its front. "That depends on what you need."

"Oh, it's nothing terrible, just a little quest to find a little something in the vault. I can't go hunting, so I am passing the quest onto you."

The wechun snorted. "Task away, Your Highness."

CHAPTER 52

Juniper lay in bed until her back hurt and a headache started on the backside of her skull. Despite the tugging on the wound her movement caused, she pulled herself out of bed. Buttery sunlight streamed through the shutters. She stood; the world wobbled.

When the tilting stopped, she made her way to the window and pushed open the shutters. Sunlight burst through. The world beyond glittered as if made of gold and silver, the sunlight glinting off the snow drifts and ice-covered trees. The gilded forest stretched as far as she could see.

The wechun crawled out from under the bed, unfurling its glittering body in the sunlight. It stretched like a dog, front feet first, then back. "Ah, she wakes."

Juniper hummed a note of discontent. She was stiff and everything ached. She undid her robe and let it drop to the floor. She wore nothing else over her chest but bandages and loose trousers. She left her trousers by her robe and carefully unwound the bandage.

She examined the damage in the vanity mirror. The wound had healed remarkably. A scar would likely remain, but she didn't mind it. The new scar would intercept the curving white scar that one of Nexon's beasts had given her back in Bradburn Castle—it started at her collarbone, curved across her chest, between her breasts, and curved to her hip.

The wechun stretched in front of the fire, fur glittering in the light.

"Does this mean you're my bodyguard for the day?" Juniper asked teasingly.

"I'm far from a bodyguard," it said. "I am what my archmage decides, often unconsciously."

"Yes, what I command, you become," Juniper said, yawning.

"I'm glad you make light of the burden."

"It's too early for such dreary attitudes," Juniper said. "As my first command to you, I command you to be more cheerful."

It chuckled. "I will try my best."

Juniper pulled her robe back over her shoulders and tied it loosely. "What do you think my father would think about all this?"

"He would be honored that his daughter is living here," it replied without hesitation. "He and his wife would have hated the desolate mess their home had become, and they would be thrilled to see it coming back to life, to see people returning to this once great city."

"I am glad to hear it," she said.

It occurred to her that the wechun had lived in the castle before the civil war. She opened her mouth to ask about her parents when the woven doors to the chamber swished aside and someone shuffled through. The wechun's ears twitched toward the sound, and its nostrils flared.

A young girl of no more than fourteen entered the bedroom, carrying a tea tray. The girl had her eyes on the tray, and as she approached the bedroom table, her eyes lifted. At the sight of Juniper, the girl jumped. Everything on the tray rattled.

"You're awake!" she said in a single breath. The girl bowed, further rattling the tray. She stood straight, eyes bright and smile nervous. "It's a pleasure to meet you, ma'am."

"Ma'am?" Juniper laughed. Of all the things she had been called in her life, ma'am hadn't been one of them.

The girl paled. "Do you prefer Your Highness? I—I meant no offense."

Juniper stared. The girl trembled like she expected a lashing. "I don't care what you call me, as long as it's not rude."

The girl blinked. That had not been what she had expected.

An awkward moment passed.

"Do you need something?" Juniper asked.

"I—I brought you tea, ma'am—I mean, Your Highness." She rushed to the table and began to arrange the tea. Finished, she stood back with her hands folded tightly against her chest. "Sir Sandpiper asked to be informed when you woke. At once, he said."

Juniper started to make herself a cup of tea, then realized that the girl was waiting for a dismissal. "All right, go on and find him."

The girl bowed and scurried into the corridor.

Juniper sipped her tea. "Odd."

The wechun hummed, sounding amused.

Juniper drank a cup and half of a second before she decided on a wash. She trudged into the bathing room and set about filling the tub. With so much snow lingering just outside the windows, it didn't take long. Her magic squeezed as she heated the water. She hung her robe on a brass hook by the door.

The wechun slunk into the bathing room and curled up near the door.

The hot bath soothed aches she hadn't realized she had. She washed as best she could, and when the water began to cool, she rose. She magicked the water from her skin and hair. She pulled the robe back around her and left her hair loose.

The young girl was standing just inside her bedroom.

"Your Highness!" The girl bowed, the sudden movement awkward.

"Oh, hello again," Juniper said. "Do you need something?"

The girl blushed a fierce shade of crimson. She said meekly, "Everyone has heard about your victory over Nexon. You used your mind and your cleverness, not brute force. You have saved the realm." Her grin returned, and her entire face brightened. In a single breath, she added, "Everyone is talking about you, the Archmage of Water, the lost princess of Balendin, conqueror of evil!"

Juniper chuckled at the girl's enthusiasm. "Did you find our dear Sir Sandpiper?"

"Yes, ma'am." The girl bowed her head. "He is in the study. Would you care for something to eat? Drink? Wine? More tea?"

Juniper considered. "I would love a pot of strong tea."

"At once!" The girl bolted.

Juniper let herself into the study. A door had been made from tightly woven vines. Sunlight poured in from the windows, and a magelight of pale gold hovered near the ceiling. The mold and broken stone had been cleaned. A fire burned in the hearth, and rosewater scented the air.

Reid sat at a large wooden desk, a feathered quill scratching along a piece of greenish parchment. The desk looked freshly built and simply decorated. Already, the shelves held ink bottles, quills and nibs, and stacks of parchment. Several sealed letters sat on the far side of the desk, the blue wax of the seal drying.

"Good afternoon," Reid said without looking up. The quill paused for only a moment.

Juniper walked around the desk.

"I've written to Uncle, King Bradburn, Henry, and Adrian. I am currently writing to Queen Myrisha. Delmont has already informed her of what's happened, but it would be better to have official correspondence. I'd like you to sign this letter as well, to let her know you are considering her as well. You might consider writing to her about your thoughts on declaring yourself as Isolde."

She fingered the stack of letters. Reid had elegantly written each name on the thick parchment. The wax showed the Collatian royal seal, the sun and moon circled by laurel leaves. As Reid finished his next letter, Juniper meandered to the open windows. The same runes kept in the heat and kept out the bitter cold. She spotted the druids in the garden, tending to the plants and building another row of planter boxes with the help of earth mages. Their song drifted upward, haunting and beautiful.

A flourish of the quill, and then, "Here."

Juniper added her name beside his on the bottom of the letter, adding a little flourish. She couldn't have Reid's signature prettier than her own.

Reid blew on the ink to dry, folded the letter, and poured blue wax onto the crease. A beat of silence passed as she pressed the old seal into the wax, then the letter joined the others.

"I found the seal in the old desk," Reid said. "I hope Myrisha doesn't find its use offensive, considering it was your father's."

"I'm sure it'll be fine," Juniper said. Myrisha didn't seem the type to get offended so easily. "Besides, if it was my father's, then it's technically mine."

Reid didn't argue. He extended the quill to her. "Would you like to write to her? Our letters would leave the city the same day."

She waved the quill away. "I don't feel like writing. Not today. Maybe tomorrow, or after a cup of tea. I asked the girl outside to fetch a pot. She seemed very eager."

Reid half-laughed. "Be kind. She begged me for a job that would help Her Highness. I could think of nothing else. She followed her parents to Nexon. Both turned to our side."

"Poor thing," Juniper said, mostly to put off writing a letter. "To have grown up knowing only Nexon's twisted ideals."

"Would you rather dictate your letter to me?" Reid wiggled the feather at her.

"Yes, all right." She sighed and sank into one of few chairs. They looked to be made of the same wood as the desk, hastily made and simple. "Tell her...that I would be interested in...acknowledging myself as Isolde Balendin, granted it isn't going to be some odious thing where the council is going to want to lock me in a gilded cage and command my daily routine and all that nonsense. I demand to retain my independence from the crown. I do not want a crown or a throne."

Reid began to write. Juniper added a few thoughts as he wrote. As he poured the wax onto the seal, a knock sounded at the door. Juniper answered it; it was the young girl with a tray of tea. She eagerly set the tray on the table in the sitting room and bowed herself out.

Juniper made a cup of tea and sat before the hearth. Reid made himself a cup, but he did not sit. He held his hand out for hers.

"I want to show you something," he said.

"Where?"

He raised a brow.

"Depending on where we're going, I'm changing clothes." She motioned to her robe.

"We won't be leaving the royal wing, so you will be seen by few others."

She considered it, then conceded and put her hand in his. Reid guided her into the corridor. He started toward the far end of the royal wing, to the parlor.

Reid led her to the balcony. The streets surrounding the main gate were busy with mages and soldiers.

"The forces from Delphine will be leaving soon," Reid said. "Delmont wanted to wait until you were in stable condition. He wants to speak with us about an archmage council. It was tradition to the Iluvin, it seems."

"You sound enthused."

Reid stared into the city with that masked expression of his. "I'm still grappling with the idea that I'm a mage, let alone an archmage. I tried to explain it in my letters to Rusdasin, but…I didn't know how. I fear my uncle's reaction. I think it is something best shown rather than explained in words."

Juniper felt a tremor of that panic. "He might distrust magic, but he loves you. He came around to me, so I doubt you being a mage will make him hate you."

"He also disliked my mother," Reid whispered. "I fear what he'll think when he learns the truth about her."

Because she had convinced Reid's father to leave Rusdasin not for love but for the sake of keeping Nexon in pieces.

"Just do what I would do," Juniper said lightly, nudging him in the ribs. "Don't let him know about that part."

Reid looked skeptical. He turned his gaze back to the street below. A few streets away, a group of water mages were whisking away the snow from a crumbled building. Earth mages came behind them and righted the walls. Fire mages burned away the brush that had long since withered and died. Juniper watched as within less than an hour the house looked somewhat livable.

"The mages have decided to stay here," Reid said. "Many have nowhere else to go. They see this as a new beginning, one without Nexon commanding them or the Order looking down at them."

"The mages and the druids have claimed this place as home," Juniper said. She thought of what the wechun had said about her father being proud that people were coming back.

"They are all eager to live in the same city as you," Reid said cautiously.

She groaned.

"They want to rebuild this city as a place for magic," Reid said. "While the mages and the Order rebuild, they can rebuild together."

Juniper considered those words. "A city for magic?"

A whole city?

"The mage council—"

"It's…perfect." Juniper flattened her hand over his heart.

His brow furrowed. "For?"

"For a place to teach magic! A place where mages can live without being imprisoned or hunted."

"You want another Marca?"

"Better than the Marca," she said. "We can teach anyone about magic or potion making or rune design. It can be an actual school, not a fortress with sealed doors and windows. We can discover all the knowledge about magic we've lost over the past one thousand years."

Reid grinned and flattened his hand over hers. "I was worried you wouldn't like the idea."

"I love the idea of *the magic city*," she said dreamily. Frowning, she added, "I'm just not as keen on meeting with any councils."

Reid laughed, but he had that look.

She frowned. "But…?"

His smile turned sheepish. "There is something else I've neglected to tell you. I thought it might calm, but it's really taken root over the past few days."

She sighed through her nose. "There's always something else."

"The mages have taken to calling you their new leader," Reid said carefully.

She rolled her eyes. "That's why the girl was so nervous and twitchy."

He nodded. "They are calling you the Archmage Princess, hero of the realm."

She pretended to gag.

He nudged her. "Oh, don't pretend like you don't like the idea of being the hero of a century."

Yes, she loved the idea, but it also filled her with a horrible, pitting dread that made her want to curl up in the secret vault under her bedroom.

The vault…which happened to be filled with gold. She supposed, if they were to rebuild a city, they would need funds.

She heaved a sigh. "It's all happening so fast. I was Juniper Thimble, fearsome and unstoppable thief, then Isolde the lost princess, and now I'm supposed to be this archmage hero?" She blew out a breath. "And everyone knows who and what I am."

She missed pulling a mask over her nose and mouth and going unnoticed.

"Indeed they do," Reid said. "And word will only spread of how Isolde Balendin returned and saved the realm."

"Isolde…" Juniper whispered.

Reid raised a brow.

"Everyone is talking about Isolde," she said. "And if everyone is talking about Isolde, no one is talking about Juniper."

It was a brilliant idea. Isolde could have the attention and glory, and Juniper could fade into the background. It would solve her problems.

Reid shook his head. "If that is what you want."

"It is," she said firmly.

"Then we should head to the meeting chamber," Reid said. "I told the mage council that I would arrange a meeting with you today, and Delmont wants to get this archmage business underway as soon as possible. I think Jarek wanted a word with you as well."

Juniper groaned. "Do I get to eat first?"

"I will send for a meal while you get ready." Reid offered her his arm, and they started into the corridor.

"Why can't I eat with others?" Juniper whined.

Reid hesitated. "It might not be wise, at least until you are fully healed."

"Why not? I can handle myself."

"It's not that," he said quickly. He chewed on his next words. "We've already added guards to the royal wing to keep your...more *avid* fans at bay."

She blinked. "I have avid fans?"

Reid laughed nervously.

Juniper glanced around the royal wing. Indeed, she spotted twice the number of guards than before. Two druids stood by the main door that led into the rest of the castle, and two Sentinels stood guard by her suite.

Juniper tugged on Reid's arm. "Don't ignore the question, Reid. Do I have those?"

EPILOGUE

Winter had not yet released its hold over Rusdasin. Ice clung from the edges of rooftops and balconies, silvery clouds hung low on the horizon, and holly decorated every shop window. Silken banners of red and gold hung from every building, bearing the Bradburn crest. Despite the reconstruction following Nexon's insurrection and subsequent defeat, the city buzzed with excitement for the royal wedding of Prince Adrian and Lady Roslyn.

Royal Guard and City Watch lined Royal Avenue to welcome their honored guests, Sir Reid Sandpiper and Her Highness, Isolde Balendin, and their entourage from Delphine.

Even if *Isolde* hadn't fully accepted the title or the role.

She rode a lovely Collatian mare beside Reid, her auburn hair braided back, a circlet of silver denoting her title. Myrisha had chosen her dress, a deep ocean blue with details of silver and pale gold. Reid wore his silver armor, which had been shined and fixed in Delphine before they had started the road back to Rusdasin. At the behest of Roslyn, who implied the *necessity* of their wedding to banish the darkness of Nexon's rule.

Isolde had her suspicions, but she would not say them aloud.

Word of their arrival had spread, and soon people lined Royal Avenue, eager to see the lost princess who had led the army of deserting mages, druids, and battlemages against Nexon and won. She didn't even have to add her own flourishes. The rumors developed on their own, creating an epic battle and brilliant, beautiful princess.

Young girls crowded the sidewalks, eyes wide and smiles bright.

Isolde sat tall and proud, returning their smiles and waving.

"You're enjoying yourself," Reid said, a soft smile on his otherwise impassive face.

"They're so happy to see me!"

"And you're still all right with this?" Reid turned a questioning gaze toward her.

She flashed him the royal smile she'd been practicing: clever and intelligent without arrogance. According to Rue Bellamy, who had volunteered to accompany Princess Isolde on the dangerous trek back to Rusdasin, her smile had gotten much better since leaving the dead city.

"I can't go back on it now," Isolde said without letting her smile wan.

The plan was so simple. Isolde wore the public eye while Juniper hid in the shadows. She could be both.

Reid hadn't been sold on the plan, and by the skepticism peeking through the subtle cracks in his stoic mask, he still wasn't.

Bradburn Castle loomed over the city, decorated with the red and gold of Duvane and the silvery green of Galamond. The crowd thickened as they approached the castle gates, as did the guards. The gates opened with a dramatic grinding of iron, and Reid and Isolde led the entourage into the front garden of Bradburn Castle. This time of year, the trees were bare, and the flower beds were brown.

They led the party to the grand front steps of the castle, where Captain Sandpiper and members of his royal guard stood waiting.

Reid dismounted first, and Isolde climbed to the ground, mindful of her gown. She'd worn traveling leathers until the edge of the city. They'd stopped at a quaint little inn to fix themselves up before parading through the streets. Reid approached his uncle. The two shared a respectful handshake, but then Captain Sandpiper took Reid into a warm embrace.

"Thank the gods you're all right." Captain Sandpiper let go of Reid and gave Isolde the warmest smile she had ever seen. She thought he would bow or hold his hand out, but instead he embraced her just as tightly. Releasing her, he said, "It is good to see you again, Princess Isolde."

She offered him a small nod. "And you, Captain."

"I will show you to your chambers," said the captain. "My men will take your party."

Reid offered her his arm, and she looped hers through. They followed Captain Sandpiper through the halls of Bradburn Castle. To her surprise and delight, magelight glittered in the vestibule, a warm yellow light akin to real sunlight. Magic and smoke still lingered in the air. Servants bustled, far too busy to pay attention to Reid or Isolde. She spotted signs of distress, missing paintings or tapestries, dented suits of armor, missing torch brackets. Captain Sandpiper took them to a suite in the Royal Chambers, the hearth roaring and air scented with the florals of magic and lavender. Tea had been brought up and arranged at the sitting room table.

"The reconstruction has gone well," Captain Sandpiper said. "There is still much to do, but we have made considerable progress."

With the doors closed, Isolde dropped her perfect posture and Juniper collapsed into the cushy armchairs by the hearth. An unladylike sigh escaped her lips.

It felt like a lifetime ago since Reid had escorted her, the criminal scum meant to die in Adrian's place, through these halls.

"I have heard stories of your actions," Captain Sandpiper said. "I expect a full account."

"And we will give one." Reid sat at the table and poured a cup of tea, then a second. "After a rest."

"King Bradburn will also request a full account," said the captain. "For the scribes."

"The scribes?" Juniper chuckled.

Captain Sandpiper nodded. "But that can wait until after the ceremony. You barely made it in time. It begins at midday. Your aunt would have been here to greet you, but she has been busy with preparing the food and organizing the kitchen staff. We have far too many new faces to host such an event without mishap, yet Roslyn and Adrian refused to wait."

Juniper accepted a cup of tea from Reid, catching his eye as he did so. He knew what she thought about the rushed wedding date.

"Everything will be fine, Captain," Juniper said. She sipped her tea loudly.

The captain huffed.

A moment passed in silence. Juniper glanced at Reid. He wore a sheepish look. He met her stare, and she reached out to his magic with an encouraging caress.

Tell him.

Reid swallowed. His left index finger tapped against his teacup, a fidget she'd only noticed in the past few weeks.

"He'll find out eventually," Juniper had argued on the journey to Rusdasin. "Better that he hears it from you than someone else."

"He has too much to worry about right now," Reid had argued. "I will tell him and my aunt after the wedding."

"Adrian's or ours?" she had joked.

Reid's frown deepened.

"I will leave you to settle," said the captain. He stepped toward the door. "If you need anything, the staff is available, just…scarce."

"Thank you, Captain," Juniper said. "We will have dinner, won't we? All together."

The question caught him off guard. He blinked, then nodded. "Of course." He cleared his throat. "Glenda will ask after you, Isolde."

"Isolde to the realm," she said. "Juniper when I want to be."

The captain hesitated. "What name should we call you?"

"For the time being, Isolde is visiting Rusdasin for the royal wedding of Prince Adrian and Lady Roslyn, along with her betrothed, Sir Sandpiper, so Isolde will do. Better get used to it, Captain." She winked.

His guardsman's mask did not budge.

He left, and Juniper laughed.

"He is your uncle," she said, tipping her tea toward Reid.

"I think," Reid started, that serious lilt in his words, "while we are here we should only call you Isolde."

She flashed him a wicked smile. "Even in the throes of passion, sir?"

He blushed. He started to speak, but a knock at the door signaled their luggage had arrived. Isolde lounged while the servants carried her clothes, shoes, and jewels—gifts from Myrisha and some she had found in her parents' vault—into the dressing room. Reid stood dutifully at her side, watching their every move. The servants bowed and whispered her title as they came and went, all looking at her like some inhuman creature. In a good way.

Yes, she could get used to this.

The wedding took place in the largest of the rooftop courtyards. The decorations were holly and wreaths, winter flowers and silken banners. Adrian and Roslyn stood before the priestess, both looking regal in ivory and gold. Roslyn's dress hung loose from the waist, layered in silks. Her black hair curled down her back. A delicate golden circlet shone in the sun. King and Queen Bradburn stood on one side, and a burly man with raven hair and a petite woman stood on the other. Roslyn's parents, she assumed.

Among those gathered to witness the ceremony were several of the council, the king's advisers, Cecil Hurst and Rourke Hendle. Hendle looked like a ghost of a man. According to the gossip Isolde had so far heard, Rourke Hendle had taken the death of his son hard. A handsome, umber-skinned man in blue and green silks sat with several in decorated attire—Prince A'Ralen of Janti. Juniper spied Sir Isaac and several other old men with that knightly look about them, as well as Henry Julian. Captain Tinnly and his wife, as well as the newest addition—a bundle that Mrs. Tinnly gently rocked in her arms.

And of course Captain Sandpiper and his wife, Glenda, who sat beside Reid and Isolde. They sat beside Reid—Rue had named herself Isolde's guardswoman, and she sat between Isolde and the aisle.

To be honest, between Rue and Reid was the safest place in the entire kingdom. Likely the next too.

Seeing so many familiar faces set something loose in her chest, something that had been wound tight since she had left Rusdasin. There were other faces she had not yet seen or had the chance to ask about, but she would.

The ceremony ended with a blast of trumpets and a rather chaste kiss, and the wedding moved inward for the traditional meal.

It didn't take long for Reid and Henry to meet. They embraced as brothers. Isaac followed a step behind.

"Sir Julian," Reid said. "I am glad to see you alive and well."

Henry waved his finger. "It's Knight Commander Julian."

"Seriously?" Isolde asked before she could help herself.

Henry stood a little straighter. "Turns out, I proved myself in the eyes of the order and the king during the mage crisis. Enough to be promoted to the top. Never mind that the old knight commander is dead."

Reid's smile flattened. "So he is gone?"

"He made some sort of deal with Nexon," Henry said. "He was dying the whole time. Nexon was prolonging his life. But that is a dreary story for another day. We'll talk about all of that at the meeting the king has planned. Today, we celebrate!"

"The king passed over you, Sir Isaac?" Isolde turned her gaze to Isaac. He would have been her first choice. Wizened. Older. More mature.

Isaac's hesitation caught Henry's notice. Clearing his throat, he said, "He did ask me. I declined."

Henry's brows rose. "You declined?"

Isaac set a hand on Henry's shoulder. "After this season, I am retiring. This has proven more than anything that I am needed at home."

Henry looked distraught, but Isolde understood. In Delphine, Isaac had a wife and son.

"Besides, I'm sure you will do wonderfully in the role," Isaac said. "One day, you will be as old and cranky as Fowler, and the young upstarts will be looking for ways to do you in."

"What are you going to do with the Order?" Isolde asked.

"That is the question I've heard often tonight." Henry's humor vanished.

"And I am still waiting to hear an answer," came the charming voice of Prince Adrian. His lovely bride hung on his arm.

Isolde squealed and embraced Roslyn, and she hugged her tightly back. Isolde hugged Adrian just as tightly.

Oh, she had missed them both.

"It is so wonderful to see you, Isolde," Adrian said, testing the name on his tongue. "We have heard so much about you."

"All good things, I'm sure."

"A healthy mixture of both," Roslyn added.

Adrian turned his attention to Henry. "So, the Order."

Henry frowned. "I've given it some thought. I want to rebuild the Marca."

A stiff silence followed.

"Rebuild it?" Isolde asked. "But I did so much work bringing it down. Or, I mean, someone very clever and beautiful and talented did."

"The building, I mean. We make it a school, but a real school, not like it was. A place where anyone can learn about magic during the day and then go home in the evening." Henry wore no humor as he spoke. His honesty warmed Isolde's insides. He had indeed changed from the goofy squire she had met and grown into a knight.

"That is a lovely idea," Isolde said. "I was thinking of doing something similar in the dead city. Make it a magic city instead."

"Rebuilding a school is one thing, but an entire city?" Adrian's brows rose.

"I have help," Isolde said. "And there are already people living there and willing to put in the time to make it worthwhile. Druids and mages, mostly."

"Is it true the druids are staying?" Roslyn's eyes widened. "Will they teach at the school?"

She shrugged. "It is a fantastic story, which I am told I will have time to tell during this meeting?"

"Yes," Adrian said. "My father has tomorrow evening blocked off just for this meeting. The scribes will be there. He wants to record your defeat of Nexon in as much detail as possible."

Isolde liked the idea of there being books about her defeat of Nexon, about her prowess and cleverness, her sudden reappearance. She would have to come up with a story as to where she had been all these years and how she had hidden her archmage magic, and it would seem she had until this meeting to do so.

Of course, she had faced worse. She could weave a tale.

Isolde stood in the sunlight of the eastern window, stretching her arms high toward the ceiling, and then down to the floor, palms flat. And again. Reid stepped out of the bathing room, towel over his head, drying his beard.

"Don't forget, we're going into town this morning to get a few things," Reid said.

"We're having lunch with your uncle and aunt," she reminded him. "So you can explain certain things to them before we have to explain for this meeting."

"Yes, yes, I am aware," Reid grumbled. "But we need things in the city first."

"Like what?"

He bristled. "Things." He marched into the other room.

Frowning at the sitting room doorway, Isolde continued her morning stretches. She readied with leisure, much to Reid's annoyance, and then he whisked her out of the castle with only Rue as their escort. Rue, as well as Reid, knew they needed no protection, being archmages, but they didn't want to go through the city boasting about their magic prowess.

Apparently, it might cause *political unease*.

Reid and Isolde took a carriage into the market district and into the streets of finer shops. They walked along, with Reid refusing to tell her what he was looking for, until at last he pulled her into a jeweler's. The shop was small but elegant, with glass-front displays with black velvet holding an array of gold and silver bands and gemstones. The little jeweler blinked at Reid, and then a smile spread over her face.

"Ah, Sir Sandpiper, I was wondering when you would come by," the jeweler said. She reached around the back counter and rumbled through boxes.

Isolde cast a wary glance at Reid, who couldn't hide his smile. Like he'd won. She scowled. "What did you do?" she mouthed.

His grin widened.

"Here it is." The jeweler brought a little black box to the counter and slid it to Reid.

Reid slipped his hand out of Isolde's and reached for the box. She was about to say something snarky when he turned toward her and opened the box.

Inside was a ring. Silver with a single sapphire in the center, surrounded by aquamarines and moonstones.

Her fingers absently went to her ring finger, where his mother's ring had been.

"This ring belonged to my grandmother," Reid said. "She gave it to Glenda before she passed, to give to any granddaughters she and my uncle might have. She's kept it in a box, and she is fairly certain it's not cursed. Today, it is yours. If you will have it."

"*If?*" She laughed. "Reid, I love you, and you know it. Don't kid yourself. There's no 'if' anymore."

He slid the ring onto her finger. Before he could step away, she caught his lips with her own.

ARCHMAGE IN THE RUINS

Juniper knew her way around Rusdasin, its shady side streets, sprawling estates, canals, and markets. She had spent her childhood learning to survive in the royal city, stealing for Maddox and building up a stony defense. She had seen the city drenched in rainstorms, buried under snow and muddy slush, and dizzy with summer's heat. She had seen celebrations like Bala's Day in midsummer, or Espone's Festival, but she had never seen the city during a royal wedding.

Stalls lined the main streets, selling trinkets shaped like Bradburn's ax, little streams of gold and red, dolls painted to look like Roslyn and Adrian, and even a few that looked suspiciously like Isolde and Reid. Juniper resisted the urge to get a closer look.

She didn't want anyone looking too close at Juniper Thimble. Isolde Balendin was currently resting after her long trek from Delphine, enjoying time with her friends and recording her adventures with a royal scribe. Juniper had not been heard of for quite some time. According to gossip, she had been a part of the Undercity that had joined the king's forces. Some said she was still there, others said she had simply vanished.

And she hadn't even had to spread those.

Finding a way into the Undercity had not proven as easy as she'd initially hoped. During the royal occupation, the most obvious and popular Undercity entrances had been sealed. Some had been sealed far too neatly to have been done by anything other than magic. Some looked as though there had never been a secret hatch or a hidden door to begin with.

She spent hours looking, while the sun drifted to the west and shaded the city in inky shadows and splotches of magelight and torchlight. She slipped through the alley by the canal. The waters surged with the recent snow, and the same old murky depths reeked of emptied chamber pots and gods-know-what-else.

She had no choice. If she couldn't get in the old fashioned way, she'd have to make an entrance.

Might as well.

She slipped through Rusdasin, slick as a shadow, to Amery's manor. Despite the end of Nexon's reign, runes protected the perimeter. Juniper approached. Knowing Amery, eyes would be on her before she made it to the gate.

She could have slipped through elsewhere, but she'd rather not risk some ill-intending rune's effect. She let herself through the gates.

At once, she felt the sizzle of a ward on her skin. She passed through without bursting into flames, so she took that as a good sign. She lifted the iron door knocker and brought it down to the door, once, twice.

Silence met her knocking.

The door swung open, and a blonde woman stared at her. At Juniper's dark, close-fitting clothes and hooded half-cloak, her tight-lipped smile tightened into a scowl. "What do you want?"

"Is the lady of the house in?" Juniper asked.

The woman's scowl twisted deeper. "No."

"Go tell her Juniper wants a word."

"Juniper?" came a young girl's voice from the foyer.

The blonde woman turned. Blythe stood on the stairs, one foot higher than the other, dressed in dark clothes and knives—a thief about to leave for a night's work.

Juniper sauntered into the house, past the fussy housemaid. "Well, look at you. Going out for the night?"

Blythe took the steps two at a time, then threw her arms around Juniper's middle. The embrace took her back—but then she returned the embrace. She'd gotten an abnormal amount of hugs in the past several days. It also struck her how tall Blythe was.

Blythe stepped back with wide eyes. "You're all right, and you're here."

"That I am. I thought I would come and say hello to the old stomping grounds." Juniper also wanted to see who had survived, though she hadn't been able to say the words aloud. Not even to Reid, though he knew what she had meant.

One simultaneously good and bad thing about their magic was that she couldn't easily hide anything from him, and neither could he from her.

"Amery is below," Blythe said.

"Below," Juniper repeated.

"The Undercity," she said simply. "I'll take you there. This way."

The housemaid clearly didn't like Juniper being allowed in, but she didn't say anything else. She shut the door and continued doing whatever it was she'd been doing that Juniper interrupted. Blythe guided Juniper into the larder and into a dirt and stone tunnel. She grabbed a mage stone that glowed green at her touch, and while they made their way down the tunnel, Blythe told her about all that had happened in the Undercity since she had left for Rusdasin.

"That is a lovely knife," Juniper said.

Blythe glanced at the dagger she wore, then unsheathed it. The green magestone glittered along the dark blade, which shimmered as if sapphires and diamonds had been crushed into powder and folded into the steel. The hilt was a masterwork of scrolling steel and crushed lapis lazuli with a bite of witherite.

Blythe tossed it up and caught it. "I found it during the siege of the castle. One of the mages was carrying it around. He's dead now, and this dagger is far too pretty to go to waste."

Juniper laughed. If only Reid had been here. He would have gone purple with rage.

"What's funny?" Blythe asked, clutching the dagger.

"That dagger is Gem Cutter," Juniper said. "Some ancient relic or whatever. I played with it while trapped in the castle, and Reid was furious about it. Apparently, it's very old and valuable or something. But I agree, it's far too pretty to go to waste. I think it suits you."

Blythe stood a little straighter and replaced the dagger at her side.

"I see you're also wearing a hairpin," Juniper said, nodding toward the pretty pin. It was gold with a red gem at the end.

Blythe flushed a deep scarlet. "It was a gift."

"Oh?"

The little girl turned sheepish. "From Ven. For not dying in the siege, he said."

A warmth surged at the story. Juniper could spot a crush when she saw one, and it appeared that Ven had developed one for Blythe.

"But don't you tell anyone!" Blythe brandished Gem Cutter.

Juniper laughed harder. "Oh, don't you worry. Your secret's safe with me. I bet that hairpin would double as a lockpick."

Blythe blinked, as if she hadn't realized it, and then sheathed the dagger. "I haven't tried."

The tunnel had several off-shoots leading to different points in the Undercity. Blythe did not lead her into Maddox's keep, thank the gods, and instead led her into Josephine's. The older mage was nowhere in sight, but the keep sounded with life.

The Undercity had changed. Magelights still glittered, and magic still flourished, but the atmosphere had shifted. Criminals no longer lingered on every street corner and sold pilfered foods in the market, and mages no longer sold questionable potions from shabby little stalls. The Undercity had…evolved. The market had grown into one to rival topside, common people came and went, as did a lot of mages.

Of course, with the king and the guard knowing about the Undercity, they couldn't exactly return to what it had once been. The criminal guilds would find somewhere else to flourish.

They found Amery at a cozy tavern, lounging with a tankard in one hand and two attractive young men on either side. At the sight of Juniper, her olive face lit up, and she shooed the men away. Juniper took a seat on the foot of Amery's chaise.

"Am I interrupting?" she asked sweetly.

"Gods, no." Amery sat up, held her drink to the side, and hugged Juniper with her empty arm. "I've thought about you. We didn't know if you'd come down to see us or not."

"Of course I would!" Juniper pretended to be shocked. "I couldn't leave the fate of the Undercity to rumors and gossip."

"Maddox is having a hard time replacing you," Amery said, relaxing into the cushions. "I think he's got his hopes high on Blythe, though I don't think she'll come out as a mage anytime soon. She's not very good with it."

"Unlike others, I've heard?" Juniper cocked a brow.

Amery's smile turned catlike, and she snapped her fingers—a little flame appeared on her thumb. "I've been practicing."

"I'm not sure I like the idea of everyone being able to do magic." Juniper had said as much to the king when he revealed the Order's best kept secret.

"Oh, this little flame took me *ages*," Amery said. She shook her hand, and the flame vanished. "According to the knights who aren't scared of talking about magic, that's about all I'll be able to do. I won't be throwing fireballs or freezing people solid, that's for sure. That's hard even for a normal mage."

Juniper shrugged. "I can't lob fireballs either."

And she was glad Amery couldn't.

"I'm thinking of enrolling in the new Marca," Amery said conversationally. "Or any little schools that open up down here."

"Will the Undercity stay?"

Amery shrugged. "If it goes away, I can go topside. I think the fresh air is better for me, anyway. And look at this tan!"

Indeed, her usual pale olive skin had gained several shades of warmth.

Juniper chuckled. She had not gotten any tan. She and the sun were not friends, and it had made it clear that it did not want to be.

"What of Xavier?" Amery sipped her tankard.

"He's not coming back, I'm afraid," Juniper said. "He said he was staying in the Magic City."

Amery frowned. "You need a better name than that."

"Yes, I'm working on it. I'm not good at coming up with names."

"And what of you?" Amery tilted her head. "What will happen to Juniper Thimble now that Isolde Balendin has returned?"

She chuckled. "Oh, Juniper isn't going anywhere."

LATER

Reid had grown fond of the sound of waves. Constant. Calm. Powerful. A wave barely whispered of the power the ocean contained, the depths unknown. His sharpened knife cut through the wood with ease, slowly carving out the shape of a woman. Shaving at a time, her curves came to life, the dress she wore, her neck, her hair.

He hadn't meant for the wood to come out as anything. He'd just started to whittle, and she had appeared.

Whittling made him feel closer to his father.

Using steel reminded him.

The breeze pushed through the shutters, briny and wet and warm.

And to think, he had been reluctant to travel so far to the coast. He was glad Jun had talked him into it.

Outside, the evening had settled into twilight. Already, stars peeked in the clear sky. Amber and plum streaked the western horizon. A fire burned somewhere, wafting smoke on the wind. A bonfire, likely.

The door to the house opened, and bare feet raced over. Small hands latched on his thigh, and the little girl followed, looking at the wooden figure with wide blue eyes. Her braided chestnut hair had come loose, and hairs hung around her round face. Her tawny skin had taken the days in the sun well, unlike her mother.

"What is that?" the little girl asked, poking a finger at the figure.

"What does it look like?"

"A girl."

"Indeed it does."

"Who is it?"

"She doesn't have a name yet."

The little girl frowned. Reid could see the workings of her mind as the idea of a thing not having a name settled. "What shall we name her?"

The little girl again frowned. Such a task.

On the other side of the room, Juniper set a basket of gathered seashells by the backdoor. Her auburn hair hung over her shoulder in a loose braid. Sand clung to the hem of her loose dress and her bare ankles.

"Mom, Dad made a girl." The little girl pointed at the figure.

"Indeed, he did," Juniper said. "Though it was a team effort."

"You didn't do anything," the little girl argued. "We were outside finding shells."

Juniper laughed. Reid glowered—he didn't want to start *that* conversation this early. He set the little figurine into his daughter's extended hand.

"Think about what name to give her," Reid said, sheathing his knife.

"The bonfire is starting," Juniper said. "They'll be drumming soon. I can't wait for a glass of pineapple punch. Come on, Lenora. Alma is meeting us there."

Lenora looked at the wooden woman in her hands, fingering a crease in her robes. "She kind of looks like you, Mom."

"Oh, does it?" Juniper knelt down to see the wooden figurine closer. "I suppose so. I do have robes that look like that."

"Those are your princess robes," Lenora said matter-of-factly.

"That they are." Juniper cast Reid a knowing glance.

They hadn't told their daughter of Juniper; she only knew her mother as Isolde.

Reid stood. "Well, shall we go?"

"To the bonfire!" Lenora squealed, figurine forgotten. She sat it on the low table before the small hearth, then hurried into the twilight.

Reid offered Juniper his arm, and they followed their daughter into the evening. Smoke billowed from a bonfire farther down the beach. The ocean was calm, the sky streaked with amber and glittered with stars, and a gentle breeze blew in off the ocean. Lenora beat them to the bonfire, laughing as she joined her cousins. Alma embraced Isolde, and Reid shook her husband's hand.

Juniper had always wanted to see the ocean, and when they had learned her sister had fled south, she had insisted.

Reid reclined in the sand as the kids splashed in the shallows. Juniper sat beside him, chatting with her sister. They would have to go home eventually. Two archmages couldn't vacation for too long, and Isolde would be missed—but for now, they could relax.

Acknowledgments

An author (whose talk I was forced to sit through as a freshman in college) said that in order to write something, you have to be a little bit obsessed with it. At the time, I had no idea how much that bit of advice would stick with me.

That author, whose name I don't remember, was right.

I remember jotting down the first notes of what would become *Thief in the Castle* way back in 2017 without having any of the characters' names, without a title, or even a plot. I had a girl with a secret who got blamed for poisoning the prince and a boy with big dreams of becoming a knight. (This plot later became the plot for book three, *Dreams in the Snow*.)

Later, the spark of inspiration came while playing *Skyrim* (shocking, I know) and traveling through a snowstorm in the icy mountains—if only the unnamed protagonist were able to summon a flame, she would have been fine, but of course, she couldn't, because her destruction skill was too low and she'd run out of mana fighting bandits. (This scene would also find a home in book three.)

The idea refused to leave me alone. It was all I thought about. It came together slowly, brick by brick, detail by detail. The characters found their names, personalities, and flaws. The plot took shape. A villain emerged. Juniper came to life. She was, in short, everything I wished I could be. Cool. Smart. Clever. Sassy. Reid was everything I wanted in a male lead. Strong. Devout to his beliefs. A good friend. Chivalrous yet flawed. (I don't understand why I'm still single with these standards. I just want a white knight, maybe with a fiery steed. Is that too much to ask?) Adrian was my charming prince with a heart of gold. Ison was my lost boy who didn't know where he was going or what he wanted.

Whether or not these characters stemmed from people in real life will forever remain a mystery—one I will take to my grave.

When I started writing Stars and Bones, I had no success in publishing. The books I'd published weren't the overnight bestsellers I'd hoped they would be. They hardly sold at all. I went through a slump where I thought I'd wasted my time writing those books, that I'd never have another idea, that I would never be a good writer.

And then Juniper happened. I poured myself into the story. More than any story I'd written, and any I've written since.

I had a working rough draft for *Thief* within a week. That was October. I used it as my NaNoWriMo project that year, and I had a first draft by the end of November. I have no idea how I wrote it that fast. I haven't written anything with such fever since. I couldn't stop—I couldn't stop thinking about the story, the characters, and the world I was building. I started the second draft almost immediately after finishing the first, and it wasn't long before I started book two.

By the time I met Authors 4 Authors and signed to publish *Thief in the Castle,* I was working on the rough draft of book three. By the time *Thief* released, I was working on book four with notes for book five.

I was obsessed.

Fun facts: Book one originally ended with Juniper fleeing the castle after getting blamed for poisoning Adrian, but that draft was somewhere around 173,000 words (way too long), so I chopped it just after the ball scene, and the rest became the beginning of book two.

I didn't know Xavier was gay until he was on the page with Ison. So much of Xavier's personality and backstory came out after he met Ison, and it still blows my mind. I considered editing him out of book one because it felt like he didn't connect to anything, but then he met Ison and they bonded and then he was there to stay.

Roslyn wasn't a real person until she saved Juniper from freezing to death. I wrote the scene where a mysterious stranger appears, and then it hit me—*what if it's Roslyn?*

I had to do an entire draft of book one and two to focus on the magic system, because the rules I created in book two undermined how magic worked in book one. Lesson learned: map our magic system before book one.

Stars and Bones would never have gotten off the ground without the incredible team at Authors 4 Authors—Rebecca, Brandi, and Renee. I would never be here, staring at this finished series, without the support, encouragement, and advice you three have given me. Brandi, these covers are gorgeous! They fit the series perfectly. Rebecca and Renee, your guidance on revisions has been beyond invaluable. I have no idea where I would be if I hadn't met you all. I have learned so much about my own writing, editing, and how to market a book in the past six years (yes, it's been six years).

I have to thank my downstairs girls—Jackie, Kaylyn, and Cathy (even though you're a quitter)—for the endless and ridiculous support even though none of you read any of my books. When I start writing mafia romance, you'll be the first to know. Thanks for being the work family I didn't know I needed. Love you guys.

I also want to thank all the coworkers over the past ten years who got excited and enthusiastic when I confessed to being an author, to every single one of you who bought a book and brought said book to work for me to sign, like I was a big shot.

I wouldn't be where I am without the support of all the other authors, editors, creatives, bookish creators, and library workers who support small and indie authors like me.

Without my parents, I'd likely be living in my car. I don't think I will ever be able to thank you enough for all the endless and unconditional support, love, and encouragement. Mom, you were always the first to buy my next book, even if you lost them around the house. Dad, you inspired my love of lost history, pirates, and sunken treasure when you made me watch the History Channel with you when I was a kid. I am truly blessed to have such incredible parents, not to mention some awesome genes.

And of course, this series would be nothing without you, the reader. Thank you for giving me a chance to tell a story. Thank you for giving Juniper a chance. Thank you for every post, every share, every review. Thank you for making it this far, to the end, for seeing Juniper's story through.

I can't wait to show you what comes next.

ABOUT THE AUTHOR

Beatrice B. Morgan lives in southern Illinois. When she isn't reading or writing, she is most likely playing a video game. She is a night owl, caffeine addict, yoga enthusiast, dog person, hopeless romantic, optimistic, and a shameless Ravenclaw.

Follow her online:

www.bbmorgan.com
TikTok: **@beatrice_author**
Instagram/Threads: **@BBMorgan_W**
Facebook: **@BBMorganBooks**
Twitter: **@BBMorgan_W**

Also by Beatrice B. Morgan
Hard as Stone

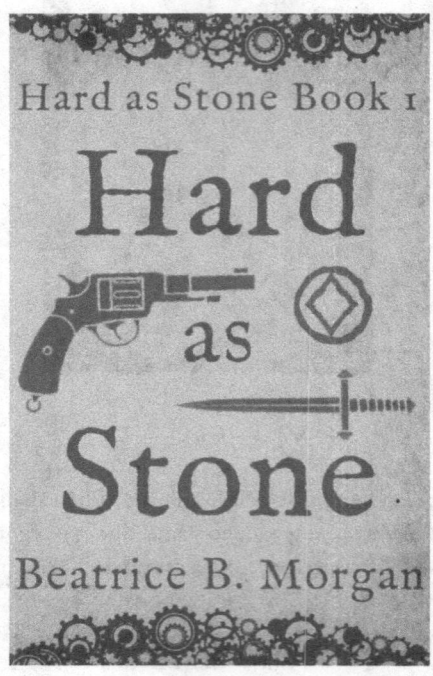

Seventeen-year-old Raven Thane wants an adventure...and she's going to get one. Just not the way that she expected. Bored and disinterested with a routine life in her remote underground community, she fails to notice a thief during her turn at guard duty. Zander, a charming sharpshooter, tasks her with helping him retrieve the mysterious stolen item. Posing as a couple on the road, they'll face deadly automatons and Gray Elite soldiers, entangle themselves in a complicated world of spies and freedom fighters, and hide secrets of their own. Can Raven fix her mistake and prove herself more than a simple country girl? Or will she create even more chaos?

books2read.com/hardstone

AUTHORS 4 AUTHORS
PUBLISHING

A publishing company for authors, run by authors, blending the best of traditional and independent publishing

We specialize in speculative fiction: science fiction, fantasy, paranormal, and romance. Get lost in another world!

Check out our collection at https://books2read.com/rl/a4a or visit Authors4AuthorsPublishing.com/books

For updates, scan the QR code or visit our website to join our semi-monthly newsletter!

Want more female-led fantasy? We recommend:

Exile

by Melion Traverse

After killing a paladin in revenge for her family, Squire Bryn is cast out by order of the god Avgorath himself. Now she seeks atonement with the father of the dead paladin. But machinations far greater than a disgraced squire are at play. Unicorn riders—believed to be only legend—ride through the land. A young sorcerer needs help in finding his father, and a mystery brews that could hold the fate of two worlds.

books2read.com/exile